*The Unraveling of Cassidy Holmes*

# The Unraveling of Cassidy Holmes

## A Novel

## Elissa R. Sloan

WILLIAM MORROW

*An Imprint of* HarperCollins*Publishers*

P.S.™ is a trademark of HarperCollins Publishers.

HarperCollins books may be purchased for educational, business, or sales promotional use. For information, please email the Special Markets Department at SPsales@harpercollins.com.

FIRST EDITION

Designed by Diahann Sturge

Library of Congress Cataloging-in-Publication Data has been applied for.

ISBN 978-0-06-300944-8

20 21 22 23 24 PC/LSCH 10 9 8 7 6 5 4 3 2 1

*For Walt*

# AUTHOR'S NOTE

Please know that this book has some triggering elements. Its contents include suicide, descriptions of depression and disordered eating, on-page physical assault, off-page sexual assault, body shaming, and body dysmorphia. If you are in a vulnerable mind space, please be gentle with yourself before you continue to read this book.

I know how hard it is to reach out when you feel like you're drowning. If you cannot talk to a trusted adult or friend about how you're feeling, here is an international resource to begin looking for help: https://suicideprevention.wikia.org. If you're in the U.S., you can call the National Suicide Prevention Hotline at 1-800-273-8255.

# The Unraveling of Cassidy Holmes

# PROLOGUE

*Wednesday*

## Yumi

The day that Cassidy died, the rest of us were in London.

The three of us were good-naturedly receiving some ribbing from DJ "Dashing Jed" on the U.K.'s third-tier radio spot. Earlier in the day, Emily had made sure that the typical ground rules were laid out: Don't talk about Merry's family. Don't talk about Rose's most recent visit to rehab. Don't pry into my failed marriage. And, most of all, don't mention Cassidy, our vacant fourth.

The cubby we sat in was well worn, with yellow carpet up the walls, and a sharp scent of dampness or mold, like someone had trod into the room with wet rain boots and shut the door without letting it air out. The deejay sat next to Merry, who was drawing hearts on the table with the eraser end of a pencil.

"So, ladies, you appear in the new Stan Harold movie, *Lunch at Midnight*. Tell me, how was your experience on set with Stan?"

Rose leapt to take the lead, as she always did. "It was wonderful working with Stan. I've seen all of his films since the mid-nineties, so it was an honor having a part in his new movie." She was smiling like she knew there was a camera secretly recording somewhere in the rows of equipment, but I'd stipulated that we not be videotaped before agreeing to do the radio show. I didn't feel like having my weight discussed in the comments section of YouTube. I sat with Dashing Jed opposite me, elbows on the edge of the table and hands cradling my face.

"He's a really funny guy," I said, injecting pep into my voice. "And so kind."

Rose began talking about a funny moment that happened behind the scenes on set, but I tuned her out. The truth was, our part was only a quick cameo in a comedy movie, not worth mentioning or even promoting. It was supposed to be a nod to the adults bringing their kids to a PG-13 movie, a nostalgic "aha!" that kept us looped into the current social discourse. I hadn't wanted to take part at all, but Rose insisted on keeping her name out front and she was worth more in the Gloss ensemble. Doing the cameo was easier than agreeing to a reunion tour—a recurring idea that she'd floated once a year for the past decade. So there we were, in dreary old London, where we'd once headlined sold-out shows, sitting instead in a dingy office giggling into microphones and pretending to be relevant.

"We're only in the movie for, like, fifteen seconds," said

Merry. "Blink and you'll miss us! But if this pushes a new generation of kids to buy our old albums, more power to us."

"What, you don't think being certified Triple Platinum is enough?" asked Jed.

"I've always preferred diamonds," she said, laughing.

I forced myself to laugh too, falling right back into our usual dynamic: Merry saying something stupid and me smoothing it over. "Merry, hon, you sound way too intense."

Dashing Jed fielded a few on-air calls as Merry ignored Rose's reproachful glare. Merry had decided long ago not to concern herself with Rose's rules of propriety and instead just spoke her mind. It had led to some arguments fifteen years ago.

"Caller, you're on the air!" said Dashing Jed enthusiastically. His voice was a magnificent, melodic baritone; one could imagine that if he hadn't picked radio as his profession, he might have made it as an opera singer.

A rasping voice, lilting with a Scottish accent, came out of the speaker. "Am I on with Gloss?"

"Yes, you are!" enthused Jed.

"I just want to say how much I love you ladies," the female voice continued. "My name's Kelly and I listened to you all through high school. Tell me, since the gang is all back together, would you ever consider touring again?"

Even though there were no cameras, I arranged my face to stay completely neutral. *Why* were people always asking for a tour?

Rose answered that one too. "You're so sweet, Kelly," she teased, "and never say never. Yumi and Merry and I have been discussing it, but we have no solid plans yet." No mention of Cassidy.

"Okay, well, I know it would sell out in five seconds flat! Regardless, I'm really looking forward to seeing your parts in *Lunch at Midnight*."

This sort of praise used to fulfill me; a feast of goodwill and self-esteem. Cheering voices in the arenas, reporters with imploring tones, soda commercials with our photos on the cans. Now they were soft, touching glances that barely felt like anything. We had peaked; we drifted into almost normal.

"Thanks so much, Kelly," hollered Jed. "We're on to the next caller!"

"Yes, hello, I was wondering," said the next voice, low and masculine. "Could you play 'Wake Up Morning'? I feel like I haven't heard that song in years."

"Is it because you didn't buy our album when it came out the first time?" Merry said in a mocking tone. "Or the second, when it went Platinum and we released it with a special liner? Or the third, when we did a best-of hits album? You could listen to it anytime you like if you go to Big Disc's internet channel. But hey, *Dashing* Jed, it's one of my favorites too. Put it on. We can have a little background music while we keep chatting."

Jed had turned to the glass partition and gestured to a station worker to find the record. His body swiveled toward the microphone, but then he paused; swiveled back. Someone outside was trying to get his attention. Merry, next to Jed, had snapped to attention and was gazing through the glass.

Someone was pressing a piece of paper against it. From where I sat, I could see only an illegible scribble of block writing. Merry's hand leapt to her mouth in surprise.

Rose must have kicked her under the table, because Merry's eyes turned toward us. They were usually so bright and icy blue that even in dark stadiums, before the lights came up, I would be able to see her eyes glowing. But now—they were so cloudy, the pupils distended in distress, that I shrank back. Jed leaned into his microphone. "Listeners, I'm afraid I just learned some terrible news. While three of the members of Gloss are here with me in studio, the fourth, I'm sad to report, just passed away."

SILENCE.

Dashing Jed could not have been surprised by our collective inward shock. Who knows why he dropped this bomb on us, on the air, during a casual radio spot. Perhaps he thought that it was his duty to let us know as soon as it happened, since the media could easily find out where we were. They would have time to gather outside as we finished up on his show. Paparazzi feed off misery; they'd be overjoyed to break the news to us as we walked out of the station. A photo of us breaking down on the sidewalk in the middle of London would net some lucky photographers enough money to send their kids to a year at a good private school. As we were ensconced in a padded cell with no way of getting any other outside information, the first opportunity to hear about Cassidy's death would have been through Emily, if she were quick enough.

Or maybe Dashing Jed had his own sadistic streak and wanted to see how we'd react. Perhaps he thought that this flat little promo piece would turn into a juicy, hard-hitting interview, where our voices would quaver as we reminisced about our fallen friend. His shitty radio station would have a bump in listeners and the airplay would be repeated on countless tabloid shows, fan videos, and transcribed for magazines and blog articles. Dashing Jed would be popular; he'd be trotted out onto late-night talk shows to converse with the hosts that, yes, he had been there when the Gloss girls all broke down to mourn Cassidy, the sweetest Glossie of them all . . .

But none of that was forthcoming, and as the silence stretched on and on, he hastened to fill the space with something other than dead air. Merry, Rose, and I shared swift, passing eye contact with one another. Then we each quietly ruminated on this piece of news, lost in our own thoughts. "What a tragedy," Jed said. "She was still so young. I'm hoping that this song will ease some of the pain in our hearts." He waggled his fingers toward the window again, likely imploring that same employee to load up our album.

To be honest, I expected Merry to say something. Anything. Merry's big mouth was infamous. The tabloids enjoyed twisting any of her statements around to make her sound more wild, more belligerent, more extreme than she already was. For the first time in fifteen years, it seemed that Merry had nothing to say. Her lips were pressed firmly together into a dark pink line.

I could sense, rather than see, Rose deflating next to me. Rose and Cassidy didn't get along very well when we were all together, but it was big news anyway. I'd been the closest to Cassidy, but I felt numb.

The music began, slow and low, and I slipped the headphones off.

I worked my jaw back and forth to ease the tension and found my voice. "How?" I asked. I couldn't even recognize myself. The noise that came out was low, husky, almost a growl.

Jed flicked a look at me.

"How? How did she die?" This question was picked up, recorded, transmitted live in a fifty-mile radius. It would be played back for days on gossip shows with a picture of Cassidy's face tucked up in the top left corner.

"I'm sorry, love," said Jed. "I don't know."

THE SIDEWALK WAS crowded with cameras as we shoved out of the double doors to the car. Paparazzi in England aren't as ruthless as those in L.A. or New York, but they've had enough practice with Hollywood starlets making waves and stirring up publicity that a few bloodhounds were up to the task. Emily had the driver pull up to the curb and we held our purses in front of our faces as we wrestled our way through the throng of bodies, tumbling into the cabin and sealing the doors with automatic locks.

Rose sank into the leather seats and gave a quick look of disbelief to the tinted windows. "Lord," she said, as lenses were hastily ground up against the glass. "I'd forgotten what that was like."

Merry tugged a lock of her white-blond hair tight against her fingers, flicking the end furiously, a habit that had always annoyed me. "Shit. I can't believe this. Em," she called to the front, "what is going on?"

Emily had already started directing our driver toward a McDonald's close by. She was Merry's assistant now, but when we were together she reverted back to taking care of us all. She turned around in her seat and gazed at us steadily. "News says she was found only a few hours ago. A housekeeper found her around seven A.M. The ambulance and then the morgue guys showed up, and the paps were camped out on her lawn the entire time, snapping photos of the body bag. There was nothing they could do—she was already gone, probably died sometime last night. But everything is still very new and her parents have been notified, and they want to keep the details hush-hush."

"Is there any idea of how it happened?" Merry asked.

Emily shook her head. "No details yet."

"Was she sick? No one has talked to her in years, right?" She turned her head to Rose and me.

Rose continued to gaze out the window. "She already said that no one knows what happened."

"Yeah, but if any of you have spoken to her recently . . ."

Em faced the front of the car and repeated, "No details yet."

We pulled up at the drive-through and Emily put our regular order in, rapid-fire, via our driver. Rose accepted a Diet Coke and watched me unwrap my burger. Some things never change. I sighed. "Don't give me that look, Rose. I know what you're thinking, and now is not the time."

"I wasn't judging. Maybe you're projecting your emotions onto me."

Already the stress was melting along my jawbone and rippling down my throat. Bite after bite, I ate until I felt the clench in my stomach softening.

\* \* \*

*November 16, 1999*

# Cassidy

The finale is tonight. I'm sitting backstage in a room with a million other people, trying to collect my thoughts, jiggling my legs nervously and biting the skin off my thumb. Somewhere in the audience, my mother is waiting to see her little girl win this competition. And at home, my siblings are going to watch me on TV.

Stephen St. James is nearby. We've been vying for the crown the past few rounds on *Sing It, America!* On the stage, we look out into the audience, eyes sparkling, mouths wide, encouraging our fledgling fans to cheer louder, clap harder. But backstage, we don't talk; we barely look at each other. After each episode wraps, we're congratulated by members of the crew as we pack up our bags and leave. I've never loathed someone I've wanted to hold before.

But I can't be distracted. Not when it's the finale.

Anna sidles up to me. She's one of the last three contestants and a little vain. Sixteen, with dyed red hair and a number of crop tops, she's a wild card. When she performs well, she kills it, but she's had a few lackluster moments as well. "Hey, Cass," she says, as if we're friends. "You ready?"

I take my thumbnail out from between my teeth and rub it on my skirt. "Yeah," I reply. "Are you excited?"

"For that record contract? I can almost *taste* it."

"We all can."

"But who's actually gonna take a big *bite*?" she says in a singsongy voice.

Anna is so petite, thin all over with slender arms and shins, a pearlescent white smile permanently pasted on her face, that I feel that my tight-lipped smile looks tired in comparison. Anna is so conventionally beautiful that I have to remind myself that she's a competitor, same as Stephen, and I need to focus on winning. If I were a member of the American public voting in *Sing It, America!,* I would pick Anna just because she's *looks* like a star already. I know it's a knock against myself, but I feel that I look so . . . mediocre.

The coaches have tried to help me with my image. I auditioned in Houston with my long hair pulled back into a ponytail, a tank top and denim skirt, and a pair of cowboy boots. I figured that, with so many people auditioning, I wouldn't stand out anyway, but my friends Edie and Joanna told me to write my name in rhinestones on my shirt. *Sassy Cassidy,* I painstakingly hot-glued the night before. I don't know if it worked, but I did get a call back, and an invitation to film in L.A., and made it through the initial elimination rounds, wearing my own clothes and doing my own makeup. But as soon as I was one of the final twelve chosen for the competition, the show produced Nikki and Gary, stylists who tried to help all contestants find a "look."

Anna was already beautiful and fierce, so she was encouraged to brighten her burgundy hair to a fiery lava red. Her hemlines got shorter, her wedges got taller, and her eye shadow became dark and glittery.

Stephen, with his long, lean lines and wholesome-boy charm, was outfitted in dark designer jeans with tight tees and oversize, unbuttoned collared shirts. They lightened his hair slightly for a just-spent-a-summer-in-a-pool look, spiked it tastefully with gel, and made sure that the makeup artist contoured his jawline to maximum effect.

Me, I was a Texan with really great hair, and the first thing they did was chop it off into a shoulder-length bob. They said they wanted me to look "edgier," presumably because I didn't know how to dress myself. They advised a diet—which I promptly ignored—encouraged fishnets, and liked putting me in animal-print cocktail dresses. Every night we filmed an episode, Nikki and Gary sat me down in a makeup chair and lined my eyes with dark kohl and lips in dark plum. Tonight, I'm wearing a hot-pink-and-white zebra-print dress, dark tights, and combat boots. I don't feel like me, but they assure me I look great.

Anna wants to continue chatting, but I can feel my throat squeezing shut. "I'm going to . . . ," I mutter and then duck away to breathe in a corner.

While I'm humming my warm-up, a hand touches my shoulder. I turn and it's Stephen St. James. I can never take in Stephen all at once. Sometimes it's his long, angular nose. Sometimes I can focus only on his smell—freshly laundered clothes and a touch of cologne. Today it's his hand; his well-manicured nails and pink-knuckled fingers that are now pulling away from my arm. "Good luck," he says. It's the second time he's spoken to me directly and not in a group—the first being "hello" when we were introduced in the big room as the final twelve.

I nod as warmth starts creeping into my cheeks. "You too."

He gives a thousand-watt smile and moves on. I close my eyes and hum.

SING IT, AMERICA! is a revolution in television. Oh, sure, reality TV competitions have been around for a while—*Star Search,* for one—but for some reason the public is primed for this type of show right now. Game show contestants have too much *luck* for the audience to feel truly invested, and scripted shows seem too contrived. Some executive somewhere decided that talented members of America's public needed to be showcased and then bumped off week by week, with a record-deal contract and a shot at fame dangling in front of their noses at the finish line, and a million people leapt for the chance.

Every week, we sing. Every week, a panel of five judges gives their critique or praise. Every week, the judges, with input from the call-in audience, eliminate one of the contestants. And every week, the live studio audience and the people at home glued to their television sets have something to discuss for the next few days. And tonight our fates will be decided.

I want this so bad that my teeth ache. I tell myself to relax my jaw and I breathe slowly and deliberately through parted lips. I'm blinking perspiration off my eyelashes, blurring the row of televisions where we can see the broadcast backstage, and I'm not even under the hot stage lights yet. There's a few seconds' delay, but it's almost live.

"Find your places, please," says a PA, sweeping through the room.

Our host, Matilda Gottfried, walks her fingers over her lapels, adjusting every pleat on her outfit. She strides out of view and a few moments later, she's on the screens. As the applause dies down, she clasps the microphone in her hands and shares a giant grin. "Welcome to the finale of *Sing It, America!* It's been a long, wild ride with our three very talented contestants. *Tonight,* one of them will be chosen, *by you,* to be our next *national pop star.* They've been dreaming and hoping for this moment for all of their young lives. Will it be Anna Williams, a classically trained dancer who can also hit a high note? Will it be Stephen St. James, who has stolen the hearts of all American women since day one? Or will you choose Cassidy Holmes, our sassy sweetheart? *Tonight's the night* when one of their lives will change forever. This entire time, you in the audience and you watching at home have been in charge of their fates. We've had to let some really talented people go over the past few weeks, but now we have three wonderful, dedicated hopefuls here tonight.

"*Tonight,* we're going to hear three different songs from each of our contestants. We'll hear a ballad, a pop hit, and one of their own picks. When we give the go-ahead, call in to vote for your favorite.

"But first, let's meet our judges . . ." The screen cuts to the five people sitting genially in the first row. "Music producer Jenna Kaulfield." A blonde with gray eyes and a thin mouth, she waves her acknowledgment. "Talent agent of some of the world's greatest bands, Jonah Stern." A man with so much bronzer on his face, his arms look like bone in comparison. "Emma Jake, eighties pop icon." She still looks youthful, with a furry edge of false eyelashes shadowing her eye sockets and high cheekbones emphasized further with rosy blush.

"Thomas Reilly, voice coach who has been working tirelessly with these contestants on honing their craft." A man in tweed who smiles at the audience. "And finally, tonight's guest judge, Marsha Campbell, from Big Disc Records, who will *personally* offer a record contract to our lucky winner. Hello, judges!"

"Great to be here," offers Marsha into the microphone. Her hair is a tossed salad of brown and red and gold. She looks young, maybe in her mid-thirties, and is wearing a pair of glasses with bright red frames.

"It's wonderful to have you all here again for this momentous occasion," Matilda says, smiling. "But first, let's recap our contestants' stories." She turns toward a large screen on the side of the stage as the prerecorded medley begins.

It's our journeys from the audition to this night—five months of our hearts in our throats, of not sleeping enough, of being crammed into hotels, of eating craft services. Of Nikki and Gary controlling my hair and fashion choices. Of waking up early for our lessons with Thomas Reilly—at first all of us together, then whittled down to individual sessions.

Anna's is first. From her audition in Minneapolis, where she showed up giggling and wearing a clear plastic rain parka over her clothes, to the warm-up lessons with Thomas in crop tops and bootleg jeans (an impressive scatting session with Thomas on the piano, her standing next to him emoting with her eyes closed, hands in the air, was used for this clip), to a smattering of her best performances so far on the show; glittery dress after glittery mini-dress; her five months with *Sing It, America!* summarized into a few minutes of visual poetry. After a particularly beautiful clip of her last week's performance, the medley shows Anna at her audition again: her hair is a less radi-ant burgundy, her lips are pale pink instead of fuchsia, but she's giggling and laughing as the judges ask: "Why do you want to win this competition, Anna Williams?"

"Because," she said, "I'm *young;* I'm *passionate;* I'm *driven.*" Every word is punctuated with her clapping her small hands together. "I have the chops and I'm gonna blow you all away!" And there's no doubt in my mind that she *is* all of those things. I glance over at Anna, who is standing off to my side. Her hands are on her hips, her eyes are closed, and instead of preoc-cupying herself with her screen time, she's warming up.

The screen transitions and it's Stephen's turn. He had at-tended the call in Atlanta, Georgia. He'd worn cowboy boots to his audition and the judges poked fun at him. "You ride?" Jonah Stern had asked.

"If you count my sixty-five Mustang," Stephen had replied with a suave smirk.

The clips continue: Stephen guffawing in disbelief when he was asked to move on to the next round. Stephen with a few of the now-axed contestants he'd become friends with, sharing laughs over a card game. A homemade video that he'd submit-ted at some point: a grade-school Stephen singing the national anthem at a local baseball game.

He is amazing. In all the weeks leading up to this competi-tion finale, I've never seen him misstep.

Stephen's video ends with his performance from the first airing, when he blew the doors off with "Unchained Melody." The clip shows Emma Jake's wide-open mouth at the judge's table, and Thomas Reilly pumping his fist in the air. Quick

cut: "That was magnificent," says the prerecorded Jenna Kaulfield. "America is going to have to look out for you."

Fade.

My medley is the final one. Here comes *Sassy Cassidy*,
rhinestone shirt and all, at the Houston audition. The line had
wormed its way through the convention center parking lot in
the middle of a Texas June; the hair I'd painstakingly blow-
dried fluffed out to a horrible mess due to the humidity. At the
last minute I pulled it back into a simple ponytail and skittered
up to the stage with the number *1438* pinned to my shoulder.

Suddenly, a fluffy black makeup brush obscures the screen.
Nikki is whisking dry powder on my skin; "I could see you
sweating from all the way over there," she says, jerking her
head to the side. "Get it together, girl."

She is spraying a cloud of hairspray now, shellacking my
head. As the mist settles, Matilda is back on the screen, smiling
her wide smile and offering us a moment to enjoy these ads
from our sponsors.

"Two minutes," a PA announces. We're brought into a
smaller room to wait for our respective turns. A small, lit television is on the wall, and a table in the middle holds several
bottles of water. I perch on the edge of an orange sofa with my
damp hands lightly touching my knees. The waistband of my
tights is cutting into my belly button. Stephen, on my left, is so
close that his knee is inches from one of mine. I slide my gaze
from my lap to his, and I see that he's clasped his hands tightly
there: pink fingers, white knuckles, crescent-moon nail beds.

The television is muted, but Stephen half-stands, finds the
remote, turns the sound on low, and sinks back down into the

couch. A waft of warm cologne and oranges trails across my body. An advertisement for a truck, shampoo, and a sitcom flicker across the screen. Then *Sing It, America!*'s logo appears again, and the camera pans across the hundreds of viewers in darkened auditorium seats. The judge's panel is illuminated in the very front, and the camera cuts to Matilda once again.

A head pokes into the room. "St. James," the PA says, not looking at any of us. I feel the couch shift as Stephen gets to his feet. The back of his neck looks flushed and I can tell that he's perspiring too.

"Hey," says Anna, a specter in the chair to my right. Her voice is small and her body seems to take up no space at all. "Break a leg, Stephen."

His eyelashes flick toward her once, and he smiles with his lips closed—I'd never seen him smile that grimly before—and he walks out the door.

* * *

*Wednesday*

# Rose

We arrived at the Savoy, hiding behind our purses again until we were in the lobby. The other girls wanted to stay at a normal hotel, but I talked them into swinging the Savoy. The studio financing *Lunch at Midnight* had given us a per diem for the promo, but it was pitifully small. I told the others that they should use some of their Cherry Cola money to cover the rest—or, in Merry's case, to just pull out her black Amex.

Emily shepherded us into a waiting elevator and we stood silently as we ascended to our floor. Yumi's and Meredith's eyes were unfocused and staring off into the distance, and I imagined that their brains were clicking and whirring, measuring up what had happened with Cassidy—plucking thoughts of obscure, bygone days, mentally profiling any number of stalkers, wondering if maybe she'd fallen down a rabbit hole of painkillers. I stared ahead at the double doors, mentally patting down my appearance and taking inventory of what might be published in tonight's online gossip rags: neat face, no mascara smearing, just a composed countenance. Soft leather jacket, hair in honeyed curls, ring on a necklace hidden under my crew neck, nice designer jeans that flatter my ass, good heels. My purse matched my shoes, but not too obviously so.

"I'll change your flights," Emily said, leaning back into her role as assistant to all of us. "Get packed and meet me back at this elevator in fifteen minutes."

The elevator dinged and the golden doors slid open. Merry and Yumi, nearest the doors, slowly emerged from their thoughts and exited. As I made to follow, Emily caught my elbow. Stunned, I snatched my arm back and glared at her.

We shared eye contact for just a moment, then she dropped her gaze.

I went left; she moved off to the right, to the opposite end of the hall.

Upon entering my darkened suite, I kicked off my shoes and sat down on the edge of the mauve bedspread. The entire room was glazed in warm pink, and with the curtains drawn there was only a slice of blue light making a line across the carpet. The bureau had a shadow where the television had been removed, per my usual request the day I checked in. My throat hurt, and I could feel the dry swallow ripple down my curved spine. I let my eyes lose focus on the white sliver on the ground and dabbed a dented toe into the soft nap.

*God.* Cass was dead. She was not coming back. And even though we barely heard from her anymore—no one did—we'd been through so much together that it was like feeling a part of my distant family had disappeared.

A hiccupping sob tore out of my body and I brought a hand to my mouth to stifle it. I could feel the pain of her death shivering upward, from the base of my hip bones toward my neck. Clamping my hand over my mouth, I bit down the tears and stood up, casting my eyes quickly around the room. Pack.

I was the closest one in the group to Cass. I was allowed to take a moment to mourn.

I needed to know more, but did I really *want* to hear it? Could I just imagine that maybe, for a little while, Cass was just fine? I itched to look at my phone but resisted.

Without any regard for organization, I dumped armfuls of clothes into my suitcase. My hands trembled, and when I touched my face they were ice-cold. I applied pressure to my eyes with my chilled fingertips, checking for wetness and dabbing at my eyelashes to keep any mascara from smearing.

I needed a drink. But the minibar had been cleared out by strict request. I touched the ring on the chain and said an affirmation: *I do not need a drink.*

Taking a deep breath, I slung the suitcase to the floor and sat on it to zip it up. I jammed my sunglasses on, did a once-over of the room, and hauled myself to my feet.

Emily was waiting with the other two. We wordlessly filed into the elevator, and Em had had the foresight to ask the hotel for additional security as we rolled our bags to the car and headed for Heathrow.

In the VIP lounge at the airport, I slipped away from the other girls to the bar for a glass of seltzer water, but asked the bartender to throw in a thimbleful of gin. Just a taste, not even a full shot, just enough to warm my sternum when it went down. I didn't need to get drunk, or even tipsy; I only wanted my insides to stop shivering.

It was impossible to avoid televisions in airports; but surprisingly, Cassidy's death wasn't making a big splash. Her body had been found only hours earlier. Conjecture is always thrown about in these types of cases; I imagined that we'd hear all sorts of nonsense before the truth came out—if it came out at all. One of the screens nearest to the bar shared a snippet of news.

A talking head spoke. "The body of Cassidy Holmes . . . ex-member of the once-chart-topping girl group Gloss . . . humanitarian . . . found just a few short hours ago . . . other three members of the Gloss girls . . . not reachable for comment . . . they have tweeted that they are . . . by this unexpected loss. There is no word from the Los Angeles medical examiner as to the reason . . . death. We'll keep you updated, here . . . BBC One." The scene switched to the London Eye for another story.

I got off the barstool and rejoined the others, slumping in a lounge chair. Merry put a hand on my arm.

"Rose, you okay?"

Had I told the bartender to splash a thimbleful of gin in that glass? Or had he seen past the sunglasses and sympathetically poured a long shot? My neck was loosening, swinging as if on a light hinge. My back felt pleasantly numb, a far cry from its usual twinging. I remembered now why I relied on alcohol so much—all pain, emotional and physical, dulled. I pulled the bridge of my sunglasses down on my nose and squinted at Merry through one eye. "Mm-hmm."

"Come on," said Emily, as she clasped my forearm and hauled me to my feet. "First class is boarding."

Yumi tucked me into my seat and then sat down next to me. "Hey, should I be worried?"

"Chill, I'm fine." I wanted to snarl that Yumi didn't know me—all she knew were rumors, and rumors can be wrong. I accepted a glass of champagne from a flight attendant. I'd already slipped a little bit today—but it was not a normal day, and champagne didn't *really* count. Yumi didn't say anything else.

The tarmac grumbled beneath us as we rolled down the runway. It magnified in my bones as a warm rattle, massaging me from the inside out. I buried my face in a pillow and dozed off. My dreams were nondescript: black, quick, dissipating like incense. At one point I woke up and saw Merry across the aisle watching a free movie on the seat-back screen, and Yumi dozing next to me. I finished the last of my flat champagne before settling back into my recliner.

Twelve hours later, we touched down in Los Angeles. I didn't wake until we were at the gate. I could sense the residue of the alcohol on the inside of my mind, like a window fogged with grease. My mouth tasted sour and my eyes felt sticky, like they'd been closed for too long.

The monitors in front of us were streaming the red CNN banner as the plane rustled with the sounds of disembarkation: the puckering noise of all seat belts releasing, people standing in the aisle to reach for overhead bins.

I fiddled with the ring on my necklace as I jammed on my shoes. Yumi clutched my arm suddenly, and I flinched away. But she wasn't looking at my jewelry. "Rose," she said, pointing at the seat-back screen.

Though we couldn't hear the sound, it was obvious that the subject of the news story was Cassidy. A photo of Cass from the shoulders up, taken a decade before, popped up in a box next to the newscaster's head. Most people, when they are relegated to a photo box on CNN, have the indignity of a driver's license photo, but this was an old professional picture from the height of Gloss. Head shot. World tour. Short blunt bangs and honey-eyed highlights, glossy pink lips. The anchorwoman looked very serious as she spoke, but our eyes were drawn to the caption below Cassidy's photo.

*Cassidy Holmes: suspected suicide.*

\* \* \*

*November 16, 1999*

# Cassidy

I've never felt more alive. The crowd is eating out of my hand. My teeth are glittering, my eyes are shining, my voice is strong.

Once the initial jitteriness passed and I got out onto that stage, my confidence ballooned up inside me. I can feel the energy quivering off my body; I can almost visualize the rays moving outward and settling like a stupefying mist on the audience.

*I can win this.*

The final notes of Madonna's "Frozen" linger in the air as I take a flourishing bow. As I unbend, I can see the audience on their feet, clapping and cheering, and the judges look pleased as well.

Matilda is beaming. "Wow!" she exclaims. "What do you think, Jenna?"

Jenna Kaulfield says, "It was splendid. You were splendid, dear."

Jonah, Emma, Thomas, Marsha: their words are a blur. I can register that my mouth hurts from my ever-widening smile, and Marsha's last words: "If it were based on this performance alone, I would offer you a contract in a heartbeat. *In a heartbeat,*" she repeats, as the crowd continues to whoop.

I am ushered off the stage to find Anna near tears. "You were so good," she whispers, as she takes the microphone.

We've made it through our ballads, and Anna is finishing up our pop round. We're more than halfway through this nerve-racking evening, and my insides are slowly untwisting.

I follow a production assistant back to the yellow room with the couch. A bottle of water is shoved into my hand and I drink. I keep shifting my feet, dancing a tiny jig on the ground, tap-tap-tapping my shoes, wiggling with my hands, which are clasped around the water bottle. I feel like a figure skater who has come off the Olympic ice and is awaiting her score. I want to whip around and grab the fingers of my coaches and smile and grip hard. But it's only me in the room, and the television is flickering Anna's image on the stage that's only fifteen feet away from where I sit.

I reach for the remote and turn the sound up. Anna is smiling her perfect grin as she wraps her elegant fingers around the microphone and shakes her hips to the beat. It's "Girls Just Want to Have Fun."

Joanna and I discovered this song when we were in middle school and played it nonstop during sleepovers, so often that I can tell that Anna's rendition right now is way too close to a karaoke performance. Something about Anna's voice, her soft lilting tone, reminds me of a sleepover with Joanna—and my first kiss. Between giggles, with Cyndi Lauper in the background, Joanna and I practiced kissing on pillows, then on each other. When her lips were on mine, I'd experienced my first tingle of excitement, but just as I leaned forward to deepen it, she pulled away abruptly and said, "This is boring! Let's watch *Sleepless in Seattle!*" I knew then that we were different from each other.

And that's when I hear it. Anna's voice ripples like a bull-frog. The note is flat, dead. Short, and she shifts back, but it's horrified her. Anna's expression is mildly terrified and, though she continues the performance, she's off by a beat, rushes to catch up again, and doesn't fully recover. She ends with a quick bow, a mortified hand leaping up to her mouth as the judges praise her.

As soon as they're done, she's running off the stage like a figure skater who's tripped after a triple axel.

Two songs down, one to go.

\* \* \*

I'M BACK TO biting my nails. It's the final round of songs, and the camera sweeps over Stephen in an arc, showing the left side of his face, mouth agape. His full face comes into view, contorted in concentration and feeling, arm outstretched; now the other side of him, in silhouette, his perfect long nose and rounded lips outlined in streaks of light. The accompaniment tapers, he lowers his arm, he smiles.

Beside me, Anna is praying. I haven't talked to a deity in a while but think that she has the right idea. Stephen hasn't blundered. She has. And I'm up next with all of the pressure.

Stephen and I pass alongside each other in the backstage wings, one person leading him away, another leading me forward. My nerves are jangling again but I think my arrangement is a good one. My friend Edie picked it out for me, and she's a music expert, so I trust her taste completely.

The lights are in my eyes, but I can hear the audience's presence. There's a transmission, a low-level hum, like a lightly plucked guitar string, that emits from a person. This auditorium is full of these little hums, a packed vibration, rippling out of their bodies and into mine. Their energy feeds me. I break out into a smile.

"Cassidy," Matilda says. "It's the last song. Of the last show you'll do with us. On *Sing It, America!* Are you ready?"

"I am." I breathe in deeply. I embody the song. I part my lips and exhale.

Stephen sang of lust and yearning, I sing of loss and love. We're yin and yang.

\* \* \*

THE NIGHT THE votes are counted is excruciating. The finale is a two-parter and we're sent back to the hotel for the tallying. I find myself tucking my knees to my chest and thinking too much. What will I do once I win? Because I can't imagine myself *not* winning. I was so good. So strong.

The night of the crowning, the three of us are one mass, holding hands as we enter the stage, clinging to one another in support. No matter how annoying I find Anna, I can't let go of her, and no matter how much I want to beat Stephen, I find myself gripping his palm. Matilda draws this moment out long enough that the crowd is fiery with anticipation.

We're squeezing, we're squeezing, we're squeezing.

"And the audience voted . . . and the winner of *Sing It, America!* is . . ."

The crowd's screams drown out the sudden hum in my ears. It's like someone turned the sound off in the room. There's a shimmer of shiny confetti floating continually down onto the stage like snow, as if we are on a daytime game show. I see Matilda in her tottering heels, backlit by stage lights, as she hugs Stephen St. James. The auditorium is an electric blue, reflecting the cool light off all the shining surfaces. Anna is crying and hugging me. I realize that my eyes are wet too, and I'm hugging her back. This, this isn't happening. This can't be real life.

It wasn't my name.

# PART I

# SELF-TITLED
# (2000–2001)

**The *Los Angeles Times*. November 18, 1999. Arts & Entertainment.**

"Sing It, America!," the singing competition that has taken the television world by storm, ended Wednesday after Tuesday's two-hour, heart-stopping voting finale. Anna Williams, 16; Cassidy Holmes, 17; and Stephen St. James, 20, were the three chosen finalists. Mr. St. James, of Atlanta, Georgia, won the audience's hearts—and hands, as they dialed in overwhelming numbers to vote for him at the end of Tuesday night's performances.

The show creators are happy with the outcome and are planning a "bigger and better" "Sing It" season two. "It was an amazing experience," said Mr. St. James. "I feel incredibly blessed." Mr. St. James's grand prize includes a three-album contract with Big Disc Records and a spokesperson role with sponsor Mountain Cola.

The *Houston Chronicle*. November 18, 1999. Entertainment. Page N2 (blurb).

Houston's own Cassidy Holmes, 17, failed to win her coveted "Sing It, America!" crown on Wednesday evening's show finale. The Meyer Park High School student was one of three finalists in the competition, but was voted as a runner-up instead of the grand-prize winner.

Stephen St. James of Atlanta, GA, was the champion of the night, beating out Ms. Holmes and fellow contestant Anna Williams, of St. Paul, MN.

The series' premiere season was one of the most popular on its network, with more than 20 million viewers watching Tuesday's performances and Wednesday's winner reveal.

# 1.

*December 27, 1999*
*Houston*

## Cassidy

Clouds of white blew off the top of the beaters as I dusted more powdered sugar over the running mixer. Finely milled fluff settled on Katie's head, giving her eyelashes and her hair a gray cast. Melanie sneezed.

"Not into the mixing bowl!" Katie exclaimed, shoving her body between the cookie dough and Melanie, who wiped her nose with the back of her hand.

Mom was relaxing after our frenzied Christmas, watching reruns of *The Jet-Setters* while sitting on the overstuffed living room couch. During a commercial break she muted the TV and glanced over the tops of her glasses. "We already have enough Christmas cookies to last us until Valentine's."

Katie snorted. "Patrick and Robbie will eat all those before supper." From our spot at the counter, covered in baking trays, measuring cups, and spoons, we could hear the intermittent *slap-pop* of a basketball in the driveway. Every now and then there was a shout of indignation that carried into the house.

Mel washed her hands and picked up a wax-wrapped stick of butter to grease a baking tray. She was the quieter of the two, and—I suspected—the late bloomer. Until this year, the twins had been happy to dress alike and do everything together, as a pair. Now, as they were entering their teen years, they were growing more into themselves and branching away from each other. Katie had cut her hair short while Melanie kept hers long. While Katie was starting to get a little attitude, Mel was still wide-eyed and sweet. I hoped she'd stay that way.

The front door slammed and Patrick appeared, stretching over us to reach into a cupboard for a glass.

"You smell like armpits," I complained. "Your stink will get in the batter."

"You mean, it'll *improve* it," he said, filling the glass with water from the sink.

"Shut up," I grumbled. I was a little put out that I had to give up my room—which had been *Patrick's* room—during Christmas vacation, but such is life when you have four siblings, three of whom still live at home and one who comes back for the major holidays. I knew Patrick was stinking up my mattress with his smelly feet and displacing my stuff with his.

"Don't be so *sensitive,* sis," he said, gulping the water down and heading back out to his game. I deflated a bit.

When I lost the contest, I'd cried on national television—live. The entire time I had been in that Los Angeles hotel, dreaming, scheming, and singing, I'd thought ahead to the point where I'd *won*. Of all the doors the record company would open, of singing for a living and having my voice heard around the world. The possibility of losing was always there, of course, but I'd refused to acknowledge it, for fear of bringing that outcome to fruition. The more positive I was, the more positive the results would be.

Perhaps I should have thought of the alternatives, so I could be better equipped to handle the disappointment. As it turned out, my blotchy face was transmitted to over twenty million viewers.

My mother found me in the yellow room after the airing was complete, when the industrious bees that worked for the show started sweeping away the confetti mess. I was on the same orange couch, fighting to breathe through my stuffed-up nose. She'd sat down next to me and touched my back with one hand. This tiny gesture made me dissolve into tears again. She let me cry for a few minutes, rubbing the spot between my shoulder blades, then said, "Let's go home."

Mortification turned me into a recluse. I didn't want the outside world to see me after that loss and had hidden myself away ever since. I'd begged for time off from school, and, having never been embarrassed on television before, my parents conferred among themselves about what to do. In the end, we sat down at the kitchen table and they agreed I could skip school until after winter break, when I would be responsible for making up all the assignments I'd missed.

Christmas had been a welcome respite, even though I had to bunk with Mel and Katie. Gifts were always sparse on Christmas; we preferred quality over quantity. The twins had the great idea to pool our money and get the entire family tickets to a Rockets game, even though only our brothers cared about basketball. The smiles never left their faces. Now, two days after Christmas, the glow from the day was starting to fade and my thoughts strayed back to the competition; the wound was still so fresh that it filled my eyes with tears when I touched upon it.

Where was I supposed to go from here?

"Ugh, I hate this storyline," Katie said, bringing my attention back to the kitchen. Her eyes were trained on the TV in the adjoining room, intent on the show. "Madelynn would never have shared her first-class tickets with Yvette! And then Yvette goes and meets Dante and it's this whole big thing."

Mel, ever attuned to my feelings, said to me, "You're okay though?" I gave her a side hug with an elbow bent like a chicken wing, but still got a little bit of powdered sugar on the crown of her head. She shook her hair out like a puppy.

"Let's not share any cookies with Patrick when they're done," I said.

Katie attacked the dough with fervor. "Deal."

Mom sighed and switched off the screen. "Sugar is not going to help you get over this disappointment."

I was quiet, pretending that I hadn't heard her, even though the mixer was off and for once the noise in the house had paused. I worked quietly on the cookies with my head down and shoulders hunched over one of the baking trays, but I knew that the twins would exchange glances and flounce off, a tactic they used any time a parent was about to have a serious talk with one of their siblings. They were courteous enough to hastily plop dough balls down and wash their hands before escaping.

I pressed one of the misshapen cookies on the sheet with my index finger, mashing it. I was wondering when she was going to broach the subject. Maybe she figured that Christmas was over, so she couldn't ruin the holiday by bringing it up. "I know that."

"The best thing you can do now is to get your assignments from Joanna, make up your tests, and graduate on time. And we think you should see a therapist."

"You mean, get psychoanalyzed?"

"Cassidy, you're a bright girl. And a *nice* girl. Your father and I were—we *are*—so proud of you for what you accomplished in L.A. Getting to second place is really amazing. But we can see how badly this devastated you, and we don't want you to get hurt again. Therapy will at least help you get over *this* disappointment."

It was more than a disappointment. The truth was, I was absolutely crushed and had spent the entire winter holiday baking cookies and hoping eating them would hold back the raw feeling of failure.

I put the cookie tray in the oven as an excuse to turn my back to her. Just the thought of not pursuing singing anymore made me feel tired—when you know you can give something up and it'll be easier, but if you don't go doggedly on you can already feel the regret. "I can't *not* sing anymore, Mom," I said tersely, choosing the more important battle.

"Right. I'm not saying you should give it up entirely. But you can still sing at home in your room, or school musicals, you know, like you don't have to keep pursuing this *professional* thing . . ."

"Mmm. I'll think about it."

I already knew I wouldn't think about it. Yes, I applied to *Sing It, America!* on a whim, but it wasn't lack of determination or lack of passion that kept me from applying in earnest. It was a lack of confidence. I surprised myself by getting as far as I did in the competition, but once I was in the game, I didn't want to leave. And no matter what my mother thought or said, I'd tasted how close I had gotten. I'd proven that I was good enough to be considered near professional. People had *rooted* for me. People had *voted* for me. Marsha Campbell had told me I was worth signing. Even though she hadn't, in the end.

If I were a petulant teenager, this conversation would have me storming off into my bedroom to sulk. Instead, I set the oven timer and walked away like her words had not hurt, and sat down on my bed, which was covered with Patrick's stinky socks. I closed my eyes as I lifted my new phone—blue, cordless, my Christmas gift from my parents—to call Edie.

Edie was the one who found out about the *Sing It, America!* competition in the first place and brought the flyer over to Joanna's. Once we figured it was not a fake contest, Joanna, Edie, and Alex urged me to audition.

"You have the best voice in the entire school," Joanna had said, exaggerating my talent.

"You *have* been taking modern dance since the first grade," Edie pointed out, neglecting to mention that I stopped dancing because my parents couldn't afford lessons anymore, what with Robbie's soccer expenses.

"And you're not totally tragic to look at," Alex added, his wide face split into a grin.

"That shouldn't matter, but it does," Edie said.

It had been Edie and Joanna's idea to add rhinestones to my shirt. Alex recommended the cowboy boots, to add a touch of "Texan flair." But Edie was the one who waited with me at the Astrodome for seven hours and suggested all of my song picks. She had always been on the money with trends and taste.

"Yeah?" came the voice on the other line. Edie claimed that people who called her were either her friends, who knew what they were doing when they called, or telemarketers, who didn't deserve a proper greeting. She had a point.

I blew out a long, exasperated breath. "Guess what? My parents don't think it's a good idea for me to try to pursue singing anymore." I didn't mention the therapist part. I knew I should take the offer—I was feeling so low—but I didn't want my friends to know about it.

"Um. That's bullshit. You're good at it."

"Yeah, well." I sighed, brushing Patrick's socks onto the floor. "Good isn't good enough."

"You're right, though. I mean, you're both right."

"What?"

"Here, listen." I heard a scuffling as she dug around in the massive piles of junk stashed around her room. Edie was always beautifully put together when you saw her in person—a dyed-black pixie cut, smoky black eye shadow on her delicate pale face, and all-black clothing bought in the children's department to fit

her four-foot-eleven frame—but her organization extended to
her makeup drawer and that was about it. "I read this article a
few weeks back on this new band Lunatix out of Tucson. You've
heard of them?"

"No . . ."

"I guess you haven't been listening to the radio, then. They're
*amazing* but no one in the industry gave them the time of day
until this talent guy from a record label heard his niece playing
their tape at a family reunion or something. Dude heard the
song and dropped his plate of hot dogs, that's how amazed he
was. Here, let me quote: 'I thought I knew every band in this
genre and with this sound, said Bradley Garner'—that's the talent guy—'but I asked my niece where she'd gotten the tape and
she pulled out a homemade cassette with the band name inked
onto a sticker that they sold for five dollars each at house parties.
Their reach was just maybe a one-hundred-mile radius around
Tucson, Arizona. I was on the phone five minutes later with my
guys convincing them that we needed to bring them in.' Now
Lunatix has a million-dollar contract with these guys and are
already talking about touring nationwide."

I sat digesting this information. "I don't get it."

"See, they were *so* good! They're probably going to win a
Grammy. But they didn't have publicity. They'd mailed their
tape to the same company last year but apparently those record
label guys just get *flooded* with tapes and they can't keep up. So
the band was just trucking away for *forever* and it's just this dumb
luck that they were recognized. My point is," Edie summed up
hastily, "they were working their *asses* off but they could have

been drudging forever. Your parents are right, there's a lot of rejection in this business. And you might never make it."

"Oh." I felt gloomy again. "Thanks for the vote of confidence."

"But I'm also saying this!" she barreled on. "You have contacts now. You did that show and people are aware of your name. Cass! Seize your chance! Call Emma Jake or, like, milk other connections you made while out there. Get cozy with that St. James guy. But, like, don't put all your eggs in this basket, okay? If none of this stuff pans out, you want to be able to go to college and become, like, a veterinarian or whatever. So don't flunk out."

I heard the buzz of the oven timer and padded back out to the kitchen, as Edie repeated, "*Don't* sit on your *ass*. It's not going to happen just because you're good. You're going to have to go after it."

WHILE I WAITED for the cookies to cool, I mulled over Edie's words. Before *Sing It,* I had signed a lot of papers—model releases, confidentiality agreements—without giving it much thought. But I'd inadvertently also signed away many rights to Big Disc, who basically owned my likeness and any potential choices I wanted to make for the next few years. Even if I wanted to eke out a living as a singer after *Sing It,* I couldn't do it without Big Disc unless I wanted to violate one of many contracts. And with my parents having five kids—one in college, the rest still living under their roof—I didn't want to tempt the record company's ire and risk any kind of lawsuit.

The game over, the boys tromped into the kitchen, Robbie clutching a basketball under one long arm. He snatched a cookie, dribbling powdered sugar on the table. "You should've made something chocolatey."

"A thank-you would be appreciated."

He disappeared into the depths of the house. Patrick hovered over the tray, grabbing handfuls of cookies, but I was too distracted by what Edie had said to smack his hand away.

I drummed my fingers on the table, thinking. My only options seemed to be to ask Big Disc for a place with them or wait out the option period and finish school before trying to break into the professional music scene again, which I was sure my parents would prefer. But by then, the iron would no longer be hot enough to strike.

I'd call Marsha Campbell, I decided. I would be cool and collected and wouldn't grovel.

"What time is it?" I asked, realizing that I would have to hustle to catch her.

Patrick consulted a hideous calculator watch on his wrist. "Six thirty."

That meant it was still before five on the West Coast, and even though it was a few days after Christmas, I figured Marsha would still be working. Adults always seemed to be working. "Pat, can you put these in the cookie jar for me when they've cooled down? I have to make a call. And *don't* pick up the phone while I'm on it!"

I spun upstairs and hoped my parents wouldn't mind me calling long-distance. I had to shift through a pile of stuff on my desk—homemade Christmas cards from my sisters, a snow globe from Patrick from his last trip to Boston—to find Marsha's direct line.

"Oh, um, hi! This is Cassidy Holmes. I was on the show . . ."

"Hello, Cassidy! What can I help you with today?"

I realized I hadn't rehearsed what I wanted to say. "Um. I was wondering if perhaps your company would be interested in taking me on. You know. As a singer." It was all coming out wrong. It was as if all the blood was leaving my brain and pooling in my stomach. I could feel a spasm of nerves twitching in my cheek.

"I thought I'd be hearing from you." Her voice softened and I remembered the enthusiastic and supportive woman who had been in the judges' stand only a month earlier. "I know how much you wanted this, and you are a wonderful talent, but unfortunately, I can't offer you anything right now. How bad would it look if you were given a contract right after *not winning* the competition where *the grand prize* is a contract? It would undermine the entire contest. And since the producers of the show are already going ahead with a second season, it'd set the wrong precedent for any future nonwinners. I'm sorry, but I can't. My hands are tied."

The spasm in my cheek turned into a quivering jaw as I fought back tears. "I understand," I quavered. "No, that makes perfect sense."

"You're a very gifted young woman," she continued, "and I have no doubt that you will do well for yourself. But maybe, sometime down the line . . . there may be a place for you here at Big Disc."

"Thank you."

I hung up, dejected. I walked down the stairs to find the cookies, cold and now hard, right where I'd left them. Sitting down heavily at the table, I picked up the fattest one.

"You'll ruin your dinner," Katie said, passing through the dining area with a glass of milk in hand.

"A lot of things are ruined," I said, taking a big bite.

# 2.

*Thursday*

# Merry

The light of the digital clock on my nightstand glowed red: 2:22 A.M. My body radiated like a furnace. The arm draped heavily over my bare back was piping; Raul always felt ten degrees hotter than me, no matter what the outside temperature was. Sleep was fitful. I used to be able to sleep through anything—grabbing snatches of shut-eye from hour to hour on tour buses and planes—but I suppose something in my body chemistry changed. As it was now, my body seemed to get too warm too easily.

Using my phone as a flashlight and padding barefoot down the stairs to the kitchen, I listened to the internal tick of the house. Raul and I bought this house a few months ago and I was still learning the noises. Every house has its shifts and creaks. My childhood home rumbled with thunder when it rained, and framed photos would jitter on the walls when a fire truck drove past our street. This Beverly Hills Spanish-style villa had an errant water pipe that whistled when the fridge started making ice cubes. Sometimes it was difficult to tell whether it was Sunny or just another specter.

I tucked my feet under myself in a kitchen chair and flicked on the television, flipping through channels. CNN was covering Cassidy's death, and this time I watched it entirely, without disruptions, as I gnawed on handfuls of dry marshmallow cereal. They hadn't discovered anything new since the earlier broadcast, though of course it was still labeled "breaking news."

After we'd landed, Emily warned all of us to keep off social media, but her eyes were on me, as usual: don't open your mouth, Merry; don't say something you'll regret, *Merry*. Yumi had pocketed her phone immediately without checking her messages, but Rose started sliding through texts before we'd even left the baggage claim. Yumi invited us to her house the next day to talk more about it, but I think Rose agreed because she actually wanted to discuss the upcoming movie premiere.

Rose always thought about the "big picture."

My hired car had deposited me at the house, and Raul was home early from the set, fresh red roses placed in a vase on the kitchen island, the burners set to warm, an inviting simmering scent rich in the air. Sunny was out, so the TVs were not in their usual active and blaring mode. Usually I hated when she watched anything too loudly, but this time I had hoped to catch more of the news. Raul stopped me from reaching for the remote and attempted to feed me warm pasta sauce straight from the pan. I love Raul, I really do, but he was doing the opposite of what I wanted: I was starved for information, not for Italian food. When I pulled my face away from the wooden spoon, he gave me a wounded look. "You need to eat at a proper mealtime," he urged, his voice warm caramel, "to readjust to our time zone." I acquiesced by nibbling at a small bowl of pasta.

Almost immediately after dinner we were in the bedroom, his arms were around my waist, warm mouth nuzzling my neck, nose-tip tracing a trail of heat from earlobe to cleavage. He smelled like thyme and aftershave, his almost-signature scent. I responded in kind, and we fell into bed together, warm and sticky with travel residue and want.

I'd been asleep for only a few hours.

The anchor said, "The body of Cassidy Holmes, former member of the pop group Gloss, was discovered in her Hollywood Hills home early yesterday morning by a housekeeper. Though initially treated as a suspicious death, medical examiners have since released a statement that the marks on the body are consistent with a suicide." The video playing behind her voice was footage from a helicopter camera. The grainy video showed official-looking people closing the trunk doors to a van parked outside Cassidy's house, and walking around to the passenger doors.

"It is unknown whether Ms. Holmes had a history of mental illness, though she was once hospitalized for exhaustion after her abrupt departure from Gloss in 2002." An image of the four of us at the height of our popularity filled the screen—Cassidy, on the far right, looked as if she could be cut away from the photo with a pair of scissors. No doubt the news crew picked that particular promotional photo to highlight her isolation.

"While the other three members of Gloss were not reachable for comment, they have tweeted and posted on their official Facebook page that they are saddened by this unexpected loss. Quote: 'Rest in peace, Cassidy. We will always love and miss you.' Her family asks for privacy during this difficult time."

This segment was only a few minutes long and didn't mention anything she had done in the fifteen years since. I'd heard, though not seen with my own eyes, that Cassidy was involved with a charity project of some kind, but of course the news wanted to discuss only what was flashy. The news piece ended with a short clip of Cassidy from the "Prime" music video, of her floating in water like an ethereal angel. I cut my eyes away—a now-ingrained reaction to that video—and muted the television while pulling up Twitter on my phone. The internet is always ahead of broadcast news.

#RIPSassyCassy I can't believe you're gone

---

heaven has another angel #RIPSassyCassy i hope you got ur wings

---

HMMM there was no NOTE guys i dont think it was really a suicide #RIPSassyCassy #conspiracy

---

Good, I'm glad she's dead. She deserved to die after she broke up the best girl group EVER. #AssyCassy

---

#GlossGirls former member 'Sassy Cassy,' 35, hanged herself at home, says anonymous source 'close to the family'

My thumb paused over this ribbon of information. No one had mentioned yet *how* Cass had died. I followed the link to a gossip site.

A source CLOSE to the Holmes family tells JMC that Holmes's body was discovered in her Hollywood Hills kitchen, and that she had hanged herself. The WEIRD thing to note: Holmes's main residence was in Pasadena. Though she owned this particular house (purchased in 2002 at the height of Gloss's popularity), sources tell us that she RARELY stepped foot into the home in the past 10 years. The 10-bedroom, 5-and-a-half bath stucco mansion was on the market in 2008 during the economic downturn, but NO buyers snapped it up for over 8 months before the listing was withdrawn. A maid service visits every other week for maintenance.

We at JMC believe that Holmes PLANNED her suicide on a date that coincided with the housekeeper visit so that she would be discovered as quickly as possible.

Holmes was 35 years old.

Sunny appeared at the threshold of the kitchen door. She resembled me more than her father, thank goodness. She was wearing a hideous pink tank with a pizza print on the front, shorts, and her feet were bare. I laid the phone down.

"You're up," I said, hiding my surprise that she was home at all. So far this summer, she had been staying out all hours with little regard for rules I put out. At least she wasn't looking at me disdainfully like she usually did.

Sunny glided over the tile and folded herself on another

chair, grabbing the box of cereal. She barely glanced at me as she picked out the marshmallows. I fingered the wheat pieces and slid them in front of me, making a triangle of them on the table. I remembered when Sunny would sit on my lap and I could feel her delicate bones through the fabric of her soft pajamas. I remembered her strawberry-scented baby shampoo, that little head of platinum cabbage and its fruity-sweet scent. At fourteen, she now smelled like teenage sweat and bad perfume.

The television light flickered blue and white against her skin, and she looked ahead at the screen, absorbing whatever rays the news wanted to share.

I had my reservations about my child growing up in this crazy world. I knew, as a former Gloss girl, that Sunny would never have a normal childhood like I had. Flashing cameras and faceless voices never chased me when I was her age. I'd always known that she would face different obstacles growing up, but I imagined that the tabloids would cut us a break at first—for the newborn's sake. It was the moment I was leaving the hospital after giving birth, swaddled in a big blanket in the back of an SUV, with yet another blanket wrapped around my hours-old baby, that I realized how wrong I was. If nothing else, her parentage made her even more of a target. Strobes blasted at the tinted windows over and over, and I pulled the fabric's edge over her eyes in case they could somehow get damaged from the flashes. I'd wondered if she was going to be affected by this spectacle later in life, if she would end up dealing with the same shit I had but at an earlier age.

She was already starting to ask me if she was too young to become a model.

"Sad," she said now, breaking the silence. The news had moved on to a shooting that had happened earlier in Indiana, but I knew she was talking about Cassidy.

"Yes," I said, feeling the meaning of the word echo somewhere inside me.

"You hadn't talked to her in a while, right?"

"No," I said, unsure of how to discuss it further.

Sunny picked up her phone and slid the screen on. I thought that was the end of our discussion, but she had opened Instagram, tapping through. "She seemed like such a normal person. I mean, look." She faced the phone display toward me. Older Cassidy, drinking wine. Older Cassidy, hugging the neck of an elderly dog. She thumbed down, showing a grid of unretouched, unprofessional snaps. I reached for the phone and looked through them as Sunny hovered and said, "You weren't following her, right?"

"I didn't even know she had an Instagram." I wondered why I hadn't thought to look her up before.

"I don't follow her either, but no one does. It's set to private. Well, it was. The account is getting more followers right now even though she's, you know."

Cassidy's photos showed nothing important or discernible about her life. No location tags, no hashtags, no verification check. A vase of roses on a desk, a handheld plaque noting her third anniversary working for a water charity. She updated maybe once every few months, with her last image posted half a year ago.

"This isn't even her name—how did you find her?"

"I dunno. Somebody tagged me." I'd gotten to the bottom

of the grid and my daughter took her phone back. "Anyway." She patted my hand and, noticing that I was lost in thought, left the kitchen. Sometimes, my sweet teenage daughter's cool exterior could thaw. I heard her door close upstairs, and I was by myself again, looking at the flickering lights of the television. I swept the wheat bits from the table into my palm and dropped them back into the box.

My own phone was on the table. I flicked through contacts and pushed "call."

The warm, dulcet tones of Cassidy's voice mail did not flow out of the speaker like I expected. The phone rang only once before a shrill noise introduced a mechanical operator's words: "The number you are trying to reach is no longer in service." I hadn't talked to her in a long while. Why hadn't I tried to make contact after everything we'd been through? Sure, I'd been upset about the tour but we'd been friends too. Out of all the Gloss girls, I was the closest to Cassidy.

I tapped the edge of the phone on the counter, thinking. Why couldn't I have put those feelings aside and helped her? Now I didn't know what she'd been up to, how she'd felt, for a decade. The years yawned backward like a chasm.

# 3.

# Cassidy

I watched my friends walk across the stage five weeks ago. I sat with Joanna's mother, Mrs. Sherman, who screamed when her daughter's tassel was flicked to the opposite side of her cap. By the time the caps flew up into the air, my throat was raw from cheering and my heart ached that I had been left out of the celebration. I found my friends after the ceremony, Edie ripping off her black graduation gown to expose yet another black dress underneath it, and Joanna combing her fro back into place after removing her cap. One of our classmates, Elana, was having a party at her house in the Heights. Even though I knew Edie and I would've preferred eating ice cream at her house and watching Drew Barrymore movies until five in the morning, the four of us planned to go because Alex was dating Elana's best friend, Brittany.

"You'll be good, right?" Mrs. Sherman said to us. "Don't do anything I wouldn't do."

Joanna rolled her eyes. "I'm premed. I'm gonna study to find out how to *save* people, not kill them."

"I know, baby girl. I just have to be a mom sometimes."

At Elana's, there were bags of chips and bowls of queso, and anyone who had an older sibling found a way to bring alcohol, but the good beer was claimed immediately and the rest of us were left with the dregs. I held a plastic cup of Mad Dog 20/20 and sipped it cautiously as the people around me tried to dance to *NSYNC.

"How's that?" Edie asked, pointing at my cup.

I shouted over the music. "It tastes like sweet death."

"Gimme it." She took a gulp from my cup and made a face. "God, why would anyone make banana liqueur? Why would they color it red? Hey, where'd Alex go?"

"Probably went to find Brittany," I replied. Edie's sour face deepened. "I'll take my gross mashed banana drink back now, please."

Alex pushed through a throng of people on the stairs and grabbed the cup from Edie's hand, draining it immediately.

"Um, you okay?"

He stormed into the kitchen and came back with the rest of the Mad Dog bottle, drinking directly from the neck. Joanna trotted behind him with a bottled water. "Dude, that isn't a beer," she said, making a move as if to take it from him.

"No shit," he said.

Joanna gave me a look—Alex didn't really listen to her or Edie, but I could exert some influence over him. After he gulped a few more mouthfuls, I eased the bottle away and said, "Look, you can't hog this delicious banana daiquiri. I'm gonna need some too." I sipped it, shuddering at how bad it was.

"It was the last thing of liquor in there," Alex said morosely. After a beat, he added by way of explanation, "Britt broke up with me."

"Oh, honey," Joanna said tenderly.

"Yeah." A note of anger came through in his voice. "What's worse, she had *Elana* do it for her. She couldn't even break up with me to my face! We're at the *same party!* How hard can it be?"

"Well, you can't drink alone," Edie said, and the three of us passed the bottle around until it was done. Then Alex saw Britt dancing inside so we moved to the porch, even though it was still ninety degrees out and my face misted with sweat immediately.

As I watched some of my former classmates kick cans in the yard and make out in dark corners, my thoughts turned inward, self-critically evaluating my life. As stupid and aimless as they seemed right now, they were all going to move on to the next phases of their lives, while I—well. It turns out that when you miss five months of school for an out-of-state, televised singing competition, there is no feasible way to catch up on all of your studies.

From being on 20 million television sets to not even finishing senior year on time. My future felt stalled. Something to discuss at therapy the following Tuesday, I supposed. My parents had me checking in with Dr. Brant every two weeks.

Edie, all four feet ten inches of her, felt the effects of the alcohol first. She hugged us fiercely. "I'm going to miss you guys."

Joanna patted her back. "Aw, come on. We still have all summer."

Alex spoke up. "I've got that poli-sci internship." He loved all things political; Alex spoke of wanting to run for office one day: President Hernandez, he'd joke. "And Edie has her thing in Portland . . ."

"Well, I'll be here serving pizzas until the very last day I can, and then I'm off to Michigan," Joanna said. "But it's not a very demanding job. I can still hang out in my off time."

And I'll be going to summer school, I'd thought to myself. My tongue felt blurry as I said, "You know what? I just want to say thanks for being there for me after that TV shit."

"Oh, girl," Joanna waved a hand dismissively. "You don't have to go through that again. We *know*. We're good."

"Well, I know I checked out pretty hard during winter break. I've been so wrapped up in my own head . . ."

"Hey." Edie put a tiny, sticky hand on my shoulder and rubbed hair out of my face. "It's fine, okay?"

"This party sucks," Alex said abruptly. "There's no more alcohol and they don't even have any cookies. Wanna go?"

Joanna had driven us back to her apartment. I'd puked in the parking lot and Alex laughed as he held my hair away from my chin and told me I couldn't hold my liquor. I remember gazing up at him from the concrete where I crouched—his dark silhouette against the brighter night sky—and arguing that banana wine didn't count as liquor. It was after midnight and the world seemed to have no depth at all: the sky was a milky blue slathered in a glaze of thin, stretched clouds.

Edie had gone off to her summer program; Joanna's schedule was so erratic that I barely saw her; and Alex picked up a second job—he said it was to offset the future costs of his dorm expenses, but I figured he was trying to keep his mind off Britt—so he was too exhausted to hang out more than once a week. Summer was a blur of air-conditioning and ceiling fans, sitting in a boring classroom for hours on end, and shuttling my siblings around town.

But then I got a phone call.

"I have a proposition for you," Marsha Campbell said. "We have a girl group. They need a fourth."

"And you want *me* to be the fourth?" I squeaked, looking in disbelief at the receiver. No one else had answered the phone; my parents were at work, the twins were at the Y, and Robbie was shooting hoops.

"Not quite. We'd like to *audition* you to be the fourth."

"I—"

"You're the right age, the right voice. We already know you can sing," she added. "We just need to know if you'll *vibe* with these girls. Are you interested?"

"Wh—Yes!"

"Perfect. I'll leave you information on the details. Can you fly out this week?"

When I hung up, I was in a daze. Then, shrieking, hopping out of the kitchen chair so violently that it fell over in a clatter, I tore around the house.

My parents did not like it. "Your education is first and fore-most," they said. "Don't you want to finish summer school?"

"But this is the opportunity of a *lifetime*—I'll be back in a few days and will only miss two days, tops. I won't even miss my session with Dr. Brant."

They finally relented, and my father walked me to my gate at Hobby Airport and sat with me while I waited for my flight. "We wanted to give you this," he said, pulling out a box. It contained a little silver brick with a blue screen—my first cell phone—and I clasped it with surprise. "Promise me you'll call every day," he said.

It wasn't my first time flying alone, but it *was* the first time I felt like an adult while I was flying. It was a new experience, to fly out *for a job interview.* I didn't even have time to check in to my hotel; a driver whisked me away from the baggage claim and deposited me neatly on the front steps of Big Disc's offices. I was passed around from receptionist to assistant to a maroon chair outside an office door that swung open to reveal Marsha Campbell. She gestured me inside, already standing to greet me at her desk, arm outstretched for a handshake.

"Hi, Cassidy," she said as we shook hands like grown adults. "How are you feeling?"

"Good," I said, resisting the urge to wipe my sweaty fingers on my jeans, determined to put my best foot forward.

She gave me a short once-over with her eyes, gray-flecked and serious. Then she smiled. "Let's meet the girls, shall we?"

I FOLLOWED MARSHA'S tousled red head down a maze of corri-dors until we reached a door with a long, rectangular window.

"Here we are," she said, twisting the knob and revealing three girls seated in various stages of boredom around a conference table. There was a warbling voice that I realized was not emanating from any of them but streaming from a shoebox-size cassette player.

Three faces turned toward me, all blank in expression. The girl in the middle, with ice-blue eyes, stopped the tape and gave me a small hopeful grin.

"This is Meredith," Marsha said, as ice-blue waved a hand. "Yumiko, Rose."

Yumiko half-stood from her chair and reached out a hand without changing expression. I put a hand out as well and shook it. "Usually people call me Yumi," she said with a touch of warmth, then sat back down again. Her voice was soft and wispy.

Rose, however, did not move. Her hands remained clasped on the table and her back was rod-straight.

"Well," said Marsha. "Girls, Cassidy's vocals suit what we're looking for, so *I* think that she's a good fit. I'll just leave you four in here so you can get to know one another. Buzz if you need anything." She closed the door behind her.

I pulled out a seat. We stared at one another.

Yumiko was one of the most naturally beautiful women I had ever seen. Long, black hair framed a delicate oval face. Her brown eyes were slightly far apart, giving her a sly, cattish sort of look, and a long flat nose led to a perfect cupid's bow on a small mouth. When she'd stood up for our handshake, I'd noticed she was an hourglass of curves, clad in a shiny metallic jacket and shimmering dark jeans.

If Yumiko was warm-toned, Meredith was the complete opposite: blond curls and pale white skin, offset by berry lips. She wore a cropped tank top and bleached jeans with enough space between the two that it was apparent she was the most confident of the three about her body. She wore her skin like it was an expensive coat that she took for granted. I'd known girls like her in middle school—while the rest of us worried about our early-blooming breasts or sudden six-inch growth spurt that left our legs looking like sticks, she was the one that puberty was kind to, sharpening the childish angles of her face, growing hips gradually instead of overnight. The ones who were cheerleaders, the ones the sixth-graders worshipped.

Rose's eye contact was unnerving. She was petite—Edie's size, maybe—but her small body was coiled tight. One Doc Martens–enclosed foot tapped against the chair leg, unable to reach the ground. Aside from a fairly unremarkable face, which reminded me of a gerbil with its long dark lashes and tiny pointed nose, I realized it wasn't just her staring that immobilized me. It was her unblinking eyes: one was brown, the other blue.

I suddenly found my voice. "So . . . hi. I'm Cassidy."

"Don't get too comfortable, Cassidy," Rose declared in a soft, clipped tone. "We've been interviewing dozens of girls." She gestured to the tape player, which I gathered had been playing their other choices before I'd walked into the room. Seems like my parents didn't have much to worry about, after all.

"Rose, do you always have to be nasty to every new person

we meet?" chided Meredith. Her attention swiveled to me. "We saw you on TV. You were good."

My mouth involuntarily lifted in one corner. "Thanks."

"Not that we regularly tuned into that show, but Marsha sent us clips when she wanted to throw your name in."

"Thank you," I repeated. "Um . . . so what is your band?"

"We're from San Francisco. Well, not actually San Francisco, but the Bay Area?" Meredith said.

"We, minus one person," said Yumiko.

"We got this deal here," Meredith said, in my direction, "but our fourth—Viv—had to back out unexpectedly. But the group just doesn't sound right with only three people, you know? It's, like, unbalanced."

"Why did she leave?" I asked, while also wondering if maybe I shouldn't ask.

"None of your business," Rose said, flint in her voice. She hadn't shifted position, hadn't moved her arms from that clasped position on the tabletop. But her foot continued to skitter against the chair leg.

Admonished, I looked down at my hands. Long fingers, pink nail beds. I had a flash of the last time I was in Los Angeles, of that boy whose hands I'd looked at before he went onstage. Stephen St. James. This was his label. He might have sat in this room. He might be in the building right now. The sudden thought streaked across my mind before I remembered why I was there.

"Oh. Sorry," I murmured.

"Anyway," Yumiko said brightly, trying to change the subject, "we're also figuring out a new manager. We're all up in the air but hopefully we'll get it all figured out soon."

I nodded. Yumiko continued, "Why don't you do a quick song with us? Just so we know how it'll feel? We'll do 'Mary Had a Little Lamb.'"

I took a moment to warm up—after the plane ride, my throat felt a little tight. I could feel Rose's withering stare. Merry flipped the cassette over and hit RECORD on the tape player.

As I launched my voice, the other girls chimed in. It felt electric, like everything just slid right into place. Merry's alto tones were deep and fluid, and I could hear the soft, lifting vibrations of Yumiko's soprano.

We let the song taper off, but there was no doubt that we all felt the mood shift of the room.

"Let's try another one," Merry said. It was even better than the lullaby. The silence afterward was so thoughtful that Merry forgot to stop recording, and Yumiko had to lean over and hit the button for her.

They were both smiling. Even Rose tilted her head, regarding me with a new look.

"Did you do much performing before the show?" asked Yumiko. "Just wondering how you lucked into all this."

"I've taken singing lessons since I was a kid and done some school musicals . . . but *Sing It* was the biggest thing I've done so far," I admitted.

"But you sent in demos and stuff, right? The typical hungry-artist thing?" Merry asked.

"Not really . . ."

"Hold on," Rose said, and leaned forward on both elbows.

"Are you telling me that you *only* just realized *last year* while on that *singing show* that you wanted to *be serious* about it?"

I was suddenly ashamed that I hadn't tried even harder, that summer or any of the summers before.

"Damn." Rose slapped her palms down on the conference table with a resounding thud. "We worked for every inch that we could gain and now here you are, fresh off the televised mayhem, waltzing in for a spot. Ridiculous."

I didn't know how to respond to that. A beat; the room darkened as a cloud shifted under the sun. Rose caught herself and intertwined her fingers together, bent her head forward as if she were praying. She breathed in and out. The other two girls seemed to understand that Rose was making a decision. They kept their mouths shut and just watched. "You're good," she said finally. "You have to be serious, okay? You have to be serious, because *we* are serious."

We'd been in this room for less than twenty minutes and I didn't know these girls at all, but I could sense the lingering sweetness of our harmony, like a perfume hovering in the air. I knew we could do great things. I looked into her mismatched eyes and nodded. "I am."

She nodded her head toward the door, dismissing me. "We'll let you know."

# 4.

## Thursday

## Yumi

W hat's this one called?" Rose said, feet drawn up onto the couch and gesturing with one hand. Her orange-colored drink wobbled perilously close to the lip of the glass. I'd considered mimosas for the early hour, but thought it was too festive a drink to serve the day after learning our friend had died. I'd tucked the booze away before guests arrived, but as soon as Rose came in she asked where the vodka was. She was drinking a screwdriver, light on the orange juice, heavy on the vodka.

I wrenched my eyes away from her drink and looked at the painting. It was oversize, fit into an overwrought gilded frame, and hung opposite the couch. I took a gulp of my own drink to soften the memory. "Something about a storm on the sea. He was obsessed with buying fancy paintings for me and he came home saying it was by Rembrandt."

"You think it's a fake, though?" She quirked an eyebrow, looking at it some more.

"It has to be. But I liked the energy of it and he gave it to me."

"Just like that—gave it to you? Even after all that mess?"

She'd probably followed the divorce in the tabloids; I hadn't discussed it with her and Kevin wouldn't have, either. "I think it was *because* of all that mess. Probably an act of kindness or pity, I think. He didn't even tell the lawyers about it."

Growing up, my parents had one couch, wrapped in a plastic liner. I considered their wisdom, protecting their polyurethane couch with even more plastic, as I watched a sweating orange droplet fall from Rose's over-full glass onto my eight-thousand-dollar dove-gray sofa.

She made a grunting noise as we heard the front door open and slam in echo. "Sorry, sorry," Meredith sputtered, kicking off a pair of pink sneakers and folding her feet underneath her next to me on the opposite couch. "I was up with Sunny last night and then took a nap. My internal clock is still on London time. And there's a thick camp of paparazzi right outside your gate."

Rose's eyebrow remained raised as she sat sipping her drink. Merry used to adjust to time zones instantly; motherhood had blunted her edge and evidently Rose judged that. "How *is* Miss Soleil?" she asked.

Merry blew out a breath. "Sweet. Tiring. Teenagers," she said with a knowing smirk, before realizing that neither Rose nor I had children. "Well, you remember what it was like, being that age."

I was sure that my upbringing—kids picking on me because I had a funny last name, being the only nonwhite face in a sea of students, before we moved to the Bay Area when I was twelve—was vastly different from Merry's teenage years. She'd told us before that she had been on the JV cheerleading squad and asked to the senior prom when she was only a sophomore. But I said, "I can imagine."

"Only"—she fussed with a throw pillow—"She's been asking about doing more in the entertainment world."

"Like stripping?" Rose said, obviously joking, but Merry's head snapped up.

"No, but almost as bad as." She gave a grimace. "She thinks that because she's the *daughter of Cherry Gloss* and the *stepchild of Raul X. Martinez*"—this she said in a hoity-toity accent, although from what I knew, Soleil did not speak like this at all—"and she has sixty thousand followers on social media, she is entitled to leverage that into something."

"Like stripping?" Rose repeated, smiling harder. Merry threw the pillow at her. Luckily, she missed.

"No. Like modeling. When I asked her who would hire her to walk their catwalk, you know what she said? *Any one of your designer friends.* Can you believe that?"

"Nepotism wins again," I said lightly, trying to keep the sour note out of my voice.

Merry poured herself a glass of white wine and gulped down half of it. "I already hate that she's on Instagram so much, with her life so public like that, but at least I've given her basic safety pointers so she's not posting where she is when she's actually there. But you remember what it was like before. All that *attention*."

Attention can be loaded. Attention can be good or bad.

We murmured, commiseration or agreement, I wasn't sure. Rose sucked in her cheeks and jiggled her glass of ice cubes in the ensuing awkward silence. Merry looked around. "I like what you've done to the place," she said, changing the subject. We hadn't spent so many consecutive days with one another in a long while. I'd had the painting for months but Rose hadn't been over to my house for probably years.

"Thanks."

"So have you considered the reunion tour?" Rose asked, setting her glass down on my coffee table and getting down to it.

I shook my head slightly, confused. I'd thought this meeting was about the movie premiere. Or Cassidy. "But without Cass—"

"I was reading stuff last night," Merry began, then closed her mouth.

"I read about it too," I said quietly.

The worst part about the tabloids is that they find things and publish them with little regard for how people might feel about the information. When I stumbled upon the method of Cassidy's death, I wondered if her parents would want that out there. And something squeezing her beautiful throat—her soft, sweet vocal cords—was almost too much to bear. Was it symbolic?

Merry's voice became firmer. "I don't think she did it."

I reached out a hand to gently touch her. "Mer . . ."

"It's just not *like* Cassidy," she repeated.

"How do you know, though? We hadn't spoken to her in months. Years," I said.

"Why would someone like Cass just decide, out of the blue, to kill herself? It doesn't make any sense. I could *maybe* wrap my mind around it if it was fifteen years ago and she'd just left the group, broke the contract, lost endorsement deals, was a social pariah, but *now*? After all this time?"

"You don't know what was going on in her personal life," I argued. "Stuff that has absolutely nothing to do with us, or money, or other friends."

"I just say there's reasonable doubt, that's all."

"I don't," Rose interjected, crunching down on an ice cube. "We knew from the start that Cassidy wasn't really ready for any kind of confrontational lifestyle. Do you remember the first time we met her? How she said she was never interested in being a real artist until a reality show competition? She buckled whenever she was told to do something. She was too sensitive. People like that don't do well in this business."

"But," I said slowly, "she *wasn't* in the business anymore."

I'd known Rose for twenty years and knew she could spew some vitriol, but I didn't know where this animosity had come from.

When Cassidy had soft-auditioned for Gloss—when Marsha brought Cass to L.A.—Rose could have been nicer. After we'd left the label's building and gotten lunch, we chewed on our straws and mulled over Viv's replacement. Rose had been critical of Cassidy's meek demeanor, of her disinterest in pursuing the dream, of the brown color of her hair. But Marsha liked her, and it was undeniable that she made us sound better.

"We'll make her pull her weight," I'd said, and the others had agreed. "Otherwise, we'll toss her out," Rose had said.

Cassidy had done what she was told to do. She'd signed her contract within twenty-four hours of our meeting and the label asked her to move out to L.A. immediately. Within a week, we were installed in the same three-bedroom apartment, with Cass and I doubling up in the shared room. She was on the quiet side and kept to herself around the rest of us. She tidied her portion of the living space, took great lengths to work out and keep to her diet, and made it to all of the appointments we were obligated to keep.

It had been nonstop preparation leading up to the album release. Big Disc emphasized Cassidy's role in the group as a means to pump a little more publicity, flaunting the fact that yet another *Sing It* contestant had found success in her chosen profession. They wanted to time the album release with the second season of *Sing It, America!* as a cross-promotion, since they had a stake in both ventures. So all four of us were working, though not really *being,* alongside one another. Cassidy's assimilation into Gloss was pushed to the backs of our minds. My immediate concern was to not fall asleep from the slowly creeping exhaustion that spread over my limbs and settled behind my eyes. Merry, who grew up with morning swim meets and fitting in cheerleading practice and seven hundred extracurricular activities, seemed to keep up fine, and Rose, with a determined grin that bared her teeth when she was especially tired, did better than Cassidy and me. We two were a little out of shape, a little more overwhelmed.

But even though Rose believed that Cassidy was a pushover,

that didn't automatically mean that Cass would voluntarily leave this world *now*. Meredith's point of view was more appealing. I reconsidered. I turned to her.

"Well, who else would want Cassidy gone?"

"I made a list," Merry said, pulling out her phone.

"Oh, *please!*" Rose sounded exasperated, but Merry went on.

"Maids, groundskeeper, anyone who worked on her house. Former stalkers—who could still be *current* stalkers—the roommate of the guy who probably never got over her . . ."

"This is ridiculous," Rose interrupted. "It could have been a postal worker. Someone who got mad if she cut him off in traffic and then followed her home. Anybody. Why don't we talk to the detective? The police know more than we do, anyway. Maybe you'll listen to someone with authority about this and start to accept that, yes, Cassidy was a sad person."

"I mean, after that boyfriend—it was probably hard," Merry said.

I nodded in agreement. At least the world hadn't been convinced that Kevin broke my *arm*. He'd broken only my trust.

"We should talk to them anyway," I said. "The police, I mean. We might be able to give them more information if it *was* a stalker. All those piles of letters . . ."

The phone on the couch cushion next to Merry began to vibrate. "Hello?" She clapped two fingers over the speaker, a holdover from when phones actually had large mouthpieces. "It's Em." Eyes downcast, she focused back on the voice in her ear. "Uh-huh. Okay. I'll write it down. Yeah, I'm with them now so I'll just tell them . . ."

Out of the corner of my eye, I could see Rose's body jerk quickly, like something had surprised her. She slid her phone out of her purse and read whatever was on the screen, smiled a strange smile, and swiped her finger across the text to respond to it. If I didn't know better, Rose had a lover she hadn't told anyone about. I knew Rose's modus operandi, and it was to splash her (and our) relationships far and wide, as quickly as possible, for maximum headline impact. She had been linked to a number of high-profile men, but as soon as they started talking about settling down and having a family, she found a way to get rid of them. I'd always wondered if Rose even *liked* the men she dated; every single one stank of a personality clash and a publicity stunt to me. If Rose was keeping someone under wraps, there had to be a good reason. Or she was waiting for an opportune moment.

She caught me looking and her smile changed from that tender indulgence to a self-righteous smirk. Sometimes, even after all we've been through, I had to wonder if I knew Rose at all.

Merry ended her call. "Cassidy's funeral arrangements. Her parents want to hold the service in Houston. Once they release . . . the body . . . they'll set the date. Probably next Wednesday. We'll attend, right?"

Rose clucked her tongue softly. "As long as it's not during the premiere. What shitty timing."

"The premiere? Of course we'll go to the funeral," I said. Rose glared at me. "We had two minutes of screen time in that, versus three years with Cassidy."

Merry turned her face toward us again. "Okay, so, the letters?"

**Excerpt from the beginning of VH1's *Behind the Music,*
episode "Gloss," first aired September 2008**

They began as a humdrum girl group on the West Coast;
they exploded into a worldwide phenomenon seemingly
overnight.

*Black-and-white photographs pile in a montage; they in-
clude a shot of young Rose in a star-spangled outfit, waving a
baseball cap, and another of a dark-haired, dark-eyed girl in
jean shorts smiling from a tire swing on a playground.*

The story of Gloss began in 1993. Eleven-year-old Rosalind McGill and her childhood best friend and neighbor,
Vivian Ortiz, spent their days singing, dancing, and partici-
pating in church choir. When Rose decided she needed a bigger spotlight in 1997, she did something unusual: instead of
ditching Vivian to try to make it as a solo act, she chose to
expand their group, adding members Yumiko Otsuka and
Meredith Warner, from outside of their small town in Northern California.

The group practiced relentlessly, covering popular songs
and penning a few of their own. Finally, after two years of con-
stant toil, touring in one of their mothers' minivans up and
down the California coast, they caught the attention of Marsha Campbell at Big Disc Records.

*A clip of Marsha in 2008, her hair a bright blond:* "I knew
there was nothing like these girls in spirit and in sound. We
had to sign them."

There was a problem as soon as the girls signed with the

company. Vivian, one of the founding members of Gloss, had to pull out for health reasons.

*Marsha's head again:* "Vivian was extremely sick. It wasn't just nerves."

*Another head, this time of a more mature-looking Meredith being interviewed:* "We'd been working so hard to get to the signing stage, so I thought she was just exhausted from that. But it turned out to be far more serious."

Vivian was out; now the group needed a replacement. Marsha, who had recently been a judge on the wildly popular TV program *Sing It, America!*, knew just the one: season-one runner-up Cassidy Holmes, who was the same age as the girls.

*An audio clip plays the cassette-tape recording of "Mary Had a Little Lamb" from the girls' first introduction to one another. A photo of the girls in their early days—a candid from their first tour bus, with Rose in the foreground sipping a can of Diet Coke, Cassidy and Yumi in the shadowed aisle behind her—is in sepia tone on the screen.*

As soon as the girls heard Cassidy sing with them, they knew they had found the missing piece of the puzzle. The ensemble was complete. The girls quickly cut half of their debut album with producer Jake Jamz and embarked on a mall tour spanning more than forty cities.

Meredith, though not the eldest, often remarked that she felt like the mother of the group. She was loud and not afraid to speak up when something seemed out of line. *A video clip of Merry in 2001: she is arguing with manager Peter Vincent on a sidewalk, one finger held aloft in a stabbing motion. The video is grainy, taken from across the street. There is no audio accompanying the video, but it's obvious she's having an argument with him.*

Despite a few setbacks caused by Meredith and her diva antics, by the time Gloss had a full album ready in 2001, the girls were poised for stardom.

# 5.

*September 2000*
*L.A.*

# Cassidy

When I blew out my candles on my seventh birthday, I wished I could be a ballerina. I coaxed my parents to sign me up for dance classes. On the first day of ballet, the girl next to me took an instant dislike to me and stomped on the back of my heel. I wish I could say that I moved to a different part of the room or transferred to a different class, but I didn't; I told my parents that I didn't want to take ballet, and they let me move to modern dance instead.

I have always been bad with confrontation. Which meant that Rose's finger pointed in my face, her two-toned eyes bright with fury even in the dim glow of the recording studio lights, was very off-putting.

"This isn't fair." She glowered at Jake Jamz. "You're giving *her* all the good lines!"

It was clear from the way that Yumiko and Meredith deferred to her judgment when I auditioned for the group that Rose had a temper, but although I'd spent all of August worrying that we would get into a fight, we'd been able to shrug off conflict in the apartment. I'd hoped that I wouldn't be on the receiving end of Rose's ire, but any fragile politeness ended when she realized our producer had chosen only two of us for the main verses. In the control room on the other side of a giant glass window, Jake furrowed his brow. His voice came over the intercom: "Cassidy's voice is better suited for—"

"I don't give a crap. I'm *not* singing *backup*. I started this group!"

"This is dumb," Yumiko said. "Why aren't you mad at Merry? She's also singing lead here."

"*Merry* has earned her place." Rose spun around to glare at Yumiko. "She's been a member of Gloss for longer than six weeks."

Our new manager, Peter, leaning in next to Jake, clicked in. "Every minute in here costs you money. So I'd suggest recording the way Jake wants it and leave your bickering for later."

Rose leaned into the microphone and growled, "No."

I moved my gaze away from Rose, worried that any eye contact would set her off, and saw Peter rubbing his temple in the control room. I hoped he'd come into the studio to break up a fight if Rose decided to jump me.

Meredith snapped, "Stop being a child. So you'll be background for this song. You won't *always* be background on all songs."

"Look, if the tables were turned and *I* was singing all the lead parts and you were stuck in the background, wouldn't you be mad?"

"I *am* stuck in the background, and I'm not mad," Yumi volunteered.

"I wasn't asking you," Rose said. "I didn't come all the way over here just to be in the chorus of my own damn group."

Meredith sighed. "This is one song and it's not worth fighting over. I'm tired. You're tired. It's going to get even more tiring. We should save our energy for a bigger fight ahead."

"What could be bigger than the sound of our first single?" Rose snapped. "The song that will introduce us to an audience? If *you* were in the background, and your mom listened to it and couldn't hear *your* voice, what would you say then?"

"My mom wouldn't be listening for me," Yumi said quietly.

"Spare me your sob stories," Rose bit back.

"It's fine, I'll sing backup," I said quickly, not wanting to see what happened next. I brushed my lips hastily into the microphone. "Hear that? Jake? I'll sing backup for this one."

THE LABEL TOOK us under its wing, providing housing, a driver to take us to our appointments in a big blue Suburban, and Peter Vincent. Peter seemed like a nice enough guy. When he arrived at Big Disc for our initial meeting, Meredith had let her gaze roam up and down his body, silently assessing. He looked as clean-cut as a mid-century milkman, with bright blue eyes and sandy-blond hair. Although his voice was grating— "Seriously," Meredith had said, "he has zero control of his voice. How do people live like that? Talking, without under-standing what speech is supposed to sound like?"—people sat up and listened to him. When I mentioned it to Joanna, I could hear her shrug through the phone. "He's a guy. People auto-matically listen to white men for some stupid-ass reason. At least it benefits you."

The complex that housed us was large and sprawling, and typically used for migratory parents and their children aiming to make it big in Hollywood. Pilot season was now over and the apartments were decimated; only the evergreen hopefuls stayed year-round in the temporary housing, and those lucky enough to have been chosen for projects but hadn't found new homes yet. We could see them dotting the parking lot from the vantage point on our little balcony, coming and going on their own exhaustive schedules, tiny bodies with beautiful faces and their handlers. I sat outside on our sparse balcony, the darken-ing concrete warming the backs of my thighs, and pulled out my little silver phone.

Edie had mentioned that my forced rooming with Yumiko was a positive, that I'd get to know at least one of the girls in-stead of shutting myself in isolation every night, but the only way to get privacy on the phone was to talk out here with the glass door closed. It was still light enough that the sun burned low in the sky, a yolk breaking on the low flat roof of the build-ing across the parking lot.

Though I'd tried Edie and Joanna, reaching their respective voice mails, Alex picked up for the first time in a week. My mood buoyed when his voice came through the receiver.

"Give me a sec," he panted, as I heard some crunching and

echoes in the background. "I've got some groceries and I'm not in my room yet, but I didn't want to miss another call from you."

"That's okay," I said. "What'd you buy?"

"Pringles, Mountain Dew, peanuts, the usual dorm-room snacks."

I laughed. "It sounds sophisticated."

"You know it." The background sounds faded. I could hear a door snap closed. A muffled, "What's up, man," aimed outward at a roommate.

"Have you heard from Edie or Joanna lately?" I asked, hungry for news. I hated asking about them first, but I hadn't heard from either in a while.

"Joanna is swamped. I barely talk to her, though we hang on IM sometimes when she is still up doing homework at two A.M. It's never a full conversation though. Mostly her bitching about her classes."

We didn't have a computer at the apartment. I'd never owned one of my own and the other girls hadn't brought any along with them. The apartment was bare-bones at best, and the label certainly wasn't going to provide one for us.

"And Edie?"

"I talked to her yesterday. She told me that the last time y'all talked, you were getting ready to release the single?"

"Yeah, we shot some promo photos for it a few days ago."

"Holy shit, Cass! How was that?"

"Honestly?" I hesitated. I knew that it was a big deal. It was the first time we had ever been treated to the professional-singer experience, with an artistic director, stylists, photographer, and makeup artists. Walking into the shoot, we had been tired but excited, but as the day wore on, it dragged. "Um, it was cool."

"If it'd been cool, you wouldn't have started with 'honestly.' That bad?"

I sighed and leaned against the wall, gaze soft toward the parking lot. Rubbing my temple, I said, "We had to get up super early. The shoot started at seven, but we had to be all glossied up." I didn't even know how Meredith had come alive; after we'd wrapped work the day before, she'd come home with us, changed, and gone out with a Nickelodeon star who lived next door and could get them into a club.

The SUV had picked us up at five—birds roosted quietly in the trees, and aside from the gentle hums of air conditioners, the silence had been ruined by Rose's bashing on the door to our room to wake us up—and rolled us over to a studio space in downtown L.A. The next hour was spent with a hair and makeup team as we nodded off in chairs.

"Glossied," Alex said. "How apropos."

"Right. So this hair stylist is pulling on my head with a comb like a sadist—" I'd been so tired and so hungry that I'd almost appreciated the pain, because it took attention away from the emptiness in my stomach. Our manager had driven Yumiko and me to a dietitian almost immediately after my contract ink had dried, and we'd been given strict instructions on what not to eat. It was practically the entire food pyramid. I initially pushed back, but Peter made it clear: image was everything, and to be in Gloss meant to be on a perpetual diet. "Or you can pack your bags and go home," he'd said. I resentfully agreed to do my best.

"Sadist, huh?" Alex said. "You're learning new vocabulary while you're in L.A."

"Look who's talking. 'Apropos.'"

"I got a 760 on my verbal SATs, you know."

I knew. That's why Alex was at Northwestern, after all.

"Anyway," I went on, "the artistic director comes out and he introduces himself as *Jean,* in the French way, pronounced through the nose." I spoke like Jean had, grandiose and pinch-assed. The man had been so pretentious, even while wearing a bright white T-shirt and ripped jeans. His words to us were "Ladies, this shoot is going to be *hot.* You are *gorgeous.* Bring the *attitude.* Make at least *one person in this studio* fall in love with you by the end of this shoot."

A stylist rolled a cart of synthetic fabrics close to our stations and plucked at the name tags attached to each hanger. "Meredith," she said, passing along an ice-blue metallic jumpsuit. "Yummy-ko." A black ensemble. A dusty pink for Rose, a sequined number for me.

"It's pronounced You-Me," Meredith corrected, fingering the shimmering fabric. "Is this material even going to photograph well against the rest of all that?"

"I'm supposed to wear these?" Yumiko said, holding a pair of stilettos that were basically black-lacquered chopsticks. Her stylist pushed down on her arm and continued flat-ironing her hair.

"Sure it will," the first stylist said, answering Meredith

and ignoring Yumiko. She shoved a pair of black three-inch-platform clogs in my direction. I had to hold them in my lap while a makeup artist coated my face with powder.

When we arrived on the set, tugging our outfits indiscreetly, Meredith pinching at her underwire like a woman infected with a rash, Yumiko teetering on her heels, Jean introduced us to our photographer, Sven, who began barking orders immediately. Move here, arm there, smile this way, *no, not like that,* give it to me for real, yes Red, just like that, now shift, yes you, the Asian girl, more face, give me more in the eyes, yes! And all the while as time slid by slowly, as we were posed like mannequins, rearranged inch by inch, I could feel the horrible hollow underneath my rib cage, reminding me that I hadn't eaten and there was an apple waiting for me somewhere in the depths of the SUV.

It had been at least an hour since we'd stepped onto the set, four since waking up, and eight since falling asleep. Our smiles slipped, our hair grew limp under hot studio lights, and Sven complained.

"You there! Cassidy," Sven snapped, and a finger had to poke me in the back before I snapped to attention. "I need you to laugh like you're *actually* glad to be here. Not like that," he said, when I let out a high-pitched giggle that was nowhere near adorable or sexy. It sounded strained and anxious, a dog tied to a fence post. "Throaty. Tilt your head back a tiny bit, eyes to me, yes." His gaze was all over, flattening my body into a two-dimensional shape, stretching and pulling me with the light as he rearranged our collective limbs. "We'll have to bring in some of this waist and hip," he said to his assistant. Peter called out, "Girls! This is for the *cover art for your single*. If it doesn't look good, *it won't sell*. Please, *make an effort*." The fatigue from the past few weeks, the humiliation of the waist and hip that I was sure the photographer meant was mine, started to catch up with me.

"Come on, Cassidy," Rose murmured, her finger snaking in between rows of sequins on my bodice. "Think about how lucky you are to be here and give a little chuckle for the photographer so we can leave."

"No, no, no," shouted Sven. "Cassy! I said sexy, not sad. No tears!" He stood still, for the first time since we started the shoot, lowering his camera. "Do you need a minute?"

"I know we could all use a break," said Meredith.

"No, let's just get this over with," said Yumiko. "You can do it, can't you, Cassidy?"

I dashed at the tears that were blurring the edges of my vision and nodded silently, humiliated and ashamed. Jean signaled a makeup artist from the wings to come in and powder us all, soaking up another layer of sweat in a finely milled cosmetic dust.

"Again," said Sven, and we moved on. Forty-five minutes later, we were changed back into street clothes and pulling off our fake eyelashes in the car, where no one said a word during the drive back. It was so quiet that I didn't even try to eat the apple I found rolling along the floorboard in the backseat.

But what I said to Alex was a little less depressing. "I was in this sequined jumpsuit that I had no business being in—like seriously, my butt was like two giant disco balls, and no one needs *two* disco balls."

"It sounds very eye-catching," Alex teased.

"The clothes were all awful. And they put Yumiko in all black, with flat-ironed hair. She looked like a goth. It made no sense why Meredith and I were in these shiny clothes and she was stuck in the back."

"Maybe once the cover comes out it will be more obvious," he said, trying to sound positive. "Maybe the clothes look bad in real life but great on film."

"Maybe." Alex was such an optimist, always seeing the best possible outcome. I wasn't so sure. I thought about how the stylist ignored Yumiko when she asked about her shoes. "She does have the most beautiful face. They probably put her in black so she wouldn't overshadow the rest of us."

"There you go," he said quickly. I didn't know what else to say after that, and we both grew quiet.

The last wash of orange skimmed along the edge of the adjacent building, sliding below and out of sight within minutes.

"What ya doing?" Alex asked, when the pause had gone on for a minute.

"Just watching the sun go down. It's been a while since I've taken the time."

"How does a California sunset compare to a Texas one?"

"It's different. It's—I don't know—brighter?" Texas sunsets are warm and the golden light soaks into treetops and long grass. They herald cicadas before the mosquitoes. This one was almost frosted in comparison. "The view here is terrible though. I'm sitting on my apartment landing. I wish I could've seen this from a tourist spot. Maybe see the Hollywood sign all glowed up."

"There's so much I miss about Texas," he said. "The sunsets here suck. The blue lasts forever."

When I walked back into the kitchen, dusting off the backs of my shorts, I found Yumiko at the plain IKEA table. She cupped a ceramic mug and flipped pages of an aged teen magazine. I could hear the low murmuring of Rose holding a conversation behind another wall. Without tearing her gaze from the dog-eared leaves, Yumiko asked, "Good talk with your friend?"

"Yeah, um, fine." There was an uncomfortable beat of silence.

She turned another page. "Peter called. We have to go out and mingle again. Let the 'people know about us.'" She spoke in what was supposed to be Peter's voice.

I opened the fridge and leaned in to look. Apples, lettuce, skim milk. Meredith had an annoying habit of eating a few bites of something, then leaving the plate and utensil in the fridge and forgetting about it. A withered salad was turning into sludge on the middle shelf. I closed it without taking anything, and then our eyes met.

"Hot tea helps," she said, lifting her mug off the table in a tiny salute. "It kinda . . . coats your insides, makes you feel like maybe there's something in there."

I leaned against the fridge. "I'm so hungry," I confessed.

"I bought two kinds. Feel free. Kettle's on the stove." She turned her attention back to the magazine.

"Thanks." I flipped the burner on and found a cup. I wanted

to feel zen about this diet. If I leaned into it more, maybe I wouldn't hate it as much. If I made it into a competition with myself . . .

Yumiko snapped her magazine closed and lifted her eyes to mine. "The walls here are thin," she said. "Rose is probably talking to Viv again."

I didn't know what to say to that. I knew nothing about the girl I'd replaced. Yumiko studied me for a long moment and then took a quick drink of her cooled tea as she shoved out of the chair. The conversation seemingly over, she retreated to our room.

That night, Yumiko settled into her somewhat squeaky mattress and her deep breaths did not start immediately. "Cassidy?" she whispered, and I could tell she was facing me across the short aisle between the beds. "Are you up?"

I shifted my body weight over so I was on my back, speaking toward the ceiling. "Yeah?"

"I was just curious . . . do you feel *lonely*?"

My eyes were open now, focusing on the shapes and dollops of light that played across the ceiling as cars moved on the streets below. I didn't respond.

"Isn't it weird?" she continued, taking my silence as a yes. "We spend all this time together, and then with all of these people, but it's like we're not social with anyone else. It's like we're in a bubble."

"Yeah, I know," I murmured.

Her springs squeaked again and she resettled herself on the bed. I stole a glance at the lump beside me in the dark. Yumiko was on her side, facing me, her legs balled up under the blanket. I could see the glitter of her eyes from several feet away.

"This must be hard for you," she whispered. "I'm with my best friends here, but yours aren't around. Cass, don't be afraid to become our friend too."

From then on, Yumiko and I continued soft conversations in the dark. It was easier for us to share anecdotes and thoughts when the lamps were off and the words could breeze across the room, light and fluttering, like autumn leaves drifting from branches.

# 6.

January 2001
Southwest Leg of the Mall Tour

## Cassidy

Texas blurred by in a bright gray-and-yellow carousel outside the bus window. Meredith sat next to me in the back of the bus, rhythmically flicking the ends of her hair with a thumb.

Yumi snapped, "Can you stop?"

Meredith rolled her eyes but released her hair without saying anything.

We'd been traveling for a few weeks now—since the holidays—on a mall tour, and at last we had returned to my home state. I'd been excited to show off Houston but it's nothing to note in January: cold, gray, with excessive amounts of plastic bags that blow around in the wind. We had visited one mall and then moved on without staying a night. The only positive was that Mom brought Melanie and Katie to the performance, grinning and proud, and I was able to let them hang out with us on the bus for a few minutes before we had to leave for Dallas. The twins had acted as if it was the coolest adventure in the world.

Our mother, while interested in the bus, pulled me aside as the twins picked through my show costumes. "Are they feeding you enough?" she whispered in a concerned tone, plucking at my forearm. "You've lost so much weight."

"We're fine, Mom," I said placatingly. "Touring is just very energy-consuming. We dance a lot and have rehearsals on top of that." When she didn't look convinced, I lied and said, "We even have a nutritionist on call. Seriously, don't worry."

The truth was, over the weeks, not eating had become easier than actually eating. The more praise Peter heaped on me for losing weight, the better I felt about the diet. This was one thing I could do well, one thing I could control.

Because the rest was out of my hands. Peter planned everything: he had us following a crooked line across the southern United States, touring malls every day of the week. It was low-budget but respectable, with a small stage set up like a kiosk near the food court, and we'd perform four songs from the album, dance a choreographed routine, sign photos, break everything down, and move on to the next mall. We'd shuffle the Midwest a little bit, then hop back to California to shoot our first music video for "Wake Up Morning," and debut our single on the radio.

Even though we knew the tour, the bus, the small entourage, and the managers were taking precious dollars out of Gloss's record deal, everything felt very inexpensive. Peter was in talks with a director for the music video, who described his vision as "charming"—which probably meant we'd be wearing ten-dollar sundresses from Walmart while we lip-synced.

"We'll take a second tour out to New York if the first is successful," Peter had promised. "Likely with nicer buses."

"Or a plane," Rose had muttered.

The bus didn't bother me too much, but tensions were running high while we were confined for hours at a time. At the apartment, we could at least retreat to our own bedrooms; here, we could only duck into our bunks for semi-solitude. Rigid privacy curtains closed off the triple-bunked beds from passersby in the aisle and blocked out light, but not sound. Anything that could be flung around in a sharp turn was belted down with Velcro or in a pocket attached to the walls. This is where I kept my cell phone, which had become my lifeline to the outside world. Meredith showed me how to send text messages—since real conversations were often drowned out by both road noise and loud conversation—by pressing numbers multiple times until the correct letter appeared on the screen.

Most of my texts were with Alex, who was my long-distance cheerleader. We sent messages back and forth throughout the day, as he kept me abreast of any news happening in Chicago or with Edie and Joanna, who did not have text plans on their phones. The information was few and far between, but it kept me occupied.

I'd gotten to know Meredith a little better over the past few months. She continued to act as a buffer between everyone in the group, adjusting attitudes when Rose grew headstrong or Yumi was too reluctant. When Peter insinuated that Yumi wasn't losing weight fast enough and that he was concerned she was slipping on her diet, Meredith gave him an earful. After he'd left, she murmured to Yumi, "You gotta cut down on the secret Mickey D's."

"I don't know what you're talking about," Yumi had said.

"Oh please. I can smell a chicken nugget from a mile away."

If Meredith was the casual enforcer of the group, Rose was the dominant head. She had the last word on everything, even if it meant a few of us were dissatisfied. We had looked through the photo proofs for the single cover and narrowed it down to five; in the one Yumi liked, Rose self-criticized she was hunched over; in the shot Meredith liked, my smile was halfway to a grimace. Rose picked the shot where she presented well and convinced the rest of us that it was the best look for every member. And because Rose had that infamous temper, only Meredith pushed back for a moment before we let it go.

Now, somewhere between Dallas and Tulsa, I sat chewing on a thumbnail and gazing at the glossy print that we'd be autographing postperformance. Rose's phone rang; she glanced at the caller ID and gestured to the other girls. "It's Viv." They scooted closer to Rose on the padded benches at the front of the bus. I still hadn't met or talked to Viv, and one look from Rose told me that I was not privy to this conversation. Even at night, speaking across the aisle in our shared room about her disapproving parents or my sisters, I didn't dare ask Yumi about the original fourth; Viv was an ethereal other, existing in a plane that I could never cross.

Their moods were subdued after, and I followed them at a distance into the mall, the last one on the stage, feeling weary.

I knew well enough that I had to smile as soon as I entered through the doorway and until we could get back on the bus. By the end of the performance, as we sat at the edge of the stage for the meet-and-greet, my mouth felt like it was held up by twine.

For a split second, as my marker hovered over a glossy print of our four faces and I asked a high-school-aged boy his name, I existed outside my body and viewed the scene in the food court from a bird's-eye perspective. These kids were excited about us, because they were *told* to be excited about us. Hyped by radio stations. Endorsed by ICEE stands. We were shaped to fit into the little cubby hole that these teens were hoping to see filled.

"Nick. I'm so pumped to be here," said the teen.

"Nice to meet you, Nick." I signed "Cass" as the marker bled ever so slightly at the edges of my name. Since I was at the end of the table and the first Gloss girl that the fans met, I had the responsibility of writing the fans' names on the top of the photo too. Yumi buffered me from a chatty Merry, and Rose was happy to urge people along at the far end.

I could feel the dampness in my armpits and a slow trickle of sweat was moving from the back of my neck into the waistband of my pants. I could smell the warm, moist breath of every person facing in our direction—a cloud of burgers and pizza, spearmint gum and sour apple gummy candy, Starbucks Frappuccinos and Jamba Juice smoothies. I practiced breathing with my mouth. As I watched a local news station take a few sweeping shots with a giant video camcorder, I wondered if my grin was looking more like a grimace.

"Hi, beautiful," said a voice, and another 8 x 10 print slid into view. I snapped my gaze upward to see the speaker's face, but I couldn't place him. He was older than most of the others who had come through the line; there were crinkles around his eyes, skin as soft as crepe paper. He wore rimless glasses and had day-old stubble on his upper lip. He held out a bundle of tissue-wrapped flowers—expensive-looking, not the cellophane packet type sold at a grocery store.

"Thank you," I said, feeling flattered. I glanced at his hands, which were at my eye level, to see if he'd brought flowers for any of the other girls, but apparently he'd brought a gift only for me. "What's your name?" I asked, still smiling.

"It's Jerry! Don't you remember?"

I felt my cheeks warm, and tried to jostle my memory. "Umm . . ." I fumbled with the marker.

"We met in L.A.," he continued, speaking softly yet firmly, like we were the only two people in the world. "At *Sing It*."

"I'm sorry, I meet so many people . . ."

"I've been following your success since the show."

Something about this man was unsettling. He looked at me like he knew me well. Like we were acquainted, had a history.

We had never discussed what we would do if someone creepy came to one of these tour stops. I wished there was a code word I could pass down the line, so that mall security could materialize out of thin air and whisk Jerry away. Instead, I signed "Cass," slid the photo away from me, and looked at him dumbly. He pointed at my flowers. Still in a soft voice, one now laced with rage, he said, "I used my miles just to see you again. You inconsiderate bitch."

Had he shouted, or spoken harshly, I'm sure the other girls or people in the line would have snapped to attention, but his voice was so low that it probably seemed like Jerry and I were having a normal conversation. Someone next in line jostled him, and Jerry ignored the other Gloss girls, almost running into the news cameraman in his rush to leave. I wondered how else that could have played out when I heard a shriek nearby.

Merry was standing and ripping up a photo in front of the teenager who'd preceded Jerry. Tiny pieces rained down onto the table like confetti. "Get out of my face," she said, loud enough that I could hear her in the din.

Rose was trying to shush her while Yumi hastily scraped the confetti pieces into a pile with her hands, away from any curious eyes. In the crowd, the cameraman squinted into the eyepiece, aiming the lens. Merry shook out her hands, smoothed her clothes, and sat down again. Baffled, I followed suit, and soon the easy chatter resumed in the food court.

I flicked my smile back on as the next fan demanded my attention. The Sharpie felt greasy in my fingers. "What's your name?" I asked.

When we got back to the bus, my body was shaking so hard our driver, Gus, had to help me climb the steep steps. "You okay, dear?" he asked, dark eyes warm with concern. I gave a half-smile and nod, but rather than congregate in the back with the other girls to discuss what had happened with Merry, I lay down in my narrow bed, took off my shoes, and covered my eyes with the pillow. I listened to my heart beating in my ears and breathed in and out slowly.

I hid in my bunk until my hands stopped quaking; the bus

quieted down as people dropped off to sleep. I cracked the blackout curtain on the window, and the night scene rotated a repeat of the same visual: streak of a street lamp, painted white lines on the black road, dark clumps of trees on the other side of the divider. We were going to zip through the night on a seven-hour cruise and get to the next stop.

The tiny reading light clipped to my bunk illuminated a circle about as wide as a coffee cup. I slipped my journal out of the Velcro pouch on the wall and uncapped a ballpoint pen. No sooner had I written one sentence than my phone buzzed: Alex.

"Where next?" *St. Louis.*

"So close 2me!" *Chicago isn't close.*

"Closer than L.A." That was true, I conceded in my head.

I realized then that I really needed to talk to him about the signing today. I was still so shaken up, and a friendly voice would soothe me.

He answered on the first ring. "Cass? You okay? You never call." There was tinny laughter in the background, but it cut out when he waited for me to speak.

"It's been a weird day. I thought I could use some friend therapy. Are you busy?"

"Nah, just watching Leno."

"Thinking about L.A.?" I teased.

"Imagining the beach and sunny weather. It's kind of cold and damp today."

"Oh." I dragged a thumbnail across the page I'd been writing on.

"What's up?"

"Just . . . weirdness. I know I should be grateful for what's going on right now—for me, for the group—but it just boggles my mind how people can be so in-your-face, you know? I feel a little bit like a zoo animal. People *expecting* so much from me, people I've never met. Some guy today told me that he followed me since *Sing It*."

A guffaw on the other end of the line: "Well, that's good, right?"

"No, Alex. Listen to me. Like, he was acting so focused and so *intense*. I'd never even *seen* the guy before." Deep breath. "It genuinely scared me."

"You tell anyone?"

"I'm telling *you*."

"He sounds like a creep. You should've had security throw him out."

"I wasn't thinking. I mean, I was, but it happened so fast, and then Merry started shouting at a guy—a different one—and I just didn't know what to do."

"I hate to say this, Cass, but this is going to keep happening. Your star is going to get bigger and more weirdos are going to fall in love with you. I wish I could protect you."

My eyes were open in the darkness. The cubicle was so small and narrow, but it didn't *feel* small and narrow because I couldn't see the edges. Rolled up in my little cocoon, with the vibration of the diesel engine and bouncing tires beneath me, I imagined being in a warm, safe space with Alex, the one friend who still made time for me despite our new lives. "I wish you were here with me."

And I meant it. Alex gave a laugh I'd never heard before,

like he'd breathed from low in his throat into the mouthpiece of the phone. "Yeah," he whispered.

There was a twinge. A small, short one, at the base of my spine. I didn't know if I missed my friend or if I missed Alex, specifically.

"Yeah," I whispered, smiling, puzzled but pleased.

After we'd hung up, I unfolded the privacy curtain from my bed to brush my teeth. I jostled my way down the narrow aisle as the bus rumbled along.

Rose bumped into me at the sink, grabbing a bottle of water from the fridge, and leaned against the attached cabinets as she sipped and watched me brush.

"Who were you talking to?"

I gave her a quick glance but didn't answer.

"My bunk is right under yours. I usually can't hear anything with all the bus noise going on, but I couldn't fall asleep, I felt so grimy. And I heard your voice yammering on. So who was it?" She crept closer and wiggled her eyebrows at me mischievously. "Could it have been . . . a certain . . . Monsieur St. James?"

Her remark landed flatly; it felt more personal than a probe into my romantic interests, but I didn't know why she would care. I rolled my eyes and pointed at the toothbrush in my mouth.

"Look, *chicas,* you're on the local news," Veronica, our sound technician, called from the back of the bus. She and Yumi sat cross-legged on the bench facing the mounted TV. Rose and I stepped to the side and watched as the screen switched from the establishing outdoor shot of the mall we'd left earlier that day to one of the food court where we'd set up our stage. A quick pan of the tween audience, cheering; a few seconds of us dancing our choreography; a shot of Rose smiling wide at a young fan at the signing. A teenager's face showed on the screen, her smiling mouth full of braces: *I made my dad drive me and my sister.*

The closed-captioning read: *Not every Gloss girl was on her best behavior tonight.* The cameraman had been filming down from an elevated spot, so he caught Merry's outburst. There was the back of Nick's head; he gave an 8 x 10 piece of paper to Merry to sign, and her face changed from smiling to hostile as soon as she saw it. That's when she stood and shredded it. *But for the most part, it was a big success.* A man's face, eyes highlighted with round-rimmed glasses, and my heart jumped: Jerry. *I came in from out of town to meet them. I know I'm a little old but I know talent when I hear it.*

"What was she so mad about, d'ya know?" I asked, words garbled from the foam in my mouth.

Yumi said, "It was her tits."

The screen shifted to its final feel-good anecdote of the night, a goat-petting zoo, which closed the broadcast. Veronica changed the channel, blue tinting her and Yumi's faces in flashes.

"*Whose* tits?"

"Merry's. The guy had pictures of Merry with her boobs out."

I held up a finger, ran to the sink, spit, then ran back. "Um, *how*?"

Yumi shrugged. "*Apparently,* she did some amateur modeling

for some artsy-fartsy photographer. She told us that kid had a print of it somehow."

"Gosh, I'd scream too if that happened to me." With all of those middle-schoolers around, I wasn't surprised she ripped up the photo as quickly as she did. I then wondered how many other prints of Meredith's breasts were out in the world.

Rose said, "Hopefully, only the local news ran that clip. We don't want the entire world to think that Merry is unhinged." On that note, she walked back up the aisle and zipped into her bunk.

Veronica glanced at me and replied nonchalantly, "It's such a small story, I doubt it will be aired anywhere else. Now, if the *tits* were on television, that'd be a different story. They'd be everywhere."

When I pulled the covers up to my chin, it was so dark in my bunk that the carpeted cubicle surrounding me was black as tar. I cracked a curtain so that the passing streetlights would create a hypnotizing repetition as I took stock of my thoughts. Meredith. Alex. I'd never thought of Alex in any way except as a good friend. He, Joanna, and Edie were my three bedrocks while in Houston. We'd grown up in the same neighborhood and attended the same schools. All of those shared experiences, our similar humor—we were just on the same wavelength most of the time. Sure, Edie was an artist, Joanna was a scientist, and Alex was Alex (and on that note, I was just me), but we just *knew* one another. And Alex and I had known each other for so long that sexual attraction just didn't seem to be on the table.

Until that laugh.

I closed my eyes.

# 7.

*Friday*

## Yumi

Merry texted me to say she couldn't make it—probably because of whatever Sunny had done this time. That girl attracted attention like nothing else, much like her mother. I stood inside the police headquarters awkwardly, scrolling through Twitter headlines waiting for Rose, when her text came through as well: Hey, can't make it. No apology.

I sighed and hitched my handbag to my shoulder and ventured farther inside. I'd made a note of the police spokesperson that had been quoted in yesterday's news reports, but when I asked for whoever was in charge of Cassidy's case, I was steered to a desk with a nameplate that said DET. D. LAWRENCE. Though the LAPD building was new, with sharp angles and several stories' worth of tinted windows, the budget apparently hadn't trickled down to the department wares: Detective Lawrence's desk was small and shabby, and its surface was covered in a hodgepodge of manila folders and stacks of paper. The detective, phone clasped to his ear, had a young face—maybe in his mid-forties—but his close-cropped hair was all white.

He slid the receiver back into place. "Yes, what can I do for you," he said, voice flat, as he shifted his attention and brandished a hand toward a desk chair.

"Hi, I'm Yumi Otsuka," I said, sitting down. I was glad I'd never changed my name.

Fifteen years ago, the detective hadn't been our target audience; while we had been selling tickets to stadium shows to teenagers, he was probably already out of school and more concerned with marriage or his mortgage than to keeping up with the Billboard charts. But he *had* to have recognized me. Gloss had been more than a national phenomenon. We were global. Universal. Our likenesses had been on lunch boxes and thermoses, our voices in soft drink commercials. And he was leading the investigation as to what had caused Cassidy's demise. He must have researched her past—and with it, us.

Detective Lawrence's expression did not change when he looked at me. He waited a beat and then leaned forward, his badge tumbling along his tie on its neck chain. "Ma'am, I think I know what you've come here to ask, and unless you have additional information for me to help with the investigation, I can't discuss anything with you."

"Of course not," I said, feeling stupid that I'd tried to do this in person instead of on the phone. The conversation stalled for another long moment. I shifted uncomfortably in the chair and tried again. "Maybe I *can* help, though. We've had so many stalkers over the years. The rest of us—that is, the rest of our, um, group . . ." I coughed lightly, feeling embarrassed. "We thought about it and wanted to give you as much information as you might need. Housekeeper. Groundskeeper. Ex-boyfriends. Superfans."

"I did look at old complaints she filed, over a decade ago. Stalkers and harassers. We are looking at many angles here. We treat all unattended deaths as suspicious, so until the medical examiner says it's self-inflicted, we will be pursuing all avenues of inquiry."

My arm hurt and I realized it was because I was digging the nails of my right hand into my left wrist.

"So it *is* her, then?" I asked. I guess I had been holding out hope that maybe it hadn't really been Cassidy's body that they'd picked up.

The detective's eyes were very blue behind his lenses. "Yes, ma'am. Her family flew in yesterday and identified her."

I swallowed.

"What we *don't* have are any *current* stalkers or harassers. Do you ladies still hear from your obsessive fans?"

"Yes," I said. "One of our employees has boxes and bags full of letters."

"How many, would you say?"

"Thousands. It used to be more." Rooms of letters. Some adoring; some not. Some *too* adoring. Some frightening. As the years passed, the nostalgic fans tried to talk to us through the internet: Twitter replies, Instagram comments, Tumblr tags. These days we couldn't keep any in-box for very long. I disabled all of the direct messaging features on my social platforms so that I could sleep better at night. If someone I truly knew wanted to reach me, they could call. But it was only the very devoted who continued to put pen to paper and affix their stamps. These were what Emily collected. "We could have her drop them off."

Detective Lawrence leaned back and steepled his fingers. It was only a moment, but I could sense his hesitation to have to read through bags of letters, each one with a person behind them, each one a potential threat that had to be crossed off. But duty spoke: "Yes, I would like to see them. Your employee can leave them with the front desk clerk and they'll make their way to me."

"I'll get on it right away."

The detective handed me a business card with his contact information. "If you think of anything else."

"If you learn anything, will you let me know? Here." I pulled a Post-it pad on his desk close and jotted down my number. "Please don't share this widely. I normally don't give this out but Cassidy is important to me."

"Of course, ma'am."

"Thank you. And if you could call me Yumi, instead of ma'am, I'd appreciate it."

He reached out for a handshake. I grasped his palm firmly.

Outside the station, I pulled on my oversize Dolce sunglasses and walked quickly to my car, parked in the nearby covered lot. I began dialing before I could forget, asking Emily to drop the letters off. "All of them?" she said, sounding disbelieving. "That'd take at least two trips, even in Merry's Land Rover stuffed to the brim."

"Maybe you could sort through them and pick out only what was sent to Cass."

"That'd take even *longer*."

"You're right. I'm sure they have an army of people to do that sort of grunt work at the police station. I guess you're stuck." I unlocked the door and climbed in, turning the engine on to get the air-conditioning going, but made no move to start driving.

She heaved a huge sigh in my ear. "I'll get it done."

"Thanks, Em. What would Merry do without you." I said it as a statement.

"She'd be doing a hell of a lot more by herself, that's for sure."

"Tell her I'll see her tomorrow."

"Tomorrow?" Emily sounded confused.

"Jordan's wedding. Ian's son?"

"Ah, yeah, no. She has a schedule conflict and can't make it. But she did send along a beautiful set of Waterford crystal wineglasses."

"Oh." I chewed the inside of my cheek. It was just like Merry to bow out of attendance even after saying she'd go. Like the tour extension; she'd signed up for it like the rest of us, but when Cassidy left she supported Peter's suggestion to let it go, citing her pregnancy as a reason to halt. Rose was livid; she demanded that Merry pay restitution for the amount she'd lose not touring. I was outwardly neutral, but silently agreed we'd needed a break. Cassidy had left, we were a mess, and my relationship with Kevin was just getting serious. I didn't want to be on tour, either.

Before I could say anything else, I heard a beep from call waiting. "I have to run, but thanks for dealing with the letters." I clicked over without recognizing the number. "Hello?"

"Hi, Ms. Otsuka," said a male voice. "My name is Mike Parsons. I'm calling on behalf of the FPZ Network. We would normally contact your agent about this sort of thing, but seeing as how you dismissed your agent—"

I closed my eyes and leaned back in my seat. "What is this regarding?"

"You're on our short list to be a judge on *Sing It, America!* We're hoping to narrow it down by the end of the month."

"Is this a joke? *Sing It* was never on FPZ, and it ended five years ago."

Mike's voice on the line was saccharine and upbeat. "Both of those things are true, but FPZ acquired rights to the show and we're heading a revival."

"I'm retired."

"We're aware you're retired from, ah, singing. But this is being a celebrity judge. Listen, if you're just the slightest bit interested, would you consider coming to our offices on Tuesday for a quick chat? Bring whomever you need to—new agent, lawyer, whatever. We're very eager to talk to you."

"I'll think about it," I said, weariness creeping over me.

"Although I'm a little busy next week, accounting for, you know, my friend dying."

"Our condolences." Mike's voice did not change an iota. "If you could make it to our offices at three o'clock, we'll be expecting you."

*Hell if I'll be doing anything in the public eye again.* My big mouth had done so much damage already. Sometimes I woke up in my quiet, lonely house and remembered what I'd done. The lush carpet, the king-size memory-foam bed—I didn't deserve any of it.

# 8.

## Cassidy

The Gloss that appeared at their single release party was not the same ragtag group of girls that had congregated at Big Disc headquarters eight months ago. Before leaving the apartment I checked myself over, and reflected back at me was someone who could pass as a star. When I flipped through fashion magazines, the women on the covers looked a lot like I did at this moment: draped in fine fabric, groomed, and polished. Hair not grown out or in a weird stage, nail color applied evenly, legs smooth from recent waxing. What the celebrities and music journalists at the party couldn't see were the insides of my cheeks, bitten raw; my spasming stomach, empty as always. And it wasn't just my stomach that felt hollow. As I followed Yumiko through the doors of the industrial building, I told myself that I should be happy, because I looked good

in this dress and our single was being released, finally, after
months of buildup in suburban malls.

Marsha Campbell spotted us and broke away from a conversation. She waved us over and gave a smiling, appraising
up-and-down look to take in our ensembles. "You ladies look
amazing," she said, reaching out with tentative arms to give
us each the briefest and lightest of hugs. Her embrace barely
touched my shoulders, and I had the feeling she kept her touch
light so as to not disturb any delicate fabrics or hairstyles. "So-
cialize. Mingle. Don't get stuck in one place for too long," she
instructed, and smiled again before plucking something from a
passed appetizer tray.

We dispersed, each wandering to a different area of the
room. I sauntered to the bar, feeling daring as I did so, but
asked for sparkling water in a champagne flute.

My feet already ached and my stomach was so shriveled that
it had stopped hurting. The only sense I had of my malnourish-
ment was a soft buzzing in the back of my head, which amplified if I stood too still. So I took a turn about the room, sipping
my fake champagne, and found Meredith entertaining a little
group of people with a wild anecdote about our recent music
video for our single.

"I can't say *much,*" she said loudly, "but we wear the most
ridiculous outfits. Trust me, this video is going to make a *big*
splash." She smiled conspiratorially.

Someone in the group said, "So they're quite revealing,
then?"

Meredith gave a theatrical wink. "We were *very* wet."

Yumi, who had sidled up next to me, laughed giddily at

Meredith's comment. "Omigod, Merry, you can't give it *all* away!" I'd noticed she'd do this often, edge in with a supportive comment that took the jauntiness out of Meredith's declarations.

The truth was, the music video for "Wake Up Morning," which took two eighteen-hour days to shoot, did not involve any pool or beach. We wore hot pants and sequined bustiers and Rollerbladed on a flat track. There was a scene with a water hose, a clichéd moment when one girl splashes the rest and then we dance, drenched, on wet concrete. Cue slow-motion shots of hair flinging droplets, trickles of sweat running down an exposed midsection. Combined with the typical music video fodder of girls singing longingly into microphones on stands, wearing leather leggings, the video wasn't excessively expensive or fancy. Rose had grumbled about that too, but Peter told us that the label wasn't going to spend a million dollars on a first video.

Yumi and I separated from the rest of the group. "Look who it is," she said, nodding toward a figure halfway across the room. I recognized that side profile immediately. The face I'd seen for weeks on end the first time I was in L.A., the cheekbone I drew and redrew with my eyes during that finale: Stephen St. James, the crown of his head partially obscured with a decorative cowboy hat, as if to make the space around him larger.

Crushes are strange things; they narrow rooms to corridors, reduce our senses to just the sound of a deep breath. If this were a movie, the entire warehouse would constrict to show just him and just me, the rest of the crowd dissipating into smoke.

I took another breath. I hadn't realized that I still had feelings for him until this moment.

The room regained noise. The piped-in music, pops of champagne bottles relieving pressure, susurrus of voices, snapping of high heels, and occasional bursts of laughter came roaring back into my ears. "The man we can thank for our album getting shifted to the fast track," Yumi mused. Jake Jamz had told us that Stephen's new album wouldn't be ready in time for the mid-season finale of *Sing It,* which is why our single—and Gloss—got the promotional slot. It would coincide with our wide release the following week. "Who's that with him?"

He turned as if he'd heard this criticism, spotted our pointed stares, and held up a hand as if to say hello. A tall, lithe brunette, made taller by stilettos, clutched his other elbow. Yumi raised an arm in return, but by the time I could command my limbs, his attention was back on his date.

Meredith removed herself from the group and came over, following our gaze across the room. "He's cute, I guess. What do you think, Cassidy?" She was smiling at me, but there was a hint of knowing. I twisted so that my back was to Stephen and I was facing her. While it was excruciating to look at Meredith and her arched eyebrow, it felt safer than to continue staring at the cowboy hat bobbing across the room.

I cleared my throat self-consciously.

"I knew it!" she crowed. "Your face can't keep a secret. You got to know each other on the set of *Sing It,* right? Maybe you can make a love connection. I bet Big Disc would *love* that—

keep it in the family, twice the publicity, like Nickelodeon stars do. Or maybe they'd hate it—you know, 'don't shit where you eat,' that sort of thing. Oops, he's coming this way."

"Please don't say anything embarrassing." I tried to remember what a normal facial expression felt like.

"Ladies," said Stephen St. James. I hazarded a glance at his face and was relieved that it was mostly in the shadow of his hat brim. The leggy woman trailed behind him, as if in afterthought.

I murmured out a weak hello as Meredith said, "Hi there!"

"Stephen St. James," he replied, extending his hand.

"I'm Yumi." Yumi briefly accepted his hand before he held it out to me.

His hand was warm, large. Even though it was dim in the room, I could imagine his perfect, crescent-moon nail beds. I felt a callus on his palm.

He tried to shake off his double-take, but I saw it. "Cassidy! It's good to see you again."

"Yeah." My lips stuttered and then stopped. I tried to think of something else to say, but my throat constricted. The brunette filled in the gap by pushing past the wide brim of Stephen's hat and extending a delicate hand. "Jeannette."

"She's a model, was just in Milan." Stephen regained our attention and stepped closer to our circle, edging Jeannette out. "By myself, I only get to see below the Mason-Dixon line, but maybe Jeannette will take me international one of these days."

Meredith took that opening. "How's the tour been?"

"Oh, it's been wild. I've still been promoting my first album everywhere while recording the second. Been all over, lately. Atlanta, Nashville, Dallas. You know how it is."

"We're about to open for Illuminated Eyes, which should be cool!" Meredith said, as she reached out and held my arm. "I'm excited to not dance in a mall again, and move on to real stadiums and stuff. Are you touring mostly in the South?"

"Ha, I defy genres, but I'm still a Southern boy at heart." He grinned, cratering a deep dimple in one cheek. "Though I think our label would like to list me as R&B with a hint of country. Hence the"—he tapped his hat.

"And Jeannette, what were you doing in Milan?" Yumi asked politely.

"Well I—"

"Oh, will you excuse me," Stephen interrupted, and brushed past us, breaking our circle. I watched as Jeannette smiled apologetically and followed. Stephen grabbing at Jeannette's delicate hand as they left our group was all I could see before they both melted into the crowd.

"Rude," Meredith remarked.

"She barely spoke. How can that be rude?" Yumi said.

Meredith glanced at me. "I meant St. James. He didn't let her get a word in at all. It was just about him, him, him." She grabbed my shoulders with both hands, turning me toward her. "Never mind *either* of them," she said emphatically, but the back of Jeannette's dress plunging low, showing an intricate mandala tattooed between the delicate wings of her shoulder blades, was now carved into my mind. "Look! We're at this amazing party that's being held in our honor and we're awesome, right? Let's have fun."

Rose sidled up and rested her fingertips on my arm, as if in warning. "I hope you're not just hanging out with one another here; we can do that anytime at the apartment. We're here to do a job."

A face in the crowd turned toward me just then, and though it was dark, there was no mistaking that fringe of false eyelashes, thick as a moth's wings. Her cheekbones, razor sharp, emphasized the hollow of her jaw. I marveled at her face, wishing my own bones would protrude like hers did. Suddenly, my own newfound slimness wasn't enough.

The woman glided over, gesturing widely with one undulating arm, like she was directing an orchestra. "Ladies," she murmured.

"Miss Jake," I said reflexively, gazing at one of the women who had judged me from afar during *Sing It*.

Emma Jake was in head-to-toe tangerine orange. She wore a crepe muumuu with slick orange pants underneath, glasses with tiny oval orange-tinted lenses, and orange ballet slippers. It was an outfit for an eccentric old woman—or an aged pop star. I supposed that once you made enough money and built up your name, you could wear whatever you felt like without your industry peers judging you.

"Congratulations," said Emma Jake, her voice lilting slightly, as if she were imitating a British accent. "I persuaded Marsha to let me have an early listen of your album. It's pure pop magic."

We chorused our thanks.

Emma waved her hand at us quickly, fluttering it like an energetic bird. "Oh, don't be sycophants. You are all very lovely." Here she paused, dipping her orange-tinted sunglasses down the length of her nose. She looked us up and down, taking our image in with calculated interest, before dropping the glasses on the ground and grasping at our arms. "Ladies," she said in a stage whisper. "You're going to be big. I have a sense about these things. I knew that that St. James fellow was going to win even before he actually won it. Pardon me, dear," she added swiftly, tugging on my forearm a little tighter. Her breath smelled like the beach, coconutty—not what I expected. "I liked you, but St. James was going to be the solo star. You see already."

"Of course, Miss Jake," I stammered.

We were interrupted by a squeaky male voice ringing out over the speakers. Peter had an awful speaking voice, but he *was* our manager. Since he was standing on the stage holding a microphone, people stopped chatting to turn toward him. Peter smoothed his suit lapels and straightened and said, "Welcome to the launch party for Gloss! Everyone having fun?" The crowd whooped.

Emma patted at us again, giving her parting words: "I'll see you this week for the season finale? There's so much I need to tell you before you dive headfirst into this pageantry." She shifted away, leaving Meredith and me looking at each other.

"You've heard them on the radio already with their single 'Wake Up Morning.' And now, maybe we could persuade the beautiful ladies of Gloss to sing it for us live?" The cheers intensified. "Yes! Come up here, ladies! I'd like to introduce some very special friends of mine . . . Rose, Meredith, Yumiko, and Cassidy! The girls of Gloss!" The thunderous applause didn't stop, even after we'd climbed the stage in designer clothes and stiletto heels.

These weren't students in a gymnasium, fidgeting during a school talent show. This crowd wasn't a room full of teenagers brought in by record stores at the mall. These were industry insiders, promoters, journalists, all interested in what was happening in the room. I didn't care that the lyrics were a little too adolescent, that I didn't write them, or that I hadn't really felt any of those feelings keenly before. All I cared about was delivering them with emotion and conviction. I needed to sell the feeling and make others believe that I believed it. When Meredith, Rose, Yumiko, and I blended the chorus, I took a peek at the glittering eyes closest to the stage. People were smiling. They were clasping their hands together, clenching their fists. They had tension in their shoulders and were biting their lips. I felt my chest do a double-thump—though it could've been the percussion reverberating through my back. I thought, *We got this.*

I wasn't going to let the doubts creep in this time.

BEING BACK ON the *Sing It* lot was not as unnerving as I expected, now that I was on the other side of the competition. The stage was just a stage; the little yellow room was just a box with a dingy couch.

I didn't need *Sing It; Sing It* needed *us.* We were *Gloss* and our single had debuted with half a million copies sold—*on its first day.* Peter had hummed excitedly about its climbing rank on the Billboard Hot 100. We were walking on air by the time we rehearsed for the show's season finale.

Emma Jake caught us after soundcheck and smiled benevolently, her thick eyelashes fluttering. "Are you hungry?" she asked. "We could have lunch." She commandeered a van and had a driver take us to the Ivy, where a waiter led us straight to a table in the back. "Iced tea, Jerome," she said, her grandiose lilt even more pronounced. "We'll also be needing another chair. Thank you."

She tucked her napkin on her lap daintily and smiled around at us. Her face was lit with two bright pink spots of rouge on her cheeks. If she were a normal civilian, I would say she looked clownish, but because she was Emma Jake, I thought she looked only a little ridiculous.

Emma Jake was an icon. According to legend, twenty years ago you couldn't walk down the street and run into a kid who *didn't* have at least one of her albums, or a poster of hers on their bedroom wall. Cyndi, Madonna, Emma. They were uttered in the same reverent breath.

I was born a few years after her peak, as her star was losing momentum. She fell in love with a backup dancer, planned for a short break to have a baby, and then it died at birth. She left the dancer—or maybe he left her—started recording a comeback album, and lost heart halfway through. The delay kept extending until she finally released it two years behind schedule. I'd grown up hearing her new, matured sound; it wasn't the high-synth pop that her old fans wanted, and Emma Jake faded into the background. And though she'd made albums since, they were rarely in the top charts. Still, she was respected in the industry: she *had* come back. And she had come back with integrity; she'd penned autobiographical folk songs about the life she'd never have. I wondered if she'd chosen to join *Sing It* as a judge because it was a way for her to reenter the mainstream conversation.

"Ladies," she said, raising her glass. "I want you to remember this day. This is the last day where you can walk around L.A. feeling anonymous. It's the last precious day of your lives."

It was strange to sip iced tea and leaf through menus while sitting across from a woman whose backstory I knew as well as my own. To think that she had had dreams of where her life would take her, and the world learned as soon as she did that they wouldn't pan out. If it had happened to me, I would have dropped out of the public eye immediately, crawled into bed, and never wanted to take off the covers.

And yet, she was smiling at us like a benign bird, almost pitying how naive we were. "It's going to be a doozy," she told us. "Everything you say will be amplified. If you don't misstep after this album, the news will report about you as much as they'll discuss stocks, the weather, and presidential addresses. I'm serious. Ah, Lucille! Yes, you're late. Sit."

Her attention was usurped by a teenager with blond hair and a heart-shaped face who had approached our table. She was wearing metallic jeans and a casual black V-neck that was so dark it had to be new. Lucille gave a quick, breathless hello and slid into the chair in between Emma and Rose, directly across from me.

"Ladies, this is my niece, Lucille."

The young woman wasn't wearing much makeup, but her cupid's bow was so pronounced that I stared at her mouth, certain that I'd seen that uncommon feature somewhere before.

"Oh my god!" Yumi exclaimed. "You're Lucy Bowen!"

I tried to rein in my surprise, but a noise escaped my lips. Necks were already craning at other white-topped tables nearby. Emma Jake was the kind of presence that people understood, and they quietly let her be, but Lucy Bowen of the hit TV show *The Jet-Setters* was small-screen royalty.

Lucy smiled politely, used to this sort of reaction. Even though I knew she was younger than us, her mature response made an impression. I would have had my eyes hidden in the menu if this were me. "Yeah! Nice to meet you. Are you a fan of the show?"

"We haven't been able to watch recently—I mean, we've been working so hard—" Yumi chattered excitedly.

"My sisters would *scream* if they saw me sitting here with you," I blurted out.

Emma took control of the conversation again. "Yes, well. I invited her here because she's young like you, but has a lot of experience in the industry. I thought she could be a good influence for you. Luce, these ladies are from the pop group Gloss. They're about to break out with a hit album and I have a feeling the transition is going to be swift. They are going to need help." The waiter arrived with Lucy's iced tea and stayed to take our orders.

"Aunt Emma, I grew up doing commercials. I've been on *sets* my entire life." Lucy pursed her mouth a little and addressed the table. "Television is different from the music industry, but apparently she thinks that *I'm* the best person to help you?"

"Oh, hush. Sets, sets. We were just on a set, weren't we, girls? I asked because you're the same age and you owe me a favor. Listen, ladies, the money *isn't* in the music. I tell all new working chanteuses this because I don't want them to fail. The money: It's in you. *You* are the brand. Become spokespeople. Shoes, perfume, whatever." She waved her hand as if she were fanning away ephemeral fog.

"Isn't the album enough work?" Rose said. "We busted our asses getting here. Now isn't it time for us to be on *TRL*? Well, *we* busted our asses. Cassidy here just hopped on at the last minute."

I took my time spreading my cloth napkin across my lap. I could simultaneously believe and not believe that Rose would say something like this in front of Emma Jake, and our new mentor, Lucy Bowen, who busied herself by tearing Sweet'N Low packets.

"Oh?" Emma Jake said archly. "She hopped in, did she?"

"Well, yeah. We worked so hard to get the attention of the label and finally did. Then they just added her on after she lost *Sing It*."

If Emma Jake had a stern face, she didn't show it. But her voice lost some of its lilt and there was some flint to it. "The label did what was best for the group," she explained slowly. "Heaven knows I don't always agree with them on things, but they knew what they were doing. I listened to your record: it would not have worked without Cassidy. Whether you like it or not, and whether you agree with the way that she was brought on or not, the four of you are a team now. You can't have in-fighting. You can't act like you resent one another in front of the press. You must get along and you *must* support one another." She paused. "You may not be friends after all of this, but you *will* be like family. And you will have to learn to trust one another, because the rest of the world will love you and hate you and support you and then turn on you. You can rely *only* on one another. Do you understand?"

Meredith, Yumi, and I nodded. Rose was still, her eyes flickering on the water glasses. She probably wasn't used to being spoken to like this.

"Rose," Emma said, and the flowery tone was back. She touched one of Rose's hands.

Rose jerked her arm a little but not away. "Yeah."

"I don't mean to lecture you, especially here. This was supposed to be a celebratory meal."

As if summoned at the perfect moment, Jerome placed our dishes in front of us. I ate as slowly as I could with half-bites to make the food last longer, and I noticed the rest of the table did the same, picking gently at plates and eating around any oil spots. Only Emma Jake ate with gusto.

When the check arrived, Emma said, "Cassidy, dear, please stay a moment." The others excused themselves and I waited, wondering what Emma wanted to tell me alone.

"Listen, sweetheart." She straightened up after signing the check with a flourish. "I can see you're going to have a little bear of a time with Rose. It's not easy being the odd one out, but I know you are good for the group. Rose is very headstrong and she's in it for the long haul. Be careful not to get hurt. I don't think she means everything she says, but keep your guard up just in case."

"I know," I said. "I will."

Emma Jake walked me to the door, patted my arm like a

doting grandmother, then, to my confusion, she meandered back inside. I stepped into the sun, blinking brightly, and rejoined the others.

Lucy smiled as a shiny silver Jag was pulled forward by the valet. "Who wants to sightsee in Malibu?"

# 9.

May 2001
NYC

# Cassidy

"Would you like a drink before takeoff, Ms. Holmes?" A flight attendant hovered by my elbow. I accepted a sparkling water and glanced over at my companions in our private jet, courtesy of Big Disc for landing *The Sunrise Show.* Our tour manager, Ian, messed with his PalmPilot; Merry was asleep, head lolling off to one side, blond curls bobbing. Yumi was flipping through in-flight entertainment, and Rose surprised me by pulling out a Sudoku book and filling in one of the grids with a pen.

Rose saw me looking at her and a faint tint of red appeared on her cheeks. I wondered if she was still upset with me after the talk with Emma Jake. We'd barely exchanged two words after our lunch at the Ivy, not since Lucy had driven us, somewhat jerkily, toward the lowering sun. The road had gotten narrower, a little twisty. We'd popped out on the coast, and she'd made a right turn on the PCH, which ran parallel to the beach. I had sat on the right rear side, having been squashed on the edge with Yumi in the middle seat as buffer. Meredith had claimed the front passenger seat, chattering away with Lucy about boys.

We'd made it all the way to Malibu, where the Jag climbed another twisty road and stopped near a wrought-iron gate at the end of a cul-de-sac. "This *totally hot* A-lister lives here," Lucy said, waggling her brows. "He won't mind if we park in front of his house."

We got out and stretched. It'd been at least an hour crammed into the back seat of the car. Rose walked away from all of us, facing the ocean, which we could see through a small smattering of trees among the manicured lawns. The horizon line was a gray smudge in the distance, perfectly bisecting the sky and water.

Meredith whistled. "Gorgeous. I'm going to have to buy a place over here."

"It's prettier down by the water, but if you've never seen the houses up here, you don't know what you've missed out on coveting." Lucy laughed.

"You don't live out here?" Yumi said, sounding surprised.

"Ha! I wish. I'm still a minor, remember? I live with my parents in a boring old ranch house in Sherman Oaks. But once I'm eighteen . . ." She clapped her hands together forcefully. "I'm going to buy myself a nice birthday present with a pretty chunk of my *Jet-Setters* money."

Rose, I noticed, kept her distance. Yumi stood next to me and murmured, "Ignore her. She's in one of her moods."

"I don't get her," I said fiercely.

Yumi touched my elbow. "I'll explain later, okay?"

Lucy was still waxing poetic about real estate as Meredith loudly agreed. We returned to the car, drove down to the beach, and began to dig our heels into the sand with wind whipping our hair. Yumi motioned me over to her. She glanced over at the other girls, but with the wind they wouldn't be able to hear us anyway. "I wish you'd be a little more patient with Rose," she began. She held up a hand when I started to protest. "It's still hard on her that Viv isn't with us."

"Oh." I looked at Rose, who hadn't joined us down on the strip of beach. She was still leaning against Lucy's car. I had so many questions, but could never bring up Vivian without feeling like I was intruding on something personal. "What's she like?"

"Beautiful voice. Same register as yours, but different. And pretty. In an unconventional way." Yumi touched her cheek with a finger, remembering. "Dark hair, curly, kinda wild. We all kind of grew up together, but Rose and Viv knew each other the longest. It was Rose's idea that we become a singing group. She saw a music video on MTV and decided we should do that." She smiled. "Rose said it was important that we *blend*. That none of us overpowered the other. We were all equals in the group, she said." She was hugging herself against the wind.

"And then what?" I asked.

"We were pretty good. I mean, without a band, singing along to karaoke a lot. We made a tape of ourselves singing a *blended* version of different covers and sent them to a bunch of companies. Big Disc actually wrote back."

I was quiet, looking out into the endless surf. Light danced on the waves.

"The company invited us to come in and sing. They really liked us. Said we had p-potential," Yumi stuttered, and I realized she was crying. "They wanted to add a fifth voice in; said we'd sound even better. Rose said no, that it was the four of us and that's it. We went home. I loved that she stood up for the integrity of our group. Then Viv got sick." She swallowed hard. "She was feeling really low energy for a while, had these headaches. She went to the doctor and they ran tests. Cancer. It was her idea that we go to Big Disc and say okay to their terms, because she knew she'd be replaced anyway. That's when you came in."

No wonder Rose was so callous. She was expecting one of her best friends of the last ten years there, and instead saw a stranger. A stranger who usurped Vivian's place that she had worked so hard to create.

"It's not you, Cassidy," Yumi said, dabbing at her eyes with the heel of her palm. "She doesn't mean to be cruel. Please be patient with her."

"Why didn't anyone tell me this before?" I was mortified, having harbored so many ill feelings toward Rose during the past months. "I have all this resentment—and so does she—and I would've been more understanding . . ."

"I guess I thought she'd settle down and you'd get along. But you were kind of clueless, and she's still upset . . . so yeah. I figured I should probably tell you so you could tread more carefully around her." She smiled a shaky smile. "She's a bitch, but a bitch for a good reason."

A shout warbled across the sound of the waves. Meredith was waving us back.

"Just try, okay?" Yumi said, and held her hand out for me. I twined my fingers into hers as we made our way across the sand.

THE FIRST EXHILARATING, live television performance of "Wake Up Morning" began its rounds on the *Sing It* finale, to much applause, but *The Sunrise Show* would be the real test—its live audience consisted of *Sunrise* fans, not *Sing It* ones.

With a rumble, the cabin door closed and, before I knew it, the world below us miniaturized, fell away, partially hidden under wisps of clouds. Rose was halfway through her inked grid before a drink materialized on her foldout table.

"What's on your mind, Cassidy?" Ian asked.

He sat sideways in his seat with his long legs swiveled out toward the aisle, scribbling in the margins of a sheaf of papers. Barrel-chested and tall, with a default scowl on his face, Ian was intimidating at first, but we soon saw his softer side. He always asked if we had any requests when he managed the tour schedule, even though we knew that Peter had locked down every possible minute of our time.

"I thought that was already finalized," I said, noticing that the top page was a calendar grid. Every available space was jammed with tiny print.

"Peter wants another radio spot. Gotta add it in." After a beat of silence, he looked up at me, making eye contact. "You okay?"

"Yeah, just thinking about all the stuff that we're going to do. I'm kind of anxious about *The Sunrise Show*."

"But you've been on TV before?" He said it like a question, even though he was well versed in my *Sing It* experience. Eyes back down on his makeshift office, pencil working. Even Ian wasn't capable of filling out a grid in ink! My begrudging admiration for Rose grew.

"Yeah, but . . . that was singing. I can sing." I stated this matter-of-factly. I might have been insecure about many things, but my voice was not one of them. "But what if Melina Vaclavik asks me a question and I give a silly answer? At least on *Sing It* if I was being interviewed, it was taped so I could start over if I messed up."

"So don't mess up."

"I'm not good under pressure."

"That's bullshit."

I bit down on my lip as I peered at Ian across the aisle. The truth was—and I began to realize it while flicking my eyes over to Rose—that I was worried I would be up there on that stage and Melina Vaclavik would ask *Rose* a question and she would delegitimize me right there on live television. *A reality show competitor who didn't even win the final round. A girl who skipped half her senior year just to become a background singer.*

"Take it easy." I must have had a terrible expression on my face. "I watched *Sing It* with my little boy. He thinks you're talented. I do too. You'll be fine."

The anxiety still threatened to climb out of my throat. I clutched at the soft leather armrests and tried to take my mind off it. "Your son?"

"Yeah. Jordan. I get to pick him up on Tuesdays and hang

out with him, and what he wants to do is watch *Sing It.* So that is what we do."

I let out a breath.

"How old is he?"

"Twelve, going on twenty," he said, mouth finally cracking into a full smile.

"Did he vote for me? Be honest. Or did he vote for Anna?"

"I never let him vote," he said firmly. "I won't have him calling phone numbers that show up on the bottom of a TV screen."

"But *you* could have called *for* him," I pointed out.

"See, just bring that sass, Miss Cass," Ian said, jabbing the tip of the pencil toward me emphatically.

"That didn't answer my question," I said cheekily.

He turned back to his work. "He made me vote for St. James. Thought he was a *hunk.*"

I laughed.

I HADN'T BEEN to New York since I was a little kid. My family and I drove up from Houston, like ridiculous people, in a minivan, when I was eleven. I didn't remember much of the trip except for the crowds and bleak weather. We'd come during Christmas break, and though I thought the many buildings would have insulated us from the cold, wind sheared through the corridors between buildings instead, creating tunnels of absolute misery. We had walked in a miniature tour group, all in a clump with my Astros-capped father leading the pack, while the kids whined about wanting to just sit down somewhere there was heat. I distinctly remember my toes going numb in my sneakers.

Returning to New York with this tour group was a different experience altogether. As we made our descent in our private aircraft, it was in the twilight hour between sunset and evening. Skyscrapers glowed blue, rimmed warm pink from behind. Millions of beads of light lit uneven clumps of buildings and major thoroughfares. I squinted and made out the Empire State Building, taller than all of the other buildings around it, and toward the edge of the window, the unmistakable ridges of the twin towers stood at the tip of Manhattan.

Twenty minutes later, we slid onto a runway, disembarked, and within moments we exited JFK and climbed into a glimmering black SUV. We rode through sticky streets, an hour and a half of low murmurings, as Merry had fallen asleep again in the middle seat.

It surprised me then, and it surprised me again, how *dense* New York is. Coming from two highly populated cities, it shouldn't have caught me off guard, but those were cities of sprawl. The millions of people on this two-mile-long island are stacked upon one another, sleeping above one another, crowded next to one another, walking in a giant sea of anonymous faces. It made me dizzy.

While Big Disc may have spared no expense getting us to New York, they were slightly less accommodating when it came to our hotel rooms. We slept in modest adjoining suites, two to a room, with Ian across the hall and various other members of our entourage scattered across three floors. Merry had sprawled on a bed as soon as Ian unlocked the first door, and Yumi followed her in. Rose and I uncomfortably realized we were roommates for the night.

We moved into the second suite room, still without dialogue, barely acknowledging each other. As if she knew she couldn't be the first to talk, Rose perched on her bed and flipped through channels, stopping when she found a rerun of *The Jet-Setters*. She left it on low volume, as if the walls were thin enough to wake Merry in the next room. I watched the pronounced cupid's bow of Lucy Bowen's mouth undulate on the screen, though I was unsettled to feel Rose's eyes flicker on me instead.

AT DAWN, THERE was already a crowd outside of *Sunrise*'s first-floor studio window.

We were whisked away to the dressing rooms in jeans and wide-collared shirts. Even at this hour the hallways were bustling with personnel. Yumi, Rose, and I sat quietly, eyes closed and listening to Muzak, in our separate little chairs as the hair and makeup stylists worked. Our bodies, on West Coast time, had hit the snooze button. Merry, on the other hand, had banked so many hours of sleep during our travel that she was wired and chatty.

How strange, I thought, as someone soothingly combed out my hair and spritzed it with spray. That we were here, doing this. That we'd be on television and my mom would tape it for the rest of the family. That Alex and Edie and Joanna would catch the broadcast in different time zones, if they weren't sleeping through it. That the next few months we'd be working continuously, and that this soft tiredness on the edges of my eyes, in between my brows, was going to be pleasant compared to the bone-deep weariness that would be setting in over the course of the coming weeks.

As blush was being applied to my cheeks, Merry uttered a gasp of disbelief. "We're going on stage in *those?*"

*Those* turned out to be full latex suits in different colors. Laid out on hangers, they looked like doll's clothes. I thought I knew what we'd be wearing on tour, and this had not been in our fittings.

"Will they fit?" Yumi asked doubtfully, examining one.

Ian, who had merely checked a box ensuring the clothes had been in the cargo for the tour, also looked at them apprehensively. "I'm sure they had your measurements," he said slowly.

"They'll stretch," I added, but I didn't know how I could go out in that. All other performances I'd seen on *The Sunrise Show* had been flamboyant, sure, but nothing as gratuitously skintight as this.

"Someone call Peter," Merry said, looking with disdain at the tiny catsuit. "I doubt this will end well."

But Peter did not budge. "They're hot!" he argued on the phone. "The designer assured me they stretch just fine. And what else can you wear while you're out there—jeans? Don't bother me with petty stuff like this. Just put the damn things on!"

So Ian left, and we tried to change. Merry tugged on her suit while a stylist was still chasing after her with a can of hairspray. "Cassidy, zip me up?" she said, wriggling her arms into the long sleeves. The suit was ice-blue and covered her entire body, from neck to ankle, but it hugged every curve like a second skin. Every time she moved, she squeaked, and she pulled at the crotch with both hands. "This is more invasive than a visit to the gynecologist," she groused.

With thick-soled shoes that added three inches to her height, she looked like a genuine pop star. Our debut on national television was going to get tongues wagging, that much I knew.

"This doesn't *breathe*," Yumi complained, as she zipped into hers—black, of course. Mine was dark blue.

The makeup artist was aghast. "You're supposed to sprinkle baby powder inside the suit so that your skin isn't sticking directly to it! Didn't your costumer tell you?" She shifted bottles around on the table, searching for some.

"You'd be surprised what they *don't* tell us," Merry said wryly. She pulled at the neck of her suit and sprinkled the proffered powder down the front and jumped up and down to disperse it.

Yumi opted to peel hers off and sprinkle powder inside before yanking it back on again. There was no costumer to wipe away the white spots that made it to the outside, so the makeup artist did that for her.

Rose twisted into her pink suit. "I blame Britney for this."

Merry shifted in the mirror, looking at her body from all angles. "My boobs are stretching this thing within an inch of its life!" she commented. "I can barely breathe."

"That's not your boobs, that's your ass." Rose flicked an eye toward Merry's rear end. "Less regular Coke, more Diet, Merry."

"Aw, screw you, Rose!"

We were ushered outside to wait behind the patio stage. The crowd was a wavering blob of colors and noise and rectangular boards. The fluorescent poster boards were easier to read than the people holding them; they expressed birthday wishes, anniversary kisses, hellos to people at home, all wanting their tiny slices of broadcast fame. I could see Milena Vaclavik's side profile as she spoke to a camera amid a spattering of enthusiastic viewers, and then we were tipped to ascend the shallow stage. I nervously looked at the faces, trying to single out anyone who shouldn't be there. I wondered if those people would be fast-forwarding through our parts on the VCR while slowly parsing the crowd scenes. Perspective. We may have flown in on a private jet, but to thousands across the nation we were just the musical filler, the background to their loved one's tiny moment of fame.

"This is Gloss with their debut single, 'Wake Up Morning.' What a perfect title for our viewers!"

It was barely ten and already the buildings were baking in the summer sun. The unforgiving latex made me feel like I was encased in tin foil. Merry and Rose, both so fair, began to turn pink.

We took our places—Rose and Merry in the front as main vocals, Yumi and me in the back, and waited for the backing music. While we grasped a hold of our microphones, I found myself reading the signs.

**HI DAD**
**NANA PAPA WE LOVE YOU**
**LOUISIANA GIRLS LOVE NYC**
**GO SASSY CASSIDY GO GLOSS**

A quick pang of fear quivered down in my stomach, ricocheted off every surrounding organ. I glanced up at the face to see who was holding this sign.

I squinted. Was that . . . ?

Teeth glinting in a large, smiling mouth; sunglasses wrapped around his eyes so it was hard to tell, but . . .

There went the opening bars to the music, and I snapped back to the task at hand. We were a well-oiled machine and our dancing was crisp.

> *Every morning when I wake up*
> *I feel a pang when I remember you're not here*
> *But then I recall that you kissed me goodbye*
> *And told me that you'd always be near . . .*

We were in the middle of the second verse when the crowd began to buzz with agitation. Normally I lose myself when performing, but out in the daytime like this, on an outdoor stage without extra lighting, the audience was visible and took up more attention than usual. It wasn't the typical grooving or hand-clapping that we'd grown accustomed to—they seemed distracted, pointing at the stage, murmuring. I wasn't sure what was going on. They whooped and clapped when we finished our set.

As we exited the stage, the crowd shifted away from us, homed in on the camera crews like minnows. We were being led back toward the building, but I craned my head and looked for that guy again. Maybe he'd fight his way inside.

"God!" Merry said as soon as we were inside. "Fuck!"

She was clutching her chest.

Yumi was incredulous. "What happened?"

"This damn suit *ripped open*! What do you think happened?"

Her jumpsuit had torn along the left armhole seam and across her chest, and a gash had opened up along the nipple line.

"What did you *do*?" I exclaimed, staring at the rip.

"What *could* I do? I put one hand up to hide what I needed to and kept singing. The show must go on, right?"

"I'm going to kill whoever made these costumes," Rose vowed.

"It's like your boobs couldn't be contained," Yumi joked, "now or any other time."

Merry set her jaw and glared at Yumi. "I can't help what happened with that guy in Oklahoma. I *could* help not flashing all of New York if the costume person hadn't made these suits so minuscule!"

Ian finally met us at the dressing room door. "What the hell?" he barked, looking straight at Merry.

She was indignant. "I can't help it! The suit ripped! It was live! I couldn't just leave!"

"But you—"

"This is *humiliating*! Can we just drop it?" She pushed into the room, her hands scrabbling at the zipper on the back of her neck, and I followed her in to help. Ian saw her starting to disrobe and turned to face the door.

As I helped to peel Merry out of the garment, Ian sighed and said, "They can't air a topless pop star on morning television. Maybe they cut away in time." But I knew from the murmurs and pointing in the audience that Merry's wardrobe malfunction couldn't be ignored, and I was sure that *The Sunrise Show*'s audience got more than they bargained for this morning. Merry knew it too. She wadded the suit up, threw it in the trash, and grabbed her original shirt from her dressing chair.

She angrily buttoned her top while glaring at Ian. "You tell Peter that I will not wear a stupid pleather, latex, whatever-the-fuck-that-was jumpsuit *ever* again!" Without waiting for an answer, she stormed off, bumping into a man in the hallway.

A man I recognized.

# 10.

*Friday*

# Merry

I was on my third cup of coffee, even though my limit was supposed to be two. Dousing fires coming for my fourteen-year-old daughter required caffeine. Tons of it.

What possessed my sweet, lovable girl to post such a stupid, idiotic thing on her Instagram? Where were my parental controls? Why did I let her run amok? Even though it had been deleted for twelve hours already, the screenshots kept coming up with speculation and commentary. The internet always has receipts.

Then calls began coming in from gossip rags and TV shows. It was Friday and they needed fodder for the weekend, I supposed. The same questions that had come up over a decade ago that we had tamped down and buried—or so I thought.

I'd had to call my publicist for reinforcement. She worked steadily on her end, sending me texts every so often on the steps she had to take. When I'd called to tell her what Soleil had done, she huffed a long sigh into my ear. "Are you sure you don't want her to just let her learn from her mistake?" she said wearily. "Sometimes teenagers just have to stick their foot in it."

"I'm not asking you to scrub the entire internet. We just need to control this a little bit." I chewed the inside of my cheek.

"The best thing you could do is tell her to apologize. A real apology, not something that shifts the blame on anyone else. *I'm sorry you were offended,* et cetera, doesn't work here."

"And what do *I* do? People are blaming me for this. I've said some shitty things in my lifetime, I'll admit that, but I never could have seen this coming."

A beat, like she was weighing what to say. "I'm aware."

"I *know* you're aware. You've cleaned up more than your fair share of my messes. But the chatter now is a smear campaign. I'll be damned if this will hurt my bottom line."

Justine sighed again. "Roger that. I'll get to work."

I slugged my coffee. Pawed through my calendar. Emily was fielding questions, adding meetings that were stacking up on Monday to calm the board, soothe investors. There was a setup at four on Tuesday that looked suspicious. I texted her. "What does FPZ want?"

"A meet. Looking for a new *Sing It* judge," she typed back.

I paused. "FPZ? *Sing It?*"

"New network acquired rights. Rebooting show. Need celebrity judges."

"*Damn it, Emily,*" I muttered under my breath. Didn't she see what else I was dealing with? I didn't want to be a part of some cheap reboot on a small network, which would take attention away from my businesses that actually made money. "Not interested," I typed. "Cancel it."

"I think they're asking other Glossies too."

Hmm. It would be interesting to see Yumi and Rose at each other's throats for the job, but no. "Even more of a no," I wrote.

"Okay."

Raul popped into the kitchen, hair still wet from a post-workout shower. "Hello, my love," he said.

Despite my attention being pulled in multiple directions like taffy, Raul could crystalize my focus like nothing else. I smiled up at him. "Hello."

"Oh, you have that tired-but-caffeinated look." He nodded at my mug. "What number is that?"

I slurped the last dregs from the cup. "I'm not telling."

He leaned over the kitchen island and wiped foam from my lip with his thumb. "Try to behave yourself," he whispered, the lines around his eyes crinkling.

Love in Hollywood is a strange beast. It feels two-faced and duplicitous when you're *trying* to find someone; everyone has a star meter, where they judge how important you are in the industry, even if they don't mean to. Some will say that they don't care about your level of fame, but they really do. I've had boyfriends who couldn't handle the demands of my schedule, asked me to slow my hustle. If I listened, it inevitably tanked the project I was working on: solo record, makeup collaboration with a well-known brand, a cookbook that I failed to promote hard enough. Or maybe my name just didn't command enough attention anymore.

I had faced the inevitable: individually, we just weren't that interesting to people. We needed to be the cohesive foursome.

We needed to be Gloss.

Eventually, I slowed down because of Sunny. She was getting old enough to realize when she was getting passed off to nannies and babysitters, and I didn't like that at all. I wanted to raise my own child. It was just her and me in this world, and I was fine with it.

Meeting Raul was an accident. I was meeting with a consultant for a lipstick line and dating a B-list movie star at the time. What is it about B-list movie stars that make them so insufferably insecure? He was self-conscious and asked me to visit him on set that day, and texted me during my meeting. I irritatingly obliged. While merging onto the 5, he texted me again, and I took one second to glance over at the phone, a reflexive habit. I tapped the bumper of the car in front of me and when we'd settled to a stop to assess the damage, a beautiful, dark-haired man with dazzling white teeth emerged from the other car. He was pleasant as we swapped insurance information.

That might have been the end of it, but I bumped into him again at a bakery and he asked me out then. I dumped the actor. Raul and I didn't talk shop on our date. We just talked, ignoring the live jazz band that we'd agreed to go see. We ate three meals over the course of the sixteen hours we spent together on our first date, and that was that.

Raul was an unknown, a struggling actor who baked bread at a Los Feliz coffee shop. His shifts started early, so our dates after that were interrupted by his three A.M. wakeup calls. On the positive side, his workdays ended early enough that he could quickly wipe the flour off his forearms and attend auditions while still smelling like fresh bread. And to boot, he was perfect with Soleil.

The soap opera role came a little later, and while it's difficult to become a breakout star in an ensemble cast as large as a soap's, somehow his character made an impression. And there we were. I sold my Malibu house and together we bought a place closer to the heart of the city. I was happy to make some sacrifices to be with him. Wasn't that what love was about? Doing what you think is best for someone else, because their well-being is important to you?

"What are you thinking, my love?" he said to me, busily slicing cantaloupe into thin pieces and setting them on a white plate. He had such a beautiful accent. Rich and decadent, like when you let full-fat ice cream melt in your mouth.

I considered mentioning what Soleil had done, but decided not to ruin the moment. I popped another coffee pod in the machine, but then remembered how many I'd had and didn't push the button. I spun to look at him. "How much I love you."

"Ah, but how much do you love me?" he asked, wiggling his eyebrows as he set the plate in front of me. He knew how much I liked to snack while he made the main course of anything. I saw his array of ingredients laid out in front of him and hoped for an omelet.

"So much that I feel bad for asking if you want to go to a funeral with me."

"Your friend?"

"Yes. It's probably next week, once her family makes arrangements. Wednesday? I am going to have Emily make the flight arrangements but wanted to check with your schedule first."

"Hmm, I wish I could be with you, but the schedule is too tight."

"I thought as much. I'm going to bring Sunny with me." *And keep an eye on her,* I added to myself.

"So I will be a bachelor for a few days? How will I behave myself?" He began slicing vegetables quickly and easily, not even looking, the knife gleaming and his knuckles acting as a guide for the blade.

"Hopefully work will keep you out of mischief." I grinned at him. He smiled back. I felt a small cushion of contentment. It was a nice change after the past few days of feeling a sense of reeling.

I still remember the way that Cassidy gained her first boyfriend. It was completely out of the blue: one day she was unattached, the next moment they were together. Alex. He'd known her for years, was one of her best friends, encouraged her to try out for *Sing It.* Out of all her close-knit friends, he was the only one who really kept in touch with her when she moved to L.A. to be a part of the group. Familiarity begets flirtation—or something like that.

She'd told him about our television appearance on *The Sunrise Show,* and though he didn't even live close to New York, he surprised her with a custom sign and stood in the crowd while we performed. We were ushered back inside, where he couldn't follow. Somehow he got a hold of Ian and shared a handful of photos of him and Cass when they were in school together.

Ian—good guy that he is—begrudgingly allowed contact while he contended with the *intense* matter of me flashing a live audience. I'd stormed out of the dressing room and nearly mowed Alex over, but that didn't stop Cassidy from nearly jumping out of her skin when she saw him. They hugged and he spun her around in a circle, like they were in a movie. "Alex! I *thought* that was you! What are you *doing* here?"

Something in her voice made me turn around and look. She had never sounded like that, not the entire time I'd been living with her and working alongside her. Cassidy's voice was tinged with wonder, dipped in gold: she sounded *happy*.

I had a clear view of his face, and he looked at her like he thought she was the most beautiful creature he'd ever seen. With both of his hands clasped on her thin shoulders, he asked her if she wanted to grab lunch or take a walk or something.

I'd only ever seen that kind of face on a guy when he was trying to build up the courage to ask a girl out on a date, to the prom. My cousin Kasey's boyfriend proposed to her at one of our Thanksgivings, and his earnest expression mirrored Alex's. Lord, the girl needed some happiness and companionship besides the rest of us, but Ian, ever the killjoy, said no. "We have a schedule," he said. Alex's excited face fell away, and he dropped his hands to his jeans pockets.

"But . . . but Cass, you have to eat *some time,* right?" Alex coaxed.

"She gets to eat from twelve-thirty to one."

"Oh, give her a break," I griped to Ian. I blame myself for what happened next. All the months of happiness don't make up for the ensuing years of turmoil. I will always remember that I helped start this. "Let her grab something at the café with her old friend and then she can join us at the hotel before we have to go."

Ian paused, glanced at his watch, at his PalmPilot, and I knew he was considering the length of my fuse after the jumpsuit fiasco. "Fine," he acquiesced. "Meet us in the hotel lobby no later than one o'clock."

Rose added, "Cassy, remember there's a photo shoot scheduled for tomorrow. Try not to pick anything that will bloat you."

Cassidy nodded. She turned her face back toward her friend and he held out his hand. She took it and they didn't walk off, they *skipped* away, like kindergarteners on a school field trip to the zoo. We watched them go. I remember being glad for them.

I regret it all. It's terrible, what happened to that boy.

## 11.

# Cassidy

The ground floor and basement of 30 Rockefeller Plaza is a concourse of food and shops, an air-conditioned mall of sorts. I'd changed out of my catsuit and dabbed off my lipstick with a tissue. Alex was waiting for me outside the dressing room and I reflexively grabbed at his hand, as if touching him would bring together the strange two halves of my old self and my new self. Now, we walked hand in hand through the underground levels, taking in the gilded walls advertising coffee and sandwiches.

Hungry as I was, my more pressing concern was uncovering why Alex was in Manhattan and had been holding a sign bearing my name.

I twisted his hand and tugged it closer to get his attention.

He'd slowed down to look at a pasted menu but refocused on me. I asked, "What *are* you doing here?"

"I'm here to see you, dummy!"

"No note, no call, you just decided, *Oh, let's go see Cassy in New York?*"

"Here, want something? I'll buy." He led me into the shop and told the woman at the order counter, "Two pastramis on rye."

"No," I chimed in quickly. "Spinach salad for me, please."

We sat at a small table with our bottled waters. "You don't have to listen to that Rose all the time, you know," he teased. "You can eat my sandwich if you want."

I shook my head. "Start talking."

"It's summer vacation and I wanted a change of scenery," he said, fingers playing with his cellophane wrapper.

"Please. You are so bad at avoiding the subject. Just talk."

"Ugh, you know me so well."

"Well, duh. We've been friends for forever."

He shifted in his seat, his body hunching over the small round table between us. "Here's the thing," he said slowly. "I'm transferring to Pomona. I'll be in L.A. with you." His eyes were on me, awaiting my reaction.

"You did what?" I had a quick twinge of anxiety. "You didn't do this because of *me,* right?"

Abruptly, he leaned back in his chair and took a gulp of his drink, creating a larger space between us. "Nah. I can't deal with another Chicago winter. I'm a Texas boy. All that snow . . . I couldn't ever get warm. I don't want to go back to

Houston, so, I thought, why not try L.A.? It's supposed be the same season all year long."

"That's good. Probably good, anyway. That you're doing it for yourself. I mean, we're always traveling. We're going to be on tour for months, probably." I was babbling, miming the motion of a bus traveling down a wavy road with my free hand. Alex caught it and held it still on the table.

"The thing is," he said again, "I feel like you've been needing someone, right? Someone who knows the real you, not just this glossy girl who is beautiful and sings real nice—"

I faced the open stall of the busy concourse. The crowd, which had been moving evenly in the space behind Alex and the café stall, suddenly changed composition. I felt myself stiffening, hands curling into fists, heart on overdrive.

And then I saw him. A man, stopped in the middle of the flock, making people change direction to avoid walking into him. Before I could consider anything else, he was rushing toward our shop. But this was not Jerry.

"Alex."

There was fright in my voice, but Alex didn't react like I expected he would. He continued, "It's just, I think—"

"*Alex!*" I said it more urgently. He turned to look, and the man was upon us, grinning widely.

"There you are!" he hollered as he bridged the last few steps to make it to our table. "I've been looking for you, darling!"

Alex stood up to intercept him. "Whoa there, I think you have the wrong person." He was blocking the guy with his wide body, but the man stepped around him, swatting away Alex's outstretched arms.

"Cassidy," the man said, reaching out toward my face.

I was too frightened to scream.

The man flopped to the ground, collapsing a couple of chairs. The noise reverberated in the wide space, catching the attention of a few passersby. Alex had tackled him from behind, trapping the man's arms in a bear hug. "Cass, get security!" he hollered as the man tried to wriggle free. I found myself on my feet, backing away from the table, the man, Alex, but I'd lost my voice.

The man continued to yell. "You—get off of me! She's my wife! My soul mate from a past life! We belong together!"

Another man rushed forward—polyester, blue, a working security guard. Another officer arrived and the three of them wrestled the man into submission. When a hand touched my shoulder, I gasped in surprise, but it was the cashier who had rung up our food. "You all right?" she said, and I surprised myself by falling onto her bright orange shirt and sobbing uncontrollably. She wrapped her arms around me, patting my back. "It's all right, it's all right," she repeated. I could only register that her chest was soft and her hug was reassuring.

"Has this ever happened before?" she said, and I shook my head no, getting my tears all over her shirt collar, but in my head I thought, *There was Jerry, once. Jerry was scary. But he wasn't as scary as this.*

The woman transferred me to a new hugger, one I knew. Alex clutched me familiarly, protectively. "He's cuffed and gone, Cass. Holy shit!" He was shaking just as much as me.

"I'm going to find a way to get a hold of one of your friends. You *have* to talk to the police about this."

When he loosened his grip, I hugged him back harder, desperate. "Alex, don't leave me!"

"It's okay, it's okay. I'm not leaving. I'm just making a call," he said calmingly, gently removing my hands from his shoulders. By the time we were through talking to the police about what had happened, Ian's deadline of one o'clock was far gone. He would be blowing a gasket.

I walked into the hotel lobby with Alex on one side and a cop on the other, hugging my arms to my chest, and saw Ian. He stalked toward us, eyes blazing. "Where the *hell* have you been—" he began, but Alex cut him off.

"What the *hell* are *you* doing, man?" Alex screamed. "Do you not realize the *danger* these girls are in? Some psycho tried to grab Cassidy out in the middle of a crowded building! *Why* aren't they given any protection?"

Ian faltered. "What?" He noticed the cop, then. "What happened?"

Alex sputtered out the story, and the officer chimed in to say, "We do recommend that you provide some security detail for your client. Unfortunately, being in the public eye can and will draw some dangerous people."

Ian thanked the officer, who left with a curt nod. He then switched back to teddy bear mode, his voice velvety soft. "Cass." I found myself tearing up again. I sniffled.

He sighed and turned to Alex. "You better come with us for now."

We had a group meeting in our hotel room, where Alex

offered to be an extra pair of eyes and hands while Ian got approval from upper management to hire a security detail. Ian acquiesced gruffly, but warned, "I can't pay you for volunteering."

"Him?" Rose said. "He doesn't look very intimidating."

Alex drew himself up to his full five feet, eleven inches and puffed out his wide chest. "I know how to handle myself."

"Don't get too cocky, guy," Ian continued, pointing a finger. "You'll be riding on the other bus with the roadies. No special bunking privileges." I was shocked with embarrassment by this remark. Ian checked his watch. "Remember, photo shoot tomorrow, then concert in Jersey. Get packed. Get moving. We're already running late."

THERE YOU ARE. *There you are.*

Despite my exhaustion, it had taken me hours to fall asleep that night. I kept replaying the incident with the man in the bowels of the Rockefeller buildings. I couldn't remember much about him except his gravelly voice—"There you are!" he'd shouted, and then my silence—the fact that I couldn't even *scream,* god! That was unnerving. When I closed my eyes, I could see his outstretched hand reaching for my face. By the time we arrived at a photo studio in downtown Manhattan, I still hadn't slept more than a handful of hours. I was dragging and didn't even care that my outfit was a dusty blue, a shade that flattered no one.

Ian paced behind the photographer and his assistant during the shoot, talking low on his phone. After it wrapped, he hustled us to the doors, talking a mile a minute. Apparently,

Peter had been making new connections and pinging his contacts to try to get ahead of the *Sunrise Show* fiasco. He'd hired a publicist, Justine, who would be joining us in New Jersey and walking us through any other issues that might arise from the incident. Luckily, while the show did air live on the East Coast, it was tape-delayed for all other time zones, so the network opted to run unused footage of a different angle for all subsequent broadcasts.

"I won't lie, this could be bad," Peter began on speakerphone when we were back on the bus. "Yes, most people are making breakfast or getting ready for work when they are watching *Sunrise,* but there are a lot of housewives who watch the entire show from start to finish and they would be the ones to complain to the network."

"It's not like I could *help* it," Merry snapped.

I was worried about her, especially once we caught a glimpse of the controversy on a TV tabloid show called *JMC* while on our way to a show in Pittsburgh a few nights later. "Pop group Gloss made unexpected headlines when one of their singers accidentally flashed the crowd at *The Sunrise Show,*" a voice-over narrated. They'd obtained a video copy of the original airing and played the exact moment Merry's catsuit ripped. There we were, lined up and singing on the *Sunrise* stage. I could make out the sheen of sweat on all of our faces except for Rose's, which was starting to match the color of her suit. "During a simple move, singer Merry, here, suddenly lost part of her costume." *JMC* slowed the playback and pixelated Merry's chest. "The Federal Communications Commission is considering suing NBC for indecency in broadcasting. On the plus side, we've given Merry the nickname Cherry, for reasons you could *probably* guess."

It was absurd.

It was disgusting.

But damn, if it didn't highlight Gloss. We were already making headway with our single, but there was an increased surge in sales right after the *Sunrise* fiasco. Peter couldn't tell if it was something that would've happened anyway, or if the sales outperformed the projections, but despite Merry's repeated objections to her sexualized nickname, he didn't seem to do anything to discourage its use. He told us that letters were pouring into Big Disc about us—he hadn't read all of them, but their volume was promising. "Only big acts get the kind of fan mail you're getting," he said, pleased.

A few days later, we were dressed and waiting in our dressing room as the arena filled up in Ohio, when an assistant brought a magazine in. We clamored around it and Yumi read the headline out loud, "Gloss: Pop's Newest Sensation!" We posed among one another, each positioned on a seamless white background. Alongside our figures was a line that emphasized why our personalities were so perfectly suited for our nicknames.

Yumi, with her perfectly symmetrical face straight to the camera, lips parted sensuously, looked like an Asian Barbie. I recoiled when I saw that they called her *Tasty*. "Oh, *that's* rich," she whispered, staring at the caption. In my photo, my body was swiveled away from hers, with one leg straight and one bent and my chin tucked against my shoulder. I looked smirky, like I had a secret, and my bangs fell over one eye mysteriously. Rose, with one arm folded over her chest and the other hand cupped under her chin, looked like Audrey Hepburn incarnate. Her head was tipped off to the side and she smiled genuinely and warmly, her eyes striking. Merry looked like she was mid-squeal laughter, tugging with both hands at the bottom of her tiny shorts, though in this shot it looked less like she was adjusting the middle seam from her crotch and more excited about showing off her legs.

I read the rest of the blurb:

> The polished girls of Gloss are complements to one another, in looks and in sync. In their debut album, *GLOSS,* in stores June 3, the foursome deliver pop hits and power beats sure to make you dance in the car as well as at the club. With their soulful harmonies and immaculate production thanks to producers Xavier X and Jake Jamz, we can overlook some of the blander lyrics in favor of what Cherry, Rosy, Sassy, and Tasty can deliver: surefire hits that will just keep coming.

Alex, who joined us after we were dressed (in sequins, not catsuits), read over our shoulders as well. His hand held the small of my exposed back, a light touch reminding me that he was there.

"God, I can't believe they called you *Tasty,*" Merry said. "That's disgusting."

"How hard is it to pronounce *Yumiko,* really," Rose agreed.

I squeezed Yumi's hand. She squeezed back.

"And *Cherry* is now in print," Merry groaned.

"It's just one magazine," Alex said, trying to sound positive. "I bet no one else will say it again."

But the magazine's reach was long. When we took the stage in Cincinnati, there were already fan signs in the audience for the Glossies: Rosy, Sassy, Cherry, and Tasty. As we continued through our winding tour with Illuminated Eyes, Yumi's energy seemed to flag, as the multiplication of *Yummy* and *Tasty* signs dimmed her spirits even more.

We'd had a few long days in the bus traveling through the northeast, so to appease us, Ian finagled an overnight stay at a decent hotel in Ohio, which was a welcome change from showering at the venue and hopping back on the road. I was ready to get the greasy show makeup off my face and soak in a bath. Meredith dropped off her overnight bag and skipped out the door: "Later!"

I barely acknowledged her leaving and started filling up the tub with hot water. I was wiping cold cream off my face when a knuckle rapped on the room door.

Presuming it to be Merry without her room key, I pulled it open with one eye closed, tissue in hand, distractedly rubbing off mascara.

But it was Alex.

Alex, who had seen me barefaced for years; Alex, who had gone swimming with me while I was heavier and his only comment on my appearance was the way my wet hair dried into beachy ringlets instead of straight wisps. Here in this hotel room, the sound of the water galumphing into the tub behind me and wearing only a robe thrown over sweaty underwear—"Oh!" I said, stumbling backward a step.

"Hi," he said, assuming permission to enter. He clicked the door shut behind him. "Your roomie in here?" he asked.

"She stepped out for a few minutes."

Alex came a little closer and, softly, hesitantly, tried to touch my hand. I was still clutching the damp tissue and swiveled my head to the side to search for a trash can.

"Oh," he said, embarrassed. "Sorry. I thought . . ." His voice trailed off.

"No!" I was embarrassed too. "I didn't mean it like . . ."

"So you're okay with . . ." He was so close now, breath warm with peppermint. I didn't step back.

Our lips met. I let him kiss me.

I hadn't been kissed often before this, but even with my limited experience I knew that we weren't in the most romantic situation to start a make-out session. I was acutely aware that the polyester tour outfits, which were tight and airless, left me with an unpleasant and sharp odor anywhere that my skin had been encased. "Hold on." I said it softly, but it sounded high-pitched and weird. He pulled back long enough that I could wipe off the rest of the makeup and deposit the tissue in a bin.

I turned back to him and he had gained confidence with my consent; hands still gentle and warm, cupping my robe-wrapped hips. "I've been waiting to do this . . . ," he murmured into my mouth. He pressed the front of his body against mine, and I skirted back a bit, not sure if I wanted to feel anything below the belt just yet. We continued this dance, which shuffled us both toward the bed. My calves hit the bottom of the bed-frame and we teetered for a moment before he guided me to sit on the edge. We were rapidly moving horizontal. I hoped he wouldn't try to peel off my robe; I could almost imagine him unwrapping the layers like a sandwich and getting a whiff.

"Is this okay?" he said, moving his attentions back to my neck: long, slow kisses with occasional tiny nibbles closer to the earlobe. "Mmm," I managed to say, mind flicking wildly, unable to calm down and process the moment. What was happening? This was my *friend* Alex. We had flirted, yes. We had been moving toward this. But it all seemed to be happening too fast. The bed gave a little creak as we shifted on it, slowly sliding up toward the headboard so that our legs were no longer hanging off the side.

I listened for any noise outside the door, wondering if Merry would return and interrupt this so that I could have a moment to think about it, but heard only the muffled roar of the hot water in the tub. I pushed him away and sat up. "The water!"

"Hmm?" The lights were still blazing in the room, but the look on Alex's face was of someone waking from a deep sleep.

"The water in the tub . . . it'll overflow . . ." I was on my feet, hurrying to the bathroom, robe clutched tightly closed at the neck—he hadn't touched the knot. I sat on the closed toilet seat and turned off the tap, but made no move to return to the bed.

Alex had followed me to the bathroom but didn't enter. He leaned in the doorway and my next thought was that he was going to invite himself into a sexy soak. "You've had a long day," he said, giving me a lazy grin. "I'll leave you to your bath."

Relieved, I stood up and walked him to the door. "Thank you," I said. He gave me a soft kiss on the mouth and left with a wink, bumping into Merry, who was returning. I let her in and then closed and locked the door.

"What was *that* all about?" She wiggled her eyebrows and grinned. "I go out for *one* cigarette and you get all frisky in our room! Bad girl! Bad Sassy!"

I turned to the bathroom and said over my shoulder, "You shouldn't smoke."

"Yeah, yeah," she said dismissively to my back.

"I'm going to take a long bath."

"Not too long, 'kay? I want to shower off some of this glitter before I ruin this hotel's good sheets."

While in the hot water, I let my mind unspool. Thoughts of New York, the energy we helped to carry over for Illuminated Eyes before their show, our burgeoning popularity, Alex's reconnection with me ever since *The Sunrise Show* . . . The way he stepped into the hotel room—not insistently, not frighteningly, and not like he was entitled, but in the gentle familiarity of a friend going out on a limb—except everything after that was so close, so intimate. I wasn't sure how to feel.

He had been a gentleman, though, I thought, turning the hot water tap on again to heat up the cooled bath. Hadn't we been dancing around for the past couple of weeks in our new situation, getting closer to this moment? I had to know that he liked me, to volunteer as a bodyguard. And I liked Alex. I liked him with me. I liked that he was going to be close when we returned to L.A. I would know somebody who knew me before I was Sassy Gloss. And as far as make-outs go, this had been chaste too: all clothes had stayed on and he hadn't even tried to put his hands anywhere besides my waist. We were still firmly on first base. The logic was sound, but then again, I was very tired.

I wondered if Alex thought that this brief, passionate exploration of each other's mouths was supposed to inspire something in me; that he left me with a wink because he assumed
I was so riled up that I'd touch myself in the bath. But I was
bone-weary. I popped the drain with my foot and listened to
the gargle of water down the pipe, toweled off, and went to
bed with wet hair splayed out over the hotel pillow.

# 12.

# Cassidy

Coming off the stage, you're aware of only a few things before the rest of the world starts returning. The bright lights
have blinded you, and as the green cast fades from your vision,
you see the ropes and pulleys, the unevenness in the floors, the
crew members hiding in all-black outfits as they do their jobs.
Moreover, your body feels as though it's been infused with
starlight, and the light leaks from your limbs and hands and
eyes and mouth in little pinpricks, so if someone were looking directly at you, they'd see a constellation coming out of a
silhouette. Slowly, you realize that the heat emanating from
your body is the heat of the stage lights that has been absorbed
into your hair and the dampness between your skin and your
polyester outfit; the sharp pain in your pinky toes as your feet
pitch downward in those uncomfortable stage shoes. Scent

returns last; the air suddenly, inexplicably, creates a singed taste in the back of your throat, and everything smells a little bit like cardboard and melted plastic. You become aware of your face, contorted in a giant smile, so tense that it's not just your mouth that is spread wide, but your eyebrows and ears are tensed too.

This was the state I was in when we discovered Stephen St. James outside our dressing room door in Chicago. Giggling, we whooped down the corridor, our shoes clacking on the linoleum. The gangling figure was not a surprise, since crew members were always on the move, but his stillness was. The hat was. The *person* was. Our new security detail had let him through.

"Hi there," said Stephen St. James, and we slowed, wondering who he was addressing.

"Hi," Merry said after a beat.

"I hope this is all right," he said, waving his backstage pass. "Grant gave it to me." Grant was the drummer of Illuminated Eyes.

"Yeah, sure," Yumi said. "I need to get out of these *shoes*." She hobbled forward, pushing the door open.

"Want to hang with us?" Merry added. He didn't say anything, just followed her in. We took seats at a long set of mirrors and in unison slipped off our heavy stage boots with a collective sigh. Our gym bags of supplies were where we'd left them on the floor, strewn with plastic bags of ponytail holders, extra socks, makeup brushes, nylon shorts. Flip-flops and laceless sneakers were aligned next to the base of each of our vanity mirrors, even though we'd kicked them off before the show.

It was always a little unsettling when you knew someone had been in to clean up after you, make the edges neater.

I hadn't seen Stephen since the launch party, when that enviously skeletal brunette was hanging off his arm. I began removing bobby pins from my hair, all the while glancing at his reflection in the mirror. He was seated on a spare stool by the door, slightly out of range of the bulbs glowing from our mirrors.

Stephen St. James looked the same—but *not*. His face was a little more angular, his cheekbones in high relief. His teeth looked bigger and whiter, possibly veneers. And though he was dressed in his signature paisley collared shirt and a pair of blue jeans, they were fitted so closely to his body that they had to be tailored.

The other girls were conversing lightly, easy stuff that Stephen could jump into if he wanted. My silence could have been interpreted as fatigue, but it was possible to be seen as rude.

"So Cassy, what were you doing earlier?" Merry asked, fluffing her hair out in a halo.

"Nothing really," I said, my voice sounding unnaturally loud. I was punishing my thumb with a bobby pin, the little bubble at the end dragging repeatedly under the nail. "Just a little sightseeing."

Since the hotel in Cincinnati a week ago, Alex and I couldn't find time to be alone, so we just held hands. More often than not, we were on the road at night, in our respective buses, and I was silently thankful that Ian didn't let Alex spend the night on our bus. I wondered if maybe the boundary between friendship and relationship was just too hard to cross. Alex's role had always been friend, protector; *boyfriend* was proving difficult to understand. When I was able to reach Joanna a few days after Ohio and tell her about the kiss, she sounded happy for me.

"Honey, he's always been a little sweet on you," Joanna had said, the phone lines crackling between our hotel and her parents' house in Houston.

"You're making that up." In our group of friends, I always considered Edie the delicate and elfin cute girl and Joanna the intelligent beauty. Either of them would've been the better pick if I were in Alex's shoes.

"Never. Still, I'm amazed he's switching schools for you. What happens when you go on another tour?"

"Mm, don't know," I'd said. "He'll probably stay put. He's only along with us right now because it's summer break."

"And your album? It drops soon?"

"On the third," I'd said. It was a good thing Big Disc had thrown that incredible party for our first single because we worked without breaks during the album release. The big machine had hummed in the background, pressing discs, printing covers, stocking boxes, and shipping to stores while we were dancing and singing on the road with Illuminated Eyes. And just a week after our conversation, the album had been unleashed in the real world; but in our little bubble on the bus, in hotels, in the bowels of stadiums, we didn't get to witness its ascension.

"I can't seem to ever get a hold of Edie," I had added, before we'd ended the call. "If you reach her, tell her I said hi."

This morning, in Chicago, Alex took my hand as I got off of the bus and said excitedly, "I asked Ian if I could show you around before tonight's performance and he's giving us the afternoon. Come on."

He and I sat on the Blue Line for a little while, hip to hip, our fingers intertwined. We didn't talk much, nor did we kiss. I liked this. I liked his reassuring heat against my thigh. I liked his presence. We exited at Grant Park and walked hand in hand toward the lake.

"It's so beautiful compared to Houston, right?"

I took a deep breath of the air, which was light and honeysuckle scented. Houston in June gives the uncomfortable feeling of breathing hot water into your lungs; this was a refreshing and crisp change, even if it was over ninety degrees out. A breeze swept over the lake and ruffled our hair.

"I might be willing to overlook snowstorms and cold weather if the summers feel this good," I joked.

"Oh, Cass, don't even *say* that," he said, shaking his head wearily. "Cold weather is the worst. I spent every day last winter huddled up next to my radiator and cursing when I had to go to my microeconomics class. Come on." He tugged at my hand and guided me toward a looming bronze lion, green with patina, flanking the entry steps of a gorgeous beige building. "The Art Institute," he said, while pulling out a pocket-size camera. He pulled me in close, large warm hand at my back, and tried to aim the lens so that we'd fit into the shot. Click. The camera advanced to the next frame automatically with a little whirr.

"Your parents will be happy to get some confirmation that you're not just working all the time," Alex said, wrapping the camera's hand strap around his forearm and rubbing my shoulder. "Here, I'll take one of just you now." He stepped away and squinted through the viewfinder.

"Yeah," I said, smiling at him, but feeling oddly hollow.

We continued on our mini tour of Chicago, wandering around Grant Park and seeing the construction of Pritzker Pavilion. A kiosk nearby sold snow cones in paper cups and Alex paid for two.

Hand in hand, slurping our melting ice, we passed a gaggle of teen girls on the sidewalk heading in the opposite direction. One did a double take. In a plain tee and jeans and without the other three girls, I'd been comfortable thinking that I could blend into the crowd, but she'd recognized me.

Alex drank the last of his grape slush while we stood at a crosswalk. "Incoming," he said, smiling. I glanced back. They had switched course and were following us indiscreetly, whispering and giggling. When they caught me looking, they burst into shrieks and charged forward.

"Omigod, are you Sassy Gloss?!"

I turned on my signature Sassy Cassy smirk and nodded. The girls dissolved into more screaming. *Can we get a picture with you? Will you sign my shirt?*

Alex grinned and brandished his camera. "Cass, it's your first time being mobbed in a public place! You gotta take a photo." I acquiesced, but while he took a photo with both his and one of the girls' disposable cameras, I felt like I was outside of my body watching the entire interaction. My mouth stretched the way it should, my hands floated to the girls' shoulders like a friendly pop star's would. But I wasn't *really* there.

Now, in the dressing room of the stadium, Merry sighed and

leaned over Yumi. "That must've been nice," she said. It was even nicer, I thought, that Alex had met up with one of the friends he'd made while at school and was missing the concert. I didn't want him to feel obligated to be next to me all the time.

The others were still riding the buoyant wave that the crowd had given us, but my feet had reached the shore as soon as I'd seen that cowboy hat waiting for us after the performance. I felt as though I'd drunk six cups of coffee and my ribs were quivering, but when I stopped running the pin through my fingers, I found that my hands could stop completely still. It was only inside me.

There was a knock at the door and Ian—cell phone in hand, with the echoing sounds of Illuminated Eyes' wild drumbeats and a hissing roar of the crowd—joined us inside. "Ladies," he said, then saw Stephen. "Oh, hi there. You can be here if you want. It's Peter with some news." He jabbed a button on the receiver. "Putting you on speaker, Peter."

The reception was, as usual, a little spotty, but we could understand him perfectly when he said, "Ladies, as you know, your debut album went live last week. We have numbers for you. You are . . ."—he paused for dramatic effect—"*Number one on the Billboard chart!*"

The room exploded in a cacophony of sound. We hopped around the room and shrieked.

Ian calmed us down and Peter continued, "And . . . you've been invited to the Music Video Channel MVAs."

We screamed some more.

". . . You're not eligible for an award, but the producers want you to perform instead. Meredith, we have to make sure there are *no* more missteps, so keep a lid on it and a bra on until September. Ian?"

Ian took him off speakerphone and clapped the phone to his ear. He smiled a huge smile at us, so big that his eyes disappeared into the mass of his brown cheeks, and he spoke into the receiver as he backed into the corner of the room.

Rose turned to me and yelled, "Can you believe it?"

"I can't believe it!"

We grasped each other's elbows and jumped up and down. It was the most interaction we'd had in weeks. As if realizing it at the same time, we disengaged and then hugged the other girls. Even Stephen got in on the hugging, though he barely brushed me.

Two years ago I was the loser on a reality show competition. Now we had *the* top-selling album in the country and were invited to a *huge* industry event. I couldn't wrap my mind around it. That night, I floated back to the hotel without feeling my feet touch the ground. It wasn't until I was kicking the covers back in the morning that I saw the other bed still tightly made with its hospital corners and realized Merry hadn't come back to the room at all.

# Soleil

Soleil waits until she can hear her mother's footsteps recede down the hall before she thrusts open her closet doors and pulls out a large cardboard moving box, filled to the brim with envelopes. They're all different sizes and colors, different levels of worn and torn, with handwriting of all types scratched on the outside. She had sauntered into the garage to take a phone video of Raul's newest car to share on Instagram—she wasn't sure if her mother would have approved but she knows that she can share car videos as long as the license plate is obscured. Besides, Merry was so busy, she couldn't keep up with everything, especially something as ephemeral as her Instagram stories. Soleil figured she could share the videos there, so they'd be available for twenty-four hours before disappearing into the ether, and Merry wouldn't know.

When Soleil entered the garage, she noticed that someone had carelessly stacked a set of big cardboard boxes in a corner, taken down from the adjoining storage area. Soleil had seen these boxes before—a few of the many items that had been transferred by movers from the Malibu house to this one—but had never actually looked inside them. She pried open a corner of a box and dipped her hand in: paper. Her fingers swam through a disorderly collection of envelopes, all crammed without care into the box. She pulled out a fistful of letters and read the mailing addresses: some to Rosalind McGill, some to Meredith Warner, Yumiko Otsuka, and Cassidy Holmes, and some to just "Gloss" or "GG," care of Big Disc Records. The post dates on the envelopes were from over a decade ago.

Her heart had soared. Fan mail! Who knew that her mother was so sentimental that she'd keep her fan mail? Maybe these were destined for the trash. Soleil needed to save some for posterity.

A thought struck her immediately after: people loved this sort of thing. Nostalgia. Fan appreciation. Soleil was sure that this would be more interesting to her followers than a fancy car. She'd hauled one of the boxes to her room and stashed it in her closet. She was almost sure her mother wouldn't mind if she looked through the fan mail, but Merry had also been so touchy about Soleil's latest Instagram post that maybe it was worth keeping quiet, for now.

It wasn't Soleil's fault that she didn't know who her father was. Didn't it make the most sense to ask her thousands of followers who she looked like? Have the mob do the detective work for her? "Just another bastard who doesn't know her dad." It was the perfect way to gain sympathy—and virality.

Soleil opens her window blinds to let in pretty natural light and carefully does her makeup the way she's seen the influencers do. By the time she is done, she looks sixteen and her cheekbones pop. She changes into a cute cropped shirt with glitter rainbows on it before she decides that she looks too young and switches to a black V-neck. Then she studies herself in her phone's camera, making sure her look translates well to selfie.

Going live on Instagram, she starts with a big smile and a toss of her shiny blond locks. "Hi guys," she says, in her best imitation-YouTuber voice. "I'm here with a special treat. FAN MAIL!!!" She indicates the box. "In here is NOT fan mail for me, but mail sent to my mom in her Gloss glory days. We're going to roulette this bitch and open a few live on air. I might make this a weekly segment, what do you think?"

Her interaction count is rising, so she chats a for few more minutes, letting them join in, and sets her phone at an angle on her desk to have both hands free. Then she pulls open a corner of the box and fishes for an envelope somewhere in the middle. "We'll keep this anonymous, to protect the innocent and maybe not-so-innocent." She waggles her eyebrows while opening the envelope. It had already been sliced open, so she doesn't feel bad about going through this one: it is already vetted. "Addressed to my mom," she announces, "and sent from Georgia." She unfolds it and begins to read: "Merry Gloss, as talented as you seem to be, you set a terrible example for our children. You should be ashamed of yourself, wearing those slutty clothes . . ." Soleil trails off, pressing her lips together. This woman who wrote to her mom really did not like the stage outfits and was pretty mean to her mother. "Wow, this lady is unhinged," she says aloud. "She doesn't like that my mom had a wardrobe malfunction, but it's not like she could've helped it. Let's see the next one. To Yummy." She flips the envelope toward the camera, gesturing, but so quickly that it's illegible to anyone watching. "It's actually spelled out as Yummy. How gross." She'd heard about Yumi being called Yummy or Tasty, but in this day and age, even she knows that is unpleasant for any woman. If it is this easy for a fourteen-year-old to grasp, Soleil wonders why this person with neat, adult handwriting was rude enough to address a person this way.

She is glad she reads a line or two before reading it aloud, because this is in no way PG-rated and she feels the color rise in her face. "Ohmigod," she squeaks, setting it down. "Okay, there were some real weirdos writing to the group, people. Ew ew ew," and she places the letter down with two fingers gingerly, like it is wet.

"Maybe roulette wasn't the best choice. I should've checked a few beforehand," she says into the lens. "What do you think?"

More chatter pops up on-screen, none very intelligible. Even though she is young, people call her Mom, they scream #goals, they comment on how pretty she looks. No one really seems to care about the content of the letters, just that she is there and they know she is streaming live. A famous person sharing their time is more valuable than a lot of things to these fans.

"Here's one to Rose," she says, finding one with distinctly female handwriting on the envelope. She figures a woman might be harsh to Rose, but it would be safer than the explicit garbage written to Yumi. She rips the envelope a little to get it out and begins, "Rose, I thought to call you but I didn't think you'd answer. I'm better at writing, anyway. I just wanted . . ." She stops abruptly, her eye skimming to the bottom, and then she checks the envelope for the address. "Oh. I think this is actually a personal letter that got sent to the wrong place."

The people on the other end of the ether are curious now,

urging Soleil to read it to them anyway. Others are cautioning her about opening other people's mail, which is a federal offense apparently, and to stop. The comments are devolving into people yelling at one another over what Soleil should do. She shrugs her shoulders and stuffs it back into the envelope, setting it next to her. Even she knows that there are some things you don't share, and an actual, personal letter to another member of Gloss is probably off-limits. If it'd been to her mom, all bets would be off, but she likes Rose—while also knowing about Rose's temper.

"Never mind," she says, smiling at the camera. Her overlined lips stretch thickly and she waggles her head slightly so that her cheekbones catch the light. "That was boring. I'll take questions about my makeup now." The comments surge forward again, this time with people berating her for wearing too much, while others tell her how pretty she looks. Her eyes stray once back to the letter on the bed: a letter Cassidy wrote to Rose in 2002.

## 13.

# Cassidy

The rest of the summer passed in a blur; it didn't feel as though we had twenty-four hours in a day at all. Between early-morning workouts before the buses set off for the next spot, a cat-nap on a bunk before the night's performance, and exhausted showers before crashing and doing it all over again on five hours of sleep, the days and nights lost their defined edges.

At least we got into a groove with our performances, gaining a better sense of banter with the audience between songs and hyping them up for more energy. Actually, the shows were the easiest and best part about being on the road. We devoured the crowd's cheers, but after reaching number 1, getting to and from the shows was the worst. Security now followed us everywhere, and overzealous fans tried their best to jump lines or break through cordons. Merry had had a close call with a male fan who had gotten too close after slipping through two bodyguards. And now Peter could forward us only the *good* fan mail. The rest he left in the care of Big Disc.

We finished our long road trip the same week that classes at Pomona began. The university opened its residence halls, and students, including Alex, started their migratory trek back. He left our tour group early to move, and he left me a voice mail giving me his hall information and the phone number to his dorm room. Physically, Alex and I hadn't gone any further than what happened in Cincinnati, and I was too exhausted to give it any more thought.

After our penultimate show opening for Illuminated Eyes, Yumi spent most of her time subdued on the bus, upset about the excessive signs that called her Tasty. Merry had chosen to ride with the main band, and the three of us sat in the diner section of the bus with Veronica, our sound tech, who was eating a pint of Ben and Jerry's with a spork.

Rose clapped her hands in irritation. "You know what, screw this!" she snapped. "Yumi, I'm tired of you moping around."

Yumi glanced up with a sharp look.

"Yes, it sucks that they've made you into the geisha of the group. But look at all of us! We're *all* sexualized in some stupid way." Rose pointed at me. "The vixen." At herself. "The naïve virgin." At the front of the bus, ostensibly where Merry would be. "And, you know what they did to Merry. We're more than that, and we all know you are more than that. But do you see me sulking? Do you see Cassidy wandering around going *poor me, poor me*?"

I spoke up—the first time in a long while that I addressed Rose. "That's not fair. It's different."

"How's it different? We're all characters, aren't we? So hers is Asian." She swiveled to Yumi. "You *are* Asian, in case you haven't noticed."

Veronica hastily stuffed the spork into her ice cream and left the section, presumably to avoid the awkwardness. I watched her go, wishing I could do the same, but I didn't want to leave Yumi alone with Rose. I explained, "It's different because being a *vixen* is like a desirable thing. But they're treating Yumi like she's some sort of ornament."

"It's racist," Yumi stated simply, eyebrows furrowed.

"Welcome to the world," Rose told her, getting up to grab a Diet Coke from the mini fridge. She popped the top and licked the foam off her hand.

"Do you *always* have to do that? It's so gross," Yumi snapped.

"Do what?"

"Slurp soda off your hand like a *dog*. Can't you open your soda cans like a person?"

Rose took a giant sip and ignored that. "Listen, we're all being objectified. Yours is a little shittier than most. But if you let it bother you, you're not going to get any enjoyment out of life. Look at Merry. They're out there talking about her *nipples* and she lets it roll off her back. Just . . . *lean* into it!" She snapped the fingers of her free hand. "I bet if we changed your outlook, you'd love the nickname in like two months."

"I sincerely doubt that," Yumi huffed, arms folded defiantly.

Rose winked and took another sip of soda. "You'll see. I just need to talk to Peter."

I wondered what she had planned as the bus stopped in Las Vegas and we moved toward the exit. As soon as the doors opened, Merry jumped up the steps, back from her visitation on the other bus. "Say cheese!" She snapped a photo with a familiar-looking small camera.

"Where'd you get that?" I asked.

"Alex let me borrow it." Merry smiled winningly at me. "I hope you don't mind. He asked me to take a bunch of photos so he didn't miss anything."

"Ah, young love," Gus said.

"Gus?" Rose drained the last of her soda and handed our driver the can. He accepted it with his gnarled fingers, not with disgust like I'd expected, but with a polite smile. "Do you see a lot of *young love* on these sorts of trips?"

"I've been hauling tours for years," our driver said. "I've seen everything."

"Hear that, Merry?" Rose raised one eyebrow high. "He's seen *everything*."

Merry and Rose descended the bus steps, playfully shoving at each other. This arena was fenced off, so I could hear the fans screaming from beyond the chain-link, but they weren't pressing up against the bus, which was a welcome change. Rose made a head start for the stadium door without waiting for the rest of us, enjoying her freedom. Yumi and I exited the bus, stretching our legs. The drummer from Illuminated Eyes, standing by himself a few yards away, gave us a deliberate nod. "Gotta go," Merry said and joined him. They walked toward the arena together.

All that Yumi could utter was a flat *hmm*.

After Merry had failed to turn up in our Chicago hotel

room, and then in three cities after that, I deduced where she was going. And while Yumi didn't have much to say about it, the tabloids had paragraphs to share. *Inches* of column space. Grainy photographs in color. Grant, Illuminated Eyes' drummer, was married, and he and Merry had been caught on film sharing a lighter and cozying up next to each other in the space between two tour buses.

The news broke as we were coasting back into Los Angeles, and Ian got a heads-up from Peter about the sticky situation: Grant's wife was the famous actress Marisa Marcheesa. If no one knew who Merry "Cherry" Gloss was before, they certainly knew now. An accidental nip slip was *nothing* compared to cavorting with a married musician.

"Did you even *ask* him if he was married?" Rose asked, annoyed.

Merry tossed her golden curls back. "Of course I knew; I'm not an *idiot.* But he isn't happy, and there are no children involved. So why should I give a shit about how badly his marriage is going? It takes two to tango and he was more than willing."

"You *can't* say that sort of thing in public, you understand?" Rose hissed. Merry shrugged.

Peter's voice was thoughtful on speakerphone as the bus cruised over the Los Angeles county line. "Normally I would welcome a little controversy, since any press is good press and this is doing *great* for your name recognition. But Marisa's roots in L.A. are deep. She's third-generation Hollywood royalty, an Oscar-nominated actress who can make life sticky for us. It's already cost you one brand deal, *but,*" he hastened to add, "there was a surge of interest and you're now the faces of Kit shoes, so I can't tell you off *too* much."

As soon as Justine put out as many of Merry's fires that she could, we were up at six again, filming short commercials and being prepped to photograph for ads—sandwich companies, shoe advertisements, Cherry Cola, cinnamon gum.

For Cherry Cola, Merry was given the opening line of the commercial and Yumi was given the final. Merry rolled her eyes but had accepted that her breasts were always going to be a topic of conversation and left to get fitted in a pair of white shorts speckled with tiny cherries.

Yumi, however, blanched at the direction to "sip from the can through the straw, turn to the camera, and say 'Yummy' seductively. End with a wink." I felt so bad for Yumi, who didn't deserve this treatment at all.

Yumi turned to our manager. "Peter, can I talk to you for a second?"

Peter, already bored with the shoot, didn't even glance up from his PalmPilot. "What's up, Yumi?"

"I don't want to do this."

Peter smiled indulgently as he turned his attention toward her. "Look. I know it's a little embarrassing, but if Merry can do her part, you can too."

"This is *humiliating*!" Yumi looked as though she would cry.

Rose interjected, "You're turning their stupid nickname for you into gold."

"Instead of people forgetting about it, this will just make them remember it even more!"

Rose pointed a finger at the bustling set: the operators testing lights, assistants scurrying with coffee, the director chatting with cameramen. "One, everyone is waiting on us to go out and deliver this commercial. Two, we're getting paid *buckets* of money to say this. Three, being remembered isn't a *bad* thing."

Peter added, "Rose was smart enough to get this campaign on my radar, and it's going to be *huge*. It'll make the Gloss name recognition skyrocket! It'll be good for your pocketbook, in the end." He shooed Yumi away. "Several hours of work for an easy contract! Go!"

Yumi stomped back to the set and bore through the commercial shoot like a professional, but she refused to sit next to Rose on the ride home and sulked in our shared bedroom. I popped open a tab of complimentary Diet Cherry Cola, but before I could take a sip, Rose stole it from my hand for a taste. "Blegh," she said, her breath tinged with cherry scent. It smelled like cough syrup. She offered the can back to me, but I tipped the remains down the sink. Rose said airily, "Believe me, she'll thank me one day."

In addition to pallets of soda, gifted stacks of shoeboxes and cases of cherry-red lipstick were strewn about our shared apartment. I arranged my portion to be sent to Houston, but there were still three other girls' deliveries to maneuver around. We pushed pathways between boxes and the living room was generally clear, but quickly the rest of the place looked like a hoarder's lair.

"Damn it!" Rose shouted from her room, and through the wall we could hear cardboard tumbling. She emerged in our bedroom doorway, glaring at Yumi and me as we packed toiletries for the trip to New York and the impending Music Video Awards. "We need to move out of here, I swear. I just knocked over like fifty shoeboxes! We. Don't. Have. Storage!"

Yumi still refused to talk to Rose, so I picked up the conversation. "Where would you move?"

"Somewhere in the Hills or something. We are making fat checks now. Why're we still living like we're poor?"

"It's not like we haven't been spending some of the money," I said. "Didn't you just buy a BMW?"

"I'm just saying," Rose went on, "that when we get back from this trip I'm going house-hunting. Where is Merry, anyway? We leave early tomorrow morning."

"Over at Grant's. But she's already packed and brought her stuff with her. She'll meet us at the airport."

"Grant lives over in Malibu, doesn't he?" Rose mused aloud. "I'll have to ask him about real estate when I get a chance. It's ridiculous that Marisa let him keep his own place. No wonder he's fooling around while she's filming in Europe."

The doorbell rang. Rose immediately had her guard up. "Are you expecting anyone?"

Yumi and I both shook our heads.

Rose rustled out of the room and to the front door. She greeted the guest perfunctorily in a low voice, then shouted over her shoulder, "Sassy! It's Alex."

Alex stood in the living room, smiling, holding a pizza box with both hands. He'd never seen where we'd lived before and a shot of self-consciousness struck me unexpectedly. He picked his way to the kitchen and set the pizza down as Rose disappeared again. "Alex! What're you doing here?"

"If Mohammed can't come to the mountain . . ."

I realized with a pang that I hadn't kept up with my supposed boyfriend for the past few weeks we'd been home. "God, Alex, I'm so sorry I haven't called. It's been chaos!" I gestured to the clutter. "All of *this* happened in the last week."

He peeled the top of the box away, revealing a large combo pizza with extra olives, my old favorite. Meaty steam and the smell of sausage permeated the air, and I felt almost stuffy with the heavy scent of grease and cheese.

"The first few weeks of classes have been busy too," he said, coming toward me for a kiss. "I finally have a minute to get away from my roommate, who, by the way, is an actual fan—"

"That's so sweet of you, Alex," I said, then swallowed. I hadn't been in such close proximity to pizza in what felt like years. I was both hungry and repulsed. It reminded me of our high school cafeteria, its scent of bleach and fried oil; of old friendly hangouts with Joanna and Edie, half a lifetime ago. I felt a pull to take a bite, feel the hot cheese burn the roof of my mouth. Then I thought of the consequences, the uncomfortable bloated feeling I'd have in my stomach later, the pounds I'd worked so hard to lose. Every bite counted.

"The others are welcome to share," he said, taking a seat and pulling out a slice.

Rose, who was apparently within hearing distance, called, "I don't need any new cellulite, thanks!"

"How did you know where we lived?" I asked, busying myself by getting him a plate.

Knowing that it would be an even bigger deal if I *didn't* eat, I found a sliver thinner than most and dabbed it with a paper towel to soak up the grease, taking a bite when the cheese took on a matte appearance. After months of sauceless chicken and lightly dressed salads, the pungent flavor of olives and spiced sausage was a revelation. I chewed slowly to make the most of it.

"I asked Ian where to find you. He's a pretty great guy, but a bit lax with your security."

"I think he knows you're not a stalker," I said wryly, picking at an olive.

Alex's smile disappeared and he put down his slice. "Listen," he said, his words coming out slowly, "I'm sorry I can't go with you to New York for this thing."

"Oh! It's okay . . . I didn't expect . . ." I hadn't put Alex down as my date, or even let anyone know that he might be coming along. The hired stylist who whipped up outfits tailored to each of our individual personalities didn't have a special outfit waiting for him. Meanwhile, I was just excited about mine because it had a corset and reminded me of Drew Barrymore's Cinderella gown in *Ever After*. Guilt suddenly washed over me for not even considering Alex.

"I know it's been hard keeping in touch since I moved into the dorm," he continued. "I told Ian about it first, and he suggested that I come over and tell you in person, in case you got upset. I'd love to go to this awards show with you, but my classes are just starting to get serious and I don't think I should miss a few days so early in the semester."

"It's fine."

"Ian did say that they've got hired bodyguards for y'all, so I'm not really worried. But I wanted to be there as support."

"Oh, but that's—"

"Just know I'm cheering you from the West Coast." He grinned at me, all canine teeth and bright eyes. "I'll watch you! I guess the broadcast will be tape-delayed, so I won't know anything until three hours later."

"I'll call you right after, no matter what," I promised.

He seemed brightened by this idea. "Yeah?"

"Yeah. Oh!" I suddenly remembered. "Merry has your camera. She's not here, but I can go find it."

"No, don't worry about it. Take it with you to New York. I want to see all the glitz and glam."

I slowly finished my slice and shook my head when he offered me another. "You're getting a little thin, Cass," he said, wrapping his fingers around my wrist. "You sure you're eating enough?"

"I'd just eaten before you came over," I murmured. "Thanks for bringing the pizza over, though, I hadn't had any in a while." When he left, taking the box with him, he kissed me with warm, garlic-scented breath. I wondered why I hadn't considered taking Alex as my date to the show. Was I selfish? Or was I just not that interested in him? The pizza sat heavily in my stomach.

## 14.

# Cassidy

The thing about red carpets is: they are chaos.

When I was younger, before all of this, I used to see the best-dressed red carpet rankings in entertainment magazines that lived in dentists' waiting rooms. Sometimes, when watching the Oscars' preshow, you could see a star emerging as if by magic onto the carpet, posing with a perfected arm-bend and leg-shift and thousand-watt smile, and sashaying on down the line. *Pop pop pop,* camera flashes going off, a gentle and fawnlike blink, and the starlet is sauntering off to talk to Joan Rivers.

We had been on a few other red carpets before this one, but they were for smaller parties. Nothing could have prepared me for this.

As we emerged from the limo, I *felt,* rather than heard, the screams, a noise that almost physically pushed me back into the car. I kept myself from staggering and gazed at the ruckus. Ropes and barriers, erected on the edges of the carpet, segregated frenzied fans from the music elite, their arms outstretched, a sea of open mouths. The wide strip of crushed burgundy velvet that was laid out before us was the only calm path between our glistening car and the throng of news service cameras ahead. Someone escorted the four of us plus Peter to the awards backdrop for photos.

Though we'd been coached on how to be photographed for this type of opportunity, my knees quivered as we carefully choreographed hands and poses, sweeping our gazes out along the 270 degrees of shutterbugs so that every one of them caught a straight-on look. The photographers shouted, and while they kept their distance, their voices were oppressive, pushing at us from all sides, wrapping us in noise. My face was outwardly calm, poised, even a little smirky, as if this entire moment was amusing or beneath me, but inside my heart beat wildly and I could feel dampness under my armpits.

"Sassy! Sassy! Look here!"

"Rosy, Rose, where's your smile? Smile wider, Rosy!"

Merry was next to me, and between clenched teeth she throatily growled, "Holy fuck, this is like a nightmare." But it was like we were blanketed in the photographers' screams and the words didn't reach past our small, shared space. Her indignation was heard only by me, and maybe Yumi, who was on her other side.

Camera crews and interviewers from the channel were up ahead; this red carpet was a minefield of tasks to complete before we could sit down in relief. Rebecca Hamm, the main interviewer for the past three years, set her sights on us and waved us over. She peppered us with questions about our clothes, who we were excited to see, and if we had predictions for who would win Best New Artist in a Video. Rose, as usual, spoke for the group. I tried to keep my eyes trained on Rose or Rebecca but darted a quick glance over my shoulder to check if Stephen St. James had arrived yet.

Of course, I didn't *see* all of this when it happened. Being on the red carpet is a disembodying experience. An invisible hand is guiding you forward, plying your mouth to smile, to laugh, to form words that you think the world wants to hear. You are affable, you are charming. If you are me, you give just enough sass to live up to your moniker. But in your mind, the world is just a blur, sped up like videotape on fast-forward. There were small moments that jumped out in surprising clarity: tripping on a stair and looking down to see that a strap on a sandaled heel had come loose, a hand brush from someone next to you that was surprisingly warm and intimate compared to the hands-off voice-directed commands given by various members of the crew, the sudden urgent need to pee after you've sat down in your constricting, corseted dress.

I watched these scenes on a tape a few days later, safely back in L.A. Unlike in choreographed music videos, where every movement was anticipated and planned, I found my motions embarrassing. I never looked directly at anyone, except Merry when her mouth moved, cursing out the photographers, and I'd given her a sharp glance of what seemed to be admonishment. When looking for Stephen, I gave the impression of being lost.

Even the decor of the theater came to me in detail after watching the televised program, curled up on a couch at Lucy Bowen's house with my socked feet tucked under me. It was as if everything had been inked black and red when I lived it, but as the TV washed its yellow and blue glow over me, the world took on more color. Presenters and their beautiful dresses and smart suits. Gleaming shoes on glistening floors. The tiered seats with plushy backs, and the gift bags containing jewelry, designer water, glass bottles of perfume. We performed our second single, "What Did U Say," to much fanfare. The ceremony was set up with a main stage, where presenters gave awards, and an attached secondary stage, which was spotlighted when performers were singing. We glittered and smiled from our point on the secondary stage after our song, and the spotlight stayed bright on us so we weren't sure when to exit.

There we stood while the nominees for the Breakthrough Video were announced. We smiled stupidly, looking toward the wings for someone—*anyone*—to motion us to leave, but without squinting obviously into the shadows, we saw nothing, and waited for a lighting cue. Later, I could only remember the presenter because I focused on a forty-foot-tall enlargement of her mouth, filled with Barbie-pink frosted lipstick, on the screen in front of us. With a flourish, she slid open the envelope.

"Stephen St. James, for 'Rockabilly,'" she announced, and we clapped, still on the stage, as awards music played. Merry elbowed us to get us to move—finally, there was someone trying to usher us off, but in the playback I could see that my rigid dress did not yield to her touch, and so I continued to hobble in one place on my tall heels in ignorance. The other Gloss girls were moving away, inching into the shadowy recesses of the side stage, with their arms outstretched as if to pull me along by an invisible rope. But I wasn't budging.

Stephen walked up the steps toward the presenter, but instead of accepting the trophy, he detoured to the secondary stage, like maybe he'd assumed I was still standing there to congratulate him.

"Watch this part," Lucy giggled, chewing a fistful of popcorn noisily. She'd invited us all over for a movie night, but Merry was with Grant and the other girls chose not to come. After being attached at the hip to the rest of Gloss for the summer, I was excited to spend time with *anyone* else. "Here." She jerked a finger at her television screen at the moment the idea seemed to come to Stephen. He opened his arms for an embrace. The girl greeting him on that stage—me—had a look of surprise on her face, but she didn't resist when he put his arms around her.

"Did he stick his tongue in your mouth?" Lucy asked, and, giggling, flicked a kernel into my hair. "Did he slobber?" I wiped my mouth in memory.

Quick as a snake, he'd dipped her and gave her a giant kiss on the mouth in front of the entire live studio audience—and the ten million viewers at home.

"*WELL,*" GRANT SAID, climbing over the back of a booth and sitting down on the edge, balancing two drinks, "here's to the Gloss girls, who don't know when to leave a stage." He handed Merry a glass of some amber liquid and clinked his beer bottle against it in a cheers-ing motion. "And here's to winning the big one next year."

Illuminated Eyes came and went with passing head nods in our direction, but Grant stayed behind, smiling crookedly at all of us, then pulled Merry to him and met his lips with hers.

Yumi blew a strand of hair off her face. "I'm going to go mingle," she said, getting up and brushing off her pants.

We were at a Manhattan nightclub after-party, shmoozing, though I was still ruminating over what had happened at the show.

I left my purse and Alex's camera on the table with Merry while I grabbed a drink. I sidled up to the bar, which was long, glittered with black mica, and packed with svelte bodies, but there was only one bartender that I could see. "Excuse me," I shouted over the noise, but he slid farther down the bar, hands flying over bottles, dipping and pouring and shaking. I waited a minute as he slowly made his way up the bar, chatting effusively with clients and handing out glasses. As he approached, another body slid past me and stood in front of me, effectively blocking the bartender's view. "Hey!" I said, tapping the offender on his leather-clad shoulder.

The ear, at first, was a perfect seashell that slid into view. Then a stubbly cheek, that beautiful nose, and two piercing blue eyes. "Oh," I squeaked.

"We meet again." Stephen gave a quick grin and turned back to the bar, ordering for the both of us. He handed me a gin and tonic. In the dark room illuminated by various neon sconces along the wall, Stephen's eyelashes cast long, sideways shadows across the bridge of his nose and onto his cheek, giving him a boyish appearance. Instead of a battle-hardened cowboy, he looked like he could be a student at some preppy college.

"Thanks." I liked Stephen—but *did not* like that kiss. I didn't like the questions that it would bring up when I got home. I hated how flustered I felt around him—how he'd made me wonder if yes was no or no was yes—and how he'd made me feel like this ever since I first met him in 1999.

There was only one thing to do in this situation: evade. I drank the entire gin and tonic in a few unladylike gulps and raised the empty glass to him like a toast before moving off to the dance floor.

My feelings were complicated. He'd kissed me in front of that entire audience without even asking. *But it was the heat of the moment,* I thought. And another: *Maybe he actually likes you.*

Something bubbled up inside me. A curious finger of want. When he caught up with me, as I'd half expected him to do, and moved against me to dance, I acquiesced.

The music was loud, beating consistently. My shoes were sticky on the ground, dragging through dropped straws and the glaze of drinks already lost. We didn't talk anymore, just danced. One song, two. We took a break to down some shots. I eyed him critically, wondering when he was going to give up and grind against someone else, but after we'd slugged whiskey together, he was on me again. After a few songs, Rose tipsily joined us, bouncing loosely to the beat.

The alcohol flowed into me, heady and light, loosening my limbs. I rubbed up against Stephen, and Rose rubbed up against me. I didn't know where my feelings started and where they ended, as each stumbling bounce brought forward a myriad of feelings toward the two. Rose flung her arms around my shoulders and faced me, and I was surprised at how close she drew toward me as she danced, eyes closed, lost in the beat. After months of walking on eggshells to stay out of her direct line of sight, here was Rose, acting friendly as her lips brushed against my ear, saying *something* that I couldn't understand. The vibration from her voice sent goose bumps down my arms. "What?" I shouted, and she tried again, but when I couldn't hear her a second time, she shook her head and smiled. Stephen cut in and began to slide alongside my body, and I lost Rose in the crowd.

The alcohol was getting to me. I was confused, over-whelmed, and overheated. Without excusing myself, I lurched from the dance floor and groped my way to the restroom. Under the fluorescent lights, my skin was green. I splashed water on my face and tried to breathe deeply, swallowing the thickened saliva that comes before getting sick. The door banged behind me and a leggy brunette appeared in the mirror behind me. I had only a vague idea that she was sharing a sink with me, pulling paper towels out of the dispenser without having used a toilet.

She dabbed my forehead lightly with a dampened paper towel. "You okay?" she said.

I was able to squint to see her. "It's you," I said.

"You're Cassidy, right? Do you remember me?"

I leaned forward over the sink, swallowing hard. "Mm, yeah." The insect from the release party with the mandala tattoo.

She put a chilled hand on my arm. "I don't know how much

of this you'll remember," she said slowly, like she was talking to a toddler. "But I wanted to tell you not to get too close to Stephen."

I twisted around on the sink, the ceramic jamming into my pelvis. "Possessive, much?"

"I didn't mean it like that," she said, almost kindly. She wadded up the damp paper towel and tossed it in the trash. "I'm just looking out for you. When we were together—"

"I can take care of myself, thanks," I scoffed, pushing past her. "All I'm doing is *dancing*. I have a *boyfriend*!" As I walked out the bathroom door, I almost ran straight into Yumi. She grabbed my wrists.

"Shit is going down," she whispered, worried. There seemed to be a *very* public argument happening in the middle of the dance floor between Grant and a tall, beautiful redhead. Yumi continued, "Marisa is giving him hell right now."

"Oh shit," I said, my tongue heavy in my mouth. "Is Merry okay?"

"We should probably round up the others and go." She tugged on my hand.

"Go? It's still early. I'm finally having *fun* for a change."

She let go. "Well, I'm not. Everyone's calling me *Tasty*. I'm going back to the hotel." She began walking away.

"Remember, that nickname made us quarter of a million dollars," I called after her, sounding a lot like Rose. Marisa pushed past me toward the bathroom I'd just vacated, but Grant didn't follow.

Stephen had found a table of people to talk to, but when I emerged, he handed me another shot. Rose was nowhere to be seen. "Sassy! You're back. Let's show 'em how it's done." We got lost in the beat.

A REPETITIVE SHRIEKING assailed my ears.

Slowly, I realized it was a phone. I cracked one eye open a slit and reached out at the air, grasping nothing.

"Oh, for fuck's sake, she's super hungover," said a voice, and something was jammed into my hand. "Cass, it's for you."

My throat felt as though it had sandpaper lining. "Mmmph. 'Lo?"

"I was so worried," said a male voice. It was familiar. Harried. Frustrated.

"Dad . . . ?"

"Not *Dad*. Alex. Remember me?"

I wiped a hand down the front of my face and remembered, suddenly, that I had promised to call him after the awards ceremony. Instead, I had slunk into the car with the girls and tossed drinks back at Slice, then danced with—

"Ohh. Shit. I'm sorry, Alex." Cracking the other eye open as well, I saw that I was in a hotel suite, having apparently fallen asleep on the first flat surface that would absorb me. Yumi, who had handed me the phone, now wordlessly placed a glass of water and ibuprofen on a side table littered with our goody bag items, cellophane peeled away in a pile. I shuffled forward on my elbows, using the phone as leverage against the plush carpet, to reach Yumi's act of kindness. Alex was still speaking, his voice loud enough that even with the receiver clapped to my shoulder instead of my ear, I could hear him clearly.

"When I hadn't heard from you, I called my parents in Houston. They were watching it live, and they told me you were there, so I knew you'd actually made it to the show, but . . ."

"No, yes," I croaked, gratefully sipping water.

"Are you okay?" he demanded. I took a languid inventory of my body. I was fully clothed, though missing shoes. The underwire of my bra was cutting deep into my rib cage and I rolled to my side, but the pressure of the ground against my belly had apparently held my nausea at bay; I moaned.

"Yes, no, maybe," I whimpered.

His voice softened somewhat. "Did you overdo it? You know you don't handle liquor well."

I clutched at my stomach and slowly rolled myself into a ball, still on my side. "Ughhh."

"Call me later," he said, his voice rising at the end like he was asking—but not quite.

There was no way to hang up the phone, so I left it clasped under my hand until the dial tone began its intermittent growl. With a weak arm I hurled it away, skittering the receiver across the floor until it clattered to a stop, anchored by its coiled cord.

Yumi appeared once again as a pair of legs wearing white cotton socks. She stooped over to pick up the phone and set it back in its cradle. Then she perched on the edge of a chair nearby. I closed my eyes, wishing that the room would stop spinning, so I heard rather than saw her sitting there, studying me. "Are you all right?"

"Will you help me get this bra off? It's cutting off circulation to my arm."

She sighed and unhooked it, helping me to slither out of it.

"What's this?" she said, dumping one of the cups out. A

soggy piece of paper towel, damp with sweat, peeled away and floated to the floor.

"I'ono," I mumbled. "Can we order some food? Need some Alka-Seltzer."

Yumi ordered two plates of dry toast, poached eggs, and fruit bowls with a side of seltzer. I was able to pull myself to a sitting position but stayed cross-legged on the carpet and sipped at the water when it arrived. It was hard to look at the eggs, which glistened like gelatinous white fish on the coffee table, and when I averted my eyes I spotted empty McDonald's bags on the side table. I was sure I hadn't eaten any burgers last night. I cut my eyes over to her. "So . . . how much of an ass did I make of myself?"

Yumi was nibbling on a corner of her toast. "Not too terrible," she said. "But I didn't stay until the end. Peter had to drag you up here."

"And the others?"

She glanced down and brushed crumbs away from her legs. "When I left, Rose was fine. Tipsy, but fine. Merry, however . . . She probably feels about as bad as you do right now. Maybe worse."

I felt for Merry right about then, but my own self-pity won out. "Mmph," I grunted.

"It's probably going to be everywhere soon, if not already. Grant and Marisa Marcheesa had a huge blow-out fight last night."

"Over Merry?" I sipped the water slowly. "Merry wouldn't be stupid enough to get involved with him again after the tabloids ripped her apart earlier."

"I don't know. Both of them were yelling, though. I'm sure we'll hear about it soon enough, if Merry's involved." She slid one of the plates closer to me. "Chin up. We fly back today."

I WASN'T THE only one who emerged from the hotel room slightly hunched and wearing sunglasses; Merry was so pale, she looked blue. Yumi and Rose slipped on their sunglasses as well, to quell any invasive paparazzi. When we stepped out of the Suburban at JFK, Merry vomited on the pavement next to a trash can, bought a pack of spearmint gum immediately inside of the entrance doors, then cursed when the remaining change set off the metal detector. But once we were through to the terminal, we ducked inside a first-class lounge and waited without harassment for our flight to be called.

Throughout the flight I thought about Alex. We had maintained our friendship over years of physical closeness—the same schools, same classes, same homework, same hangouts— and now that our lifestyles were diverging, it was obviously going to take more work to keep the connection. Everything I did now was work—so should a relationship *also* be work? At what point do you say that it's *too much* work?

I hated that I had doubts about us. He was my roots. He was the only one who seemed to know the real me. I couldn't just throw that away.

Above all, he was a good person. He'd traveled all the way to Hollywood to bring me pizza and break it to me gently that he couldn't go with me to New York—not that I'd minded, but he'd *thought* I would, and that's what counted.

I made up my mind and hired a car to take me to Pomona. I

needed to make things right. What if he was angry right now, still stewing, talking to Joanna or Edie about how I was cheating on him with Stephen St. James?

When the car pulled up to a corner of the campus, I realized I didn't know where I was headed. Nervously pulling my hoodie up over my head and donning sunglasses, even though it was dusk out, I approached a couple and asked where I could find the dorms. "Follow this path and turn right," the guy said.

"Thanks."

When I turned away, the girl hissed, "I think that was Sassy Cassidy."

". . . Who?"

I speed-walked away and came to a dorm with an arched, and very locked, door. As I ruminated on how ill-thought my plan was, a girl swiped a key card to enter the dorm and I followed her in, removing my sunglasses to see. A guy with a shock of brown hair opened the door to room 202. I backed away. "Oh, I'm sorry, I must have the wrong—"

"Holy shit," the boy breathed. "Holy *shit!*"

I pivoted on my heel to flee, but a second guy framed the doorway.

"*Cass,*" Alex said, in a strange voice. He breathed it, like he had been afraid that I was lost and that he was relieved I'd returned safe. The soft tenderness made my eyes water. How could I have been blindsided by the glitz and glamour when Alex was more genuine than anyone I'd ever known?

I was out in the hallway, one with many doors lined up on either side, all of them opening and closing, people walking behind me on their way around the building. I felt vulnerable, even with my hoodie rendering me anonymous from the sides and back. "Could I come in?" I whispered, clutching an elbow with my other arm self-consciously.

He took one hand off the doorframe, making an opening, but I found myself walking into him and wrapping my arms around his middle. He wrapped his arms back, giving me a bear hug. "I'm sorry, I'm sorry," I whispered, tears coming again.

"It's okay, it's okay," he said, soothing my back. We held each other like this for a few long moments before I remembered the other guy. I wiped at my face with the sleeve of my hoodie and discovered him sitting on his hands in a computer chair, his eyes as wide as saucers.

"Cass, this is Joseph, my roommate. Joe, my girlfriend, Cassidy."

"Hi," I said, extending my hand, before realizing that I had probably snotted on it. A self-conscious laugh bubbled out of my chest. He grabbed it anyway.

"Hi there." Joe was grinning. "Oh man. We all knew that Alex has a girlfriend but he didn't say her name, ever. I can't *believe* this!"

To Alex, I said, "You didn't tell people about me?"

He scoffed a little. "Are you kidding? No one would believe me. They'd think I was making it up."

"But we have all those pictures from high school, and . . ." I trailed off. Pictures when I was ten sizes bigger. Pictures when I had crappy hair, pictures before my teeth whitening. All of those *before* pictures. I didn't even recognize that version of me.

Alex must have sensed where my thoughts were going, or

maybe he just wanted to talk to me without an audience, because he said, "Joe, do you mind stepping out for a little bit?"

Joseph seized upon this idea with gusto. "Oh, yeah. Cool." His hand swept through stuff on his desk for his key card. "I'll go grab a bite." We waited a few awkward moments in silence while he laced his shoes and closed the door behind him.

"Are you hungry?" Alex asked. "I should have thought of that."

I'd eaten a salad on the plane, chewing slowly and thoroughly on the iceberg lettuce, hoping to keep my stomach in good order. The thought of food still turned it over and I shook my head.

He sat down on his bed on his side of the room, and I sat next to him. We faced the thin aisle between his and Joseph's beds, and I leaned into him, looking at the decor of the room. "This reminds me of the room I share with Yumi," I said out loud. It was white, not lavender; the posters were of sexy movie stars—Joseph liked Angelina in *Tomb Raider,* apparently—but the setup was somewhat similar.

"I bet your room smells better," he joked, his arm warm around me.

"I like the way you smell," I said, burying my face in his shoulder. I was warm in my hoodie, but I felt more comfortable with it still on. A little security blanket. It was easy to talk into his shirt. "I'm a terrible person. I can't believe I forgot to call you after the show."

"It's all right," he murmured. "I was pissed but only because I was worried."

"Did you watch it?" I was sure he had, but he shook his head.

"I only watched your performance and turned it off right after."

"So you didn't see . . . ?"

He understood the question. "I didn't see it. I did hear about it." His eyes were troubled. "I don't know what to think now, either."

"It was completely out of left field," I said quickly. "I had no idea he was going to do that. And I swear, it's the only time anything like that has happened." I didn't mention dancing with Stephen at the after-party. What Alex didn't know wouldn't hurt him.

He nodded distractedly. "I wondered . . . but I knew you'd tell me if something was up. Right?"

"Right. I'm not *that* big of an asshole and loser."

"I don't know, you stayed inside all winter break and baked a million cookies after you lost *Sing It*," he said, cracking a smile. "Ow!" I had poked him in the side with a finger.

"My baking days are over." I pulled back and rubbed at my eyes, which were now dry.

"Why, Cass? I liked your cookies."

I shrugged. "Not allowed to eat them anymore."

"That's dumb. You can still make them for me. Ow!" I'd poked him again, but I was smiling this time.

I leaned back into his pillow, stretching out my legs. He followed suit, laying on his side to look at me. We were quiet for a minute. "You really are gorgeous," he said.

"Oh, stop. I'm puffy and smelly. I woke up hungover and nearly puked on the plane ride back. I'm wearing the same clothes I had on in New York, so basically if you were to take off my hoodie you'd reel from the stink."

"Is that so?" His fingers played with the edge of the sweatshirt, down by my hip. "Let me sniff."

I gave a little squeak and crossed my arms on top of my chest. "I don't think so."

"Just a little one," he said, sitting up and using more leverage to peel the corners up again, taking the edge of my T-shirt with it. My navel was exposed. I giggled and he used that as an excuse to pull the shirts up all the way to my bra line. He left me a row of kisses on my stomach, getting me relaxed enough to uncross my arms and touch his hair in response. We locked eyes.

"Are we okay?" I said.

Alex moved a little bit on the bed so our chests met. "We're great," he said, and his lips met mine.

about, taking in the scenery. The ceremony was set up on a green lawn, but if the couple wanted to walk a block to the beach and take photos in the sand, it wasn't out of the question. As it was, they would be wed under a grand archway of lavender and pastel pink flowers, standing amid a semicircle of lush palm trees, and surrounded by more green.

The air smelled like sea salt and camellias, and as I perched on my toes to keep the backs of my heels from sinking into the lawn, I thought to myself that stilettos weren't the best choice for footwear.

"Excuse me," said a voice, and a young woman appeared at my elbow. She was in her early twenties and wore a navy blue dress, a little austere for the light airiness of the occasion. Her eyes flickered with recognition, a look I knew well, but instead of saying the typical *Aren't you Tasty Gloss?* she spoke professionally and courteously. "We're asking everyone to take their seats."

I picked a chair second from the back row and watched as wedding attendants, clad in pastel-toned long dresses and suits and beach-waved hair, swept down the lawn aisle. When Jordan finally emerged, resplendent in a Vera Wang tuxedo, the crowd stood until he was at the altar with his husband-to-be.

Seven years ago, in the same season, I said the same vows as Jordan was saying now, in the same warm dusky light. It hit me suddenly, as it always did—the pang of the dissolution, burning hot in my chest.

Rose had attended *my* wedding. Cassidy had not. We'd hired a high-end planner and every time she had suggested something, I'd run it through my head, wondering what Rose

## 15.

# Yumi

I had sent an RSVP to the couple last month, out of a combination of pleasure and obligation—it was our old tour manager's son, and he had put us on the invite list, sending one to each of us in turn, though apparently I was the only one who mailed a positive answer back. Rose had admitted she was terrible at checking her mail, and Merry sent crystal in lieu of her presence. Cassidy, as far as I knew, hadn't responded at all.

And she couldn't make it now.

After we'd disbanded, Ian had moved out to San Diego. He and his ex-wife had put Jordan through private school and—judging by the tasteful and elegant decor of the wedding venue I was now stepping into—he had probably made some contribution to the couple's wedding costs as well.

I accepted a program from an usher and stood at the back of the vast ceremony seating area as other early arrivals milled would have to say about it. How she would judge it. How it would photograph and be in *Us Weekly*. And yet, it had been a beautiful wedding.

Yes, our relationship had started as a PR move, and I had been wary. I wasn't a big sports fan and I wondered if maybe dating an actor would have been a better pick than an athlete. I understood Hollywood types, I'd said to the other girls. I could understand their motivations, their wants. Even more significantly, I could understand their schedules. But Kevin had been a "safe" choice. He was a great Clippers player; had a toe in the entertainment industry (his sister, Kate, whom everyone now knows as *the* Kate Rodgers but at the time was a budding actress on a long-running soap, had taken him as her companion to a few red carpet events); was good-looking *and* a gentleman. It was hard to find a pro athlete who checked all the boxes. After what had happened to Cassidy, our cautionary tale, we needed to make sure that the men with whom we were aligning ourselves were not violent or scary.

But it turns out cheaters cheat. We'd been together for three years, off and on, on and off, culminating in an "all or nothing, it's forever or it's over" proposal that sounded more romantic when he said it. We planned a wedding in six months, and then six months after the wedding he was caught with his pants around his ankles and a twenty-year-old in his Lotus. In hindsight, I'm grateful that I knew I wasn't ready for kids when we found ourselves accidentally pregnant in the early days of our dating, and I took care of it swiftly. Children with him would have made the separation infinitely more complicated. As it was, when the news of his cheating came to light it was years after the abortion and it was one thing I whispered thanks for.

A bloom of anger rushed through me when I thought again of his betrayal. The ensuing hurt was amplified when more women came out of the woodwork. Tabloids paid for stories, real and fake; well-meaning family emailed the highlights to me, as if I hadn't seen them already. He came out with a story about how he fell in love with some teenage starlet, and he filed for divorce to be with this girl who couldn't legally buy alcohol.

I should have dragged his name through the mud; it should've been me who ended it. I should have been more forthright about my pride. I took the tabloids to the lawyer and I made bank off them. I made him pay for every cent. The media then took his side, calling me a shrew. You can never win. He was the one who was wrong, and everyone was happy to pity me until I grew the strength to fight for the truth, fight for what was mine, and then I was a headstrong bitch who took her ex-husband for all he was worth. The world hates strong women. Just look at how they treat Rosalind McGill.

Inside, I gave a quiet wish that Jordan and his beloved would have a better life together. That they got it right.

"I now pronounce you husband and husband."

I clapped fervently with the rest of the crowd, hoping that our collective enthusiasm would seal their union with joy and permanence. The couple grinned and danced back down the aisle.

Once the wedding party had dispersed, the photos had been taken, the dinner served then plates cleared, the sounds of the wedding relaxed into a pleasant buzz of conversation and clinking coffee spoons. A deejay set up in a corner let the last notes of the ceremonial dances fade away, flicked on a mobile light machine, and segued into the Jackson 5. Guests crowded the dance floor and, one by one, tossed off their heels to cavort barefoot. My table-mates left to dance.

I was stirring a Splenda into my black coffee when a hand floated into my vision. It held a dessert plate of cake, an offering. "Oh, no thank you," I began to say, but it wasn't the catering staff making the rounds with wedding cake, it was Ian. I jumped up to give him a hug. "Ian!" I had to raise my voice over the music, which was now blasting something in the Top 40. "Congratulations!"

"All alone there, Yumi?" His voice was kind. There were smile lines around his eyes and some of his hair had gone gray, but he still looked as he had fifteen years ago. He flashed me a happy grin and sat down in one of the vacated chairs.

"None of the others could make it," I said, sitting down again and eyeing the cake. It was white and looked to have a stripe of fruit jam in between layers. I could smell the buttercream. "Merry is handling a Soleil crisis and Rose is doing god knows what . . ."

"I thought as much." He nudged the plate closer to me as he leaned forward. "I was hoping that Cassidy would come. It would have been nice to see her."

"Yeah. Well." I felt the sudden lump in my throat and swallowed, rubbed my nose with one hand. Fuck it, eat the cake. I picked up the fork.

"I'd like to attend the funeral, if I can."

"Fuck, Ian, why are you sitting here with me? You should

be happy. You should be cutting up the dance floor. Why do we have to talk about Cassidy now?"

He reached over and took my hand, fork and all, in between both of his. "Because." His giant paw was warm and comforting. I brought a shoulder up to my cheek to dash a tear away, letting out a small breath.

"Thanks." I cleared my throat. "It's on Wednesday. Houston. I'm surprised Em didn't send you the info."

"I haven't been on your payroll in years. I don't know why your staff would bother to tell an old man like me where a service would be held. But thank you. I'll call the office and get the address."

The music, pulsating noisily in the background, started the opening bars of a familiar tune. A quick cut of the eyes at the dance floor: the grooms and all of their friends shrieked with recognition, and they began to chant while shimmying and flailing to the beat.

> *What did you say what did you saaaay*
> *When I told you I wanted it that way*
> *You couldn't cut it, you weren't the one*
> *But I still wanna have some fun*

Our voices were young, almost childlike. We were eighteen when we recorded those lyrics. "I swear, I didn't request this." Ian leaned back, seemingly content to watch the group pantomiming with grand arm gestures. "One of the guests must have asked for it."

"It's a nostalgic song," I agreed, pushing my empty plate toward the centerpiece.

"He was in middle school when this came out," Ian said. "He loved it. Remember how you all signed one of the album liners for him? He kept it on display on his dresser for years." He gave me a look then. "I hope you know how important your music was to these kids. It may have felt like fame to you, or you may have bad memories after Sassy left, but these were formative songs to the youth of America."

I chuckled. "The words are so silly. They don't even make sense!"

"It's still history, Yumi."

The song ended and flowed into a ballad. The dance floor emptied as the youngsters took a breather and parent-age couples swayed demurely back and forth. Sensing that our conversation had tapered to its natural finish, Ian excused himself from our table and approached his son across the room. Jordan accepted his flourished hand and they rotated slowly by the head table.

It was still early, by wedding standards. I guessed that more hours of dancing and merriment awaited the more dedicated of the wedding-goers. But I was suddenly exhausted. My eyes felt prickly and my legs hurt, like I'd been cramped into a chair too hard for my body. Families with smaller children cleared off after the cake cutting and I didn't think anyone would miss an ex–Gloss girl fading into the night. I gathered my purse, licked the last of the cake from the fork tines, and found my way to the exit.

**September 10, 2001.** *JMC* **magazine. Column: "Hookups and Breakups"**

Tongues are wagging and divorce papers are being drawn up between actress Marisa Marcheesa, 24, and musician Grant Kidd, 25. The Illuminated Eyes drummer has reportedly been stepping out on his famous wife, who was best known for her turn as Jane Eyre in the 1997 adaptation of the Charlotte Brontë novel. The two were seen sparring at a Manhattan club after the MVC MVAs on September 6. Contributing to the breakup? Pop's newest heartbreaker and home-wrecker, Meredith Warner, 19, aka "Cherry" from Gloss. The two were photographed canoodling while on tour last month, and rumors are flying.

# 16.

## Cassidy

How soon is too soon to move in with someone?" mused Merry, picking through real estate listings. "Grant's Malibu place is just so beautiful."

"I like this one. Oh, but the fixtures in that house are terrible," Yumi said.

"Fixtures? You can *buy new fixtures*, Yumi." Merry peered at the listing with her. "Oh, you're right, those are ugly."

"This one would be perfect if the driveway wasn't positioned like that," Yumi continued.

We were eager to move out of our current apartment, which we'd long outgrown. To look at the swathes of listings, we had to move a pallet of soda off the kitchen table.

It was almost peaceful with Rose missing from the apartment. She was already out seeing a house and didn't invite us along. I hadn't realized how tense I was when she was around. We hadn't discussed how close we'd gotten while dancing at the after-party, and I chalked up any lingering feelings as inebriation on that night. But lately I had the feeling that she was sizing me up even more than usual, and the added scrutiny made my cheeks hot and my stomach twist.

"What's this?" Merry said suddenly, plucking an envelope that was mixed into the real estate listings.

"It's addressed to you, Cass." Merry passed it over to me. "But it doesn't have a postmark."

The envelope wasn't sealed, either. I slipped a piece of paper out while looking at Yumi's rejected house with the imperfectly positioned driveway. "I like that one," I said, and then began to read the note.

*Dear Cassidy,*

*Let me show you what love really is. Don't hang around with that Stephen St. James anymore, he's bad for you. I'll prove to you that I'm the best for you. I'll be watching you.*

*Yours,*
*Jerry Dalson*

"What the *fuck*," I screamed, letting go of the paper. It had clearly been placed in our mailbox with the real estate pages or—I shuddered to think—had been set inside the apartment while we were out. No one guarded the apartment door while we were gone, and the lone sentry driving his golf cart around the complex would have probably missed Jerry if he'd timed his entrance correctly.

Yumi read it and shrieked, "Omigod!"

Merry called Peter, and Peter called the police. It wasn't obvious how the letter had appeared in the apartment, but since Jerry had signed his name, the police would use that as evidence in a court order. By the time they were done, my skin was crawling and I didn't want to be in that apartment any longer than I had to.

*The Jet-Setters* had just finished shooting a scene that required the main cast to be in Moldova, and Lucy's return meant an intimate bash at a rented beach house. When my car pulled up to the gate, I recognized it as the "friend's" house where we had parked the day Yumi confided in me about Viv.

Although Lucy had told me it would just be a few industry girls and some close friends, it was strange to find her entire team there, along with one of the biggest A-list celebrities in Hollywood. Lucy hadn't warned me in advance about Sterling Royce, who greeted me shirtless while slathering sunscreen on his washboard abs. A wired stereo system piped some R & B to the outdoor speakers as Lucy sashayed about in a microscopic bikini.

Sterling caught my gaze and gave me a haughty smile. I flicked my eyes away toward the pool and said hurriedly to the group, "How was Moldova? Did the scene work out okay?"

"The food was weird," said one of Lucy's assistants, and the conversation stalled there. Lucy had brought along her personal makeup artist and her stylist, without whom apparently she could not exist, and another soap coworker, Amanda Tate.

I didn't see either of her parents around, but maybe our adult supervision was supposed to be Sterling Royce.

While I filled a cup with a skinny margarita, I whispered to Amanda, "What's going on? How does Lucy know *him*?"

Amanda cut her eyes toward me. "No one is supposed to talk about it. He's *into* her. You know."

"But he's, like, *forty*."

"Thirty-two. Girl, you think he's *forty*?"

"What's all that whispering!" Lucy chided from her deck chair. "Manda, will you find the help and ask where the food is, already?"

I settled in a lounge chair, tilted my wide-brimmed sunhat so that it covered most of my face, and tried to relax my shoulders and hands. The rhythmic sound of crashing waves hushed any other conversations and I willed myself to breathe in and out at the same tempo as the music. I reminded myself that I was in a yard full of people, and that security had followed me here. A guard was parked in the kitchen, watching everything.

"Hi, everyone," said a voice, as another person stooped through the patio door. Shirtless, already tan, towel in hand.

"Stephen!" Lucy said, waving him over. "You made it. Please, eat our fruit. Drink our alcohol. Enjoy our view."

Sterling said, "Baby, you're the perfect hostess."

I could see Stephen out of the corner of my eye, framed by the black-and-white-striped edge of my oversize hat and the tops of my giant sunglasses, as he accepted a drink from the server and settled into a chair next to me. He creaked back and forth a few times as he applied a dash of sunscreen to the bridge of his nose, capping the bottle and placing it on a nearby table next to his cup. Then he stretched out and gave a warm, heavy sigh of contentment, as if settling in for a nap.

I slipped the edge of my draped towel over my legs. My bikini, cute as it was, was also suddenly uncomfortably revealing, squeezing the sides of my hips and accentuating love handles.

"Hi, Stephen," I said. A moment later I realized how slow I had been to acknowledge his presence, and after everything that happened at the MVAs last week, I didn't want him to think I was giving him the silent treatment. I wondered if Lucy had invited him because of that kiss—playing matchmaker, as seventeen-year-olds do. Quickly, I feigned a yawn, pretending that I'd fallen asleep in the chair and had only just woken up from dozing to find this pleasant companion next to me.

"Hey, yourself." He slurped at his cup, squinting my way. He wasn't wearing anything on his head—no sunglasses, no ridiculous hat. The edges of his cheeks were already turning pink after ten minutes of direct sun.

"Aren't you afraid of burning?" Amanda interrupted.

"Hmm? Oh." He poked one finger on his sternum, leaving a white mark. "I don't burn that easily."

"You're so pale. Don't be dumb." Amanda threw him a tube of SPF 50 from her own bag. "I'm brown and even *I'm* wearing this stuff."

"In that case." We watched as he began painting his arms in white.

"Sassy?" He was holding the tube out to me. "Will you get my back?"

He sat on the edge of his chaise as I swiped sunscreen along his spine, spreading it outward in circular motions. His skin was already hot. He had a freckle between his shoulder blades. He was due for another appointment at the salon, as there was prickly looking growth at the nape of his neck. I didn't mean to take these little mental pictures, but I couldn't help myself. At that moment the CD ended, leaving a hole where the sound had been. There was only the waves, and clinks of ice settling into glasses as drinks melted, and Amanda's occasional page flip of her magazine. It felt uncomfortably quiet, before the CD changed over and music resumed its flow.

"You know," I said, doubling back up and focusing on the tops of his shoulders, even though they already glistened with sunscreen, "you don't have to call me Sassy."

"That's your name, though, right?"

"That's like my stage name. You knew me before, as just Cassidy."

"It's hard to think of you as *just Cassidy,* though." He twisted around to reach for the tube, helping himself to a big blob that he then smeared on the tops of his feet. "You were like a different person then."

I hesitated, hands slowing as I pondered if I should be upset by this remark. He wasn't interested in me during the reality show, so maybe *Sing It* Cassidy was like a kid sister or friendly competitor, whereas the stylish and scantily clad Sassy Gloss was a siren calling to his base animal appetite. He must've replayed his remark in his head because he added, "I just mean, you've come so far since you were on the show. New hair, new ensemble . . ."

"New body," said Lucy. I gave her a look that she must have understood through my shades, because she propped her head up on one hand and flipped her hair over one shoulder. "Whatever, I watched the show. You were a *lot* heavier then."

Stephen swiveled around, raising both hands in surrender. "I didn't say it. Though"—he grinned in my direction—"You *are* looking good, Sassy."

I knew that the way a normal girl would react would be to laugh and shove him playfully and say something like, "You're such a jerk," and continue the conversation for a few more minutes before retiring back to her lounge chair. If this had been any other person or any other situation, I may have done the expected. Instead, my reaction was to flatten myself in my chair and bring the towel up to cover the rest of me, and I clamped my eyes shut.

There were just too many thoughts roiling in my head. This wasn't what I expected the party to be like. I was supposed to have a calming time at the beach house with butler service and fresh papaya; I was going to unravel my thoughts, forgetting for a day about Jerry, real estate, and impending tour schedules. But what I felt instead were even more obstacles to get through, little pinballs bouncing around inside me, each pinging noisily, demanding attention, rowdy.

One of Lucy's assistants complained, "These skinny margs are so boring. I'm craving sugar. Hello?" She called to the woman in the black linen shirt who was hovering inside the door. "Could we get some fun drinks out here? You know, something fruity, with extra umbrellas?"

"Yes, miss." She emerged with a tray of raw fish and what looked to be tacos filled with shredded meat. "I also have your sashimi and kalua pork."

The smell of pork overpowered the fragrance of fake co-
conuts from Amanda's sunblock and salt from the ocean. The
other assistant hopped up and took a bite of a taco without using a plate, dribbling oil onto the ground. "This is fantastic,"
she gushed, slurping juice from her thumb. Lucy found a pair
of chopsticks and stabbed at the fish, ignoring everything else
on the tray.

It was all too overwhelming. My stomach turned suddenly
and I rolled out of my chair, wrapping the towel around my
waist and dropping it only when I'd slipped my feet into the
infinity pool. Swimming to the farthest corner from everyone else, resting my elbows on the edge and looking out
at the waves, I wished for a quiet place where I really *could*
vacate my thoughts, a spot where all of my brain could stop
clicking and just be still. I submerged my head under the
water and listened to the thrum of the pool pumps. It was
easier than hearing anything else.

I WAS JOSTLED out of sleep by an insistent shaking. Lifting myself up on one arm, I realized that I'd fallen asleep on the slippery couch in the living room and Amanda was pushing me
awake. I hadn't had much to drink, but had laid out on the sofa
while the party died down. Blearily I glanced around and spotted Stephen with his head cradled in his crossed arms, slumped
against the soft back of an armchair. "What?" My voice was
groggy and thick. "What time is it?"

"Your phone keeps going off." Amanda's voice was irritated.

"Huh?"

"Your cell phone."

I had forgotten about that little silver brick in the bottom of my bag, but it trilled, indicating a voice-mail message. Yumi's voice: "You should get back here. Viv is back in the hospital and Rose is going off the rails. I can't handle her alone."

*Viv?* After being relegated to the sidelines for any mention of Viv, now I was suddenly summoned to Rose's side because the original Gloss fourth had a downturn? I glanced up at the slumbering forms all around me, brow furrowed, but picked my way through the bodies. Stephen St. James gave off a snore as I passed by, and my security detail took me home.

When I got to the apartment, Yumi was pacing while Rose sat at the kitchen table with her cell phone clasped to her ear. Her face was tear-streaked and stricken; it was the first time in memory that I'd seen her cry. There was a bone-deep chill of fear that I could taste in the air, heavier than anything I'd sensed before even though Jerry's letter had given us all a big scare that morning.

Yumi snapped her cell closed and looked at me taking in the scene. "What's going on?" I asked.

"She's been stable, for the most part, but had a sudden fever." Yumi gave a helpless shrug and glanced over at Rose. "She was rushed to the ER. That's all I know. Viv's mom called us."

Merry was nowhere to be seen. "And Merry?"

"Useless. Went off with Grant and hasn't answered her phone, even though I called her, like, fifty times. I know it's unfair to call you, since you don't even know Viv, but, like . . . I don't know what to do about *her*."

*Her* was Rose, who had finally hung up the phone and sat with her head in the crooks of her elbows, sobbing. I set my

fingers gently at the little knob at the base of her neck, pushing her damp hair out of the way, and let my hand rest there.
I expected her to duck away or slap my arm aside, but instead,
she sagged farther into her seat and let the phone dangle from
her fingers until it clattered onto the table.

It was weird to see Rose like this, completely vulnerable, all
of her hard edges softened with tears. If anyone needed a hug
right now, it was her.

I leaned in close and let her soak one side of my shirt. It was
a little awkward, leaning in like that, with one foot braced
against her chair and one of my hands accidentally tucked under her damp armpit. My other hand clutched against her head
and I found myself patting her hair. Words jumbled in my head
and I realized I'd never been in a position like this before, comforting a friend who was in near-mourning. What do you say?
My mouth was up against one of her ears. I smoothed her hair
and murmured, "It'll be okay. It'll be okay." I rocked her back
and forth as she cried.

Yumi didn't say anything; in fact, I'd almost forgotten she
was there. All that mattered right then was Rose and her fear
and my fingers in her hair and her smell—her warm head and
hours-old conditioner and perspiration and that earthy smell
that you can sometimes sense when there's been a fresh rain,
only it was Rose's tear-laden breath. Her hands scrabbled for
something to hold on to and she found me, found my back,
squeezed my hips, hugged me tighter.

"It'll be okay."

She pulled away, dashing at her pink-rimmed eyes with both
hands. Her nose was clogged and she breathed heavily from

dry lips. "Th-thanks, Cass," she wavered, and Yumi snagged the paper towel roll and passed it along in lieu of a tissue box.

We listened to the refrigerator tick in the silent apartment.

"I want . . . ," she said slowly. I pushed a lock of hair out of her face to see her better. "I want to see Viv. Yumi, will you go see Viv with me?"

Yumi laid down on the couch and dropped an arm off the side. "I get that you're worried, but it's a *fever*. You want to risk Peter's ire for just a fever? We have work to do today."

Rose's eyes swiveled to me and she said entreatingly, "A fever can mean anything. Infection. Recurrence. Will you take me to see her? And my mom?"

I hesitated, but one glance at Rose and I knew I couldn't say no. "Are you sure that's what you want?"

She gave a tiny nod.

"Okay . . ."

Rose's new BMW was parked outside and she handed me the keys. "Are you sure you don't want me to call Gus or someone?" I said. She was unnaturally quiet, drawn into herself with worry.

She shook her head. "I want to ride with you."

I fingered the keys as a flicker of doubt traveled through me. Despite all that we'd been through together so far, I didn't think that we knew each other all that well. And I didn't think I was a better driver or roadside companion than a professional. And I was tired, having fallen asleep late and woken up early. But she was already gathering her purse and waiting expectantly for me to join her. So I did.

## 17.

September 2001
San Jose

# Cassidy

The drive to Oakland from L.A., even without traffic, is a good five hours. We told security to take the morning off and to stick with Merry, who'd probably need them more, counting on the unexpected nature of our visit to be anonymous enough.

The car was so new, it smelled like sweet leather and there were no fingerprints or smudges on any of the glass or mirrors. The California state map tucked in the glove compartment had never been unfolded. Rose hadn't had time to personalize the car in any way—load the six-disc changer with CDs, find any dangly rearview mirror tokens, stuff a blanket in the back seat—so there was nothing to listen to except the radio, which we kept switched off. The day was just beginning; sunlight slanted in an unnaturally crisp and white way across the passenger-side window as we headed north, bathing Rose and her rose-tinted chapped nostrils and rose-rimmed raw eyes in a light that made her almost translucent. She was quiet, grasping her phone in two tight hands, looking between it and the view out the window every few moments, as if she were afraid she would miss an important call.

We'd been on the road for several hours when I glanced over at her, this petite girl with her arms crossed over her chest, though she insisted she wasn't cold. In the year and a half that I'd known Rose, she had never shown much of herself to me. Behind her narrow face and large, unmatching eyes, I had the sense that she was always calculating her next move—*our* next move. She was the leader of the group, the mouthpiece, even though we had said over and over again that we were all equal members. We'd never seen her with a guy, and she'd never expressed interest in one. But somewhere underneath her thin breastbone, a heart beat there.

She gave me a sharp look. "Why are you slowing down?"

"Hmm? Oh." I'd decelerated without realizing it. I mashed the pedal down again with new resolve. The 5 rolled beneath us, a smooth curve. We were quiet for another long stretch, and Rose flipped on the radio, which played a countdown of the Top 40. "Wake Up Morning" had slipped to number six, but "What Did U Say" was still number one. I asked, "Do you think you'll be moving soon?"

"Maybe. I found a really cool spot right above the Sunset Strip."

"What's it like?"

"Big. Six bedrooms, a pool, lots of glass. It's gorgeous." A small, excited huff that could have been a laugh. "It's a little much, but I fell in love with it. And the location is perfection."

"A little much? How much?"

"A few mil."

The idea that a house could be anything *but* a particular number of "mil" was astonishing. I mustered a "wow" as I followed signs for 580 toward San Francisco. My hips hurt from sitting so long and it'd been hours since we'd eaten anything.

"What about you? You think you'll move out? Well, obviously you will, but any idea where? Hold on." Her phone was ringing. "Yeah? Okay." She listened quietly, then said, "Okay, see you tomorrow." She clicked the phone shut. "Cassy. There's been a change in plans."

"What do you mean? We aren't going to Oakland anymore?"

"Oakland? Well . . . About that." A note of hesitation crept into her voice.

"I'm going to pull over." I pulled the humming BMW over to the shoulder and set it in park without cutting the engine. I asked, "Where are we going?"

"We're not going to Oakland."

"What?" I took my hands off the wheel and turned in my seat to look at her. She was fidgeting with a ring on her right hand, hair draped over her eye like a shiny brown curtain.

"We can't actually go to the hospital to see Viv right now; only family is allowed and I don't want to be mobbed if we're recognized in the waiting room. Let's go to my mom's until we get the okay. It's been a while; it'll be good to see her . . ." Her voice drifted off, as if uncertain.

I reached over without thinking, pushed a lock of her hair off of her forehead with two gentle fingers. It wasn't what I expected to do—it seemed too personal, and I could feel her soft exhale on my inner arm as I held her gaze for a moment, before quickly withdrawing my hand and placing it on the wheel. How had I never noticed how absolutely beautiful she was? How had I thought she had a gerbil-like face when we first met?

The flicker I'd seen in her eyes convinced me that this was a topic that I shouldn't pry into. I swallowed.

"Okay, let's go." I shifted back into drive and we eased back out onto the road.

We STOPPED FOR gas, protein bars, and a bathroom in a town called Lacy, taking a short stint on a gravel-paved highway back to the 5, past Stockton. "Would you mind telling me how much longer we'll be driving?" I asked softly, as the afternoon got even brighter.

"A little longer."

It seemed like *a little longer* was a continuous refrain, but finally Rose said, "Turn off here." There wasn't even a sign for the town, just an exit number. We rolled past a population sign that was skewed to one side, having been broadsided by a car at some point. We sped past a gas station and a dry-goods store, taking straight roads toward a residential street. "Stop at the second on the left." We parked in front of a modest house with an older 1980s Ford sedan sitting in the short driveway. The silence after I turned off the car made me rub my ear in surprise.

Rose was already stepping out of the passenger side, tugging at the back pockets of her jeans to keep them from riding up. I stretched and folded the state map, jamming it into my bag as I plodded up a dirt drive behind Rose. She stopped in front of the door, hesitating, then pulled it open.

The front door led directly into the living room, which was lit by only one lamp, and filled with large, overstuffed furniture. One wall was completely covered in crosses of different sizes and materials, some of them lumpy like they'd been shaped by a child. I shifted my gaze to a woman in a fluffy couch, sipping from a straw in a convenience-store Styrofoam cup. Her hair was dyed red but her light brown roots were showing.

"Hi, Mom," Rose said, reaching down to give her a hug. Her mother glanced over Rose's shoulder at me. "This is Cassidy. She drove me."

"You can't drive yourself?"

"It's a new car."

Her mother seemed perturbed by this comment. "And you still couldn't drive yourself? Drove my Ford all over Northern California, but you can't even make it out of L.A. on your own." Rose didn't respond. Her mother reached out a hand to me. "I'm Clara. To what do I owe this pleasure?"

"It's nice to meet you," I said, clasping her damp hand. "We're just here because . . ." I faltered, not sure if it was my place to say.

"Just here to visit," Rose said.

"You girls hungry?"

We shook our heads and Clara took a long pull from her straw. We watched the muted television screen, which was playing *Judge Judy.* "I suppose you'll want to stay the night," Clara said, eyes still on the TV. "It's a long drive. Your room is still as it ever was. You know where the spare blankets are."

Rose turned toward the depths of the house. "Cassy, let me show you where you'll be."

She took me around the corner to a small bedroom with only enough space for a bureau and tiny desk that butted up against the bed, so one could potentially do homework while sitting cross-legged on a twin mattress. All four walls and the ceiling were covered in posters and magazine clippings of celebrities a tween-aged Rose would have idolized. A mirror over the bureau doubled as a scrapbook: glossy photos of Rose posing with friends, arms slung around each other, graying *Calvin and Hobbes* comics trimmed from the newspaper, and inspirational quotes written directly onto the silver surface in dry-erase marker made it difficult to see a reflection. The room seemed too juvenile for the taste of the Rose I knew; a pink ruffled bedspread adorned the bed and her pillows were covered in eyelet fabric. She twirled around in the gap between door and bed frame. "Ta-da."

"I don't understand," I said. "What about Oakland?"

Rose blew out a long breath. "We're only a couple of hours from Oakland. If I said I was from Bumfuck, California, no one would know what I was talking about. And it's almost true. The other girls in the group are sort of from there. Our talent competitions were in the Bay Area. It just made sense to say Oakland."

"What's the point, though?"

"The *point*," she said emphatically, "is that we're selling sophisticated, savvy, sexy women from a big city. What if we did a profile in a magazine and they said we were from Podunk, Nowhere? I bet you if *Rolling Stone* said that I was from a town of twenty thousand people we wouldn't have had our big rise."

I rubbed behind one ear. "But you are. And we *have*."

"Doesn't matter. And now that we've said Oakland for so long, there's no point in clearing the air now."

"And your dad?"

Her lower jaw jutted out slightly and she hugged a pillow to her chest. "What's there to say? They're divorced and now he lives in the city."

I sat down next to her on the narrow bed and then laid out, stretching my tired legs. She remained with her back to me, spine curved. We were quiet, and the entire world was quiet too. What I wanted to ask was why she didn't confide in her mother about Viv's ill health. Instead, I tapped her lightly with one socked toe. "We can't stay in here forever."

She grabbed my foot. "I know." She exhaled through her nose. "But I can't talk to her about Viv. We wouldn't hear the end of it. You wouldn't understand."

The room was dim and it was so, so quiet.

It was awkward being in a strange house with two people I didn't know very well. Though Rose and I had been living together for almost a couple of years now, it occurred to me just how little I'd gathered about her life besides her business acumen. She had rolled over onto her side on the eyelet bed, alone in her thoughts, so still that I felt that the sound of my breathing was intruding.

When I stepped out of her bedroom to give her some space, I found that the rest of the house was just as uncomfortable. Clara continued to sip through her straw, alone, the flicker of the television painting her face blue. Her eyes in the darkened room seemed rheumy, glass marbles that rolled like they were weighted at the bottoms. I began to question what was in the cup.

"That girl, though," Clara said, and I wasn't sure if it was directed at me or if she was speaking to herself. "Roping another person into driving her all the way here. Lord help us." She seemed to register my presence and patted the cushion next to hers, but I remained standing. "You're not going to see that girl, are you? That Ortiz trash?"

"I . . . I don't know her," I said hesitantly.

"You should be glad that you don't. She's trouble, mind you."

Clara began to murmur words in a softer cadence, seemingly to herself, but I caught *unnatural* and *improper* in her spiel. I escaped back to Rose's room.

As the sky turned black outside and it became apparent that Rose was probably going to sleep through the night, I realized I hadn't checked in with anyone since leaving Yumi that morning. I wondered what she and Merry were doing, if they regretted not coming along. Peter had called my cell a few times, but I didn't want to listen to his messages. The lamp in the bedroom had not been lit but it was a last-quarter moon outside and the venetian blinds were still twisted open, and it was bright enough that I could see the shine on Rose's eyes. "You're awake?" I whispered.

"Been awake. Just thinking," she murmured back.

"I was just going to grab these blankets and . . ."

"Here." She scooted over, making room for me on the twin mattress. I lay as I had before, not side by side with shoulders touching, but head to foot so that it felt less intimate. Nothing telegraphs casualness like having your stockinged feet in someone else's face. Once the springs stopped shivering, she spoke again, in a low voice, "Your feet kinda stink."

"Sorry." I switched directions. I felt the fatigue in the back of my eyes; I'd slept poorly on Lucy's couch and driven for hours. My head relaxed into the pillow and I closed my eyelids, aware that my teeth had a filmy layer of grit from the sugar in the protein bar I ate.

"I can't believe that Yumi and Merry aren't here." She huffed in disgust. "How is it that *you're* the one to come visit Viv with me, and you don't even know her?"

I wasn't sure what to say to that but it seemed inappropriate to not acknowledge it. "Hmm."

"It's fucking ridiculous. You think you know somebody . . ."

I opened my eyes and she was looking at me. A tiny jolt tickled my sternum. It was as if she saw me for the first time—*really* saw me. I wondered if she felt something too, or if she was still ruminating over her anger toward the other two Glossies.

Embarrassed, I decided to deflect. "Did you like growing up here? I mean, you grew up next to your best friend, right?"

"Ugh. I keep trying to give my mom money but she says I should hold on to it. For security, she says. I tell her she can leave this tiny-ass town and live in a bigger city but she likes it here, even though there's nothing to do in a town this size.

And you can never get in trouble because everybody knows your business."

I felt the heavy sense of Rose's commitment to getting herself out of here. I could understand her anger when I slipped right into the group—a girl who tried out for a talent contest with an audition in the city she already lived in! How convenient, how easy. She would have had to plan her trip weeks in advance. A girl like this, who traveled to another city to practice her talent, who finally made it to Hollywood and could actually buy a chunk of it with money earned by herself, well, that was a girl to be commended. I could bet that everyone in her hometown, all the doubters and naysayers, were probably eating their words right now. A house in Sunset Strip. She was practically Clooney's neighbor.

She rolled away, the weak light from the moon illuminating her back. Maybe we were done talking. It wouldn't surprise me; Rose wasn't much of a talker to begin with.

"I think," she said, halfway muffled by her pillow, "it was a mistake to come see my mom. I care for my mom, but . . ."

"Sure," I said, voice floating up into the low ceiling. Clara's murmurings had worried me a bit, but I wasn't going to say it aloud.

The next moment, brightness streamed in through the single window and it was morning. I shifted awake slowly, the slanted light creeping warmly onto my cheeks. I was still fully clothed on top of the pink ruffled bedspread. Without getting off the bed, I slipped a hand into my bag and found my cell phone.

As I eased onto my back, wiping sleep from my eyes and displaying my missed call list, my elbow bumped into a curled-up lump next to me, under the blanket. Rose slept with lips slightly parted and hair strewn across her pillow like a mermaid.

At this angle, her eyes closed and face relaxed, she looked younger. Sweeter. Less intimidating. Maybe it was because I couldn't see her striking eyes staring me down.

Rose shifted and snuffled. She yawned and opened her eyes, and it was back to normal, like last night's chat had never happened. She barely looked at me as she got out of bed and ignored me as I checked my voice-mail messages.

Clara was still in the living room, still on that same couch, as we ate cornflakes for breakfast. I couldn't imagine how she had transported Rose anywhere outside of this house, especially to gigs in San Francisco. The pageant-show mom I'd imagined and the woman in front of me now could not be reconciled in my mind.

I drank the warm dregs of leftover milk, but Rose dumped hers down the sink. "We're going to go," she said in a flat intonation without looking at Clara. "We didn't, you know, bring a change of clothes and we have stuff to do back in L.A."

Clara pursed her lips together but did not argue. "Are you going straight back?"

Rose sounded careful in her reply. "We might swing over to San Jose. Cassidy's never been to the Bay Area before."

"Are you going to see . . . *her*?" Clara's disgust for Viv was palpable. I couldn't understand what Clara could hate about a sick young woman.

Rose shook her head and gave her mother a stiff hug goodbye. I climbed back into the driver's seat, gazing at Clara as she waved goodbye at the front door and shut it before we'd pulled away. It struck me as odd that someone who could claim knowledge of a god could hate someone so forcefully. We didn't discuss what her mother had said.

It was easily another hour to San Jose, and we listened to Barenaked Ladies and Savage Garden on low volume, Rose having had the good sense to pilfer some of her old CD collection before leaving her childhood house. "I thought she was your neighbor," I said, my hands clenched around the steering wheel. It felt wrong to ask about Viv, after all the secrecy, but at the same time, Rose *had* dragged me out all this way.

"They moved out here for treatment," Rose said bluntly.

"Oh."

"I heard from Viv's mom while you were in the bathroom. They're out of the ER and back at home. So we won't have to visit any hospitals."

I wondered if I could just wait in the car to avoid any awkwardness, but Rose directed me to a house near the city center and gave me a look when I didn't unbuckle my seat belt. When Rose knocked on the door, a woman appeared from behind a screened porch door. She was short, with warm brown eyes and a long braid that swung from her shoulder as she reached for the doorknob. "Come in!" she said. "She's sleeping right now but she'll be so happy to see you."

The smell in the house was all wrong. Our apartment in L.A., after days of being sealed up while we traveled, smelled like musty towels and stale perfume, the scent baking into itself. This house smelled strongly like antiseptic, the stomach-clenching scent of bleach-water that I recalled from cleaning cafeteria tables with old sponges in elementary school.

Our host made us tea with honey, served in sunny yellow mugs, which Rose looked at carefully before gripping the sides and taking a sip. It seemed an odd choice for September, but the tea was fortifying in a way. "You're getting too skinny," the woman said maternally, pulling out a loaf of banana bread. "Mrs. Foster—you remember her?—comes by every month with baked stuff, hoping to put a little meat on all of us. Here." She sliced a couple of thick portions and deposited them onto plates. To my surprise, Rose broke off a piece and popped it into her mouth without asking for a fork, wiping her greasy fingers on a paper napkin.

"Thank you," I said, and took a small bite. It was buttery and dense. I mentally counted the calories.

Now that the woman was sitting down, I could see the exhaustion. The skin under her eyes was discolored, and her mouth, when she wasn't smiling toward us, worried itself into a well-worn frown.

"I visited my mom," Rose said, warming up slightly in the presence of the woman.

"And brought a friend," Viv's mother said, looking pointedly at me. She set a hand out toward me, across the table. "Oh, where is my mind? You must be Cassidy. Welcome." She clasped her fingers on mine and the corners of her lips twitched upward, as if they had to relearn how to smile. "I'm Vivian's mother, Lorna."

This woman felt genuine. "Nice to meet you," I said, stunned at the contrast of warmth from Lorna and coldness from Clara.

Lorna turned her beam on Rose. "The worst is over, *mija*."

"What was it?" Rose asked meekly.

With a sigh, she said, "What it always is. Complications. You think it's worse than it is. Or you think it's better than it really is. You never know, and you take her in. But she's all right."

Rose's face crumpled and she began to cry with relief. "Now, now," Lorna said, patting her ineffectually on the forearm. "She's home, nothing to worry about, see?"

I awkwardly wrapped my hands around the contours of my mug. A baby monitor, set on the edge of the laminate counter near the sink, crackled briefly, drawing my attention. "Ma?" a hoarse voice said.

Rose wiped her face with the heels of her hands. "I'll go."

The chair squeaked as she escaped to a back room. Lorna shifted her weight as though she wanted to check on her daughter as well but thought better of it. She set her fingers on the table in front of her, exercising restraint, and smiled brightly at me. "So. Cassidy. How are you enjoying the group?"

Her posture, the question, together, felt like the start of an interview. "It's been fine. Great. A great opportunity," I said, mind going straight into PR mode.

"Oh, honey, it *is*, all right." Lorna was too anxious to sit still, so she got up to boil more water. "I've been with the girls since, well, forever. I'm the original Gloss groupie." She gave a laugh as she untangled the threads in the box of tea bags. "Seamstress, dress designer, chauffeur."

There was murmuring in the back room, the rise and fall of Rose's strong voice and a softer one in response. Lorna continued, accepting my silence as absorption. "I know that it's a trial, dealing with them all the time. I don't admire your position." Her back was to me as she attended to the kettle; she did not move. She *should* be envying me, I thought. I took her daughter's spot in this group. I bet the cat fights and long hours would be exponentially more tolerable than a sick child. But I didn't say anything, and she didn't correct herself.

I felt very awkward, not sure what subject to touch next, hoping that she would guide the conversation toward a lighter path. Instead, she stayed very quiet near the stove, still facing away, doctoring all the little things that one does to tea. She composed herself and sat at the table again. We sipped resolutely. I felt the urge to apologize. But when I did, she looked into her sunny yellow mug and sighed. "No, it's fine," she said. "We've had a lot of bad days in this house." Using a paper napkin from a crumpled takeout bag, she swiped at the crumbs dotting the surface of the table before picking up her cup again. "We used to live really close to the McGills. A couple of blocks away. Those two were joined at the hip. They did everything together. Girl Scouts. Piano lessons. They shared their clothes for a while, until Viv had her growth spurt and Rose couldn't catch up." She swallowed. "And they did all the singing stuff together. But then Viv got sick and while Rose helped as much as she could, we moved out here to be closer to the hospital." That was why the house didn't feel lived-in or even like a *home,* much like our tour bus didn't feel like a home. It was a tool, a transient thing that helped us get from point A to point B. For Viv, that was the medical center a short car ride away.

"That must have been hard," I said, unsure what else to say.

She nodded silently. "We used to drink cocoa out of these mugs," Lorna said, laughing sadly. "At sleepovers."

Rose poked her head out from the hallway. "I need some help." Lorna stood. I made a move to stand as well but Rose stopped me. "Better not," she said. "You probably want to meet her when she's cleaned up a bit."

So I sat again, listening to the shuffle and creaking of floorboards. I rubbed my thumbnail on the outside seam of my jeans. Takeout bags crowded the kitchen counters, plastic clamshells of grocery-store bakery items stacked up with desiccated flakes of pastry at the bottom.

Finally, after I'd memorized the groove of every paint drip that had been hastily applied to the cabinets, I was called to the back of the house. I passed other open doors as I padded down the hallway: a darkened bathroom with a tap still dripping, a smaller bedroom with sheets askew. Viv's sick room was an attempt at cheerfulness: it had a bay window and natural light, though the curtain was half-drawn. Her hospital bed had no ruffled adornments, but the coverlet, in a rich shade of maroon, was patterned with a soft fringe that gave it a luxurious look and distracted one's eye from the various medical paraphernalia surrounding her. Photographs and get-well cards covered a big bulletin board directly across the room, so that she could look at it from bed. This is where the long creature lay, legs covered in maroon, her hair close-cropped and eyes bright. Lorna and Rose flanked her on either side of the bed. I approached the tableau.

"Hello," Viv said, holding out a large hand with long, slender fingers. She did not have her mother's hands.

"Hi, I'm Cassidy. It's so nice to finally meet you." She winced when I grasped her hand. "Oh! I'm so sorry."

"It's all right. I'm just a fragile person nowadays." Her voice was raspy. "I really wanted to meet you, but I hope you don't mind that I'm going to nap a bit." She lowered the angle of the bed with a remote, taking her to a more horizontal stance. "I'm just so exhausted."

Her eyelids fluttered closed as Lorna and Rose held a conversation over her head about Viv's various treatments, her energy levels, her appetite. I watched her as she fell asleep softly, gently, one finger twitching against the side of her face, the gliding rise and fall of her rib cage shifting the cover's fringe. She wore a ring identical to the one Rose had on her right hand, and I wondered if they had bought each other friendship rings. My eyes traveled over to the bulletin board and there were photos of all the Gloss girls at various ages, wearing silly costumes and smiling. One photo was a duplicate from Rose's room: I recognized the wide degree of teeth in the smiles and realized it was the pair of them, arms around each other's shoulders in that unselfconscious way that preteens grab their friends.

When we left the house, Viv sleeping through the afternoon and not waking to say goodbye, Lorna pressed more banana bread into our hands and gave us long hugs and a kiss on one cheek. To Rose she murmured what sounded like an encouragement and let her go. She pressed the side of her face against mine, her cheek hot, and whispered, "I'm glad she found you."

# 18.

*Saturday*

# Rose

I need something amazing," I said to Alicia, my stylist. I shouldn't have waited this long to find something for the *Lunch at Midnight* premiere, but I'd been busy. My agent had texted me some good news, for once: *Sing It, America!* was going to be revived and the producers had my name down on a short list for a panel judge. They wanted me to come in early next week for a chat. "Something that turns heads. Something to be written up in the style column."

Alicia flicked through a few wan hangers on a rolling garment rack. "These are all I could get on short notice."

"Just these?" There were only a handful of outfits. Nothing outlandish or exquisite.

"Like I said, short notice. I called in all the favors that I could, but . . ."

I knew what Alicia wasn't saying. I wasn't a big name

anymore. Dressing Rosy Gloss wasn't as big of an honor as it used to be. I wasn't about to *buy* my premiere outfit, either.

"Yeah, but *this*? I could get it at Nordstrom *Rack*," I sneered, shoving aside a rayon dress. I didn't know why I still had Alicia on my payroll; funds were tight already. It felt as though I were climbing the same ladder on which I'd struggled fifteen years ago, but now I had bad knees, figuratively speaking. "Who's dressing Yumi?"

Yumi had dismissed all of her staff aside from her house-keeper years ago; she lived in that stuffy mansion she'd won in her divorce settlement, with no agent or stylist or anything, and barely touched her money. I doubted she would wear couture to the premiere, but Merry likely still had all of her connections.

"I don't know. I could find out if you'd like."

"Ugh, never mind. There's no point. Go."

Alicia hesitated, but I turned toward her with renewed annoyance. "I said, *leave*."

She click-clacked away, and I ran my fingers over the rack again before shoving it aside. It rolled across my parquet floors and slowed at a bump near a Tiffany lamp. I lay back on my chaise and covered my face with one hand. Ever since the news about Cassidy, I'd been more irritated than usual by the incompetence of everyone around me.

"You okay?" my housemate asked.

I looked over at Viv. She'd poked her head into the room, leaning on the door's threshold. After she'd gone through remission, Viv had been desperate to have some life experiences, and I'd paid for a few tickets around the world. But soon Viv was clamoring for something familiar—some*one* familiar—and had moved in with me. After all, I had more than enough rooms to spare, and she could live as though she were independent, but my staff could keep tabs on her health as well. If anything seemed unusual, we had a world-class hospital a few miles away.

Usually she was in the other wing of the house, entertaining her own guests, but she must have heard Alicia leave. Alicia was the harbinger of frustration these days, and if there was anything Viv was good at, it was placating me.

I huffed out a breath. "It's fine. You didn't want to go to the premiere, right?"

"I'd rather die than set foot into that nightmare," she said, smiling. "I have some really good *Masterpiece* queued up for that evening."

"Just checking."

Viv disappeared from the doorway and I scrubbed at my eyes, ruining my mascara, then reached for my phone to call Emily. Maybe she could skim a few dresses from Merry's offerings and share one with me.

She picked up after a few rings, sounding breathless.

"Are you at the gym or something?" I asked, curious.

"No, I'm just getting some boxes down from the attic, something for Yumi. There are like a dozen left to go."

I got straight to the point. "Did Merry get her premiere outfit yet?"

"Yeah, Merry and Sunny both."

"*Soleil* is going? Not Raul?"

I could hear her shrug. "Sunny really wants to go. Raul has a schedule conflict."

Great. I'd have to share the carpet with a little nepotistic snot.

"Was there something you wanted?" Emily asked.

"Just wondering what they're wearing. So, you know, we don't match too much. We *aren't* really a group anymore, right?" I said it casually. The worst part about being broke is that I couldn't give the appearance of being desperate.

"Merry's in Dior. Soft pink dress with pleats, green embroidery. Sunny gets a playful jumpsuit from some up-and-coming designer that she wants to partner with."

"Anything they haven't sent back yet? I'm thinking of firing Alicia. She doesn't know how to dress me anymore and everything she brought to me was hideous and out of style." I held my breath.

"I think a few have gone back already, but we still have a few pieces. Let me look." Crunching of shoes on gravel.

I KNOW THE generic formula for maintaining fame, which is why it's so irritating that fame has been an elusive bitch for me to grasp. For some, it comes pretty easily: their family's in the business so they already have a leg up, they fuck the right people to stay in the spotlight, they strategize their lives for maximum impact. I do the best with what I've been given.

The truth is, the public wants you to stay the same as when they fell in love with you. Sure, you can "reinvent" yourself every couple of years, try on different personas. This is important for child stars to transition from adorable to being perceived as a sexual adult. Every ham-fisted kid actor on a cable television series has gone through the change, with much magazine fanfare: "Starlet acts out!" "Teen seen leaving co-star's home in the same clothes she was photographed in yesterday!" It's like clockwork. But the public wants you to be the same person *underneath*. If they feel like they don't know you or can't relate to you, they will turn on you.

Becoming a target for the tabloids isn't bad, either, though it's a lot less fun. People were already waiting for you to mess up, but now they're gleeful about it. There's nothing the public loves more than to tear down someone who was once their idol. Tabloids dictate the public's opinion, and if you don't feed the wolves, they make up their own stories. Hell, sometimes you give them the story and they print only half of it. Or none of it.

My point is this: times change and people change, but celebrities are not allowed to leave the box that we've been painted into. There are a few exceptions that everyone allows, like the sinner who becomes a saint—usually after having respectable children—or the sexpot who ages gracefully into a bombshell octogenarian, but for the most part, if the world says you're a five-foot-one, petite, rosy-cheeked, lovable woman, you remain one for as long as you can.

Cassidy, she didn't understand this. People liked her on that TV talent contest show, but they did not truly fall in love with her until she was a part of Gloss. An ironically named, shy, thin brunette who had a tragic straight relationship. Once she had her arm broken, she was frozen in time forever. The classic vulnerable woman made tragic by circumstance.

People respond to authentic celebrities—or what they *perceive* as authentic. They are too stupid to realize that most celebrities wear one face in public and another face at home. Merry was a home-wrecker with a heart of gold, so her multiple red-hot boyfriends were the norm. When she got pregnant and didn't name the father, it was a much-gossiped-about scandal, but people seemed to expect it. They didn't vilify her for long. It was like, "Oh, that Cherry Gloss, it's just like Cherry to do something so salacious," and then they wanted to see photos of the baby when she was born. I tried to get her to capitalize on the birth and sell photos to *People* magazine, but she refused. I threw my proverbial hands up into the air and had to call a select few photographers myself for her exodus from the hospital. She wouldn't do what was needed or what the people wanted, so I had to do it for her. It was a classic case of Rosy helping Merry, as usual.

When Cassidy broke off with not so much as a warning, we were all left holding the bag. We had a new album out, were lined up to tour Asia for the first time, and the public was at peak frenzy at that point, frothing at the mouth, climbing fences, clamoring with posters and CD liners and Sharpies held out for their available skin. We had to request the topmost floors of every hotel and reserve the entire floor underneath it with security, just so that we weren't inundated with overzealous fans. The howling of our names was rarely frightening; if I didn't hear the din of people shouting our names from a mob outside, twenty floors below, I would turn off the air conditioner, slide back the curtain a slice, just so I could see out but they couldn't see me, and wait. Their voices were like lullabies.

How could we tour without her? We hatched some ideas: have a body double dance her parts, rework the lighting and fog machines so that her face was perpetually in shadow. Leave the camera off the double as much as possible, except when her back was turned. Feign illness. Feign a broken leg. Feign a death in her family. Fake her own death. (That last one was my dry suggestion.) We even had the costume designer change our outfits so that we wore visors, elaborate eye makeup, silver face paint as cheek contour. Made us look like aliens, unrecognizable. We would have probably gotten away with it for a little while and not lost all of the revenue, but we had to admit that we were playing with fire. Our fans were sharp-eyed, the front rows vicious in their adulation. If they knew that Cassidy had been replaced, there would be hell to pay. All trust lost. I just thought that Cassidy was only a little upset and would rejoin the fold. We started with a lie for the Pacific leg of the world tour.

"One of our members has been admitted to the hospital for exhaustion, vocal exhaustion, and dehydration. Her doctors noticed distressed nodes and recommend an extended rest for her voice. We are excited to visit Asia but regret that it will not be under the best circumstances." It hurt to make that announcement. We said we'd be a trio and hedged around the promise to tour Australia with our full member list.

But all of that did nothing when Cassidy was spotted nowhere near Cedars-Sinai Medical Center in the days before we were to depart for Japan. She was in her old hometown outside of a Whole Foods instead, looking awful, no makeup, and hardly recognizable, but obviously not recuperating at home in Los Angeles. Rumors swirled; we denied.

Merry was photographed tripping over her heels and scraping her knee up on the sidewalk outside of a club. Tabloids gushed that there was trouble between us: a feud, a breakup. We denied.

Yumi went on several high-profile dates with the person who became her husband, just to deflect some of the negative attention (everyone loves a love story). He was a player for the L.A. Clippers, a match made in management heaven. Of course, once the tabloids tasted a tiny hint of blood in the water, they guessed our agenda there too. We denied.

Me, I was photographed shopping at Kitson like nothing was happening. I wanted it to be as normal as possible. A story was drafted that Cassidy's Houston appearance was a family visit during her downtime—a stress-reduction move, nothing more. We denied, we denied, we denied.

As the days slipped by, the countdown to the tour start neared, and we were nowhere closer to having Cassidy back. Merry tried to talk to her; the label execs made some ominous comments. The three of us couldn't get in touch. I remember calling and calling, but her voice mail was full and an automated voice informed me in clipped tones that I would have to try again later. Merry reached out to Emily, recently terminated from Cassidy's employment, who still had a spare key. Emily and Merry let themselves into Cassidy's house to find the furniture still there, but the fridge and pantry were completely empty and there was no human presence in the house.

Merry eventually got a hold of Cassidy, and though she refused to meet with the group, someone convinced her to talk to our PR rep, Justine, and the label. In the same office conference room where we'd met her for the first time, she dropped the bomb: There was no way she could honor her commitments. She was done. Finished. Out.

She surely received a talking-to. She was probably threatened with legalese and contract-waving and a firm finger-pointing at her finances. From what I heard from Marsha's assistant, Nancy, she just sat there. Not defiant, not exhausted, not really anything. "She just looked sad," Nancy had said. "She wasn't scared of them, but something else seemed to have spooked her. She said she was sorry, but she couldn't do it anymore." Nancy had thrown her hands up. "I have no idea what happened. I couldn't get a read on her. She left and that was that."

It was going to get out anyway, Marsha said. Pull off the Band-Aid. Get it over with.

We called a press conference and gathered with our manager, Peter, and Justine. We stated that while saddened by Cassidy's decision to leave the group, it was professionally done and for medical reasons. We assured fans that we were still planning to honor our commitments—but as a permanent trio. Then we left the stage. Justine stayed on a few extra minutes to field more questions. I saw a video clip on my homepage that evening. "Gloss had to replace a member of their group once before, and they don't intend to do it again," she said to one query. "The girls are very excited to begin their tour after this minor setback."

The shit hit the fan. No matter that we were still going on tour. The fans and media despaired that it was the end of Gloss forever. True, the group would not be the same without Cassidy, but it's not like the rest of us weren't there to pick up the pieces. We had been a group before Cassidy, and we could survive without her.

I FLICKED THROUGH Instagram while waiting for Emily to find the dresses. Someone reposted something about Lucy Bowen in my feed; Lucy was yet another woman coming forward about her mistreatment by the great Sterling Royce, who had preyed on her when she was underage. The video auto-played. "I was seventeen and thought I was in love. He was older and should have known better." Lucy hadn't had a hit in years; this was probably the only way for her to make her star shine again, even if Sterling *was* getting his due comeuppance. I kept scrolling.

Cassidy's once-private account was now open, and I followed a trail of tags to glean any information about her life since the fall of Gloss. She'd posted her dog, a different house, a glass of wine. But nothing that told me anything personal.

Emily's voice: "Rose? You still there? There is a gorgeous Dolce dress that would fit you, I think. If your measurements haven't changed too much. Though it might be a touch long."

"I'll swing by and pick it up tomorrow. And Emily?"

"Yeah?"

Emily had known, probably; she was too well connected not to know. But she always kept secrets. Emily was an iron vault.

I cleared my throat. "I know why you want me to talk to the others. But . . ."

"Oh," she said. "It's okay. I shouldn't have pushed you. You can tell them when you're ready."

I knew Cassidy had been upset, but it was unacceptable that she'd left without a word of warning.

And now she'd left this world with the loudest goodbye.

# PRIME (2002)

PART II

PRIME (2002)

## 19.

*January 2002*
*Houston to L.A.*

# Cassidy

Christmas of 2001 felt like a funeral.

Everything I liked about the holiday had lost its luster. I baked cookies, as I usually did, though I couldn't eat them. (I snuck one and couldn't enjoy it; I just worried about its calorie content.) My time was divided between my family's Christmas breakfast and the Hernandez's holiday dinner. Although Alex's parents opened their home to me like I was a member of their family—they'd even hung a stocking for me on their mantel—I was somehow miserable. We'd been so busy recording the second album that I had to get a personal shopper to pick out gifts, and my family squealed over their perfect presents that I'd had no hand in picking out. And even the flight had been a trial: I'd had to travel with three members of Peter's security until I reached my airplane gate, because I had the poor sense to fly commercial.

During Christmas dinner with Alex's family, off-kilter and sullen, I shifted turkey around my plate until it looked like I'd made enough of an effort. Then I found an excuse to sit on the back porch, brooding quietly to myself.

Alex found me trying to pet one of his neighbor's dogs that had jumped the fence. "Are you okay?" he asked.

I avoided his gaze and continued to hold my fingers out to the dog, which wasn't budging. "This dog is like a cat," I muttered.

He slid closer to me and put an arm around my shoulder. I wanted to lean into him, but I was tired. It was both frustrating and a relief that my boyfriend could be so understanding—and that put me into an even worse mood, because were relationships supposed to be so middle-of-the-road? It was fine that there weren't extreme highs or lows, but did this relationship always have to be so *boring*? Even the sex was humdrum.

When I saw Joanna after a long hiatus of being apart, she asked how things were with Alex. All I could do was shrug.

"No spice?" she'd asked.

I had buried my face in my borrowed bedspread. My bedroom had become Katie's room, as the twins had reached puberty and couldn't stand to share anymore. For the time being, I was bunked up with Melanie, who had kindly vacated the room to watch the annual reruns of *The Jet-Setters* with Mom while I had visitors. "It's fine." My voice was muffled in Melanie's pumpkin-spice-scented sheets. "We have moments of glorious chemistry. But then other times . . ." I sat up and wiped my face heavily with the palms of my hands. "I just can't get past the fact that he's my friend."

"You still think of him as a friend, after all this time?" She sounded incredulous. "That's *not* a good sign."

"You don't understand." I finally looked directly at her. "Jo, everyone knows me as 'Sassy.' The other girls, our manager, my friends. Alex is the only person in L.A. who knows me as *me*. He's like my partner. I can't jeopardize what we have together if I *sometimes* think he's just a friend. We are so good together."

"It's not fair to him, though," she said slowly. She flopped down on the sheets with me, belly-down, kicking her feet up behind her. "One day he'll wake up and realize you don't love him in that way."

"Maybe. But I need him, Jo."

"Needing someone isn't the same as loving them. And when you finally know that you don't need him and can be on your own, what are you going to do?"

MERRY BOUGHT A house in Malibu, close to the beach, where she could smell the ocean. Yumi finally decided on a Spanish-style colonial in Thousand Oaks, something with enough breathing room that she could sit outside and barely hear any traffic. Rose chose to do renovations on her Sunset Strip home before moving in, and I was still mulling over one of Yumi's rejects in the Hollywood Hills, which hadn't budged in the market.

We'd cut a new track last September and released it as a single—"Remember," a ballad that coincided with the attacks on New York—and segued into an announcement of a world-wide tour for our second album. The *Prime* tour was kicking off in May, starting with European dates. We were still at work recording the tracks, but our afternoons were currently open while everyone was recovering from the holidays. I decided to reach out to Emma Jake for financial advice. She suggested meeting at an animal shelter. It was a strange request, but then again, it *was* Emma Jake.

"Oh, dear," Emma Jake said when she saw me. She wore a head-to-toe metallic jumpsuit that looked like crushed foil and purple Prada pumps. Her hair was dyed lilac. "You needn't wear a disguise here, Miss Holmes."

Feeling sheepish, I removed the sunglasses and beanie I'd worn to conceal my identity. "Um, Miss Jake? Why are we here?"

Emma Jake gave a theatrical swivel of her head and waved her arms at the beige surroundings. "Why wouldn't we be here?" She blinked owlishly in my direction, as if waiting for me to disagree. "I have an errand to run."

"Oh?" We turned and started walking toward an inner door. A worker held the door open for us wordlessly and then followed us through.

"Yes. Every year I adopt a new dog."

The noise inside the kennels was sharp and loud.

"How many years have you been doing this?"

She hesitated for just a moment, but it was that hesitation that told me everything. Her stillborn baby. Her backup dancer. Her two-year record delay. "Oh. I mean—"

"Well. I have quite a few dogs now. Most of my staff is made up of pet-carers, I daresay." She continued to drift, brushing her hand against the bars of cages, looking at each animal's face and paws.

"That must be noisy."

"What?"

"Your house. With that many animals. It must be noisy."

"I live for it, dear. The best part about having a big house is giving hope to creatures who may otherwise be unlucky." She stopped to gaze at a copper-colored dog whose ropy tail banged rhythmically against the rear of the cage. I realized belatedly that Emma Jake hadn't become a *Sing It* judge to reintroduce the newer generation to her music; she had joined because it was something that would give her a little bit of joy. She was a genuinely nice person who wanted to help shape the green artists of the new millennium. I cocked my head sideways at her as she stretched out a hand and let the dog gently sniff her.

"I wanted to ask your opinion about something."

"Oh? Cassidy, pet this dog." She reached over and grasped my hand. Her skin was dry and her knuckles felt knobby. She guided my outstretched fingers toward the cage. "Now this is a sweet dog."

The volunteer, who had been chaperoning our little conversation a few respectful paces away, shuffled forward a little bit and said, "Pitbulls get such a bad rap. They can be bred to be vicious but with good people they are loyal as can be."

"How old is he?"

"This is a she. Her name is Penny and she's still young, only about a year old."

I pet her a little more, as much as I could through the bars, then withdrew. "Miss Jake?"

"Mm?" We were walking again. Penny gave a burble of disappointment as we moved past her cage.

"I need help with real estate. I'm thinking of buying a place in the Hills."

"Big?"

"Not too big. I mean, Rose is about to own a house with six times the number of bedrooms she'd need. This *is* bigger than I really need, though."

"You can get some dogs."

"Yes, but, uh. I'm not sure if I'm ready for that kind of commitment."

"If you already know it's too big for you, why bother?" She stopped at another cage and petted an inky-black mix of indistinguishable origin.

"I might grow into it . . . Have a family . . ."

"My dear." She straightened up. "We're not the normal. I could give you sound financial advice such as *Buy only what you can afford. Buy only the space you need.* But I'm not going to. You like this house. You want this house?"

"Well, it's beautiful on the inside, great light, a nice yard— not too ornate of a yard—actually, Yumi passed on it because she didn't like the yard—"

"I've seen you on cola cans." She kept petting the mix while looking at me. A pink tongue slithered out and lapped at Emma's wrist, which she did not seem to notice. "Your commercials. Your name on everything. On the Billboard Number One for over two months."

I waited, wondering what she was getting at.

"I've seen your world tour schedule. I know how much merchandise you'll be selling. How many albums you've roughly sold since last July? Honey. Buy whatever you want." She used her other hand to pat me on the shoulder. "I could tell, during *Sing It,* that you were a girl with a pretty good head on her shoulders. Self-critical, yes. Maybe too harsh on herself. But reasonable. Listen, Cassidy." She grew serious. "No matter what you hear, fame and power usually don't change a person. It amplifies who they are already. Some people grow more sinister with money. Some people grow greedier. And some people do good things. So, if you want this house, which sounds like a completely sensible purchase, buy it." Speech over, she turned her head to the volunteer, who acted as though she hadn't heard this sage advice. "Could I take a walk with this one, please?"

So Emma Jake left the shelter with the black dog, and as my driver took me to Alex's dorm, I firmed up my resolve to put an offer on the Hollywood Hills house.

Joseph, his roommate, was out, which made the cozy cuddle on Alex's narrow twin bed even more intimate. I lay flat on my back, sans pants, hair tousled over his pillow. Alex was in pajama pants and his head was nestled into the fleshy area between my breast and armpit. "So you're buying a house," he said while tiptoeing his fingers down the slope of my stomach. I reached down and pulled the covers up to my navel.

"I think so. Wild, right?"

"You're going to live all alone?" He sounded worried.

"In a big house. With tall walls and a locking gate and the best surveillance video that money can buy."

"Maybe you should get your own bodyguard," he said softly, still speaking into my shirt. Silently we both remembered the man reaching out to grab me after our performance on *The Sunrise Show*. And Jerry, leaving that letter for me in the apartment . . .

"Oh!" I said with a start. "I have something for you." I reached for my purse and pulled out his small mint-tin-size camera. "I'm returning this, finally. Merry left it when she moved out." He made a motion to take it, but I stretched it out of reach. "Under one condition."

"What's that?" he said teasingly.

"Don't give the photos willy-nilly to my parents—or even *your* parents. There might be sensitive information on here." I plucked a second roll of film out of the bag as well. "Merry was kind enough to reload for you, but who knows how much of this is her and Grant doing X-rated things."

His eyes shone in the dark room. "You're kidding."

"What, that excites you?" I giggled. "Promise me you'll double-check with me before you share them."

"Duh."

"I'm serious." I felt the laughter ebb away. The familiar chill of anxiety was now stirring in my stomach. "My life feels like such a commodity already. I don't want everything of mine being sold off. Or Merry's life, for that matter."

"Your secrets are always safe with me," he said, voice low.

I looked at him for a long moment, the bulb on the tip of his nose, the mole on his right cheek, and memorized this feeling of trust.

"And Merry's," I said.

"And Merry's," he repeated, just as earnest.

"Okay." I gave him the camera and film, which he clenched in one of his big hands. He put his head back down on my chest and we breathed together.

## 20.

January 2002
L.A.

# Cassidy

The third bedroom was bare, stripped and scattered with forgotten hair elastics and an extra pallet of Cherry Cola. A slice of sunlight, freed from the vertical blinds along the back patio door, glowed yellow on beige carpet. The living-room ceiling fan swung around lazily, shifting the handles of a plastic grocery bag lying on the floor. Rose and I existed together in the apartment like ghosts, rarely there at the same time, but little by little, our belongings disappeared from their places and moved to our new homes.

In a rare moment between recording and training, we were in the apartment at the same time, packing up the last of our belongings. I heard her ripping a roll of packing tape down to the cardboard base and cursing. A moment later, she was framed in my bedroom's doorway, wearing the worn-down tube as a bracelet. "Do you have any more tape?"

She'd been friendlier ever since our visit to see Viv; sometimes, like now, her voice softened and sounded conversational.

I held mine out and our fingers brushed as she took it from me. Her eyes flicked down to my mouth, before she quickly said, "It's weird. Us leaving."

A beat. "We'll be neighbors," I said helpfully. My four-bedroom house with Spanish clay tile was only a few miles from Rose's all-glass-and-concrete dwelling above the Strip.

"I know," she said. "It won't be the same." She seemed to want to say more, but shook her head and padded back to her side of the apartment. I watched her go. I'd miss her barking orders at me early in the morning, I'd miss her indignant sighs when we rode in the SUV together. I would just . . . miss living with her, as strange as that seemed. The realization streaked across my mind, unbidden, surprising me.

Eager to be out of the apartment and away from my confusing thoughts, I crammed the last of my clothes into a laundry hamper and left the last few wire hangers in the closet. I called Lucy. "What if I told you I could make you laugh and cry at the same time?"

She giggled. "Oh, I'm in."

"Will you pick me up?"

When she arrived at the complex, I had an old ratty towel in my arms. "Interesting . . . ," she said, eyebrows raised. I gave her directions to the animal shelter I'd visited with her aunt. She parked her Jaguar in a space and turned to me. "You're kidding, right? You're not going to put some mangy mongrel in my pristine car, are you?"

I held up the towel and smiled winningly.

"Ugh." She clutched the steering wheel until her knuckles were white and pretended to smack her head on it. "Why can't you just use your own car," she groused.

"That would require *buying* one. And I'm already doing enough. A house and a move *and* a world tour *and* a dog . . . Come on."

We exited the car and made our way to the front door. "A world tour and you're adopting a dog now?" She sounded incredulous. "Dogs are hard work. You're not going to bring this dog with you on the tour, are you?"

"First, we have to see if the dog is still there."

She was. Copper-colored Penny, her tail still thumping against the floor, was waiting for me. Lucy's expression softened when she saw her. "Oh, she's a sweetie. But wait." She dug into her back pocket and pulled out a fat silver brick the size of a passport wallet and thick as a deck of cards. She swiveled the screen with a snap, revealing a small keyboard.

"What *is* that?" I asked.

"It's called a Sidekick, won't be *officially* out for a few months," she said absentmindedly, thumbing the pad with both hands. She lifted it to her ear and glanced at me. "You can't do something like adopt a dog and not have the tabloids know about it."

"That's a phone? You're calling the paparazzi? *Why?*"

"It's a good deed! I keep trying to get my aunt to capitalize on her good heart but she refuses. I might as well bring someone else into the light."

I sighed and looked at the worker who had let us in. "Well, it looks like you're going to get some unexpected visitors," I told her.

By the time the three of us—Lucy, Penny, and myself—walked out of the shelter, the parking lot was a full circus. We clambered back into the Jag amid the frenzied clicking of cameras. Luckily, Penny didn't seem perturbed by the noise and enjoyed smearing her nose on the window glass.

"Consider this *my* good deed," Lucy said, putting the car in drive.

"Calling the paps? Hardly."

"No, letting you get my back seat all slobbery." Some of the paparazzi followed us in their own cars. I checked out the back windshield as they continued to give chase while on the 5 and even after we exited Los Feliz.

"Don't go to the house," I said suddenly, worried.

"I wanted to see your new crib!"

"I don't want them to know where I live."

Lucy rolled her eyes. "They're going to find out eventually."

"Can't I just have one minute of peace? Go to your place. We'll lose them after an hour, maybe."

"My parents will *flip* if they see a dog on my leather interior. Or anywhere on my mother's antique rugs. No." She shook her head and handed me her Sidekick. "We'll go to Malibu. Go into my contacts and message Emily Kinnerman. Tell her to meet us at the beach house."

By the time the car slipped past a set of wrought-iron gates, the last persistent paparazzo was left behind. Two other cars—a gleaming black Maserati and a more practical-looking

Toyota—and a short-haired woman in distressed jeans were waiting for us at the end of the drive. "You're still renting this place?" I asked, clipping the complimentary leash to Penny's throwaway collar.

"My parents, well, they need some alone time. It seemed easier to just keep staying here to get out of their way." Lucy waved at the woman. "Emily! This is Cassidy. Cass, Emily. And Emily, this is Penny." She turned to me. "Are you keeping that name?"

"Sure, why not."

"Em is fantastic with animals," Lucy said. "She just recently started her own business as a pet-sitter, and I figured you'd be a good client, considering you seem to know nothing about keeping a dog."

Emily and I shook hands—a little formal, I thought—before Penny jumped excitedly on the woman's legs. We went inside, where we found Sterling Royce riding an exercise bike while shirtless and sporting headphones. Surprised, I asked, "What's he doing here?"

Lucy giggled. "This is Sterling's beach villa." Sterling nodded an acknowledgment at us, but didn't break his pace. "He won't care if you bring a dog in. He has a maid service come in, like, every day. Just don't let her chew on anything." She sat down and started to sift through a cascading pile of architectural and fashion magazines to pluck out the gossip rag. "Sit. Talk."

Perching on the slippery couch reminded me of the last time I was here, the day of Lucy's post-Moldova party, but unlike that dark morning, the midday sky was so blue it was almost white and the room was bathed in an even glow. Sterling's headphones emitted a tinny beat that we could hear from all the way across the open floor plan. He pulled off the headphones and panted, "Lucy, are we having guests over for dinner?"

Lucy raised her eyebrows. "What do you think? His personal chef is the best. She makes everything macrobiotic."

We sat and chatted over a meal of beans, vegetables, and miso soup. Emily, who confided that she was twenty-five, had been a personal assistant to some B-list stars, mostly taking care of errands and pets while nannies oversaw children and drivers kept to schedules. Tired of having her agency take most of her profit, she decided to go into business for herself.

Sterling poured ionized water for the table and listened to the conversation without contributing too much himself.

Lucy was describing the fraught day she'd had on set as she popped open dessert wine—apparently, Sterling ate macrobiotic meals but drank whatever he felt like. He sipped lightly, wetting his lips on the glass, and said, "I thought you were going to quit *The Jet-Setters* if they continued to put you through that bullshit."

"Quit?" I said, alarmed. I knew that the show wouldn't last forever, but Lucy's character was my family's favorite.

Lucy seemed a little embarrassed. "Sterling thinks I should demand more, since I've been there since the start. And if not, I should quit."

"Damn straight," Sterling said. "You're more than just the small screen. You should be in movies. With me. We'll be the next Bacall and Bogart."

"Who?" Lucy asked.

Sterling looked irritated. "How do you not know who Lauren Bacall and Humphrey Bogart are? Do you not know the industry you're in?"

"If you're talking about some old Hollywood couple, I'm still catching up on my movie education," she said. "My parents didn't let me start watching the old-timey stuff until, like, three years ago."

"Don't remind me how young you are." He knocked back the wine. I could not understand Sterling. He was twice Lucy's age and seemed like too much of an adult to be playing house with a teenager. I couldn't see the appeal, unless he liked reminding himself how much more life he'd lived than his girlfriend.

Lucy refilled his glass and poured a generous measure into another for me. Emily took one too, sniffing it heartily and taking a small sip before placing it on the table. Her hand bumped one of the tabloids Lucy had left open and she gave a cursory flick-through. "Oh look," she said, pointing to a photo. "It's you."

"I love when paps get good angles of me," Lucy said, gulping at her wine like it was grape juice. As much as she wanted to act like the lady of the house, I couldn't shake the image of an enthusiastic child pretending to entertain her guests. "I bet they'll print flattering ones of you today, Cass. Just because of your good deed." She lifted the tabloid and scrutinized it. "Well, well, well."

It was a candid from the MVAs, of Yumi in the foreground sipping a drink and me in the background dancing at a club.

Merry must have taken the photo while I danced at the after-party, because there I was, illuminated in direct flash, arms over my head as Stephen bumped up behind me.

My pulse raced as I snatched at the page.

There was only one way the magazine could have gotten it: Merry had pushed the shutter button, and I had returned that roll of film to Alex the previous week.

## 21.

*January 2002*
*Malibu*

# Cassidy

My throat hurt from swallowing its sudden lump.
I wished I hadn't discovered Alex's betrayal. "Do you have anything stronger than this?" I asked, shivering at the sweetness lacing my tongue. "Something with more kick?" The wine was not going to get me through this night.

Lucy pointed a finger at me. "Now you're talking." She rummaged in Sterling's liquor cabinet, hauling out a glass bottle by its narrow neck, and drank a quick swig before pouring two more shots. We cheers'd before knocking the whiskeys back. It burned all the way down my throat and I could feel the outline of my stomach glow with warmth. I still wasn't used to the heat of drinking: it hit me in the knees, making the bones around my shins feel strange and wobbly. I must have let out an involuntary "whew!" because Lucy laughed, a genuine, deep cackle.

I couldn't look at the magazine again; the thought of Alex selling my photos to a tabloid made me thirstier. Tears stung at the edges of my eyes and I drank them down too.

Emily produced some weed and began rolling a joint. As the sky grew bruised with purple, then navy, the fog in my head grew cloudier. I could hear the surf over the disjointed laughter of the girls next to me. Lucy suggested that we play Never Have I Ever.

"How does that one go?" I asked, working thickly through the wall that was my tongue.

"What? How many parties have *you* been to?" Emily asked.

"Here, like this." Lucy touched the cup to her lip as she thought, her eyes closed and thick lashes fluttering. "Never have I ever . . . adopted a dog today!" She opened her eyes and beckoned me to drink. "See? You say what you've never done hoping to get the other person to take a shot. You *did* adopt a dog today, so . . . bottoms up!" Even though she hadn't adopted a dog, she gulped a drink and dropped the glass clumsily on the coffee table.

"I'll be the fair and impartial judge," Sterling said, tipping his neck back and laying his head on the couch cushion behind him. He gazed at us through softly slitted eyes.

"That's no fun!" Lucy shrieked, her inebriation making her louder.

Now it was Emily's turn. "Never have I ever . . . got it on with someone twice my age."

Sterling laughed and poured Lucy a shot.

"Low blow," Lucy said, and drank. "Never have I ever skinny-dipped in a hotel pool."

I was beginning to feel as though I hadn't even lived yet. It was my turn and I couldn't think of anything edgy. Even though I knew none of this mattered, I didn't want to look young and immature in Sterling Royce's eyes. I thought hard and blurted, "Never have I ever graduated from high school."

"Does getting my GED count?" Lucy mused aloud, but Emily and Sterling both took a drink.

"Joined the mile-high club!" said Emily. "Ooh wait. Joined the mile-high club *in a private jet*." Lucy and Sterling drank.

"No fair," Lucy groused. "If you've been on one, you kinda have to."

I figured the best way to understand this strange relationship was to ask. "Never have I ever dated someone who was wrong for me." And yet while I spoke, Alex's face swam into my mind's eye. Lucy waggled her finger tipsily. "That could be interpreted in *so many* ways," she giggled. "But okay, listen. Sterling here is a good example. He's a gentleman, but I'm jailbait."

"But as soon as you're eighteen, we'll go public," Sterling said conversationally, rubbing her shoulder unabashedly. "No one really cares if it's on the down low."

"My birthday is right before the Oscars," Lucy said excitedly. "I'm gonna be his date. He was nominated, you know," she added proudly.

Emily, seemingly bored, tapped her shot glass to resume the game. "That reminds me. Never have I ever had a crush on

somebody that I shouldn't," she said, making a cheersing motion with her cup. I imagined two-toned eyes as I sipped. *I must
be drunk,* I realized.

Lucy grinned slyly at me, and I didn't miss her eyes flickering toward Sterling, making sure she had his attention. "You're
so *innocent.* You've had, like, what, two sips?"

She was already sitting next to me but she moved closer as
she said, "Tell me, Cassidy. Never have you ever *had sex?*"

Although my face was numb from the alcohol, I felt a sharp
rebuke in my chest. I grinned lopsidedly to cover my embarrassment and took a big gulp from my cup.

She scooted closer, our legs touching. "Never have you ever
*made out with a girl?*"

Was this some sort of hazing? Emily just looked on, smiling
serenely, high and content. Sterling was acting nonchalant and
bored, but inebriated or no, I could tell that his interest was
peaked; his half-slitted eyes were trained on us and he didn't
twitch a muscle as he waited for his entertainment to *really*
begin. Is this what most kids our age do? Of course not, they
don't have access to gorgeous, thousand-dollars-a-night villas
in Malibu and quality liquor. But if I had been hanging out
on a college campus with Alex or Joanna or Edie, we'd probably do something like this. I was sure. Act silly, irresponsibly,
experimentally. Make each other laugh. Inch a hand closer up
a thigh.

She was so near. I realized I was leaning in, trying to focus
on her face, but she was blurry from being so close. So close
that her eyes became one green eye, her nose a shadowy slope.
I could smell her breath, boozy and not altogether pleasant, but

there was an underlying sweetness to it. She brushed hair out of my face, the strands sweeping softly against my cheek, and her fingers were gentle against my ear. And then she was on me, mouth full and wet.

My immediate thought was that it was *different,* and her chin rubbing against mine was too smooth without the stubble that scratched me when I kissed Alex. My lips worked slowly, drunkenly; the alcohol was hitting me faster and harder. Her hands were on either side of my cheeks, holding me in place, while mine were in surprised fists at my sides; I realized that my fingers hurt and I sent signals to my hands to relax. *This isn't the woman you should be kissing,* my brain said, tapping softly at my consciousness.

I couldn't hear anything else, anyone else.

Lucy's lips parted from mine and she giggled. Sterling said, with a low chuckle, "Do it again." But I forced a laugh of my own and shook my head.

Looking out, past the fence and toward the public beach, I wondered if there were barracudas of photographers out there, watching and snapping.

I AWOKE ON the slippery couch for the second time, a soft wet tongue lapping at my face as morning light streamed in through the giant windows. Sterling stood nearby, loudly cursing, a hunk of shit smeared on the bottom of a custom-made Italian loafer. My last scrap of sleep evaporated quickly when I saw his irritation. Apologizing, while shoving Emily awake, I grabbed Penny by the collar and we hauled out the front door before Sterling could lecture us.

*Serves you right, you perverted old man,* I thought.

Emily's car was an old Corolla, and dingy enough on the inside that I didn't feel bad about forgetting the old towel to protect her back seat. She burst out laughing. "It's a good thing Sterling Royce has maid service every day. You're kind of a terrible first-time dog mom." She stopped the car by a park and reached for the leash. "But don't worry, I'll help you. That is, if I'm hired."

"Shh, less noise, more quiet. And yes. You definitely are."

Penny had a proper bathroom break and we drove back into the city, where we stopped again at a pet store for essentials before finally making it to my brand-new home at the base of Runyon Canyon. Emily helped set up everything and gave me her number before backing out of the drive. Quiet settled over the house, interrupted only by the soft clicking of Penny's nails on the tile as she explored every space.

I sat on the kitchen floor watching her, thinking. Lucy was not the picture of discretion. She was a few years younger, and had been brought up in this odd Hollywood world, but I could see her possibly talking about what had happened if the opportunity arose. She and Rose were similar in that way; I wouldn't put it past Rose to tell an interesting story if it meant keeping people's attention. The way Lucy had called the paparazzi to get photos of my adopting the dog—would she publicly mention what happened last night?

The more I thought about the kiss, I wondered why I'd felt such a visceral sense of *wrongness*. Lucy was beautiful, absolutely. Her signature lips, with their prominent cupid's bow, had been pillowy and smooth, slippery and wet. Maybe it was because it didn't feel like she kissed me for me, but she kissed me for Sterling. How he watched and enjoyed it, probably. Or maybe it was just guilt—I wondered if Alex would consider a drunken kiss with a girl as cheating, or if he'd welcome it as Sterling did.

*Alex.*

I suddenly remembered the *reason* for my wanting to get into the hard liquor last night. The photo. I scrubbed at my face with one hand. My head was buzzing, like a thousand flies were trapped inside and agitating behind my ears. First things first: I needed to brush my teeth and take a shower. Then I went out and bought a car, feeling reckless and irresponsible as I picked out something cute on a whim—a new Audi that I chose because I liked the rear taillights, nothing more. I let Penny out one more time and then, figuring that there wasn't anything she could destroy yet, locked her in the house.

Rose wasn't there when I showed up at the apartment, but some of her belongings were lying scattered in the living room, ready for pickup. The apartment looked old and weathered. The carpet was well-worn in spots where we and previous tenants had traveled routine paths from the kitchen to the bathroom and the bedrooms farther in. The ceiling fan was still on and keening unevenly. We'd lived here for almost two years and so much had happened. Everything had been a whirlwind, from the first single leaping to the top of the charts to the tour and the promotions. We had all sprung from this little beige apartment; we, as Gloss existed now, had been born here. And for a brief moment, Viv's dark, sad eyes swam to the forefront of my mind. She should've been here; she should be the one buying an expensive house on a hill and impulse-buying a car. Not me. I'd felt so buoyant before, but now my heart plummeted like a rock.

My thoughts were interrupted by a trill coming from my bag: Alex, wanting to see the new house. I hauled the full hamper to my hip, locked the door, and turned the key in at the front desk.

I was slow getting back to the house because I had to stop at the drugstore, so Alex was waiting for me at the front gate. After meeting Penny and rolling around with her on the floor, Alex toured the house, taking in the high ceilings, stucco accents, and gleaming floors. He tested every water faucet and flipped every light switch, peering into the fixtures and taking it all in. Penny followed him from room to room, tail sweeping back and forth furiously. "It's a really nice place," he said when he finally saw the last bit—the courtyard outside that was bookended by two separate wings of the house, studded with newly installed security cameras positioned every which way.

I shrugged halfheartedly. "Yeah, it's fine."

His expression was incredulous. "Fine? You could stick three families in here and it's only *fine*? You bought your first house and you're not excited at all?"

My eyes wandered through the courtyard, the trees bordering the lawn, the new Audi sitting in the long driveway that disappeared over a crest in the hill. Then the two-story buildings, capped with beautiful Spanish tile and warm pink stone that looked purple in the dark. But I couldn't muster any enthusiasm. "Let's go inside," I said, and Penny led the way back into the kitchen. I sat on a cardboard box and picked through my plastic laundry basket. Alex slid down the kitchen island and stretched his legs out across the floor.

"I don't get it," Alex was saying. "If you don't love it, why did you even buy it?"

I pulled out the magazine that I'd bought at Walgreens. I flipped through to the dog-eared page slowly, deliberately. I had been shocked and angry before, and had almost been looking forward to this confrontation, but now that it was about to happen, my heart beat too loudly in my ears. I took a short breath. "What is this?"

"What's what?"

I shoved the magazine at him and jabbed a finger at the glossy spread. "This."

Alex's eyes widened and he grabbed it. "Wait. That's the—"

"Mm-hmm." I crossed my arms.

"But. Hey. You don't think that *I*—"

I leaned forward on my elbows, clasping my fingers together so that I wouldn't hit him. "I do."

"But Cass. There's got to be a perfectly good explanation for this."

"There is. Easiest one: you sold me out."

"I can't believe you'd even *think* that." His tone turned defensive now. "And besides, *I* saw a lot of things I wanted to ask *you* about in those pictures. You sure look cozy with Stephen."

"Um, wait. You're going to turn around and lecture *me*? We already talked about this. That stunt at the MVAs—"

"Look. I get it. He's a big star, you're a big star. Whatever. And yeah, you told me nothing was going on, but you're out *all the time,* and I barely see you—"

"It's not my fault that I have to work!" I exploded. "You think this is *fun* for me? I'm always *on*. If I'm not *on,* I'm sleeping. You. Me. This is the only real thing I have, and if *you* can't trust me—and I can't trust *you*—what are we even doing together?"

"Hold on a minute. Are you saying that we should *break up*? Look, you *can* trust me! I just don't know if I trust the people you're with, and—"

"Oh, that's rich." I curled the magazine into a tube and smacked my hand with it. "You, who sold our pictures. Did they pay a lot? Are you good on beer money for the year? The decade?"

"Are you listening to yourself?" he said, right as I barreled on with, "Is it covering your tuition?"

"Now hold on a minute." His neck had turned dark. "What are you trying to say?"

"That you'd make a lot of money selling a picture to a tabloid and you'd feel guilty enough to start bringing up some *other guy* like I'm cheating on you to cover it up! Which I'm not!" A flash pierced my mind: Lucy's cupid's bow coming toward me. Her blurry green eyes.

"Fine. Whatever. You're not messing around. Okay."

There was a long pause where we didn't look at each other. I said, "Fine." Another long silence.

Finally, he said, in a softer voice, "I swear I didn't sell them." His voice carried a hint of irritation. "If you were so worried, why didn't you develop the film yourself and give me only the *approved* ones?"

"Of course. This is all *my* fault." I let my head drop to my knees and hugged my legs, trying to calm my shivering body. Alex put a warm hand on my back and rubbed it back and forth. I fought to gain control of my breath again. Penny nuzzled her wet nose into my hair and licked my forehead. Something inside of me broke again, and a laugh fizzled out of my mouth. "This is all so stupid."

It wasn't just the argument. It was everything: the house, the car, the dog, the album, the photo, the security cameras, the bodyguards, the tour, the workouts, the eating, the not-eating, the loudness that was so loud, the quiet that was too quiet, the cardboard box I was still sitting on, the boy sitting next to me on the kitchen floor.

"It is. It was stupid. I'm sorry."

"Sorry you sold it?"

He stopped rubbing my back. "That's not what I meant."

I didn't say anything else.

"I know it's been tough," he said slowly, "and I'm sorry I didn't know the rules about getting prints developed. And I know you get this way sometimes so I'm going to just let it go . . ."

"Aren't you a big person." My voice was caustic, muffled in my knees.

"Cass, you're a little . . . emotional. I don't mean it in a bad way. But I have to ask . . . have you been seeing a doctor? Maybe talked to Dr. Brant since you left Houston? I just feel like you could use medication or something . . ."

My head snapped up. "You're telling me to get *medicated*?" Penny slunk away as our voices rose, tail in between her legs. "Oh great, and now you've scared the dog!"

"*You* scared her," Alex fumed, also standing. "Anyway, okay, I'm sorry I brought up the medication thing. But maybe you *should*. Talk to someone, I mean."

A laugh bubbled out of my chest. "Talk to *who*? I can't *wait* to see them on *JMC* dishing about me."

He threw his hands in the air. "Okay, never mind! But just remember, Cass, not everyone is around to sell you out. You have to trust somebody sometime. And if not *me*, who *else* do you have?"

## 22.

---

*Sunday*

# Merry

When I dragged myself out of bed on Sunday morning and started down to the kitchen, I could hear the digital murmur of voices on a television whispering through the hallway air. I paused in front of Sunny's closed bedroom door to listen. She must have fallen asleep watching a show and let it go on all night. I made my way downstairs.

Raul was cutting a fresh loaf of bread, still steaming from being pulled from the oven. When he saw me, his face broke open with a grin. "You always have perfect timing," he said. "It's as if you know that the food is ready." He dabbed a pat of butter on a piece and placed it on a plate in front of me. I bit into it, the melted butter smearing on my top lip and the hot bread burning the roof of my mouth. "Mmm. Heaven."

"Will Soleil be down soon, you think?" he asked.

"Her? On a Sunday? It's more likely she'll be eating this bread at noon."

"I heard her rummaging around in the den last night," he said, sawing a slice off for himself. "Then knocking around in her room early this morning. I think she's been up."

"How strange." I chewed another bite. "What does a lady have to do for some strawberry jam?"

"Who says you're a lady?" He winked and leaned over for a kiss. It would be cheesy for anyone else to say it, but from Raul it was beautiful. He worked long and erratic hours and still baked for me.

"Don't distract me with your dreamboat ways." I hopped up from the chair, popping the last bite into my mouth and speaking around it. "I'll grab Sunny so she can get this bread before it cools down. Cut me another piece, will you? And don't skimp on my jam!" I took the stairs two at a time, in an inexplicably good mood.

When I knocked on Soleil's door, the TV sounds muted. "Sunny?" I spoke through the wood. "Fresh bread! Want some?"

There was some muttering.

"I didn't hear that. Can I come in?"

I swung open the door, expecting to see my fourteen-year-old in her hideous pizza pajamas, lying sideways in her bed watching sitcom reruns. Instead, she was on the floor, surrounded by photo albums open to various pages and had turned the TV screen off.

"What's all this?" I asked. They were my old albums. I

wondered if maybe she was digging up past photos of herself to share on social media. Kids these days are always looking for ways to feel nostalgic, even though they haven't lived long enough to earn the right.

"Nothing," she muttered.

"Raul made fresh bread. Come downstairs and have some," I offered.

"Yeah, okay." She made no effort to move.

I turned on my heel to leave, but one of the albums caught my eye. It was small and green, a fat book that had a cellophane sleeve for one print on each side. "I haven't looked at this in a while," I said, returning to the inner part of the room and perching on her bed. The book looked the same as before, when I had it in my hands. "I should've started going through these right after I found out." Flipping the page, there was a shot of Cassidy, chewing gum. A photo of a billboard with our album cover on it. The Gloss girls in Times Square.

I thumbed backward a little, seeing yellowed pictures I'd clipped from tabloids, of Grant and me. It had been silly to cut them out, let alone save them, but nineteen-year-olds can still harbor childish tendencies. I smiled at them and kept flipping back. I knew that I wouldn't see what I didn't want to see in the album, that there were no traces left of *him* there, and that I had protected myself from the past very well. But the thought never left my mind; it was just diminished, shrunken in a tiny corner, and when I remembered that I wouldn't have to remember, it sprang up again. I slapped the album closed.

"I'll see you downstairs," I said.

"Wait." She turned the TV back on. It was paused on an old episode of *Behind the Music*. I swallowed reflexively and turned my eyes to her. I knew this episode. I'd lived it.

"My dad," she said.

"You don't have a father." The stupid Instagram post where she talked about being a bastard. The headache from Friday. I couldn't have possibly thought it would be swept away so easily, could I?

"It's Grant Kidd, isn't it?"

I squinted at her. "Honey . . ."

"The timeline matches up." She pressed play and the picture on the TV jolted forward.

Merry Gloss had a number of PR issues that the other girls took issue with—most notably her romantic entanglement with then-married Grant Kidd of the Grammy-nominated alt-rock band Illuminated Eyes, for which Gloss was an opener in 2001. Grant had been famously married to Hollywood bombshell Marisa Marcheesa when Merry and Grant started their torrid affair while on tour . . .

"Turn that off," I snapped, reaching over and grabbing the remote from her hand. "It's trash."

"I deserve to know," she insisted. "I know I'm not really fatherless."

"We won't discuss it now. Come downstairs and eat. But don't believe everything the tabloids want to sell you." I slammed the remote down on the floor, where it bounced on the carpet and skittered under her bed.

Raul was concerned when I returned to the kitchen. "You left so happy and returned with a storm cloud over your head."

I swept by him, ignoring the perfectly brown toast with the perfectly red strawberry jam and stalked to the coffee machine to pull myself an extra-strong cup.

"Maybe she should know," he said quietly. I had told Raul, of course.

"She's not the picture of discretion, is she? She's too young and has a motormouth and she will learn when she's eighteen." I slammed the cup down on the counter and shoved it under the spout. "Or old enough to show some sense. Which may be never."

"She is asking now," Raul said gently. "I do not want to interfere too much, but she is my daughter now. And I think it would be wise to let her know more about herself—and to let her know more about her mother."

I watched the coffee pour as he stepped next to me and clasped my shoulders. His lips were feather-soft as they touched my temple. "I will go out to find some new running shoes and will be gone for a few hours. You and Soleil can have the house to yourselves."

I nodded, thinking.

How do you live knowing the real version of yourself, while every other person in the world thinks they know a different version of you? Can the fake persona eat your real self, mimic so many of your truths that her falsehoods become your reality?

Raul was right, though. I did not want my daughter to know

the constructed version of Merry that was out in the world. I wanted her to know me. But how much could I tell her?

ONCE THE TESLA was out of the garage, I went back up to Sunny's room. "We need to have a talk," I said.

She sulked. "I don't think what I did was wrong."

"Justine had to clean up your mess—"

"*You're* the one who should be saying you're sorry!"

"Do you know how much of a headache this has been, for years—"

We both stopped and glared.

"There is no point in trying to dig up the past," I said. "Your father did not stick around. I raised you myself from the first doctor's appointment. *Emily* is more of a father than he was. So I would appreciate it if you would drop it."

Her voice rose into a whine. "It's not fair! Everyone else has a dad."

I held up a hand to stop her from going further. "I know you *won't* drop it, so I am willing to give you enough information that you stop telling people that you are a . . ." I didn't want to say *bastard*.

"Mom." Her brow furrowed. "Everyone else has a dad. Even if"—she raised her voice higher as she saw me take in a breath—"Even *if* they're divorced or adopted or whatever, they know. I don't get why you won't let me know about my family history."

"All I can tell you right now is that your father is *not* Grant Kidd. I'm sorry."

"But the timeline—"

"Grant and I were over before you came along. I don't want you to bother a man who is completely unconnected with you. I will tell you the full story when you are older. I promise."

I saw her shoulders slump, her neck bend forward. Her lash line started to blush as tears glistened on the rims. Her pale hair shivered as she began to cry in frustration. She looked like my tiny Soleil again, small and blotchy, round-faced and wide-mouthed. I knew how she felt. I wanted to let her feel everything and know everything. But she was only fourteen and there would be time enough for heartbreak in the future.

I stretched my arms out for a hug, but she ducked and squirmed away. Just like that, she was back to being a long-legged teenager who escaped her room and darted down the stairs. My body sagged onto her bed as my eyes raked over the photo albums still cascading across her carpet.

That bastard. That fucking bastard.

## 23.

# Cassidy

Our second tour was only a month away and everything became more intense: training, choreography, meetings, vocal coaching, wardrobe fittings. My phone stayed busy with dings and rings, and I even had a fax machine installed at my house for updated schedules that rolled in at six in the morning while Penny barked at it. I was so on edge all the time that I developed insomnia, while Rose had some sort of perfection-related anxiety. Peter palmed off prescription-strength sleeping pills to mitigate my new problem, and Rose got Xanax.

Awards season crept up as we were nearing the end of our album production. In February, Gloss's eponymous debut was nominated for two Grammys, but we didn't win either. We were working with Jake Jamz again to get our second studio album, its second single, and its music video out on time, so, though we attended as a group, our focus was elsewhere and the letdown wasn't very bitter. We knew *Prime* was the better album.

As the plans for the tour continued to ramp up, seeing Stephen St. James at Big Disc's office became a regular occurrence; he was cutting a new album and had meetings as well. We would brush past each other in the lobby or down a hallway, him going one way and the rest of us flowing in a different direction, and yet each time I still felt the jolt of seeing that roman nose glisten under a fluorescent light. He would give us a nod when we passed, a short jerk of his chin while his eyes swept over our faces and—I thought—lingered on mine. There was something about being in his presence that made me feel tense and fluttery and small.

On one of the days that I was running late to a meeting and alone in the hallway, our paths crossed again. This time, instead of Stephen's gaze pinning on mine and then shifting away, he grinned. Hesitatingly, I smiled back. He slowed down, and I did too, so that we were walking toward each other as if our meeting had been planned. "Say," he said, when our feet drew close.

"Say." I'd become much more aware of every movement I made.

"I've been invited to the Oscars this year."

"You were? Congratulations." I tried to sound gracious, but my tongue felt too swollen for my mouth.

"Nominated for Best Original Song, you know." He said it casually, as if he didn't want me to make a big deal out of it, but

I could tell that was the opposite of how he felt inside. I *hadn't* known about the nomination but pretended that I did.

"That's amazing!" I effused. I wondered if he had stopped me just to brag about this achievement, and my insides shriveled a little. I thought we were becoming friends. We'd weathered a few big moments together, and he'd *kissed* me at the last awards show we were at together, so it didn't seem outside of the realm of possibility that he'd felt something for me. "I have a meeting to get to . . ."

"Sassy, wait."

I stood still. His eyes were such a clear blue, icier than Merry's.

He corrected himself. "Cassidy, I mean. I feel like you're my good-luck charm. Would you go with me? Be my date?"

"Your good-luck charm?" I repeated. There was a quick fizz in my head, effervescence as I processed his words.

"You were there when I won *Sing It* and the MVAs. I was hoping you could work your magic again."

Reality was quickly catching up to me. "I have a boyfriend."

"I don't really care about that." His mouth quirked up. "This doesn't have to be a real date. Just be next to me."

A door behind him banged open, catching our attention and making Stephen swivel on his heel. Peter poked his head out and snapped his fingers twice. "We're going over the last numbers now. Get in here!"

I gave Stephen what I'd hoped was an apologetic smile and started moving past him. "I'll have to think about it. Let me call you."

During the meeting, we went over our finalized tour dates, which would be announced after *Prime* dropped. The first single, "Remember," had already been shared last September, but the executives were interested in a happier angle for the second and chose the hard-hitting and beat-heavy "Prime," for which the album was named. Peter excitedly announced that our fans in Japan were clamoring for more music and that we would record a special track for the international album. From early May until late August, we were going to travel three continents with more than sixty concert dates, and from where I was sitting, I couldn't discern whether I felt like this was a dream or a trap.

Thoughts swirled in my head as I was driven home. I hadn't seen my family since Christmas. Alex and I were still noticeably cool toward each other after the tabloid photo argument, even though that had been more than a month ago, and because it was midterms week, it was difficult to pin down any of the Houston crew long enough to talk to them on the phone. The only constants in my life were Gloss, Jake Jamz, Peter, and Penny—and with Penny, there was Emily, who was already there when I arrived inside my gate.

"I brought in your mail and already took Penny for a quick walk," she said, shouldering her bag to go leave.

"Thanks, Em. You're a lifesaver."

"It makes me nervous that you're only relying on cameras and don't have a guard on duty all the time." She looked around at the impeccably decorated house: all creams and pale pinks. A magazine specializing in interior design had scooped the real estate listings and knew when I'd bought the place; they'd offered to outfit the entire house professionally and for free if they could showcase the work in their magazine. It could have been a massive breach of privacy, but because the decor was nothing that I'd picked out, the article and its accompanying photos felt as personal as a hotel room. The house didn't really feel like a *home,* though, when I looked at it. A seashell motif danced around the molding and everything was the color of sand. The only part that felt like home was the smell: sun-soaked fur, my favorite shampoos and soaps in the bathrooms, the same fabric softener my mother used at our house in Houston, so the air was a mixture of lavender, Downy, and Penny.

"Why? Did something happen?" I asked.

"Nothing, just . . . you're so alone out here. And this vicious creature"—she crouched and tousled Penny's ears—"is such a sweetheart that she'd *lick* an intruder to death."

I walked with Emily to the front door. "I know. I had a panic button installed in case of intruders."

"Well, that's something. But I know a guy. Let me see if he's free."

When I brought it up to Alex on the phone that night, while I morosely stabbed at a seventeen-dollar spinach salad, we didn't mention the guy in the Rockefeller basement. "I asked Emily for a referral," I told him. "Maybe she can find me a better stylist, too."

"What's wrong with the one you already have?"

"She always dresses me as part of an ensemble. But I was just asked to go to the Oscars without the rest of the girls, so . . ."

"You were asked to go to the Oscars? Without Gloss?" He sounded surprised.

I knew that mentioning it would be like picking at a scab, but if I ended up agreeing to go with Stephen, Alex would find out anyway. "I was asked to be a personal, platonic date for someone."

His voice deepened in annoyance. "Is that *someone* Stephen St. James?"

"It might be. So what if it is?"

"Why are you immediately on the defensive?"

"Because you used *that tone*. He's an industry friend, that's all."

"You might think he's an 'industry friend,' but I guarantee you, that guy is fantasizing about you. He's already kissed you on national television! And you're going to the *Oscars* with him? The Oscars is, like, even more of an aphrodisiac than prom!"

"Stop being disgusting," I said, as the fax machine trilled and a new page began to spit out. I watched its baleen teeth unroll another schematic for the stage design of the "Prime" music video. "And standing on the red carpet is the least sexy thing imaginable. It's being sweaty and people yelling at you and getting blinded by flashes. Going would be a favor. To a friend. End of story."

"See it from my point of view." I imagined him in his dorm room, surrounded by dirty socks and his eavesdropping roommate. "I was your friend. I was *just* your friend. Then we became something more. The pathway to a relationship with you *is* friendship. And this guy—he's rich, he's famous, he's talented. He can have any girl he wants."

The last thing I wanted to do now was to have a fight on

top of everything else. I tore the fax page from the machine and balled it up without analyzing it, kicking it across the floor for Penny to chase. "Alex, I'm sorry, but I don't have time to deal with your insecurity. If you can't deal with me going to an industry event with someone who is just a friend, I can't deal with you at all."

"I just don't trust him. And the news is going to eat it up. I'll have to deal with seeing you and him in the tabloids for weeks as they speculate on whether you're pregnant with his baby, or whatever."

"I thought you didn't read those."

"I don't. But Joe already thinks Stephen is into you, and—"

"Joe, your roommate Joe? Joe knows *horseshit*! Why are you listening to some idiot who doesn't know anything instead of listening to *me*, the person who *would* know?"

"I knew that this would happen someday. You could have at least had the decency to tell me in person. God, this is just like Brittany! You know how much I hate this."

"How is this like Brittany? How? Explain it to me!"

"We're on the phone now, aren't we? You couldn't do this face-to-face?"

I closed my eyes and let them rest, feeling the soft flutter of eyelashes against the tops of my cheeks. I put a hand to my temple, keeping the light vertigo that swept over me at bay. There is something about hunger, once it passes a certain point, where it doesn't even hurt anymore. Your body accepts it, doles out comfort, as if soothing the stricken stomach. Your emptiness becomes a new fullness; you are as dense as a collapsing star; your limbs twitch, muscles tremble; but most of all, your mind gets as calm as a pond. So Alex's outburst seemed to implode in a muffled burst somewhere in the background. "I didn't want for this phone call to happen this way," I murmured finally.

I guess it didn't sound like enough because he hung up on me.

I wiped at my face with two fingers but there were no tears. I was just so tired. Another trill, and the fax machine came alive again. The paper grunted out, long as a palatial scroll. I let it roll out onto the floor.

There was always a fire to put out. I stored the salad in the fridge, made myself a hot cup of tea, and decided that Alex could use the night to cool off. Though it felt like we'd been doing that a lot lately.

THE BUDGET FOR the "Prime" music video was, easily, fifty times that of "Wake Up Morning." Big Disc shelled out for an enormous studio, a fantastical concept, and a celebrity music video director to bring it all to life. Noah Decker was the visionary behind some of the best music videos in the late nineties and the label was ecstatic to get him on the roster.

He had pulled out all the stops—*NSYNC got a rotating cube? Well, Gloss got underwater tanks and waterproof cameras. Decker's ideas included flimsy chiffon, extra-long colorful wigs, and glitter. Lots of glitter. The scene-by-scene cards had us dancing underwater, contrasted with futuristic silver outfits as we danced in a white laboratory. There was some sort of story, something about evolution maybe, but the point was that we were going to be ethereal and then hard, dream women and then assassins. Decker had helped musical acts win about half of the last few years' Music Video Channel MVAs, so it was unspoken that we would go along with whatever he suggested.

Day one was for the silver outfit scenes, which he wanted to nail down because the choreography had to be perfectly synced. We ended the first day with various close-ups. We had to have our faces wiped clean after all the sweating we did, and the makeup applied again. Though the set was bustling, I could see Decker leaning over Merry, giving her close instruction on the part she was about to film. She nodded and studied the cards, but I noticed that his gaze lingered on her neck and slid down, checking out the décolletage that her loosely tied robe laid bare.

Day two was more harrowing. The water tank was ten feet tall, standing erect in the middle of the studio. We were to lower ourselves down into the tank for individual filming. Yumi went first and took direction well; when she emerged, she was smiling. "Why are you so happy?" I asked, as she came dripping out of the tank, down the rolling step-ladder, and was wrapped in a waiting towel. I was in line to go next.

"I love the concept of this video," she panted, wiping off the bottom of her feet so she wouldn't track water back to the styling area. "Nothing about being Tasty. Just feeling the music."

Peter was on set too, and barked, "Sassy! Get in!"

Submerging myself in the water was peaceful, even with all the background lights and bustle; once my head went under, all of that seemed so far away, and I was floating in a muffled room. I trusted the director to get the footage he needed, and just sank and swam and *felt*. "Prime" was not a sad song, or even a particularly emotional one, but I pretended that it was and hoped that Decker would like it.

"Beautiful," he said, as I lifted myself onto the lip of the tank and scrambled over the side, once again graceless. Rivulets of water ran down my face, making it hard to see, and I almost slipped on the ladder coming down. "A natural," he proclaimed.

Then it was Merry's turn, but she needed more direction. After I changed out of the wet chiffon and into a dry robe, I watched as she made all hard angles, basically vogueing with her palms flat and thumbs tucked in. All those years of swim practice made her involuntarily sharp in the water. Decker tried to coach her through, but even I could tell that he wasn't completely satisfied with her performance.

She popped her head out of the top and listened as he gave her more notes, but they fell on deaf ears. Her performance didn't change.

"It's fine, your turn is over," Decker said, though it wasn't kindly.

Merry propped her arms on the edge of the tank and kicked. "If you could just give me better instruction—"

"I've tried. You're just trained to be a fish in water. I need a mermaid."

"I can do it—"

"We can't waste all day trying to get something out of you. But we probably can use something. No, no," he shouted, as she slid back in, trying to make a point. He told an assistant, "Pull her out of there."

Peter, ever the manager, barked, "Meredith, we're already behind schedule. Stop wasting time."

She was annoyed at herself, I could tell. The assistant reached for her arm but she shook him off and climbed out on her own.

Rose was waiting at the base of the ladder. "Don't," she warned, as Merry climbed down, ready to argue with Decker. "Go."

Merry was close to tears, frustrated with her performance, and stalked back to the styling area. Everyone was watching Merry, and thus took their eyes off Rose, who, at that moment, was climbing the ladder for the final turn. Three other girls' wet footprints had slicked the treads. Three other girls' palms had greased the handrails. When she got to the top, her feet slid out from underneath her.

We all heard the crash and sucked in a collective breath. Rose had grabbed the rail with one hand when she'd fallen, but that made her back slide along the ladder steps. Merry whirled, diverting her concern from her self-pity to Rose's safety. She was halfway up the slick ladder, her own feet sliding underneath her, when Rose hissed a breath. "I'm okay," she gasped, sitting up.

"Do you want to take a minute?" Decker asked.

"Let me just catch my breath."

She gingerly slipped into the water for a few minutes, but then Rose did the unthinkable: she asked to be excused.

"Are you sure?" Decker said. "We don't have much footage of you. The video will be unbalanced."

She was already hauling herself out of the tank with her

arms. "I'm going to be honest. I think I need to go to the emergency room."

"I'll go with you," I said automatically, my concern immediate and genuine.

Rose winced as she gingerly and carefully made her way down the steps. "No, don't do that. I can go by myself."

"But . . ."

Decker looked annoyed. "How about I tell you who stays and who goes? I understand if you're hurt and you think it's necessary to get to a doctor. Cassidy, we have the most footage of you, so you can go with her. Merry, stay behind and try the tank again. Maybe we'll get a few more seconds of you to put in the video."

I looked at Rose, bent over double, tying the ends of a terrycloth robe around herself. I remembered the long sheet of fax paper detailing the plans for this video and hoped it would continue smoothly without Rose and me there. "I'll stay here with Merry," Yumi said, as if guessing my thoughts.

"Whatever you want," Decker barked. "Merry, sweetheart, let's get you back in the water."

**Excerpt from *GLOSS: The Rise and Fall of the Millennium's Biggest Girl Group* by Christina Silverman, published 2013**

"PRIME": The Iconic Single

Yes, Britney danced with a snake; yes, Christina wore chaps and got *dirrty*. But the girl group moment of 2002 that blew our socks off was the entire rollout of Gloss, their second studio album (*Prime*), and their single of the same name.

How do we describe *Prime*? We first have to describe everything going on with Gloss in 2002. High off the success of their first album and a nationwide tour, the group seemed to be poised to take over the world. Gifted with monikers that showcased their personalities, Rose "Rosy," Meredith "Cherry," Yumi "Tasty," and Cassidy "Sassy" Gloss were signed to headline a world tour. Their first single from *Prime*, "Remember," was the song used on every radio and television station when the 9/11 attacks were mentioned, as the proceeds from the single's sales went to a memorial foundation.

The girls shot the "Prime" music video with visionary director Noah Decker, and it proved to be one of his most notable works. Winning every category of music video award from that year, it was a seminal piece that perfectly showcased the feeling of the early aughts: the future, hurtling into the new millennium! Beautiful women enjoying their own sexual agency!

By now, the iconic moments of the video have been seen and repeated in loops, over and over, across the internet for over a decade. There's the full group, throwing down that sick choreography in shiny silver suits, in perfect synchronization—so

perfect that there was talk that the dancers were computer sim-
ulated, but then behind-the-scenes footage unearthed in 2010
showed that the girls really did dance that tightly. There's Sassy,
floating in blue water, wearing a loose lavender dress that teases
a hint of her nipples at the edge of the frame. The only stark
color in the palette is her bright-red lipstick. Then there's Rosy
in the sensual close-ups that seemed to be required of all music
videos, but she's not smiling, she's not frowning—she's staring
with fierce intensity from one side of the screen to the other,
never making eye contact with the viewer. It was a bold choice
from the director, when all other music videos seemed to soft-
focus on a woman performer's face, gazing longingly into the
lens's eye. Rumor has it that Decker was unnerved by Rosy's
heterochromia, so he showed one side of her face at a time,
never both together.

If you watch the video closely, you'll see that Rosy has only
a few seconds of footage underwater. Sources say that she was
injured on set and fractured a vertebra. It was this injury that
began her alleged relationship with painkillers. This was also the
music video that was shot right before Sassy's broken arm that
plagued her throughout the first part of the *Prime* tour. Then, of
course, there was the infamous fire . . .

## 24.

# Cassidy

When I passed by Stephen in the hallway the next day, I felt like it was by divine design and not an accident. "Oh, the Oscars," I said. "I'll go with you."

The dimples made an appearance. "Good. I'll pick you up?"

"Fine."

"And Merry . . . she's okay?"

I felt my eyebrows lift in surprise. "*Merry?* Why wouldn't she be?"

Sliding by me in the hallway, he called, "Check a newspaper," and swept around a corner.

*A newspaper?* I could just ask Merry once I got to the meeting. But when I entered the room, the only other person there was Yumi. "Did I miss something?" I asked.

Yumi sighed and pushed a ratty copy of the *Los Angeles Times* across the conference table toward me. It was folded open to an article: "House Fire in Malibu Torches Kidd Home—Arson Suspected."

I fingered the headline. "Grant's house? 'Firefighters were called to a blaze in Malibu on Wednesday evening. Once on the scene, around two a.m., they found heavy fire blazing in the west wing of the mansion. Owner Grant Kidd was not home at the time; the fire department was alerted by a guest staying at the house.' Let me guess. Merry is the guest."

"She is still at the hospital getting checked out for smoke inhalation," Yumi said.

"They think someone set the fire on purpose?" I said, reading on.

"I think they suspect Marisa. Sorry," she said, yawning. "We didn't get out till close to eleven. How's Rose?"

"She's okay. Bruising on her spine or something. She kept mentioning the pain she had, even though they said it would go down in a few days, so they gave her a script for Vicodin. She'll be good as new in a week."

When Yumi learned I was going to the Oscars, she invited herself over for the prep. She sounded as though it was like going to the biggest prom ever. I hired Gail, an Oscars stylist who wore red-soled Louboutins and said such things as "you have the neck for this," and she in turn referred me to a makeup artist who arranged to do my hair and makeup at the house.

Now, two days later, I was sitting in a barstool in my master bedroom while the Gail-appointed hair stylist curled tiny pieces of my hair and Yumi roamed around. "Strange, about the house," Yumi remarked, as her fingers skimmed the bottom of my simple, sky-blue sheath made of slippery silk. The dress was draped over a hanger by its narrow camisole straps, and Gail had instructed me to only wear strategic body tape, which made me immensely nervous.

"What do you think of it? I know you didn't like the driveway—"

"Not *this* house," she said, sounding annoyed. "Grant's house. You know, I think it's weird how the police aren't arresting Marisa for torching it."

"Maybe it *was* an accident." I shrugged. The stylist lightly touched my shoulders to remind me not to move.

Yumi fingered my jewelry—long drop earrings and a thread-thin necklace with teardrop gemstones, nestled on velvet beds—and changed the subject. "How is Alex taking this whole Oscars thing?"

"Not great. I think we're over." I hadn't heard from him since the fight, and he'd hung up on me. Wasn't that a breakup? I'd been too busy to devote much attention to his absence in my life. And if it didn't hurt, then maybe I *didn't* need him . . .

The gate buzzer rang and Yumi's head swiveled toward the open bedroom door, as though she could see whoever was down there. "I can get it," she said, already scurrying downstairs. A moment later, she returned with a frown. "Speak of the devil."

I pulled away from Antonio's latest brush, swiveling in my seat. Alex had followed Yumi and was now hovering on the other side of the threshold. A quick glance at his expression told me that he knew exactly what day this was.

I was careful not to show any emotion. "Could I have the room, please?"

The stylist said, "Are you sure, hon? The hair's not quite finished—"

My eyes didn't leave Alex's. "I'm sure."

Antonio excused himself and started down the stairs, but Yumi lingered by the door. Hesitating, she said, "I'll be downstairs if you need me."

"No, it's okay," I said. "Could you have Antonio leave the lipstick on the kitchen island and tell him to send me the bill?"

When the house was quiet, Alex and I simultaneously let out a long breath.

"Hi," he said. His voice was low, guarded.

"Hi."

A long pause. Alex stood in a darkened corner of the room, shadowed in blue, a perfect embodiment of an unshaved college student with uncombed hair and a wrinkled T-shirt. The mirror's reflection showed me sitting under a spotlight of white, my legs exposed from under a short dressing robe. I looked almost screen-ready, minus the sapphires I still needed to apply to my ears and neck. The disparity between our two lives was suddenly very clear. I spoke carefully.

"So . . ."

He ran his hand over the chair before he spoke. It was a heavy, tense moment that felt longer than it was. "I had this whole thing planned out. But it's kinda left me." He gave a tiny huff of a laugh. I folded my fingers together, checking my manicure. When I looked up again, he had a fierce expression on his face that made my heart drop into my stomach.

"I just wanted to tell you how fucked up all of this has been. We've been friends for how long, Cassidy? And we've always talked. We've worked through our issues. I supported you throughout this entire singing career, even before you moved out here. And what do you do? You treat me like shit, like I'm some *groupie* or something, instead of a real person you knew when *you* were a real person. God, are you *even* a real person anymore?"

It stung to hear this from Alex, who was normally so mild-mannered. "*Of course* I'm a real person. Why would you say that?"

"Look at how you've been acting. Like going to this show with a guy who obviously digs you."

"Not *obviously*. Not everything you see *out there* is real, Alex. Do you understand *that*? He's acting a part, I'm acting a part. *That* is the act."

He crossed his arms. "So you don't have feelings for St. James?"

I batted this away. "That doesn't even matter. Do you have *any idea* how *hard* it is to be me? To have this pressure to be perfect all the time?"

"*Fuck*, Cassy!" he exploded. "I can't *believe* you'd *cheat* on me!"

"Are you deaf? *I haven't cheated on you!*" I hoped that Yumi and Antonio had left. It was a big house, but the bedroom door was still open and we were shouting.

He breathed fast. "Why are you *lying*?"

"You can't be serious. I think you're so in your head, worrying what everyone else thinks about me and therefore about you. Why can't you just believe me when I say that Stephen is a friend? Yes, he's good-looking and yes, I had a thing for him, like, *two years ago*. But it's not like that now. Stop reading the gossip rags and stop listening to your roommate and fucking listen to *me*."

We glared at each other for another minute.

"Or is that it?" I gained control of my voice as I struggled with my temper. "You're 'just' a college kid. You're not a superstar. So you sell my photos to tabloids. You make money off of me, just like everyone else." God, the photo. Couldn't Alex see that by releasing the MVA after-party photo he was helping the Sassy–St. James narrative?

"I've *never* done that." He squeezed his fists. "I just don't understand why I'm not your date to these things. You've never asked me to walk the carpet with you. Why is that? Are you ashamed of me?"

I rolled my shoulders back and tried to breathe evenly. "My Gloss life doesn't even *feel* like *my* life, Alex. It's all out for consumption. You should be glad that you're not a part of this fucking circus. I'm a commodity and everything I'm a part of is, too."

"And *he* gets it." He stated it; it wasn't a question.

"Yeah, he gets it because *he* is a part of it too. Being handled by like five different people. Every move we make gets dissected. And if I gain an *ounce,* I can get kicked out of my promotional deals. No one wants to buy soda from a fat pop star."

"You're joking, right? Cassidy, you're *so* thin now. Like, unrecognizable-since-high-school thin." I shook this back-handed compliment off and he said, in a monotone, "So I'm not part of your *image*."

I avoided his gaze and resisted the urge to pick at the smooth new polish on my thumbnail. "That's not what I'm saying. I'm protecting you. Protecting *us*."

"What if I don't *want* to be protected? What if I want to share this overwhelming, big-world shit with you?"

My lip twitched. "I don't want this life for you. Hell, I hardly want it for myself." There. A thought that had been circling the bottom of my heart had emerged.

"I'd do it for you. I don't care. All I care about is you, Cass." He didn't say it, but I could sense it: the *I love you*.

A pause, but to both of us it felt like a year. "I wish you could be a part of it, Alex. I do. But I don't . . . I don't think that I feel for you the way you seem to feel toward me and I don't want you to get mixed up in all this if it's temporary."

He looked as though I'd slapped him. Everything was quiet while he absorbed this news.

I murmured, "I'm sorry. I should have told you this sooner."

When he found his voice again, it sounded strangled. His words made everything feel cold. "I don't think I can be your friend anymore, Cass. It's just . . . I can't watch you with someone else, and I can't fight for a part of your life when there are so many other things going on, vying for your attention. It hurts too much knowing that I'm not a priority to you."

Breaking up with Alex was a given, but losing his friendship altogether? That hurt. I swallowed, wishing to suppress the lump in my throat that was giving way to tears. "Listen," I said, voice wavering, "I know this is the worst timing ever.

And I'm sorry. But someone is going to be waiting on me, and I can't let him down."

Alex stepped toward me, and the light on his shirt grew brighter as he came nearer. I was just in eyeline with his chest when he spread his arms and gave me a warm hug, an Alex hug. I was wrapped up in all of him, hands clasped in front of my heart, so I couldn't hug back. Swallowing thickly, I pushed away from him and patted his chest. "Don't," I said. If he hugged me any longer, I'd break. I wouldn't be able to fix runny mascara.

The front door slammed and there was the thump of enthusiastic steps on the stairs. "Sassy!" called a familiar baritone.

Then he was in the bedroom doorway: Stephen St. James. In a tux.

# 25.

*March 2002*
*L.A.*

# Cassidy

It must have looked like something, me in Alex's arms, our eyes bright with emotion.

Stephen's jaw tensed. Alex curled his arms tighter around me while I dabbed at moisture at the edge of my nose. Alex, always comforting me, even after we'd officially split. "Stephen," I said. "How'd you get in?"

He shifted a small jewelry box in his hand. "A car was leaving as I drove up, so I slipped in the gate."

"We were just having a quick conversation, and now I'm going to go." Alex stuffed his hands in his pockets and started for the door. I glanced uneasily at Alex's back as he withdrew, and Stephen reached out a long arm to bar him from leaving.

"A conversation about *what*?"

"About nothing. I don't know you and I don't have to answer you." Alex waited for Stephen to move.

"Sassy means a lot to me. If you're bothering her, I want to know."

"Her name is *Cassidy*."

They weighed each other with hard eyes. I tugged the bottom of my short robe before taking the box from Stephen's hand, calling attention to myself to defuse the situation. "This is beautiful. Thank you, Stephen." It was a coiled silver snake bracelet with emeralds studded through, heavy and clunky. It didn't match the jewelry Gail had given me, but I made a split-second decision to appease Stephen by wearing his piece over hers. "I'll get dressed and we can go."

"You know what?" Alex said. "I meant what I said before. This is over. And I want you to remember that *I* left *you*." He dashed a hand at his face and ran down the stairs.

I pulled the dress off the hanger and stepped into the bathroom to slip it on quickly, ignoring the body tape Antonio had left on the counter. "Never mind him," I said to Stephen, and tucked my chin down because I knew it was wobbling. "Let him go. Help me with my zipper." His fingers were silky as they stroked up my spine. Swallowing hard, I added, "Let's not miss the red carpet."

I'D BEEN WHISKED away to awards shows in limos before, but this was my first time arriving without the women who made me Sassy Gloss. I slipped into the back seat, careful not to crease the bottom of my dress, and was quietly contemplating how all of this had happened. Alex, my boyfriend, who likely sold my photos to tabloids; Alex, my bedrock, no longer my friend. Stephen, superstar, asking me to the Academy Awards. The next album, the chosen second single, Rose and her bruised spine, chiffon dresses in water, Merry and the house on fire. I wanted to lay my head in my hands but couldn't risk smudging Antonio's work.

"What's on your mind?" Stephen asked, as he handed me a flute from across the expansive aisle.

"Hm?" After a beat, I shook my head gently and accepted the champagne. "Nothing, really. Thinking how weird life is."

He raised his own glass. "Amen to that. Three years ago, when we were on *Sing It,* did you ever think that one day we'd be here?"

I knew he meant in a limo, cruising through Hollywood, about to get dropped off at the red carpet of all red carpets, surrounded by adulating fans. But I couldn't help but look at him, the strong jaw and sharp cheekbones that the passing street lamps outside highlighted, his Adam's apple sliding fluidly up and down his neck as he swallowed, the way that I had looked at his fingers throughout our time in that yellow room years ago, and how I'd ached to feel those hands on me. "No," I whispered, the flute still in my hand. "I didn't."

"To grand life," he said, clinking his glass against mine.

"To life being grand." I tipped a sip down my throat.

Stephen moved across the aisle to sit next to me, so close that he sat on part of my dress. He fingered one of my straps delicately, rubbing it lightly between index finger and thumb. "Beautiful," he murmured, and his face was so close that his breath warmed my cheek. I gripped the stem of my glass, aware that if I dropped it I would spill champagne everywhere. He took it from my hand and leaned in the opposite direction to tuck the glasses away. It was this short moment, when he shifted away and then back again, when I should have regrouped. When I should have remembered where I was, who I was, and what I was doing.

But the pause was so short, and he was leaning toward me with his tie silkily untucking itself from his suit vest, tickling me along the arm. His left hand came forward, gently touching the side of my face, turning my chin toward him. Our noses brushed, and then his mouth was on mine, warm and full.

His hands, the long fingers I'd imagined on my skin, were all over me now, one brushing hair away from the back of my neck, the other tracing my collarbone with the tips of his slender fingers, down into the low neckline of my dress. I accidentally bit his lip when a thumb flicked across my nipple, and he took it as encouragement to kiss me harder.

My thoughts were thick, gelatinous, wobbly in my mind.

Alex, no longer my friend.

Rose, her bruised spine.

Rose . . .

I broke away from Stephen's mouth. "Just . . . hold on." I slid on the slippery seat, trying to put a little space between us.

"What's wrong?" he said, making up the distance.

"I just need a minute. A lot has happened that I need to process before . . . *this* . . . can happen." I rearranged my straps.

The car slowed. A disembodied voice startled me out of the moment. "We're about to arrive." Our attention peeled apart from each other. The voice on the intercom continued, "Uh, should I circle around the block?"

Stephen tapped a button on an armrest. "Yes, thanks." He started straightening his clothes, but his scowl was deepening. I rushed to find words to soothe him; I didn't want him to walk outside on this big night feeling anything but happy. "You're ruining my lipstick, I mean." I delivered it lightheartedly, hoping he'd laugh and the tension would ease.

I dug into my tiny clutch for a compact mirror to show him. "And it's all over you too." I thought of all the cameras that would be turned on us, the telltale sign of our kiss magnified in magazines and supermarket tabloids, the evidence of two horny kids who couldn't wait until after the ceremony to rub their mouths all over each other. And Alex would see, and it would just confirm to him—and to that devil-in-his-ear Joe—that I'd been messing around on him.

He swiped at his mouth. "It's not that bad." Into the intercom he said, "We're ready." The car slowed again.

"Stephen. These photos will be everywhere. And my face is a mess."

"Let's go." He grabbed my arm.

"I just need a minute." I fished for a tissue.

"We can't hold up the line now," the driver said over the radio.

"Come on," he said, as someone opened the door to the red carpet. Shouts and screams amplified.

"Wait!" I slipped even farther into the darkness of the interior, hiding from camera view. Stephen was still holding my arm, and even strengthened his grip.

"Let go!" I tried to bring my arm back; suddenly I could see how thin I was in his large hands, all knobs and lines and pale skin, which was blooming white under the pressure of his thumb. "You're hurting me!"

He let go and surprised me by pulling the car door shut again. "Drive around," he yelled to the front of the car, and, smooth as butter, we took off again, circling the block. "I'm hurting you? *I'm* hurting you?" He grabbed my arm again with one hand and brought my face to his with the other. "Sassy, I'm so into you. I want to bring you as my big date to this huge fucking event. And *I'm* the one who is being hurtful?"

The dam burst. "No," I mewed.

"Don't cry!"

I tried to tamp down the tears, but his grip on me was solid and I could feel the fear rise in me like bile.

"Stop!" He shook me like a rag doll. He pinched my chin toward his face and wagged my face back and forth, making me shake my own head. "Just . . . stop crying!"

"You're scaring me," I whimpered. A face swam in my mind: the brunette with the mandala tattoo: *I'm just looking out for you.* I would crawl on the red carpet looking a mess if I could just get away from this maniac. I would tumble onto Hollywood Boulevard at thirty-five miles an hour to escape. Why hadn't the model said anything about *danger*? She made it sound like he was a playboy. Where the hell did this monster come from?

I dove at the door and tried to open it, but the handle wouldn't respond. The door was child-locked. I wondered if the driver had seen things. If other women, the brunette included, had screamed too.

"Hey!" Stephen shouted.

I didn't realize I was screaming until I felt a sudden throb against my ear, a deep pain that surprised me completely. He had hit me; it was like getting smacked in the face with a basketball. Stunned, I stopped crying immediately, cowering like one of the dogs I'd seen in the shelter kennels.

"Fuck. I didn't mean to do that." He smoothed my hair, which was probably no longer a sleek-shaped updo but a rat's nest after all my thrashing. His kindness brought me to new tears; confused tears, pained tears.

I pulled at the door handle again, kicking the door with a foot.

"Sassy, you can't go out there looking like this."

"Leave me *the fuck* alone," I screamed.

"Sassy—" He snatched at my arm again, getting a firm hold.

"I'm *Cassidy*." I pulled my arm back, but his hand was still on me. There was a loud snap and excruciating pain where his fingers had been.

"Shit, shit," he said. He pushed the intercom button. "Dave, I'm getting out. Take her to get patched up."

"You're going to leave me here?" Tears of pain made him look like a mirage.

"If we *both* don't show up, the rumor mill will go wild. The carpet has already seen me. And *you* said you didn't want rumors."

The limo whispered to a stop and I shuffled to the front of the sedan again, out of sight from the door. There was a second rush of noise as Stephen stepped out, ducking through the doorway with one arm already outstretched for a wave. Flashes popped, shading his silhouette on the far corner of the limo wall in a rectangle of yellow and white. Then the door closed once more, and I was left in the quiet to cry in stunned silence. We began moving again.

The driver spoke. "It'll just be a few minutes."

I hissed in pain. "That asshole broke my arm and you're acting like you're delivering a fucking pizza?"

"Ma'am, I don't know what you think happened, but if you spread malicious slander about Mr. St. James, I'm afraid I'll have to inform his lawyers. And I'd like to add, he hires the best in the business. You'd be lucky to find a job at Walmart before you could breathe a second word."

When we reached the hospital, I walked inside barefoot, not caring where I'd left my impossibly tall, Gail-approved heels. The pain seemed to amplify with every jarring step I took, and there were bruises starting to form on my unnaturally bent forearm, purple fingertips and a long thumb. The nurse taking my X-ray asked if I wanted to discuss what happened. I shook my head. She stressed confidentiality and gave me a card with a number in case I changed my mind; I left it on the exam table after my cast, covering my entire forearm and concealing the marks, was applied.

Who could I call? Who would believe me?

After a long moment, I dialed Emily.

"Hi, Cass! I didn't see you on the—"

"Emily," I interrupted, "can you pick me up at the hospital?"

"Sure, but—"

"I'm at Cedars-Sinai."

"Are you okay?"

"Just get me, please."

I waited for her in a room with a small flatscreen anchored to the wall, while I chewed my dry lips. *JMC*'s television show was on, playing a recap of the Oscars in a small, closed-captioned picture. I craned my head for a remote to change the channel, but my eyes were drawn back to the flickering set, as Sterling Royce escorted a beaming Lucy down the red carpet. Her makeup was too soft to age her, so Sterling looked like a teacher bringing a high schooler to her prom.

Then, suddenly, there was Stephen St. James, with a gorgeous, petite, red-haired goddess on one arm. My jaw snapped shut in surprise and I tasted iron.

*Anna.*

The closed captioning filled the bottom of the screen. "It's lovely to see Stephen again, after our time on *Sing It, America!* together," Anna Williams preened into the microphone. Her skin glowed, and in the bright lights her pupils were highly constricted, letting the green of her eyes shine. Joan Rivers asked about her outfit as the camera pulled back. "I'm in Oscar de la Renta and he's in Prada. Thank you!" The two sashayed away and the picture cut to another couple.

I wondered how Stephen had found a replacement so fast.

I wondered if Anna would be the next one in the line of fire. I didn't like her while on *Sing It,* but no one deserved to be alone in a room with him.

A commercial played without sound, and there she was, the

model with the back tattoo, sashaying in an ad for Victoria's Secret. What was her name, Jeannette? *If* the same had happened to her, I understood why she hadn't warned me explicitly.

When Emily saw me, she gasped, but stopped herself from giving me a bear hug and instead she gingerly placed her arms around me. "Are you okay?" she breathed. Her gaze drifted to my cheek, which was puffy on the left side where he'd cuffed me.

"I'm fine. Fell down some stairs."

"But your face . . ."

"Smacked into the banister. Can we go?"

I wondered if this was an isolated incident and I was just blowing it all out of proportion. The nurse asked about my periods, but it had been months since my last cycle. I wasn't pregnant, just undernourished and brittle-boned, and maybe any amount of force would have broken my arm.

In the car, Emily drove silently for a few minutes before saying, "You're lucky you didn't lose any teeth. My friend Tracy tripped at a park once and hit her head on part of a jungle gym. Her mouth was bleeding all over and now she has three fake teeth right here." She tapped her top right incisor, her face tinted green from a passing traffic light.

I acknowledged that with a guttural noise.

"I get it. You're tired. I'll just . . ." She snapped on the radio. We drove along surface streets like that for a few minutes, but after the current song finished, the next was by Stephen St. James. I turned the volume dial down and rubbed my bare shoulder. "Do you have a sweater somewhere in here?" My rumpled dress was thin and I was cold, but mostly I didn't want to hear his voice.

"I have a dog towel . . . it's a little furry, sorry."

"It's fine." Grimacing as I twisted in the seat, I pulled the towel from the back and wrapped it one-armed around myself.

"Did you get to see any of the show?" she asked.

"No, I missed all of it."

"Oh. Well, Stephen won Original Song for this." She turned the volume back up.

"Good for him." I couldn't stand it anymore, though. "Could we turn off the radio? My head hurts."

"Oh." Emily sounded chastised. "Of course." She clicked it off completely and we continued driving in the quiet.

*Tinkerbellatrix [OP]* (May 12, 2017. 6:42 pm)

Final trailer for *Lunch at Midnight* just dropped. Link.

*Formershopgirl* (May 12, 2017. 6:43pm)

I was gonna share this & you beat me to it! Anyone catch Rosy Gloss real fast at 1:40? Her face looks different.

*Tacoxxtaco* (May 12, 2017. 6:45pm)

I feel like I haven't heard about Gloss in forever.

*Pilateschick411* (May 12, 2017. 6:45pm)

True to her name, Tasty ate so much that she is unrecognizably fat.

*Formershopgirl* (May 12, 2017. 6:47pm)

That is incredibly rude. She doesn't look like she did 10 years ago because people age.

*Pilateschick411* (May 12, 2017. 6:50pm)

Then why are Rosy and Cherry still skinny?

*Bookish_Owl_8* (May 12, 2017. 6:53pm)

Rose is obviously still working in Hollywood so she's probably gotten work done. That definitely doesn't look like her original nose or chin and I bet she's gotten lipo too. I'm surprised Meredith had the time to film this movie tho. She has her entire brand empire going, plus she's probably going to start managing her daughter's modeling career (or be involved in some way). Why would she stoop to this? She doesn't need the money.

*Tinkerbellatrix [OP]* (May 12, 2017. 7:01pm)

I totally thought the same thing, Bookish. I can only imagine that she's doing it to be a good sport to Rose. It's clear to me that Rose wants to keep working even though she is the least talented Gloss. She knows she's a terrible singer so she's trying to break into acting.

*BalleRina007* (May 12, 2017. 7:03pm)

Okay, she's not the strongest vocalist but if you ever went to a Gloss show you'd know Rose is charismatic af with stage presence out the wazoo. You couldn't look away. Rose carried like 90% of their performances. You know the least talented spot is reserved for Sassy.

*Bookish_Owl_8* (May 12, 2017. 7:10pm)

Yikes. Too soon.

*BalleRina007* (May 12, 2017. 7:11pm)

I call it like I see it. She was the weakest link.

*Formershopgirl* (May 12, 2017. 7:13pm)

I don't understand how you can say Cassy was the weakest link. They were the biggest girl group in the world. When C left, the entire group collapsed. She was everything holding them together.

*Bookish_Owl_8* (May 12, 2017. 7:15pm)

Ballerina, I thought that they were ALL so talented. I still remember seeing the 2002 MVAs and I was just in awe of their live performance of "Prime." That song and its insane music video are both so iconic.

*Tacoxxtaco* (May 12, 2017. 7:17pm)

Sorry just coming back to this but you know it's just a cameo rite? They are in the movie for like 4 seconds. Stan Harold asked like ten girl groups to cameo for them. Joyride is in there too.

*Pilateschick411* (May 12, 2017. 7:21pm)

Joyride is talentless.

*Tacoxxtaco* (May 12, 2017. 7:28pm)

Anyone else think Pilateschick would be real fun to bring to parties

# 26.

## Cassidy

A grainy paparazzo photo of me with my arm in a cast, exiting the double doors of the hospital, was on every gossip site come Tuesday morning and printed in magazines the following week—covers were reserved for Oscar winners, of course, but my plight was on page six—and every one of them questioned what had happened.

*Confidentiality,* the nurses had said. Yet someone had called the paps.

I had known I couldn't trust the hospital staff. I was right to toss that card.

I couldn't trust anyone.

Before Gloss, I would sometimes have moments—a few days, maybe a week—when my mind felt like a dark room with a single, bare window. It felt impossible to do anything, and being one kid in a family of seven meant that I wasn't often missed if I skipped dinner or stayed in bed. Sometimes it would be cloudy outside, so the window would let dim light into the dark room. Sometimes it was sunny, and everything was bright. But some really low days, the window wouldn't open, and the room stayed black. After a long while, the window would open slightly, letting in light, and things would return to normal. I'd been too busy with Gloss to let the dark room bother me, but with my arm in pain, it reappeared when I took the Vicodin.

I recognized the dark room immediately. It was the place where I was told I would never be anything, that I was a bad person. That I deserved the broken bone and the pain. It was where I'd whisper to myself I wasn't skinny enough or talented enough. But it was familiar, and I took comfort in that.

Alex had betrayed me, Stephen had hurt me, and Emily didn't know the truth but at least she didn't ask for any other explanation. When Peter heard about my injury, he got the same excuse I gave to everyone, and that is what the tabloids ran with. It was great exposure, my mystery broken arm—intriguing enough for the press to ask about it, but not severe enough to limit the press I'd have to do for *Prime*.

I could see Peter's satisfaction in my blatant lie; he didn't care because it didn't affect the bottom line. Already, the music video was a hit, requested nonstop on Music Video Channel and MTV.

Merry was getting her share of the attention too. Her stint as Grant Kidd's "guest" during his house fire put a lot of attention on her. Their subsequent breakup, confirmed through his publicist and published in *People,* had raised even more questions.

An album release and an international tour waits for no one and nothing, so although I'd have to keep the cast on for the first two weeks of tour, everything went on as planned, albeit with eleven alterations to my tour wardrobe. "What did you *do* to yourself, darling?" Ang, our tailor, lamented as he took new measurements over my cast to make sleeves for all of my stage outfits.

We started in London, where Gloss was headlining not one, but *two,* back-to-back sold-out shows with more than eighty thousand tickets sold. From there, Manchester, Dublin, Lisbon, Stockholm, Copenhagen, and Paris. The stadiums were booked, with twelve trucks full of sets, seventy crew members—some of them the same crew rehired from our last tour, including Gus the driver—loaded on nine buses, and forty-four outfits among just the four of us. There could be no alterations, no room for improvising or mistakes. We had practiced every routine to perfection.

Which meant that, of course, everything went to shit.

It began with Merry missing steps and lagging half a beat behind the rest of us. The first time it happened in London, she hastily caught up by the end of the song. We attributed it to nerves. By the third time, on the fifth song of the night, Rose was staring daggers. Every show had a half-hour intermission for concertgoers to queue up at the bathroom or buy concessions and merchandise, and for us to get into our most elaborate outfits. Ang was backstage helping me with snaps and buttons, which is probably why Rose didn't chew Merry out as harshly as she would have otherwise. "What is going on with you?" she hissed.

Merry shrugged, trying to look nonchalant, but she seemed to be holding back frustrated tears. "I'm just off. I'm sorry. I'll get it."

Yumi smiled at her. "I'm sure you will. It's the first night, and you might still be dealing with the fire stuff. You're sure you're all right?"

Merry nodded, but her mouth twisted uncomfortably. "I feel a little sick. I should've eaten more."

"Want a protein bar?" Ang said, trying to be helpful.

"Nah, if I eat one of those now I'll *really* puke. I'll eat after the show."

We made it through the first London show without any more mishaps, but there was a bigger crowd than usual when we left the hotel for day two. Flashes strobed in our faces and the yelling was an indistinct curtain of our names and noise. We moved through slowly, molasses trickling through a twisted spout, bumping away microphones with the backs of our hands.

"Sassy! Sassy!"

A security guy said, "No more pictures," and waved the pap away, but he popped back up like a whack-a-mole. Now that I tuned in to the noise, the indistinct sounds weren't general hollers for Gloss, and they weren't asking the others a lot of questions. Everything was directed toward me.

"What did he do to you?"

"Tell us what happened! Sassy!"

I tried to remain stoic in the eyes of their lenses, breathing in deeply through my nose and exhaling slowly, beat by beat. The group of paparazzi swarmed, moving as one writhing mass like a school of fish. We were almost outside at our waiting SUVs. Ian opened the door and I slid in after Rose. The flashbulbs were still going off, camcorders rolling, microphones probing outward from the mass, preventing the car door from closing. Security gamely peeled fists and camera lenses away from the door when one of the grackles shouted, "Why would Alex hurt you?"

The door slammed shut, the tinted window hiding my surprise.

*Alex?*

Ian climbed in the front and I leaned back in my seat, almost too exhausted to think, as we rolled away from the curb.

"Did that guy say Alex?" I murmured to Rose.

Her eyes were closed. "I think so . . . ," she mumbled.

I reached into my bag and turned my cell phone on, certain that if Alex were involved, someone from Houston would have notified me about it. I quickly started cycling through what felt like hundreds of new voicemails, trying to glean any information before we were set to perform, but we arrived at the stadium too soon.

"Waitwaitwait," I said, as Ian hustled me out of the car. But we couldn't wait. Everything was on a timetable. We pushed through another crowd, this time mostly fans who breached the cordons and were held back by security, and when I had a moment to sit in my dressing room to continue my mission, I found that my phone battery had died.

I chased down a PA. "Find all the tabloids that mention Gloss and leave them in the bus for me," I instructed.

That night, I was distracted by my curiosity and stumbled over my steps. Merry broke away from our ensemble during "What Did U Say" and pitched to the back edge of the stage, tossed her microphone to the side, and vomited into the wings. Because it was the song right before intermission, the stage lights cut out dramatically as the stadium lights came on and we all rushed to guzzle water and change.

"Ughhh," she said, gargling.

"What the fuck was that?" Rose said, depositing Visine under her lashes and blinking hard.

"God, I have no idea. My stomach has been acting weird all week."

"Are you feeling better now?" Yumi asked.

"Tons. Maybe I just have a little bug. Or ate something wrong."

When we went back out after the intermission, we had scripted banter among ourselves to engage the audience. Tonight, Rose ad-libbed, striding out in front of the rest of us with her hands high in the air and shouting, "Whew! What's up, *London?!*"

Screams rang out from the audience, a wave of undulating adoration.

Rose took a few steps back, the cue for Yumi's line.

"We're so excited to be here tonight!" Yumi yelled.

I had to muster energy from deep within to shout my bit: "But are *you* excited? Make some noise!"

More screams.

"Merry, you were so excited, you got a little sick back there," Rose said jokingly, turning toward her friend.

"Oh, yeah," Merry responded wryly. "Well, all I can say is . . . for all the naysayers who claim that we lip sync, I think I showed them that we always sing live."

Laughter and cheers, people bobbing their glow sticks in appreciation.

When we climbed aboard the bus for our ride to Manchester, there were a few gossip rags waiting but they were all backdated. Apparently, the rumors about my arm had jumped the Atlantic some other way. I flipped through twice to be sure, but the only thing of note was that Sterling Royce had a new girlfriend—*not* Lucille Bowen.

Merry's stomach troubles persisted throughout our European leg. She blamed it on questionable food, a bug, motion sickness. While she didn't vomit onstage again, Merry was constantly sipping ginger ale and tapping out vitamin C tablets into her palm, and a bottle of Pepto-Bismol was never far from her reach. If the other girls noticed, they didn't mention it, but I wasn't talking to anyone on the bus between cities. I lay in my bunk, numbed by prescription painkillers, trying not to jostle my arm, wordlessly observing the people around me: Rose, staring out the window; Merry, rubbing her chest like she was experiencing heartburn; Yumi, chatting animatedly with Veronica, the sound tech, who was on our crew again. And a low hum of exhaustion and dizziness from the Vicodin permeated my existence, so when I could, I slept.

What did it matter if I sometimes overheard a fragment of a

conversation between two crew members about someone being "antisocial"? Or that the loneliness sometimes turned into sullenness?

By the time we reached Stockholm, I'd learned to space my Vicodin doses so that its numbness would wear off as I clumsily applied stage makeup, and I'd be fresh enough to perform, albeit with a throbbing arm. Ian stole into my dressing room before the show and slapped a magazine on the bureau beside me. "This came for you. I thought I'd run it by you."

I set down my eyeshadow brush and flipped through the pages, but couldn't read it. It was a flimsy newsprint that looked more like a supermarket tabloid than *People* magazine or *In Touch Weekly*. "It's in Swedish," I said.

"It's French. You think it's Swedish? I worry about your education that you can't see the difference." He shook his head as he took the magazine back and opened it, turning the print toward me and jabbing at a spot with one finger. "Here."

"I still can't read French. Can *you* read French?"

"A little. Jordan is taking it in school so I pick up a tiny bit by virtue of being around him."

I felt a twinge of envy. "Isn't Jordan, like, twelve?"

"Thirteen, going on thirty. Anyway, as much as I could piece together, it says that you and your boyfriend had an argument and it got violent. This paper is very slim on details."

I snatched it out of his fingers but my proficiency in French hadn't changed in the last minute. Just *boyfriend*? Not Stephen or Alex by name? "What time is it? Can we call Peter and see what's being said in the U.S.?"

Ian shook his head. "He probably knows about it and is

taking care of it. He would probably tell you to focus on finishing Europe strong, so that you can start the U.S. tour when you get back."

His words didn't soothe my anxiety for very long. I abandoned my eyeliner and walked the corridor to Merry's dressing room, thinking that if anyone knew how to handle a tabloid situation, it would be her. But her room seemed empty.

"Hello?" I said, turning around in the space, and noticed that the adjoining bathroom door was ajar. Maybe she was sick again. I knocked lightly. "Merry, you in there?" The door swung open.

She was curled in front of the toilet, looking miserable. Her face didn't move, but her eyes met mine. They were giant and sad and communicated everything.

And somehow, I knew. "Oh, shit."

Merry turned to look directly at me. "You can't tell anyone."

"I wouldn't. But Merry—"

"What." She spit into the bowl.

"People are going to figure it out. You keep complaining about feeling sick, things will start to click."

"I know." She stood on wobbly legs and pushed past me through the door. "*Don't* say anything to Yumi." Breathing shallowly, she swallowed and curled up on the couch, barefaced and still in her dressing robe and fleece pajama pants. "I swear, everyone in the media says *I* flap my mouth too much, but Yumi—she's the one who can't keep a secret."

I sat too. "We need an adult. We're really just kids, in *way* over our heads."

Leaning her head back slowly, Merry gave a little moan.

"Ian would blow a gasket. Peter would replace me in two seconds. I don't know what I'm doing about it yet. Maybe it won't even be an issue . . ."

"Justine?" I suggested. Both of us could use her right now.

"Does Justine know how to arrange a discreet procedure while on foreign soil?" She saw my expression and smiled wanly. "Hypothetically. Because I feel like she's the one who is supposed to *announce* things. Not *cancel* things. Will you pass me those crackers?"

I did, and she nibbled on a corner, staring off into space, nowhere near ready for the show. An idea formed. I said, "Let's get Emily to come."

"Your dog walker?"

"She's not *just* a dog walker. She's worked for some big names, arranging *things*. Plus she's not on Peter's payroll. If you don't want the label or management to know anything, they won't."

Merry finally finished one cracker. "Fine. How much time do we have until we're on?"

## Sassy Gloss IN TROUBLE?
## Boy Toy Tampers Top Pop Idol
## Sassy Broke Up with Him And He Took REVENGE.

Cassidy Holmes of pop group Gloss was photographed with a broken arm on the night of the Academy Awards. Her excuse? She fell down. We just learned that her ex-boyfriend Alex Hernandez, a student at Pomona, reacted poorly when Cassidy broke up with him earlier that evening. "They had a fight," one of her close friends told us, "and the next thing I knew, she had that cast on her arm. She's lying about falling down."

The PA delivered a handful of American gossip rags to Ian in Stockholm, which he passed on to me after our flight touched down in Copenhagen. I started to panic, and after deleting a dozen old voice mails pertaining to stale news, eventually I received one from Joanna: "Edie told me you're out of the country, but you have to get a handle on whatever is going on. My mom saw the accusation about Alex on a magazine at the grocery store and flipped. You're going to refute this bull, right?"

Edie: "Hey. I know you're touring in Europe but what the fuck is this?"

Melanie: "I thought you said you broke your arm because you fell down. I hope Alex didn't cause it. I always liked him."

Alex's voice was hesitant. "Uh, it's me. I don't know what is going on. Did you tell people that I hit you? It's . . . it's really scary. I keep getting hounded wherever I go. Like, not just reporters or whatever, but regular people. I was basically driven out of a Safeway by a mob. And I know we didn't end on the best of terms, but this is—can you do something?"

Yumi sat next to me on the ride from the airport to the hotel and overheard the message. We pulled into the parking lot and began to unload, security flanking us amid the chaos of fans that had scooped the hotel's guest list. "Abusive men deserve to be hung out to dry," she said, as she hopped out of the van. She was swept along the waves of arms toward the back entrance.

While I agreed with her in general, Alex wasn't the one

who had broken my arm, but I couldn't tell her that. She was already inside and I, the last girl out, was still straining to hear my voice mail.

"Well," I whispered coldly as I deleted his message, "you wanted to know what it was like being me. Now you do." And I left the safety of the van.

Flashbulbs popped in my face, hands that were too quick for security dragged along my shoulders. One fan slithered through the band of security and ran up to me, screaming. Apparently she didn't know what she wanted to do once she'd escaped the confines of security, because she continued to scream while grabbing at my hand. Someone from the team snatched her away before she could rebreak my arm and I ran the rest of the way, the tabloids clutched across my chest in my good hand, to the safety of the hotel.

When I was finally inside, I took a minute to slow my breathing and knocked on a door. Rose answered. I double-checked the room number.

"Oh, sorry. I was looking for Merry . . ." But I was pleased to see Rose, nonetheless. It surprised me, my eagerness to see her. Rose was smart, capable. She could help.

All of this passed in the split second before she answered, "Merry's two doors down, but she's probably dead to the world already. She told me she was taking motion sickness medicine and sleeping. Can *I* help you with something?"

Jittery again, I stepped into the room and dumped the magazines on the bed. "Yeah. I don't know what to do about this."

Rose sat on the bed and sifted through the newsprint as I paced back and forth. She popped the tab of a fresh Diet

Coke, getting foam on the heel of her hand. She slurped it absentmindedly. "Is this true?" she said, pointing at the tabloids. "Did Alex break your arm?"

I shook my head. "No. Absolutely not. Why would they write that?"

She sipped from the can, head down again, her two-toned eyes poring over the papers. "They must be secure with their source. If it was just one little paper writing it—but all of them?" She raised one brow. "Which means . . . it came from someone they think was there."

Stephen wouldn't want to bring attention to this, especially after his threat. "Would *Alex* be stupid enough to say this? Maybe his dumb roommate?" If so, Joe wouldn't have realized the hell that would unleash on Alex; he would be vilified everywhere.

"I *hope* he wouldn't be idiotic enough to do that. Regardless of who shared it, this shit is out there now. We should get Justine involved, figure out what to say. I'm surprised Peter hasn't quashed this." She set her soda down and began dialing the hotel phone.

Peter's phone went straight to voice mail. Rose furrowed her brow. "That's weird." She checked the time. "It's not *that* late in L.A."

"Maybe he doesn't recognize the number."

"I'll use my cell. I think he has that number saved in his phone."

But Peter didn't answer that, either.

"He's probably shmoozing or something. If I know Pete, he's on it." Rose slid off the bed and tugged at my hand. Her touch took me by surprise; in my memory, Rose had never reached out before. "Here. Let me raise your spirits." She turned off the lights so we were in muted darkness and led me over to the window. "What floor are we on?" she asked in a conspiratorial whisper.

"The . . . twelfth?"

"Fifteenth. You can still hear them. Here, let me turn off the air." She left my side to click the air conditioner off and the room fell completely silent. I could hear the shuffle of feet throughout the hallway, the honk of car horns on the streets below. Rose brushed open the curtains and we stood next to each other in the soft light that came in through the windows—the light pollution of the buildings all around us and the night sky's glow. And then, softly—

"Is that . . . ?" I whispered.

We placed our ears against the glass, my left, her right, so we were facing each other. Her eyes glittered, and again I remembered the last time I saw them like this—the last time we'd really been alone together, in her mother's house.

"Yeah," she breathed, "you hear it?"

*Glosssss! We love you, Gloss!*

"It's my favorite thing," she murmured, her palm cupping around her ear. "People down on the streets, knowing we are here, shouting our name. It's amazing, isn't it? Like being high."

We were safe where we were, a soft room done up in plush silks. No paparazzi. No Jerrys. Just fans below.

My arms broke out in goose bumps and I felt my mouth stretch into a smile. "Wow." We listened for another minute, our breath tickling our hands that were pressed against the window. She touched her tongue to her lips before speaking again. I stared at her mouth, suddenly very aware of it. The shape, the pout. I imagined what it would feel like to touch my lips to hers.

She was speaking again, and I had to refocus my attention on her voice. If she'd noticed my dreamlike stare in her direction, she didn't acknowledge it, maybe because she was in a trance of her own. "It's like my meditation." She retreated from the glass and switched on a side lamp, creating a circlet of blush-colored light on one side of the bed. She snuggled under the covers, making a cocoon. "Just me, my blanket, and the background noise of adulation. Quiet enough that I can't hear it all the time, but if I get stuck thinking about *things* too much I can tune back in and remember. Feel."

I sat on top of the covers on her bed, lying on my back next to her, and stared at the muted pink ceiling. The sound still carried, a faint chant. I could hear her shifting toward me, her hair loose across her face. "What do you think?" she asked. "A little silly, huh?"

I turned toward her and raised my head on one hand. "No, it's beautiful."

We lay there smiling at each other, and I felt my heart skip a tiny beat. Embarrassed, I stared at the ceiling, the two of us listening to the crowd and the other's breathing.

It felt like the days in the shared room with Yumi, all dark and quiet and secrets could be shared. I had to ask. "So you and Viv . . ."

"Yeah." She knew what I meant.

"But not anymore . . . ?"

"No." She was quiet for a moment. "When she was diagnosed with leukemia, we'd already been broken up for a while, and she made it clear to me that I should still keep living my life—as much as I can, with this pop deal going on, anyway. I still care for her, obviously." She shrugged one shoulder. "But it's water under the bridge now."

I wanted to tell her I could relate—I still cared for Alex, no matter what had happened between us—but it didn't seem like the right time. I had the urge to swipe her hair away from her face gently with my fingertips, but instead I said, very softly, "Okay."

Rose made no motion to get rid of me, and truth be told, I didn't want to leave. We lay in comfortable silence as the room ticked warmer and the clock ticked later. Before I knew it, I was dozing off, and I felt safe for the first time in a while.

## 27.

# Cassidy

I thought that I would feel relief once we touched down in New York—we'd be home, Emily would join us with Penny, we'd have better access to Peter—yet my anxiety about the tabloids continued to grow. Peter had been strangely quiet the last few days of the European tour and had called Ian for only a brief chat while we were in Paris. I turned off my phone because the incessant ringing was running down my battery, but when I'd switch it on, Edie's and Joanna's messages filled my in-box first with worried voices, then exasperated ones. I returned calls only to my mother, though I told her to ignore half the things that were printed. "Which half?" she asked, annoyed.

As we disembarked at JFK, the paparazzi swarm emerged.

All I could do was keep my lips together, heeding Justine's in-explicably vague advice: "Just don't comment on it."

I'd also hoped that the removal of my cast would dampen the rumor mill—with the visual reminder gone, maybe the questions and speculation would fade—but when we peeked at the Madison Square Garden crowd preshow, scattered fan signs announced their opinions on the matter. Why wouldn't people let it go? The longer it went on, the worse I started to feel about Alex. He didn't deserve this.

"Focus," Rose said over the headset. I glanced over at her but her eyes shifted away, already on task. The audio started and visuals onstage began to play, and we waited for our cue. Being near Rose now gave me a tiny thrill, as I recognized my feelings. It was as if, once I'd learned that there was a possibil-ity she could like me back, my brain gave itself the go-ahead to run full throttle into crush mode. She'd murmured a good morning in Copenhagen that had liquefied my spine.

I'd stayed in my own room in Paris, worried that another night with Rose would lead me to do something reckless and stupid.

But we played a rousing show in New York—the first of two—and after we were bussed to our hotel, Rose waved me into her room. "I figured out your leak," she said once the door was closed. "It's Lucy."

"Lucy?" I repeated. That didn't make sense. I'd been so wrapped up in my broken arm and the tour that I hadn't even talked to Lucy in weeks.

"It's just the type of attention-seeking shit she would do,"

Rose insisted. "Like going to the Oscars in a fairy-princess gown, on the arm of a man twice her age? Then he dumped her and the tabloids are going on about how lovesick she is. Wouldn't you want to feed them something in exchange for some peace and quiet?"

"How would she know about it in the first place? Why talk about *me*?"

Rose shrugged and popped an after-show Diet Coke, one of six that she had required in her rider to be in every hotel and dressing room on the tour. "Maybe you didn't kiss her ass enough, worship her fragile ego?"

"I guess it's possible . . ." Perhaps Lucy speculated just to make conversation, and hit too close to the truth. As Hollywood royalty, her word might be deemed trustworthy enough by the tabloids. I felt awkward in the ensuing silence, as I found myself staring at her mouth again. "Okay, well, good night?"

"You don't wanna sleep here?" she said, and her voice was clear and bright after her first pull of soda.

"I didn't think . . ."

She leaned back against the headboard, avoiding my eyes, and set the can on her nightstand. "Don't tell anyone," she said slowly, "but I don't sleep very well. But when you were in Copenhagen with me, I . . . I felt . . ."—she groped for the word—"I feel *okay* with you." She glanced at me, assessing my reaction. I continued to stare at her, riveted, as she flicked her two-toned eyes away again and studied her hands. "And yeah, sometimes I just need to feel *okay*. And you make me feel that."

"Oh." I wasn't sure what to say. A small quiver in my rib cage. I didn't know how to tell her that her words made complete sense. "Sure. I can stay."

I took my last Vicodin in the bottle to soothe my throbbing arm, which always seemed to hurt more when I was trying to fall asleep, and laid next to Rose with a wide berth between us. We woke up in the center of the bed, having gravitated toward each other in the night, our hair tangled together on the same pillow.

WE DROVE THROUGH the night and reached Hartford a little before sunrise. The bus slowed and bumped over speed humps in the hotel parking lot.

Ian stood at the front of the bus and barked, "All right. We have two radio promos before you get your free afternoon. Merry, you wanted off-site today, right? That's fine, as long as it's after radio. Then tomorrow: phone interviews with *Variety* and *Vanity Fair,* and then the show."

Emily, who was on a separate bus, joined us outside the hotel with Penny. Once in the room, I called my parents in Houston to let them know we'd arrived in Connecticut safely, then turned off all phone ringers so I could contemplate in silence. My mind, now that my Vicodin bottle had emptied, was sharp again, and the thoughts I'd been keeping at bay were now floating to the surface.

Was this just a one-sided crush? Or was it worth trying to find out if Rose felt the same way? Did she *feel okay* about me, the way that I *felt okay* about her?

I tried to nap in my own room but then admitted defeat and shuffled, hesitantly, to her door and tapped on it lightly. I just had to know.

She wasn't asleep, either. Her curtains were drawn save one stripe down the middle where they met, and she looked disheveled and unfocused.

"Can I hang out in here for a while?" I asked, suddenly nervous. I'd felt nervous around Rose before, but this was a different kind.

She shrugged, back to being her cold self, and retreated to the mini fridge for a Diet Coke.

I closed the door and crept toward her slowly, marveling at the soft halo backlighting her messy hair.

"Rose," I said softly, "why do you tell me that I make you feel *okay* and then ignore me later?" She went still. "I mean. You talk to me, sometimes, I guess. But when we're in the whole group . . . you always want to move on to work."

She shook her head and popped the tab; a crescent of bubbles decorated the heart of her left palm.

I reached out and clasped her wet hand.

I heard her breath catch as I drew her hand to my lips, dipping my head to kiss the foam from her wrist.

"Cassidy . . . ," she whispered. She didn't remove her fingers from mine.

I murmured into her palm. "I've been thinking . . ."

"What have you been thinking?" Her voice was uncharacteristically low, a voice I'd never heard her use.

"That . . . that I think I have feelings. For you."

She set the can down on the desk. She stepped closer to me

now, bringing her free hand up to caress the side of my face. Her fingertips were cold, the condensation streaking along my jawline. The air stirred lightly, bringing with it the scent of *her*—her spiced neck, her vanilla lip gloss, Diet Coke, her conditioner.

"You have feelings for me?"

"Yes."

"I have feelings for you too," she said softly. "But this can't happen."

But when I opened my eyes she was so close, so close.

"Why not?" I breathed.

"It's already complicated . . ."

"I don't mind complicated."

Our foreheads were nearer now. She was shorter than me so I had to slouch a little, but the fact that she was stretching to reach me brought me a thrill. I played with her hair, touching just the ends, rubbing the glossy strands with my fingers. She sighed and came just a little bit closer, and her chest was against mine, and my hand was already there, releasing that little piece of hair and grazing lightly against the side of one breast.

When our lips met, her mouth was so full, so sweet. I was fully aware of her breasts, her narrow shoulders, her small hands with dainty fingers, which were suddenly sweeping up and down my waist like she too wanted to feel the curves and hollows of the body pressed against hers. We deepened the kiss, exploring the soft, warm wet with each other's tongues; I tasted her gloss, which was flavored like cake frosting. Then she grasped at my arm where it was still healing and I sucked in my breath harshly, which made us break away.

She stepped back, slurring a surprised "Shit." Then she re-grouped. "But this needs to stop right now. I'm serious. We *work* together."

"But we're also friends, right?"

"What, even after all the mean stuff I've said to you?"

"Even after that." I came forward to try to kiss her again, but she twisted her face to the side.

She was quiet for a long moment. She held both of my hands, our fingers intertwined, and swung my good arm back and forth between us as she thought. Her half-smile reappeared. "You've made me feel happier," she admitted. "But . . ."

Those words were enough to move me into action again. I reached for her and she let me. Her mouth breathed into mine. I felt her hesitation melt and she captured my lips with hers. The gloss was gone, nibbled away; I moved my kisses from her mouth to her jawline and found myself taking deep huffs of her shampoo smell from the delta in between her neck and earlobe.

She tugged me to the bed, a gentle hint. I lay above her, relishing anywhere our skin made contact.

We took our time, a soft exploration—nothing urgent, nothing frantic. I tasted the flavor of her skin, drank in the perfume of her hair. The space between her breasts and the slip down to her navel were warmed, like she'd been baking in the sun. Her hands brushed my hair away from my face, trickled down my cheeks, hooked on my ears, scratched at my scalp.

Her bedside phone rang. Rose distractedly picked up the receiver and replaced it on its hook immediately. A few minutes later, a knock came at the door. We both scrambled up, adjusting our clothes, even though the door was locked. "Go hide in the bathroom," she whispered, and as she hopped off the bed she called out, "Yeah?"

"Something's wrong with your phone," came Yumi's muffled voice. "We have our first radio meeting in forty-five minutes and it'll take twenty to get there."

I saw my hair in the bathroom mirror and began patting it down, trying to get the teased strands to lay flat. My mouth was also pink and held a trace of shimmer from Rose's lip gloss.

Rose must have opened her room door a crack, because she answered Yumi at a normal volume. "Okay, I'll meet you in the lobby in fifteen."

Yumi's voice came more clearly. "You haven't seen Cass anywhere, have you? She's not answering her room phone, and of course her cell's voice mail is full."

"Nuh-uh. Maybe she's showering? But if I see her, I'll tell her."

"'Kay. We don't want to be late." The door clicked closed and I reemerged, twisting my hair into a fishtail braid.

"I'm sure you heard that," Rose said, looking into the hall mirror and brushing out her bangs with her hands.

"I'll slip out in a minute, once I know she's gone, and change in my room."

"Wait." She fixed the sleeve of my shirt, which had folded over, and left her hand there. "This can't happen again," she said finally. "Can you imagine it? 'Two Gloss girls come out in a relationship with each other.' Not just us, but the group would be ruined."

I'd had my first taste of her and I couldn't imagine not having more. "No one would have to know."

Her eyes were urgent, fingers hot on my arm. "It won't stay quiet forever. There are spies everywhere."

"This is the twenty-first century. People don't care."

"People *do* care." She said this flatly, warningly. "My *mom* will care. Everyone in my hometown will care. All of *America* will care." She let go.

# 28.

May 2002
Hartford

# Cassidy

We didn't look at each other during our radio spots—the two of us separated by the other Gloss girls, Merry shifting next to me—but I felt my thoughts continuing to ricochet around in my mind. Hot, cold. A residual dampness existed between my legs. Every time I remembered the way Rose had sucked in a breath when I rubbed my tongue on her earlobe, I twitched with anticipation to do it again.

When we returned to the hotel, I saw that I'd missed a few calls from my mother. Though I'd talked to her that morning, I called the house.

"Cassidy!" my mother said, as soon as I'd identified myself. "You've heard the news?"

For a split second, I wondered if she'd known, two thousand miles away, that I'd made out with a girl and that I actually felt happy. Then I registered her voice; she sounded strained, and my focus sharpened. I clutched the phone. "What's wrong? Did something happen to Robbie? The twins?"

"No, no, we're all fine." But a wet sniff echoed noisily. "It's Alex."

My curiosity piqued. "What *about* Alex?"

"Oh, honey. There's been an accident."

They had been running from the paparazzi harassing them in a Safeway. He and his roommate drove away, ran a red light, and were T-boned by a truck.

Joe had a few cuts and bruises, but Alex wasn't so lucky. My mother told me that Alex was still in surgery.

As she spoke, all I could think of were the calls from Edie, from Joanna, from Alex himself. From my mother, asking why I was letting this go on for so long. The lack of contact from Stephen St. James—which I'd considered a blessing after what had happened—now felt calculated. And then Peter and his evasiveness. Why hadn't I said anything? Why did I follow Justine's instructions when *this* could have been avoided?

"Mom, I'll call you back." I disconnected without hearing her answer. I called Edie's private line, assuming that she was back in Houston for the summer. "Edie, I just heard—"

"If this is my *former* best friend Cassidy Holmes, I don't want to speak to her," Edie said furiously. "She is a rumor-spreading, money-hungry, fame-whore who didn't give us the time of day until it was too late. *I hope you are fucking happy.*" And she hung up the phone.

I deserved it, I knew, but I called back again. "Go fuck yourself," she screamed, and the next time I tried, her line was busy.

Joanna was slightly better, but only by a slim margin. "We tried to get you and that manager of yours to help him," she said, soft voice accusing. "Why couldn't you listen?"

"It's not that easy—"

"Don't you see, your silence just made the rumors seem true. You didn't stick up for him. And now because people wanted to see him suffer, he's suffered, and he might not live to see his name cleared." She sighed. "You fucked up, Cass. I'm just so, so angry at you." She didn't slam down the phone, but she did hang up. And though she didn't hurl any epithets, I knew Joanna would not answer again if I called back to offer an explanation.

I paced the room, thinking, my thoughts frantic and angry. I could hear them in my mind, overlapping, the edges rough. I reached for the phone again. Peter *finally* answered. "Why didn't we say anything about how Alex was innocent in all this?" I said, without preamble.

"Hi, Cassidy. Nice to hear from you, too. Could you hold on a minute?" The line piped Muzak as I seethed. Then he clicked back. "Listen, I can only put out so many fires—"

"But this was just *one* fire." I twisted the phone cord so hard that my fingertips went numb. "One fire that stretched out for a month. We could've addressed it any time during Europe. Why did we wait? And now it might be too late!"

"Slow down. What happened, exactly?"

"People hated him! And they practically ran him over. He got into a wreck running away from the paps and if he dies everyone will think, 'Oh, good, that girlfriend-beater got what he deserved,' when he *isn't* a girlfriend-beater and he *didn't deserve any of this!*" This is what I'd been wanting to protect Alex from in the first place, and yet, he hadn't been able to escape it after all.

"That's unfortunate," Peter said in a deadpan voice. "I do feel for him, and you. But my job isn't to manage Alex or whatever happened to him. My job is to manage Gloss, make you more popular, make you more money. And if you noticed, people were on your side. This tour has been the most lucrative and, so far, the most successful. Even people who aren't going to the concert are buying merch off the website! We even put up a plastic cast with your signature on it that girls can snap onto their forearms, for twenty-five dollars, and I'll be damned if it isn't the number-one seller after T-shirts."

I was aghast. "You *what?*"

"Anyway, if Alex was so worried about being misrepresented, he could have hired a PR firm, same as you—"

"*He's a regular person!* Why would he have a PR guy? And are we so heartless that our sales mean more than the truth?"

Peter sighed, like he was sorry to have to tell me this. "We aren't in the business of truth, though, are we?"

"Peter, you are so far beyond—" I couldn't even form words, I was so angry. He was selfish, manipulative, and abusive. My mouth opened and closed, but all that escaped was breath.

"But I manage your career so well, you could retire on a small island by now."

Teeth gnashing, I hung up the phone and then slammed the receiver down a few more times for good measure.

After my phone call with Peter, I stormed to Ian's door and

hammered it with a fist. I demanded two days off to see Alex to set things right.

Ian rubbed his bottom lip with his thumb. "That's not possible. You have an interview, not to mention a concert here. Then two back-to-back shows in Pennsylvania."

"You can't do a show without me," I told him. "That's just a fact. Cancel those concerts."

"What's this all about?"

I looked at him, but I didn't trust him. Who knew how far the rot spread? Peter had hired Ian, and they could be allied with each other.

I left his room and began packing in a rage. In between fistfuls of clothes, I dialed Emily and left a voice mail instructing her to purchase a plane ticket to L.A.

When Rose found me, luggage and excuse at the ready, she grabbed my shoulder mid-explanation. "The show must go on," she said stubbornly.

"Are you kidding? This is a *big deal*! I fucked up *bad*. I need to see Alex and apologize to him before it's too late and I hate myself forever." I closed the snaps on the case, set it on the ground, and headed for the door. "The fans will understand. Peter will get over it. I'll be back before you know it." I yanked the handle open. "I'm going to go tell the others."

Rose followed me to Yumi's room, talking quickly as I knocked. "This is what I've worked my entire life for. I know it sucks, but we have to be dependable. Consistent. Above all, the ultimate professionals. No matter what is happening." As if our standing was so precarious, like a house of cards, that the smallest disruption would have it topple down. "Think about it, Cass! We are responsible for all of those people out there— the ones who depend on us for jobs. Ian. The entire crew. That's like, seventy, eighty people."

Yumi opened the door. I stepped inside without her invitation. "Sure, just come in," Yumi huffed.

"They'll still get paid even if we refund."

"Who's giving a refund?" Yumi asked, incredulous.

"Okay, fine," Rose continued. "Think of it this way. What can you do, anyway? If you show up and his parents are there, won't they hate you?"

"Who would hate you?" Yumi asked.

"Alex," I said.

"Why would you go running to see the guy who hurt you?" Yumi sounded puzzled. "I mean, Cassy, he *broke* your arm!"

Rose ignored her and said, "They would feel awkward around you, wonder how to treat you. And consider the security issue at the hospital if you show up; what a huge headache for everyone. Why not leave his family alone and let them be with him while he recovers?"

"It's a long story," I said to Yumi, ignoring Rose, "one that I don't have time to get into right now."

"I *know* you didn't walk into a door or fall down some stairs."

"Well, no, but Alex is a good person. *He* didn't do anything."

Rose grabbed my hand. She looked into my eyes. She licked her lips determinedly and I felt my stomach stutter. "Please. Think it through."

There was another knock on the door; Emily waved at the

peephole. I yanked it open and she blurted urgently, "I got a flight for ten-thirty. If you leave now, you can just make it."

I leveled a gaze at Rose. "I'm sorry. You had to run to see Viv when she was sick, right? I have to go see Alex now."

I HAD THE entire flight to wonder if I'd killed whatever budding romance Rose and I had stone-dead, brushing her off the way that I had. By the time I arrived, accompanied by one of the hospital's security guards and seeing the Hernandezes in the waiting room, hospital visiting hours were over. This was the family that had had me over for Christmas, had shared their table and meals with me as I was growing up. Had left a stocking for me on their mantel last holiday season. Mrs. Hernandez took one look at me and, her jaw set, turned away. The family closed ranks among the understuffed chairs of the waiting room, angling their backs to me as they huddled.

The only person who didn't was one I'd met before, only once: Alex's roommate Joseph, who had a bandage over his collarbone, a bruise spidering out from underneath the white gauze. He acknowledged me with a short nod, his palms tucked under his thighs as he leaned uncomfortably in his chair. I sat down with one seat in between us. "How is he?" I asked.

Joe shook his head. "I don't know. He's been in surgery for hours. It doesn't look good." His voice held a hint of a tremor.

"He's held on this long. That's a good sign, right?"

We were silent for a long moment. Every hospital waiting room feels the same—no matter what change in decor, whether it's a painting of a vineyard or a farmhouse on the wall, they hold the illusion of calm. I could feel Alex's mother's tempest of emotions just by looking at the set of her shoulders; she was keeping as much inside as possible.

"Why are you even talking to me?" Joe said. "I thought you hated me."

That surprised me. "Hate you? Why would I hate you? I don't even know you."

Joe gave a one-shouldered shrug that evidently hurt, because he winced. "Because of the photos."

Photos? What photos?

Realization dawned. "You? *You* sold them?" Everything I'd said to Alex crashed over me in a wave. My armpits grew damp and cold as I realized my mistake. "Why?"

"Because. He wouldn't listen." He glared at me with the tail end of his eyes. "I knew you weren't good for him. And I was right. Look at what happened. You messed around on him with St. James. Then you left him out to hang when rumors started. You and I both know he didn't break your arm, so why didn't you say so?"

We were interrupted by movement; a doctor appeared from the double doors and made her way toward the Hernandezes. The tension roiling off Alex's parents gave way to wracking sobs. Joe stood up to join them.

I realized that as much as I wanted to be there, I had more pressing things to do. With one last glance at the family, I left the hospital for my house, where I called Justine and set up a press conference for the next day. "It's time for this to end," I said.

## 29.

*Monday*

## Merry

The truth is, I could have said a lot of things. We were *the* biggest music act in 2002. We won awards for our second studio album, *Prime.* We swept the MVAs, had a sold-out world tour, and everything we said was recorded and broadcast.

If I'd opened my mouth and mentioned that a member of our production team had acted inappropriately—more than inappropriately, *harmfully*—maybe things would be different. But I'd seen what had happened to others who had spoken up. And I just didn't want to be known as a shrew, because that is what women who talked about these dark things were called.

ON THE DAY of my appointment, I'd waited impatiently for Emily to appear in the lobby, but she was late, walking Cassidy's dog.

Emily had arranged for a rental car to be dropped off at the Connecticut hotel so we could drive to a doctor with a small private practice. No taxi drivers, no big client pool to wag their tongues—the fewer people who knew, the better. But I was silent on the way there, and as we walked down the hallway to the office, my legs slowed as my thoughts ran amok. An abrupt realization: I really wasn't sure about this at all.

"I think it's this way," Emily said, walking ahead of me. She turned toward me and cocked her head. "Do you still want to go in? We don't have to, you know."

I was glad she didn't hold any judgment in her voice. I'd wondered why Cassidy had hired on a pet-sitter as a full-time employee with travel perks, but Emily seemed to be a person who was there as support, without any extra opinions.

Her face blurred as my eyes filled with tears. "I don't know. I don't."

"If you're not sure . . ." She grasped my hand. "Let's go back to the car."

"No. I need to do this."

"Meredith, you have a choice. You always have a choice. You don't *need* to do anything."

I nodded, sniffling, wiping my nose with the back of my free hand.

Emily continued, "If you're not sure, we can sit and talk about it. But probably not in this hallway."

"We're already late," I sniffled.

"You can reschedule."

"We're driving to fucking *Pennsylvania* next. I don't know

anything about Pennsylvania. You think they'd do abortions there? There's a time limit on this thing—before you know it, it'll be too late."

I felt her soft hands grasping at my shoulders. "I've signed *many* NDAs so I can't say anything in particular, but I can find a way for you to get the care you need even if you're in Egypt. So if you want to consider this a little more, we can leave."

I nodded again and she steered me back to the car. I climbed into the driver's seat, teary at first and then sobbing, making no move to start the ignition. Emily's cell phone rang but she dug around in her bag and silenced it, leaving the call unanswered. Leaning over the wheel, tears and snot dripping onto the leather, I warbled, "This is my punishment, isn't it. This is what I deserve for being a slut, breaking up Grant's marriage. And his *house* . . ."

"Okay, first, you're not a slut. And while everyone shat on you for dating the guy, *he* was the one who was in a marriage and chose to cheat, which people don't ever mention but it is the bigger fault, I think." She rubbed my back, and added hesitantly, "And you definitely shouldn't bring a child into this world if you think that it'll be a punishment."

"I don't think I can have this baby. But I also don't think I can get rid of it. Even if it was *his*."

"Does Grant know about it?" she asked.

"Grant?" I felt a momentary shock of confusion and realized she didn't know. No one did. "It's not Grant's."

"It's not?"

"It's Decker's." My voice cracked. Saying it out loud made

it more real. It was the first time I'd voiced it and the truth echoed in my ears, making them hum.

The shock was evident in Emily's voice. "Decker? *Noah* Decker? The director from the 'Prime' music video?" I looked up and saw her confusion, her thinking to any and all tabloid photos and reports.

But there wouldn't be one, would there? It was not a date.

"Pretty sure." I balled my hands into fists and clamped them against my eyes. "I can't stand that video and I can't stand that song. I can't stand to see him. I can't hear his name. Every time, it makes me feel sick."

Emily was quiet. My tears had subsided, but my nose was still runny. I rooted around in the back seat for a tissue.

"He hurt you?" she asked softly.

My silence was enough of a confirmation.

She blew out a breath. "I know it's hard, but maybe you could tell someone—report it—"

"No," I said, shaking my head emphatically. "No! I wish I could shout about what he did to me, but I know it'll just make everything worse. If it's public, it'll be my fault, and I'll just be an even more public slut than I am already." I sniffled. "I'm telling you only because, well, you're here. And you're legally sworn to secrecy so you can't open your mouth to anyone. Not even the other Gloss girls."

"No one? Not even Cassidy?"

I pressed my lips together tightly.

She sighed deeply. "Oh, honey. I totally understand your position, but I hate that it's like this. He's the one who should be ashamed, not you."

I shook my head again, wiping away more tears with the back of my hand. "I don't know. I've always wanted to be a mother," I whispered. "Just . . . not like this."

I SAT DRINKING my third cup of coffee, cradling the cup with both elbows on the counter. My head was splitting.

I thought about the last time I'd seen Cassidy. I ran into her once—just once—about five or six years after she'd left. We hadn't talked since the group broke up, though not for my lack of trying. Yumi and Rose both held a residual grudge about the way she'd left us high and dry, and the tour had petered out after Australia. Without Cassidy, Big Disc considered the extension unnecessary and had framed it as a *postponement,* until Cassidy "got better"—and I was secretly relieved that I could nurture my daughter without a huge spotlight on my changing body. I remember reading gossip sites at the time as everyone conjectured that Cass was secretly working on a solo album and was going to resurface in due time. Instead, of course, Rose tried her hand at the solo thing and, while one of her singles reached acceptable levels on the charts, she sat nursing her pride after one lackluster album.

It was one of those rare moments when I was in between projects—I think my lipstick line hadn't come to fruition, but my cookbook had already bombed—and I had extra time to spend with Soleil. The first thing she did when we were on our way to the park was to throw her toy out the car window. So we went to Target to get her a new one.

I was kneeling down on the floor as she had a meltdown, even though I showed her the toy in its box. Sighing, I removed all the packaging and thrust the doll into her hand. She stopped sobbing immediately, brightening as her fingers felt all the familiar plastic limbs.

When I got to my feet and glanced up, there was Cassidy, an aisle away, eyes skimming a shelf laden with stuffed zebras and manatees. Tugging on Soleil's hand, I guided her forward until I closed the gap between Cassidy and me.

"Hi," I said cautiously. Her eyes flicked over to me but she didn't say anything. "Did you want help picking something out?" Like it was the most natural thing in the world, us shopping together.

"No, thanks," Cassidy said.

Her first words to me in five years were a dismissal.

With a jolt, I realized she was too thin. She was in jeans and a hoodie, but the wrist reaching out and, finally, taking the manatee off the shelf was attached to a claw of a hand, tendons in sharp relief.

"Are you okay?" I asked. "We were always friends, Cass. I can help you if you need it . . ."

Cassidy looked at me and smiled. It was so unnatural, so painted on and grotesque, that the doll Soleil held had a more genuine smile on its lips. "I'm fine," she said, and made her way to the registers. I was so taken aback by the garish grin that I felt rooted to the floor for a beat, but then I followed, tugging Soleil along and picking her up when her short legs were too slow.

"Moooom," Soleil whined, kicking at me with her little feet. I set her down and pushed up against Cass.

"What's wrong? What really happened? Can't you tell me?"

The real questions almost hurled themselves out of my mouth: *What really happened with Gloss? Why did you just leave without warning?*

I was being too aggressive, and I knew it, but this had been eating away at me for what felt like forever. She acted like I wasn't there, and Soleil began to whine again. "Hold on, honey," I said, patting her. I tried another tactic, softening my voice. "Who is that for?"

I'd finally annoyed her enough that she answered gruffly. "My sister's having a baby." Then she began to walk away quickly. I huffed in irritation and picked up Soleil again, chasing Cassidy to the exit. "Cass!"

Cassidy whirled around on the sidewalk outside, and I knew it was because I'd shouted her name in public. "Why don't you go ask *Rose,*" she said gruffly.

"Ask her what? She doesn't know, either!" I started to cross the parking lot to follow her, but Soleil tugged on my hand, slowing me down. She'd dropped her doll just inside the automatic doors. A loss prevention member looked at the doll and then looked back at me.

"Ma'am," he said.

"Shit. Sorry." I went back in to pay, with my gaze over my shoulder, trying to see what car Cassidy was driving. But she was gone. I kicked myself for not abandoning the toy.

Of course I'd asked Rose what Cassidy had meant, but Rose shrugged it off. "No clue."

As I sipped my coffee, now cold, and heaved myself up off the stool to make a fresh cup, I considered once again what she had been alluding to. Did Cassidy's reasons for leaving the group—whatever she blamed Rose for, I assumed—have any residual connection with her recent suicide? Everything we do, and everything that has been done to us, can affect us. If I hadn't stayed late, if I hadn't accepted extra attention, if I hadn't been such a goddamn easy target—

My therapist has told me, time and time again, that it was not my fault. Did Cassidy have someone who would say it to her, repeat it to her, *make* her listen, like I did? The way she looked in that Target, with the ghastly smile that to outsiders might have looked real but to me, someone who knew her, was an obvious forgery, made me think not.

I was starting to consider that my therapist's suggestion to wait until Soleil was an adult was not going to hold up for the next four years. She'd keep needling. She'd keep subtweeting. She would bring it up over and over and the conversation would go around in circles again and again, an abundance of speculation.

I would keep the fire out of it, though.

**Excerpt from *Variety* Online. June 26, 2002: Exclusive Interview with Sassy Gloss**

Cassidy "Sassy Gloss" Holmes is a slip of a girl. She hardly looks like someone who would command the attention of eighty thousand people in a stadium, but it helps that she is one face of four in a pop phenomenon that has taken the world by storm—Gloss, the quartet behind hits such as "Wake Up Morning" and "What Did U Say." Since their eponymous 2001 album shot straight to number one on the Billboard 200 for seventeen weeks, starting in June of last year, Gloss has consumed Holmes's life. She looks seventeen but is actually twenty, her vulnerability exacerbated by her recent injury that also captivated America's interest.

When asked about her broken arm, which she has tended to gently throughout Gloss's second stadium tour for their second album, *Prime* (2002), Holmes grows serious. "I know there have been rumors about what happened to my arm," she says. "People have been terrorizing my ex [university student Alex Hernandez] about hurting me. This couldn't be further from the truth. He never touched me in any harmful way."

Her arm now completely mended, Holmes smiles and works her hand methodically, as if to show me that she's all in one piece. "I'm fine, really. It's Alex and his family I want to reach out to. I'm so sorry that Alex was implicated and judged for this accident." She implores the public to stop bothering her ex, who was recently hospitalized for an unrelated car accident. I reached out to the family but they did not respond.

She continues, "He is one of my best friends. I just hope

that he can forgive me for taking so long to make a public statement."

What prompted Holmes to finally address the issue now, after weeks of silence? Her brown eyes grow cold. Holmes, dressed in a gray cashmere sweater and Juicy Couture jeans that hug every curve, wraps her arms around herself even though it's still a hot summer's day in Los Angeles. "I sometimes don't understand why my team instructs us as they do," she answers hesitantly. "I usually trust their judgment. This time, I think they were wrong."

# 30.

# Cassidy

**Sassy Cassidy Claims "NO FOUL"**
**Sassy Gloss Interview: "He's Innocent"—But Is He?**
**When Women Cover for Their Abusers: What Are the**
**Reasons? A Psychologist's Look into This Phenomenon**
**IF HE'S INNOCENT, WHY WAIT TILL NOW?**
**What Else Is Sassy Gloss Hiding?**

I t didn't matter. I'd explicitly stated that Alex wasn't responsible, yet people didn't believe me. His family wouldn't respond to the stories, Alex himself wouldn't answer my phone calls, and I wondered if it had even been worth going to the press at all. Now the subject had been dredged up again, and even worse, updates were printed, spread thickly in newsprint: Alex Hernandez, once accused of abuse, was likely to never walk again. Even worse, with this permanent mark on his name, Alex would likely never fulfill his dream to serve on the city council or become governor or president. This rumor would follow him around forever.

The whole thing made me sick to my stomach. My insomnia grew more agitated; I had to take several sleeping pills a night to soothe my guilt. My eating grew even more erratic—food tasted like ash and it hurt to swallow.

We played our last concert in Philadelphia, moved on to Kansas City, played Duluth, Charlotte, Nashville, and ended in Chicago. We flew home to Los Angeles, where, I'd hoped, we would have a longer break before finishing the Midwest and the rest of the nation. And all the while, the other girls were angry with me for skipping a show and taking over the piece that was supposed to go into *Variety*.

THEY TRICKLED INTO the label meeting, loud and already in mid-conversation with one another. I walked in by myself and sat apart from everyone else.

Stephen St. James appeared with Peter, surprising me. My gaze jumped between the two men, wondering why Stephen had shown up at a Gloss meeting. Instead of sitting down immediately, Stephen ambled over to my seat and leaned against the conference table. "Hi, Sassy," he said, nonchalantly.

I immediately looked down at my hands, jittering my fingernails on the laminated table. I tried to ignore him and concentrate on breathing. "Hi, Stephen."

"I saw the piece you did in *Variety*. Riveting stuff."

The implication was clear. Say anything else, give a hint of what Stephen was *really* like, to anyone, and he'd make my life a living hell. He knew where I lived, he knew where I worked.

"Thank you," I said, throat tightening. He tipped his hat and moved to the opposite side of the table.

Yumi was there to take his place. She sat next to me and hovered in my personal space. "Cassidy, I know I'm supposed to be pissed at you about the *Variety* thing, but I have something to tell you too."

I glanced up at the source of the voice. My eyes focused on her, slowly.

She blew out a breath. "It was me."

All I could do was blink. "What do you mean?"

"While you were gone, I talked to Rose." Her eyes wouldn't meet mine. "I mentioned how I didn't understand why you would go visit Alex and do that interview after what he'd done, and she told me that he had been framed as a person he was not."

I cut my eye across the table and saw Stephen, turned away and chatting with Peter, thankfully.

"When you were getting ready for the Oscars and I let Alex in—"

"Please stop talking."

My eyes were back on the table. I really did not want Stephen to overhear this. And as much as I wanted to know about Yumi's involvement in everything that had happened, I knew that if I learned any more of it, I would blame her just as harshly as I did myself.

"I only did it because I care about you and thought—"

I made a hard gesturing motion for her to stop. She hesitated, but obligingly shut up and sat down. Peter clapped his hands to start the meeting.

It was about the Pacific leg of the tour, but I couldn't focus. Yumi was the one who leaked. No wonder she had been *so* adamant that Alex was guilty. Peter snapped his fingers in my face to get my attention again as he spoke. "We *had* lined up some local talent for Australia," he said, "like we did for your Asian shows. But because of some conflicts with our Oz team, we have had to restructure. You'll now be traveling with a fellow Big Disc client—and one of my new clients as well. Stephen St. James." The rest of the room clapped politely, their gazes in Stephen's direction, but I couldn't move. My stomach felt like ice.

"Stephen, any words?" Peter asked, opening the floor up to him.

Stephen stood. I continued staring at my still hands, but in my periphery I could see his long torso and his elegant, tapered fingers hooked on the loops of his jeans. "I've always admired you ladies for being able to travel the world. As y'all know, I've been under the Big Disc umbrella for a while but my old manager always wanted me to stick to the Southern states. I convinced Peter here to take me on so I can expand my reach. I know I'm more country than usual, but I'll be promoting my new album, which is more of a rock crossover."

Peter added, "It hasn't been announced yet, but *Sing It* is going to let Peter Vincent Management have first pick of any winners starting from season three."

Merry said, "That's great, Peter," and the meeting ended on many congratulatory notes.

It took all of my willpower not to storm out. Was this why Peter had been avoiding our calls last month? He had been busy setting up this new contract with Stephen? When the rumor had come out that Alex had broken my arm, I could imagine that Stephen confided in Peter about what had happened, and Peter, in his infinite wisdom, had allowed the lie to persist. Maybe he even fanned the flames. Anything to keep his new paycheck in the public's good graces.

The tour had been a godsend in that it kept Stephen away from me, in different states or on another continent. Even though there were only four Australian dates, it'd be a week of spending time alongside him. How was I supposed to deal with this? I felt the sting of betrayal deep in my marrow.

I arrived home to an empty house—Emily was still dog-sitting Penny—and dragged myself up to the master bedroom. All of the cushioned armchairs, soft carpets, sand-colored tapestries hanging all over the walls, dampened sound on the second floor. My feet made no noise as I placed one in front of the other, body weary, until I reached the bed. Anxiety consumed so much energy. I was spent.

Without Rose, I knew I wasn't going to sleep well here. I curled up on the bed, kicked off my shoes, and hugged an overstuffed pillow. The colors outside the window burned from fire to dusk; light in the room faded softly, until the arms holding the pillow were bathed in soft blue. Thoughts jogged in my head, a repetition, a mantra: *your fault your fault your fault.*

What could I do besides wonder how I could have changed the outcome? If I'd never gotten in the limo with Stephen St. James. If I hadn't trusted Peter so much. If I'd stood up for

Alex. If I'd never gotten involved with Alex at all. Now because of my mistake, he and his family suffered; I would never forgive myself.

My cell phone rang—probably Emily asking if I was finally home so she could drop off the dog. I picked it up without checking the caller ID.

"It's me," said a voice. I shifted and sat up, still clutching the pillow.

"Edie?" I whispered hopefully.

"No. Rose."

Her voice was lower and huskier than normal, and the reception wasn't very good in this part of the Hills so it was an understandable mistake, but I berated myself nonetheless. "Oh. I was just thinking about you. I'm sorry about the interview, okay? I just needed to get the truth out there—"

She cleared her throat. "That's not why I wanted to talk to you."

"Okay . . ." I gazed out the window. The blue was gone now too, replaced with the incandescent yellow glow of outside lights burning to keep intruders away. My yard beyond that was dark and shifting, winds rattling the leaves on the trees lining the drive.

"I'm still mad at you about the *Variety* thing. But this isn't about that."

Her words buoyed my hope. "Do you want to come over?"

"I can't. I've told you before, *we* just can't."

"You keep saying that, but I still find you in my bed almost every night. Who are you kidding, Rose?"

"I mean it this time."

"Because of fans? Rose, listen to yourself. I am not asking for an epic romance or a forever thing. I'm just asking you to be with me for a while. I think we can be happy together."

"No, not fans. Though yeah, that's a concern. It's my mom."

"Clara?" I traced the stitching on the bedspread.

"She doesn't know. Well, she knew Viv's . . . um . . ."

"Relationship with you?" We hadn't discussed it since that night in Copenhagen, the tenderness Rose had shown when we visited San Jose. The careful way Rose had carried her to the bathroom. The way Viv's mother had whispered, *I'm glad she found you,* which didn't mean anything to me until I belatedly realized the nature of their bond. Lorna knew, and she wanted Rose to be happy.

"Mom knew Viv was quote-unquote *different.* And she hated it. She thought it was contagious, learned behavior. Tried to separate us all the time. She was thrilled when Viv got sick."

"*Thrilled?*" What kind of human—

"Wrong word, but close. She knew the illness would keep us apart. Me with Gloss, Viv in hospitals. If she knew about me and you, she would have an aneurysm. And I can't do that to her."

I clutched the phone. "Maybe she's changed. Maybe she would be happy to see you happy."

"No . . ." Even though she wasn't there, I could sense Rose shaking her head vehemently. "She would never change."

"You're going to listen to her over your own feelings?" I said, incredulous.

There was a silence. "It's fucked up," Rose said, "but she's my mother."

"But how—" The ache in my stomach grew. It was as if I'd inhaled hot tar and it was gurgling through my throat, hardening in my lungs, crumbling through my body. I gagged and couldn't say anything more.

"When we are back on tour, we're going to pretend none of this happened," Rose continued. "We are two professionals doing our jobs. But no jokes. No innuendos. No touching."

"I can't *touch* you?" I blurted out.

"And no sleeping," she said with finality.

"But—" The insomniac moments without her, the quiet scent of her.

"I'm sorry about this," Rose said, "but I think it's best to lay out boundaries before we start traveling again."

"No one would know," I pleaded. "Maybe just Yumi and Merry. And I guess Ian. We can keep it quiet."

"No, we can't," she snapped. "*Yumi?* You think *she* can keep a secret? Well, did you know that Yumi chitchatted with *Veronica, the sound tech,* about what she thought had happened between you and Alex? And look what happened there! Of course, she told me and Peter too, because she was *worried about you*." Her voice dripped disdain. "We are *huge*. It will get out. *Yumi* might accidentally let it slip, or someone will see us and film us, and it'll be Merry and Grant times two thousand."

The real details about Yumi hurt more than I thought they would. I could have seen her accidentally telling *one* person about her suspicions, but to talk to Rose about them? Peter too? The betrayal stung.

"What about what *I* think? I don't get a say?" I whined.

"Sorry, no, it just . . . doesn't work that way." After she hung up, I stared at the phone display, which flashed the time and then slowly faded to gray. I curled back into a ball, wanting to cry but not feeling the wetness reach my cheeks. Everything bubbled under the surface. My heart hammered in my chest, beating in my ears; the black tar wheezed in my lungs, making it hard to breathe.

Alex. Yumi. Rose. Blame. Blame. Blame. *Stupid stupid stupid*.

I decided to black everything out and try to go to bed early. I shuffled to the bathroom for the sleeping pills and filled a glass with water. I took two while staring at myself in the mirror. Then I looked at the label and thought how hard I wanted to sleep, and took two more.

It occurred to me that I could black myself out forever if I took the right amount. There were enough in the bottle. I poured them out on the counter and fingered them with a manicured nail, watching them slide along the marble. With my hands I made a two-by-two formation of the rest, then three-by-three, then a square, which I swirled into a circle. I looked into my reflection and considered it. My thoughts scared me, that much was true—and I didn't think that I could feel fear anymore. I'd imagined that the incident with Stephen St. James in the limo had seared all the fear out of me, that my body had used up its lifetime allotment of fear. But now, feeling the capsules move fluidly under my fingers, I wondered if I was making a mistake that I wouldn't have time to regret.

A noise startled me—a bark, a clattering of shoes downstairs. "Hello?" came a voice, and Penny continued to bark resounding, echoing greetings all along the kitchen and finally short, happier tones as she bounded up the stairs. I wiped my eyes with the back of my hand and poured the pills into their container, replacing the lid safely on top and setting it in the cabinet.

"Penny!" I exclaimed, kneeling by the bathroom doorway and letting her kiss me with her mottled pink tongue. "I missed you!"

And it was true. I'd missed her happy, devoted smile and her sour breath.

And then I thought how much I would rather spend all of my time with Penny instead of around the terrible environment that was Gloss: my lover who was not my lover, my friend who was not my friend, the friend that I didn't deserve, the manager who was a cesspool of toxicity. Maybe I just wouldn't go back.

Emily came slowly around the doorjamb to the master bedroom, knocking lightly. "Hi," she said, "just checking to make sure you're actually here and Penny won't be all alone tonight."

"I'm here." I stood up, wavering a little. "Though I'm about to get into bed."

"It's barely nine." Emily consulted her watch.

"Yeah, but . . . jet lag."

Emily looked at me, really taking me in, it seemed. Penny's tail thumped on the floor in a dull clap. "Are you okay?" she asked.

I looked back down at Penny, scratching her ears, a pretense to avoid Emily's scrutiny. "Mm-hmm. Just tired."

"All right," she said, backing out of the doorway. "See you

later. Bye, Penny!" I heard her stomp across the kitchen tile and arm the alarm before locking the door. Her car crunched along the gravel toward the gate.

"Good girl, Penny," I said, glancing back up at the cabinet, knowing what waited inside. "Let's get to bed."

## 31

*Monday*

# Rose

After a lackluster meeting with the FPZ execs, where they dangled a fifteen-million-dollar contract at me and I teased a yes (I aim to have my agent negotiate another five), I returned to my Beverly Hills house to get ready for the *Lunch at Midnight* premiere, while Viv was already deep into her British dramas on her side of the house. Seeing lots of zeroes on potential checks felt like the old days. I knew that things could go back to normal soon enough.

The other Gloss girls were going to meet me there. I suggested to my agent that I walk separately to highlight my independence and position as a working actress. Merry and Yumi could figure out if they wanted to walk down together or alone.

The roar of the crowd was just as loud as I remembered. I waved genially to fans and photographers straining against velvet ropes and stepped out onto the red carpet, trying to ignore the ever-present pain in my back. Fifteen years ago, doctors said it was a bruise, but I swear to god that I cracked something.

Another holler, and there were the other Gloss girls following not too far behind me. I was surprised to see Soleil so tall—she was just a kid the last time I saw her—but now she had grown willowy and straight, all angles, with a pointy chin and sharp elbows. Her face was a reflection of Merry's if it had gone through a slightly distorted mirror: a little longer, with a narrower mouth and a higher forehead. She'd drawn her lips and eyebrows on darkly, giving herself a bolder look, while Merry stuck to her signature berry colors. Merry and Sunny had apparently invited Yumi to walk with them, because all three posed for photos together. We gathered on the other side of the publicity backdrop where I said, "No Raul or Emily tonight?"

Merry shrugged. "Just wanted to see a movie with my best gal." She wrapped her arm around her gangly daughter. Soleil scowled and tried to remove herself from the hug.

The decibel level rose, if that was possible, and I whirled around to see who could command more attention. The girls of Joyride, a young pop trio, sauntered down the carpet like goddesses. I'd never met them in person, but I hated them on sight: they were a branding company's wet dream, comprising an East Asian–European woman with full lips and blue hair, a Latina with a tiny waist and burgundy hair, and a black woman with a straight lavender weave. Not only were all three devastatingly beautiful, tall, and looked like models, I'd heard one of their singles too—it was catchy and what I expected Gloss to have created if we were still in the game.

Joyride went through the camera grinder after us, and before we were herded into our seats for the showing, the Joyrider with the burgundy hair, who was the spokeswoman for the group, stopped me by gently reaching out her arm. Her fingernails wore long stilettos with jewels on the tips, making any utilitarian use for her hands impossible. "We are so pleased to meet you," she said warmly, "and are excited to be in this movie with you. As small as our parts were." She gave a tinkling little laugh.

"That's very sweet," Yumi said, smiling lightly. She shook hands with all three women.

"Don't let the press fool you," said the Joyrider. "We are supposedly rivals with everyone and clap back at everybody, but we're actually normal, happy people."

"That's nice," I said, glancing toward the doorway as if something more interesting was over there.

Soleil shrieked a breathless "Omigod," her coolness melted away by youthful exuberance. "I *have* to get a picture with you!"

The Joyrider took Soleil's phone and flipped it to selfie mode, then began filming. "Hiii. It's Luna"; "Cherie," said the blue-haired woman; "Magenta," said the third; all together, rehearsed, they chorused, "and we're Joyride." Luna continued, "And we're here with Soleil on the red carpet for *Lunch at Midnight*." Soleil waved at her own followers, grinning like a kid who just had her first celebrity encounter.

"We're being ushered to our seats," I said, prodding them forward.

We'd gone through our part in the film during the dailies—I'd insisted on that—but the rest of the film was a surprise. Soleil was the buffer between the other two Glossies and myself, and though I was thirsty I didn't order anything. Soleil noisily slurped from a box of Sour Patch Kids next to me, spitting the gummy candy into a separate wrapper after she'd eaten off the sour crystals. I could hear Merry admonishing her for such a disgusting exercise, to which Soleil muttered a teenager's reply.

The movie wasn't much of a departure from Stan Harold's usual films—part romantic comedy, part slapstick. There was an increase in audience rustling when our cameo came up, as people recognized us: Rosy, Cherry, and Tasty, sitting in a diner booth in the middle of nowhere (it was supposed to be Arizona, though we shot it on a soundstage), blithely ignoring the she-nanigans the main character dealt with outside the restaurant. We were supposed to converse among ourselves as the actor was pushed, pulled, and wiped across the plate-glass window, a real ha-ha scene for the viewers. Finally, the character was pulled inside and slid across the just-waxed floor as we got up in our perfect heels and stepped over him to go outside. "Watch yourself," I said on-screen to the dazed boy, "you'll mess up the gloss." Proverbial wink.

The next shot was supposed to be a wide zoom-out of the restaurant as we drove away in a convertible with its top down, but Stan Harold had changed his mind. Instead, the camera focused on the perfect pouts of three young women in the diner sipping milkshakes from paper straws. The girls got up—the shot focused on their rear ends and short-shorts—and were revealed as Joyride, whipping out sunglasses and looking hot as hell. They struck a pose and Luna broke the fourth wall by saying to the camera seductively, "Oof, that's such a tired line, don't you think?" The girls left the diner and the zoom-out scene happened with *them* in the convertible.

"*What?*" I murmured. There were some whispers around us.

*That* was our role? To be ridiculed for being old and out of touch? I fumed in my seat until the screening was over, and as soon as the credits began to roll, I shoved myself out from between the rows and stalked away.

Luna caught up to me. "Rose, Rose, I'm so sorry," she said, whispering urgently.

"Don't call me *Rose* like you know me," I snapped.

"Fine, uh, Ms. McGill. I—"

"That's not any better!"

She slowed me down by standing in my path. "I had no idea they were going to use that footage like that. It was written to make fun of the guy! I swear."

"It doesn't matter," I declared, but I tried not to stomp away since there were still cameras around. "It's done, you look cool and are the *look* of a new generation; we're old has-beens."

The rest of the group had caught up to us by then. "Oh please, stop being so ridiculous, Rose." Merry scowled. "It's a joke! The movie is for kids. No one Sunny's age cares about Gloss."

"No one cares," Soleil agreed, nodding sagely. I itched to slap her.

"This isn't on you or on Joyride," said Yumi, "but on Stan and the producers, really. He thought it'd be funny."

"Personally, I thought it worked better without our bit," said Cherie. "It was overkill adding us in there."

A few straggling cameras were closing in on us having our serious-faced discussion. Magenta winced. "Uh, you know, press is here."

"Whatever, I'm tired of being a joke." I jabbed my finger at her. "I want my career back. I'm going to get it back. Watch me."

Magenta caught my hand and shoved it down. "First of all," she said, "you get that finger outta my face. Second, I don't give a shit about *your* career. I grew up watching you on MVC. *Fuck,* I even wanted to be you in the 'Prime' video. Now I couldn't care less about Gloss. Come on, girls." And the rest of Joyride passed by us, tall, leggy, beautiful, and the visual winners by virtue of being broadcast.

"That went well," Merry said sarcastically. "Why would you go and antagonize them? You played right into Stan's caricature of us. We're angry 'old' women. They're young, fiery bitches." She sighed. "Yumi, drink?" They pulled away, looking toward the after-party next door.

"Just a minute," Soleil said to them before glancing back at me. "It's understandable," she said in a bored-sounding voice now that everyone else had left. "You're in mourning. They might make an excuse for you because you're stressed."

I glanced around at the crowd and decided I didn't want to be there anymore. I'd been photographed, gotten into a tiff, would probably make some gossip channels as the relic who had tangled with a pop trio. I was done.

"I am *not* being analyzed by a fourteen-year-old," I groused, beginning my walk past the wall of paparazzi to the quiet street.

Soleil followed me, her long legs taking short strides to match mine, as she dug into her sparkly bag. "I have a proposition," she said.

"With you? Go back to your mom."

She produced a letter from an inside pocket of her clutch. The handwriting was familiar, the text purple gel pen. I stopped so suddenly, I nearly tripped. "You tell me who my dad is, and I won't show this to anyone."

I had a moment to regroup. "Your dad?" I sneered. "Why would I know who your dad is? Your mom fucked so many people. It could be anybody." That handwriting. Cassidy's? "What is that, anyway?"

"It's a letter from Cassidy to you, talking about how you two were in love." She waggled her eyebrows.

I tried to snatch it from her hand but she was taller and held it aloft. It was so unfair, being shorter than someone less than half your age.

"Why would I care if you show that letter—if it's even *real*—to anyone?"

"Well," she said, worrying at her lip with her teeth, "you haven't had a real romance in ages, if ever. So I guess you're either dating nobody . . . or dating people you're ashamed of. And I'm guessing it's the former *and* that you don't want to be outed."

*Outed*. My insides turned to ice. I'd carefully kept everything hidden, and yet, this fourteen-year-old could see right through me. "This is a shitty thing you're doing, you understand," I warned. "Like, real shitty." Didn't Sunny realize that it was fine—celebrated, even—in her generation, but mine had to be quiet about it? That I grew up hearing about the hell on earth that people like me had lived through—or *died* from? And my mother—

"I know." There was a hesitant pause as she thought about it again, but she shrugged. "I have gone through everything trying to find out who my dad is. Letters, pictures, documentaries. Everyone thinks it's Grant Kidd."

"So there you have it."

"But Mom swears up and down that it's not him. Get her to tell me who he really is or I'll send this to *JMC*."

"This is ridiculous," I exploded.

"Look, there's one of their cameramen right now," she said, waving the letter like a flag to get his attention. For a moment, I considered letting her. If an expert could match the handwriting to her diary, if the resulting attention would splash my name on the front page of every gossip blog . . . But I didn't know if I wanted my personal life out there for consumption.

I always play to win. This was not the best hand to be dealt right now.

I shook my head. "*Okay*. But I actually don't know. I'll have to ask her."

Soleil brought her arm down. I walked toward the throng of people at the after-party. It was easy to find Merry, hair so light it glowed among all the other heads, neck bent forward as she was sipping and chatting easily with a group of people. "We need to talk," I murmured to her, and she disentangled herself slowly.

We found ourselves an open corner and stood as a trio. "Merry, your daughter is blackmailing me into finding out who her father is."

Merry blinked once. "What?" She turned to Soleil and repeated, "What?!"

Instead of shrinking, as I would have if my mother exclaimed with such vitriol, Soleil seemed to grow. With hands on her narrow hips, she retorted, "I deserve to know."

"By blackmailing—wait, how does she even have anything on you, Rose?" Merry shook her hands in the air, waving the thought away. "Never mind, I don't need to hear the answer to that."

"I don't know what is going on," I continued, "and honestly, I don't care. What I *do* care about is that Sunny here is threatening to expose some of my personal correspondence to benefit herself. So rein in your kid."

I turned to leave, but Merry caught my arm after I'd taken only one step. "Rose. Wait." Her eyes glistened.

Something in her voice made me go still. A hurt that I wasn't expecting, a desperation I hadn't thought her capable of. I whispered, "What *happened* to you?" I realized that I had never considered Merry's ill-timed pregnancy as something that had been wrought by violence or coercion. I'd assumed, like everything else, it was something she'd brought upon herself.

Her eyelashes fluttered fast and I felt a pang of pity for her. Using my arm as a rudder, she steered us into a corner, where the music only echoed and Soleil couldn't hear. "I can't talk about it," she murmured. "You know what people said about me back then. Everyone will say I—that I deserved it. And what would that do to a girl her age?" Merry slid her eyes back toward her daughter, who stood quizzically where we'd left her, for once concerned that this dig for information might, in fact, be bad news for her.

I gently removed Merry's hands from my forearm. "If she keeps chasing after this, she's going to learn sooner or later. You need to get ahead of this. And what sort of example are you setting for her if you're always going to run from your past?"

She stepped away, her head backlit by a light fixture so her face was in darkness. When she spoke again, her voice was cool. "And you? What's she got on you that you're taking her side? Why are you scared of my fourteen-year-old?"

I wouldn't let her words penetrate me. My armor was back up, solid. "You know what, Meredith? This isn't about *me* being scared. So what if you were the Other Woman back then? If something bad did happen, I'd expect Meredith-Warner-Merry-Cherry-Gloss to shout about who wronged her and how that person is a piece of shit. You're not no one. You're a *Gloss girl,* for fuck's sake. Are you the woman who set fire to Grant Kidd's house or not?"

She took another step away from me. "You knew about that?"

I snorted. "You think Marisa Marcheesa, Princess of Hollywood, would set a fire? There's a bigger chance that Lucy Bowen would win an Oscar than *that* happening. I can't figure out if you did it by accident or on purpose, but I figured Grant deserved it."

"Don't tell anyone about that," she said nervously. "It wasn't supposed to burn that entire wing. I was just making a point, that's all."

"It's just lucky Marisa was around to muddy the waters, huh?"

Merry knew exactly what I was implying.

She nodded once, looking at her palms, playing with the diamond ring on her left hand. "Okay," she said finally. "Okay. You're right."

"Of course I'm right." Rosy always looking out for Merry, as usual.

"I'll talk to Soleil."

# 32.

## Tuesday

# Yumi

I popped the last bite of my Quarter Pounder in my mouth and wiped my hands on a paper napkin. My appointment with the new producers for *Sing It, America!* had me on pins and needles. I should have rehired my agent to negotiate for me, I thought, or hired a new one. I didn't know why I was so nervous; my anxiety felt unfounded, since I didn't know if I even wanted the job. I'd been out of the Hollywood scene for a while now, even if I *had* made a small cameo in Stan Harold's movie. For the most part, I'd been living modestly off my royalties and the divorce settlement, paying taxes like a normal person.

I looked in the rearview mirror, checking to make sure my teeth were clean, and reapplied lipstick. "There's no harm in being prepared to hear what they have to say." I spoke the words neatly to my reflection, blotting on the clean side of the McDonald's napkin.

When I got to the ninth floor of the FPZ office building, a young guy in a suit hopped up to greet me. "Ms. Otsuka!" He extended a hand. "I'm Mike Parsons. We spoke on the phone. Right this way."

I followed him into a small, comfortable conference room, where a few other figureheads sat.

"Hello, Ms. Otsuka, thank you for joining us," said a tall, sandy-haired man with thick-framed glasses. "I'm Henry Grafton—I head the network's programming—and I'd like to introduce Lila Landry and John Grant, executive producers for *Sing It*." I sat, and Henry instructed Mike, the assistant, to provide coffee for the room.

"As you know," Henry Grafton said, getting right down to business, "FPZ is rebooting *Sing It*. It's been off the air for a few years but has a huge legacy and we think we can revive its booming franchise. We are trying to find the right judges for the reboot—people who are known in the industry, nothing too flashy, you understand, not some hot new star who hasn't been tested. We need tried-and-true stars like yourself to be on the panel."

I smiled slightly and nodded, taking a sip of the coffee politely, even though I had no taste for it.

"For the first season," Lila Landry said, ignoring the cup set down in front of her, "the judges were a mix of talent. Some were people only the industry insiders knew, like Marsha Campbell from Big Disc. But others, like Emma Jake, were big names that had dominated the charts in years past."

"We understand you've been retired for some time." Henry picked up where Lila left off. "We were hoping that you would come out of quote-unquote retirement to help make the re-booted *Sing It* a success. Be the next Emma Jake."

The smile froze on my face. It hadn't occurred to me, even though it should have been obvious, that being a judge was a mentor role. Age hit me suddenly and I felt ancient. Cassidy had been seventeen when she auditioned for the first *Sing It,* and that was half a lifetime ago. I took another sip from my cup to give myself some time to consider the years behind me. "I see."

Lila seemed to sense what I was thinking, because she hurried to add, "You may have noticed that FPZ has been . . . fairly homogenous in the past. We are trying to become more inclusive and welcome diversity. Of course, we're not interested in you because of your ethnicity, we're interested because you're pop royalty. But we are excited to have better representation on television." She smiled graciously. "And also, we'll have judges from different generations of music. We're talking to a few so I can't name names for certain yet, but you would be the youngest on the panel and therefore the 'cool' one."

I thought back to how I felt like the token Asian in Gloss. How I was called Tasty, my name mispronounced as Yummy. All the Chinese-inspired prints I was put in, even though I was Japanese. After years of feeling like an outsider, I was supposed to be glad that I—my face and my name and my body—fit a profile they wanted to check off?

"This seems sudden, your interest in the Glossies, reaching out only in the past week?" I said to distract myself from my anger.

"We were considering another *Sing It* veteran—Stephen

St. James, winner of season one," Lila admitted. "It's just too bad about the rumors swirling around him."

"Rumors?" I repeated. My home might be in L.A., but my feet had been outside the industry for too long. I hadn't heard anything about Stephen except buzz when a new album was out.

John sighed. "It's not my place to talk about it," he said, "but rumors like the ones following St. James around are not good for business. We reluctantly had to withdraw our interest in him. Hence, Gloss. We're wondering if you'd be interested in the position at all. We are prepared to offer you a good salary for the season. Seven figures."

I shifted a little in the seat, focusing on the question at hand, as they looked at me expectantly. "I'm interested," I hedged, "though as you can see, I'm by myself at the moment. I'd really like to be able to look over everything with my lawyer before I say anything further."

They stood. "We will send the paperwork to whomever you direct," Henry said, extending a hand. I reached out and shook it, standing as well. "Just full disclosure, however—we *are* talking to Rose McGill as well, and we are not interested in having two ex–Gloss members on the panel at the same time."

"I understand." I gathered my purse, leaving my nearly full coffee cup on the table, and shook hands with Lila and John before making my exit.

My car stank of stale french fries. I looked in my rearview mirror again and studied my face. Was I old? Had Emma Jake been my age when she was a judge on the first season of *Sing It*?

I pulled out my phone and searched for Stephen St. James.

The third hit was a gossip site that spelled out the alleged rumors. I recognized the woman who made allegations, though she was fifteen years older now: the runway model Jeannette, whom we'd met at the single release party.

I read her long, sordid description of what Stephen had put her through. Physical and mental abuse, and his staff had helped with any cover-ups. He had threatened her burgeoning career if she said anything at the time, but now that she was retired from modeling, she didn't care anymore. "This man is still preying on women today," she said. "Women who are a lot more vulnerable than myself. I speak on behalf of those women, some of whom didn't extricate themselves fast enough and suffered more than I did. I am one of the lucky ones."

I physically recoiled as I remembered that we had worked alongside this man for months, had considered him a friend. Had even—hadn't Cassidy had a crush on him?

And then horror: *Hadn't* Cassidy had a crush on him, and suddenly, she was over it? Around the same time she broke her arm . . .

My stomach dropped. I'd been so fixated on *Alex* abusing Cassidy at the time, I hadn't considered someone else hurting her. But it made sense now. The way Cassidy went quiet around Stephen, the way she tensed when he showed up at that meeting before Australia. And how she quit the group right before we were going on tour with Stephen opening for us.

While I knew I shouldn't be so quick to believe my gut this time, I knew that Jeannette was telling the truth. And I also knew immediately that Cassidy had been threatened to keep quiet by Stephen and his staff.

My phone buzzed; I didn't recognize the number, but it was a local area code so I slid my finger to answer. "Ms. Otsuka," the voice said. "This is Detective Lawrence."

"Oh. Hold on a minute." I bowed my head over the wheel, taking a deep breath in and a long breath out, cleansing my head of all its bubbling thoughts before setting the phone against my ear. "Okay. I'm ready."

"Yes, ma'am," Detective Lawrence said. "I wanted to let you know that this investigation is now officially closed."

His tone grated on me. "Call me Yumi, not ma'am. There was nothing in the letters?"

"I'm sorry, m—Ms. Otsuka. The M.E. ruled it a suicide. We go by what he says. It seemed very open-and-shut to him, no matter what a bag of letters might have indicated. The body—that is, ah, Ms. Holmes—has been released to her family."

"Oh. I see."

There was a short pause, but the detective didn't hang up. I drummed the steering wheel with my fingers, my mind a series of snapshots, flipping, flipping. I'd known that Cassidy had been unhappy sometimes while we were touring. She never said it outright, but she was subdued and dismissive, evasive and snappy, especially during our *Prime* tour. We'd all had our own issues during that tour, from what turned out to be Merry's pregnancy to Rose and Cassidy getting into their giant unnamed argument that we as a group never rebounded from, and I'd attributed Cassidy's low moods to her fractured arm—the arm that I was now convinced had been broken by Stephen. But maybe there was something deeper going on—a small seed of disease that festered for years after we'd disbanded.

This couldn't be the outcome, could it? I sat in the car, weighing the possibility that there was no answer that would arise from my question.

"Ms.—Yumi. I hope that you can put her to rest. May her memory be a blessing," Detective Lawrence said, his voice softer, more personable. Like two people discussing an old friend.

The lump I'd been avoiding in my throat sprang up again, making it hard to swallow. I couldn't tell if I was angry about Stephen, angry at myself for not seeing it for so long, or in mourning. I ended the call abruptly to wipe my eyes.

## 33.

# Cassidy

The entire month of August had me in a state of perpetual dread. I had avoided Stephen St. James since the bombshell tour meeting, but as this year's Music Video Awards show loomed closer, MVC suggested that Gloss present with Stephen. Peter leapt at the idea and brought it up when he visited us at the choreographer's studio while we were rehearsing for the performance. The other girls were still annoyed with me for taking the group's *Variety* spot with my Alex rebuttal and were speaking to me only when the job required it. I could barely get out of bed to make rehearsals, and every time I opened my eyes and it was a new morning, I willed the earth to swallow me whole. Every night, I'd take four sleeping pills and collapse into bed, Penny licking my face, as I wished the tour would be canceled.

And then Peter described his vision for the MVA performance.

"They've already seen you two together from last year's show," Peter said. "Maybe we can work in some banter between Sassy and Stephen."

I studied myself in the studio's wall of mirrors as he said it, my expression deceitfully calm. Maybe Peter *didn't* know the full story. Maybe he should be let into the loop. "Peter? Could I talk to you in private for a sec?"

We walked to a different corner of the room. With my gaze off to the side, toward the other girls, who were standing separately and looking with quizzical expressions in our direction, I cleared my throat. "I'm not comfortable with this."

"With what?" Peter's head tilted exaggeratedly.

"With Stephen. Remember when I told you that I broke my arm falling down? Well, um . . ." I took a deep breath and before I lost my nerve blurted, "Stephen did it."

Peter nodded, like we were discussing the weather. "Yes, and?"

I dug into my palm with my nails, peeling a blister. "Isn't that enough?"

"Listen. I know you're feeling a little . . . *touchy* about this." Merry had been right; his voice was unbearably squeaky. My fingers twitched as an urge to claw his face came over me. "But he and I talked about this, and he told me that he was trying to help you out of the limo, you refused, and fell over. I get that you're embarrassed about how all of this went down, but you're overreacting, don't you think? You don't have to make stuff up just to get out of it."

"*That's* what he told you? He grabbed me. And when he saw that my arm was broken, he had his *driver* deliver me to the hospital. He *threatened* me."

"Listen, Cassidy. I'm your manager. I'm supposed to do what is best for you. And what you're telling me right now makes me think that the best thing for you is to spend time with Stephen, heal the breach. You're going to be on tour with him for the foreseeable future. Big Disc is thinking of extending the tour too, and Stephen has generously offered to be the opener, so that he can visit more sites around the U.S. and Europe. Make nice with him."

I walked away from the conversation feeling dazed—and it wasn't just because I was eating fewer calories than ever. After what had happened on the phone regarding Alex, I should have known that Peter would react in a similar fashion when it came to Stephen—protecting the bottom line, growing his business.

I don't know why I didn't just fake illness on the day of the show. Perhaps I bought into the hype that Gloss was a shoo-in for Best Pop Video, and after standing onstage looking at the winners—from *Sing It* to all the other awards shows since—I just wanted to know what it felt like to win *something*.

Maybe I already knew it was the end.

ANG HAD CREATED a set of patterned sequined leotards for us to wear, a medley of colors all mottled together, in different cuts for us. Gone were the days when we squeezed into lacquered pleather. Our tailor understood our bodies and seemed to have chosen an eye-catching design that disguised Merry's thickening tummy. Strategic cutouts showed off our best assets, from Rose's shoulders in a halter to my legs in boy-cut shorts. Our backup dancers would do the more strenuous moves and wore strappy little bondage uniforms like out of *The Fifth Element.*

We arrived in designer outfits—the last red-carpet appearance we would ever make together. I wore a black Chanel gown that looked like a mourning outfit with a white collar and cuffs, the meaning of which was discussed ad nauseam for months afterward. When I was paired with Stephen St. James to present Best Breakthrough Video, I had to turn on the charm and pretend that everything was fine, even though my stomach churned and my hands shook at the podium.

"*Speaking of* breakthrough," Stephen said, turning his face toward me but well aware of the audience, "do you remember the last time we were on this stage, Sassy?" The audience whooped and cheered.

I gave a smile that felt like a grimace. I recited, "I sure do."

"Should we give them another reason to cheer?"

I'd told Peter I didn't want to do this. But it didn't matter—he steamrolled every objection, citing the need to "heal the breach," and refused to discuss it any further. The crowd was on its feet, stamping and hollering, an audience of people who knew nothing of the truth and would probably not care if they'd heard it.

Stephen smiled at me winningly and scooped me into his arms. I stiffened only slightly before I let myself think of Stephen as my friend, my lover, just to endure this. His lips were pursed hard, nothing like the sensual brushes he'd begun with in the limo, and it was like kissing someone else, which helped.

I imagined Rose for a moment, and when he pulled back from me, I felt my throat constricting. I swallowed hard. The audience cheered.

Without even taking a breath after violating me so thoroughly, Stephen unwrapped the envelope. "And the winner is . . ."

Even after we'd disappeared offstage, I was fighting back tears. Our performance was soon, so I wasn't planning to return to my seat, and I tried to find a quiet corner amid all the draperies and pulleys to compose myself.

A voice hissed out of the darkness. "*There* you are." It was Rose, in her outfit already. "You're not dressed. Come on."

I felt my resolve crumble. I pulled her to me—backstage, there with everyone around us and yet enveloped in privacy in between velvet curtains—and placed my mouth on hers. I needed the last pair of lips on mine to not be *his*.

Plush, sticky with gloss, that peep of tongue that I loved. I almost lost myself in her.

She pushed me off and hissed, "Are you completely forgetting where we are?" She pointed in the direction of the dressing area. "Go change," she said perfunctorily. "We have less than five minutes before we go on."

Fog. Lots of fog. The recognizable four beats. Then red lights swirling around as the backup dancers writhed and jittered. Beats again. Now yellow lights, then spotlights on Tasty and Rosy, visible on twin metal staircase structures on the stage. Then Cherry and Sassy, emerging from cages on hovering platforms, sang the next lines and struck poses as the platforms transported them to the metal staircases. The harmony. The chorus. They danced down the staircases, tossing hair, shaking asses. The choreography with the backup dancers was so tight, they looked like they were in the military. Aerialists strapped into harnesses were lowered on trapezes over the stage and performed. Then, the much-talked about finale: amid the spectacle of fireworks and a light show, trained dancers strapped the girls into harnesses, from which giant, iridescent wings made with feathers tipped in fine glitter unfurled and flourished. A still from the performance that was shown the next day on all the entertainment news sites was a wide shot of the stage, the girls at various heights as they were hauled toward the rafters, bookended by trapeze artists, backlit and glowing.

It was a great performance. One for the ages. And in a sweep that surprised no one, "Prime" won Best Cinematography, Best Direction, Best Pop Video, and Best Music Video. We juggled our trophy statuettes during the acceptance speeches, smiling widely. Rose was the spokesperson for us on the first win, but every subsequent announcement, someone else took the microphone.

Merry thanked everyone *but* the director when it was her turn at the mike, something that Yumi corrected when she was next at the podium.

WE QUICKLY SEPARATED after the show, as Yumi opted to go to a flashy after-party and Merry claimed she was too tired to stay out any later. Rose, however, climbed into the SUV with me. "What a high, right?" she said, adjusting her dress as we began to move. I was surprised that she would join me but I didn't open my mouth for fear that she would leap out again.

The tension in the back seat was so taut, I felt my breaths come in shallowly. The driver accepted her directions without comment, completing the short distance from the theater to Rose's house in Sunset Strip, a shorter drive than finding our way to the Hills. "Do you know how *scared* I was in that harness? That I would fall and break my back *again*?"

My heart was zinging in my chest after everything that had happened, and everything that *could* happen. We weren't touching, but our hands were close enough on the back seat that I felt her energy radiating out toward me, my pinky twitching with the urge to caress hers. But no. We had to be careful.

"Grab a nightcap with me," Rose said when we reached her house. It was an all-glass monstrosity with most of the living space on the second floor. Giant windows could open up the house to 360-degree views from one corner to the other, a corridor of air and light bisecting the rooms unless doors were closed. Giant blinds could come down at the touch of a button to seal off the occupants from the outside world, which is what Rose did as we entered the house, slipping off our shoes.

It was the first time I had been invited in, and the occasion was not lost on me as I took a quick visual tour of the house, just from standing in one place, before she was on me, hands slithering under my clothes, mouth on mine. I responded immediately, allowing her to take off my dress, which pooled around my feet in a chiffon puddle.

"This is what I love about you," she purred into my ear, kissing the lobe. "Your perfect ears, your delicious neck."

Love. *I* knew it was love. But did she mean *love* the way that I did?

"Wait." I disentangled myself from her hands and took a step away. "Does this mean we can be together on tour? Because . . ." I swallowed. "I was dreading the tour, but if you say we're good, that . . . that changes *so* much."

She swept back in with her fingers in my hair, murmuring against my mouth. "We can talk about that later."

I wouldn't let her drag me along again. "No, we're going to talk about this *now.*"

She groaned, throwing her hands up in annoyance and backing away. She fell back on her sleek modern couch and dug into a box on the glass coffee table. "Fuck, Cass! You're always asking me to do things I can't do."

"Why can't you? Why can't *we*—"

"Because!" she exploded.

I squinted at her and glanced down at the table. "Wait, what are you doing? Is that *coke*?"

"Just bringing back the good mood since you're making me sag." She leaned over and quickly inhaled one of the three lines she had made on the table.

"You're fine with *drugs* but not *me*?"

"This isn't *about you*!" Rose shouted, rising quickly from the couch. "It was never about *you*. It was about *Gloss!* I'm doing what is best for *Gloss!*"

I stepped back into my dress and buttoned it roughly,

unevenly. I could feel anger in my trembling fingers. "You realize that someday we will *not* be Gloss. And you will look back on this moment and wonder why you decided to choose *Gloss* over any happiness."

She laughed gutturally. "I'll never be happy. Especially not with you. Not truly."

"And why is that?" I expected to hear more bullshit about her mother or her upbringing.

But Rose leveled a look at me. It pierced through one side of my body and went through the other, skewering me whole. "Because," she said simply, "I can never be happy with *anyone* who loves me back." And I could see it was true. It would always be true for Rose. She always wanted what she couldn't have, and rejected anything that came to her easily. Gloss's success, Gloss's tour schedule, Gloss's everything.

And then the penny dropped. "*You* sold me out to the tabloids."

She rubbed at her nose, playing coy. "What?"

I knew her well enough to understand her admission. It made sense. Yumi, concerned that I was in love with an abuser, gossiped with Veronica and then had the sense to talk to management and Rose, because *they* knew how to handle these things. And instead of *asking* me for the real story, *Rose* told the gossip rags a lie, betting that an average person like Alex wouldn't have the means or know-how to deny it fast enough before it spread like wildfire. And look at what happened: Gloss was on everyone's lips, Gloss was on the cover of every magazine. Alex had paid the price for our astronomical fame, and I knew exactly why Rose did it.

"You realize that Alex has been terrorized to all hell, right?" I asked her accusingly. "He can barely *walk* anymore. He almost *died*!"

"But he *didn't*. And we made fat checks. So what's the problem?"

The problem was that the woman I loved was a woman I hated. *That* was the problem.

And I just left, my vision bleary with frustrated tears.

I felt betrayed by everything in my life. Yumi for taking a stab at what happened between Alex and me, and getting it *so* wrong. Peter, for believing Stephen; myself, for trusting the image of Stephen I'd had in my head for years. Alex wouldn't speak to me anymore, and I'd lost my Houston friends. And Rose . . . for everything.

Everything about Gloss had made my dreams come true—and ruined my life all in the same fell swoop.

I couldn't do this anymore.

## 34.

*Tuesday*

# Merry

It was either tell or be told on, and so my hands were tied.

I'd shepherded Soleil home after the premiere and, as she slumped against the passenger seat gazing at her phone, I'd said, "Are you sure you don't want to let me know what you've got on Rose? Maybe we can tackle her together."

She'd shrugged with one shoulder and muttered, "I don't care what I have on *her*. I want to know about my dad."

"It's just . . . she has information about *me* that could be damaging. You understand?"

"Mm-hmm." Soleil didn't look up from her phone.

I didn't want to tell Soleil that, if she released whatever information she had about Rose, Rose would let people know I was responsible for arson. And, okay, I hadn't *meant* to burn down the whole west wing of Grant Kidd's house. I was upset that he wasn't listening to me—I had a weird feeling about the music video director we had just worked with, and he'd called me paranoid—and look where *that* went.

After he'd left, I'd lit some aromatic candles. Then I burned a Polaroid of myself taken in wardrobe that day at the video shoot, angry about the way I'd bungled the underwater filming, and dropped it in a trash can before the corner could burn my fingers. The can was coated in flammable metallic paint and combusted quickly. I watched it for a minute, the flames rising higher as more of the paint flaked and spat, dancing toward the curtains. I flipped a framed portrait of Marisa off the bureau and let that burn merrily. Then the curtains caught flame, red eating the blue drapery. When I finally realized my temper was probably going to get me killed, I escaped to the lawn by the guest house. That was where firefighters found me, coughing feebly and with sooty fingers, when they arrived.

Coincidentally, Marisa had been nearby as well, and she was a person of interest by virtue of being the angry wife. No one could pin it on anybody, which was just as well, but Grant and I were at the end of our run anyway.

And then Noah Decker seized his little opportunity in the guise of "discussing reshoots," and the story wrote itself.

Before our flight to Houston, I called Justine to ask for her opinion. Sometimes she's my interim therapist and lawyer wrapped up in one, but even she didn't know about Soleil's biological father or the real source of the fire. We spoke in generalities.

"I have to say that I dislike both of these ideas," Justine said frankly. "One is accusing a man publicly of sexual assault, which is a he-said, she-said situation, but to add a child to the equation . . . But the other is an actual crime? How *bad* of a crime?"

Maybe I'd outgrown Justine. "Thank you, Justine," I said, and hung up the phone.

Rose was right—Soleil would find out one way or another, and it was probably lucky that she hadn't sent off for a cheek-swab genealogy test and was instead needling me for the information.

We flew to Houston that afternoon, and as soon as we touched down, Soleil had her phone in her hand. She went very still. "Um, Mom?"

The note of fear in her voice made my stomach clench. "What is it?" What fresh horrors were in store now?

"I don't know how—" She pointed the screen toward me. It was *not* about Decker.

All of her Instagram mentions were about Rose and Cass, coming in thick and fast. "What the—" I pulled out my own phone and checked Twitter: the trending tag #glossylove. A link: *A Glossy Affair,* read the headline. I scrolled down. *Rosalind McGill, or Rosy Gloss of the former hit pop group Gloss, admits to a relationship with Cassidy Holmes during the girl group's heyday. Ms. Holmes recently passed—*

Amid all the disembarkation noise, Soleil frantically dug through her bag, her fingers closing on a torn white envelope, which she raised in triumph.

"What's that?" I asked.

"It's the dirt I had on Rose," she said ruefully. "I thought I'd lost it and someone published it, but it's right here . . ."

"No . . . the article here has an admission from Rose herself." How could this be true? And how could I not have known? Every interaction between the two of them was now cast in a different light. What had Rose said to me? *You need to get ahead of this.* After Soleil's blackmailing attempt, she'd probably known it was only a matter of time. Or maybe she was using this news for some strategic gain, to which I was still blind. "Let me see that."

The letter was from Cassidy to Rose, and I was surprised to read the pain, devotion, and love there. It was dated only a few weeks after she left the group, when we were on our way to Australia. "Where did you get this?"

She squirmed. "From the boxes in the attic that Emily pulled down."

I rubbed my brow. "Fuck."

There was more on Twitter—Sterling Royce was getting roasted for dating an underage Lucy Bowen back in the day— and I was glad to see that people were eager to blame him for being a predator. Maybe the tide was changing.

The first-class flight attendant was gesturing for us to exit the plane, and so we got up with our things, the letter still clutched tightly in my hand. We were quiet walking to our car, and quieter still on the drive to the hotel. I had thought Rose and Cassidy hadn't gotten along. Was it all a cover for their relationship?

"So now you're never going to tell me," Soleil said sadly.

"What?"

"You're never going to tell me who my dad is."

I reached over and wrapped my hand around hers. I sighed. "I don't want to. But it looks like I will have to."

The car dropped us at the front entrance of the hotel, a pink-bricked building close to parks, rather than downtown. We left our bags in the room and grabbed water from the mini fridge. "Come on," I said. "Let's go for a walk."

It was humid, steam fogging up my sunglasses as we stepped out of the air-conditioned lobby. As we crossed the street, I wondered how much I would tell her. She was already excited, bouncing on her heels with every step that we took. I'd have to quash this mood immediately.

"Turn off your phone and look at me." She did. Her eyes reflected the same blue as mine. I didn't see her father in her. Maybe in the twitch of the lip, the cock of the head. But luckily I hadn't known him very long.

"This is not a pretty story. I am going to tell you that right now."

She nodded. I licked my dry lips.

"I'm sharing this with you because you feel you should know. But I don't think you should tell others. Please."

Another nod, this one less sure.

"You know the music video for 'Prime'?"

Soleil looked confused by this apparent segue.

"The director of that."

The confusion cleared. "Noah *Decker*?" she squeaked. Just hearing the name made me swallow hard. "Wait, I figured you were embarrassed it was some ordinary guy, like maybe a camera operator, but, like, the *director*? Why would you keep *that* from me for so long?"

I peeled the label from the water bottle, giving my hands something to do. "It was not . . . I didn't want it."

Her elated look disappeared. "Like . . . *oh*." The realization hit her. She clasped her hands to her mouth. A muffled "*Ohhh. Oh, god, Mom, I'm so sorry*" came rumbling out.

I dropped the bottle and grabbed her in a hug. I knew the horror was setting in. "I love you so much. I am *not* sorry I had you," I whispered fiercely. "That man was just . . . *sick*. And powerful. And it happened."

She hugged me tighter and spoke into my hair. "That's it, though? You just let him get away with it? You're *Merry Cherry Gloss*, Mom! Why didn't you expose him for the creep that he is?"

"Because. He's a big name. He's powerful. I don't have any evidence that it was forced. And I kind of had a reputation—"

My daughter pulled away and stared at me. "But Mom, he's probably done it to others. He's probably doing it to some poor scared girl right now."

In all my years of thinking—or *not* thinking—about Decker, I'd never once allowed myself to consider that he was likely a serial assaulter. I was so preoccupied with my reputation, I didn't stop to think about his.

"You *have* to say something. He's doing Joyride's video next month! What if this happened to one of those girls?"

Magenta had said, *I even wanted to be you in the 'Prime' video,* to Rose at the premiere, and all I could think when she'd said that was, *You wanted to have a fractured spine? Be forced into a situation against your will?*

I sighed. "I don't know, honey. How would I even start? What would I even say?"

"How?" She looked at me quizzically, and her small quirked smile was sweet. "You start on Instagram, of course."

# 35.

# Yumi

'd taken the last plane out of L.A. to Houston and landed
sometime in the night, so I didn't spot Merry or Rose until
we were filing into the church for Cassidy's service. I had so
many questions about Rose's statement to the press about her
relationship with Cassidy. As soon as I saw Rose, I jumped into
step beside her and slid into the same pew.

Merry and Soleil took the seats at the end of the row, but
my focus was all on Rose, who was dressed to the nines in a
vintage Chanel dress with a black half-veil over her eyes. She
looked like a caricature of a woman in mourning.

"Is that . . . the dress that Cassidy wore to the Music Video
Awards?" I asked, noticing the white cuffs.

"This old thing?" Rose asked, rubbing her fingers along a
sleeve. "I don't think so."

"You called the paps for this, didn't you?" I accused. "You

are playing this like it's some sort of game. But Rose, Cassidy *died*. This is her *funeral,* for crying out loud." Paparazzi don't really exist outside of Los Angeles or New York City. I had to push through a caravan of news crews setting up on the other side of the road when I drove here.

She shrugged. The rest of the congregants were shuffling, sitting, murmuring among themselves. The family had not yet arrived to sit in the front row.

Frustrated, I whispered, "How did we not discuss any of this? I thought we knew all of one another's secrets. We were spending so many hours together. I thought we were friends."

"We *were* friends!"

"Please. This whole thing about you and Cassidy—it's a stunt, right? If it was true, why didn't Merry or I know?"

"Because we didn't *want* you to know. Did it ever occur to you that Cassidy was not happy about you blabbing that poor, sad Alex was the guy who broke her arm? She didn't want to talk to you after that. Her friendliness until she quit was a pretense to keep the peace."

That shut me right up. I'd tried to apologize once, but Cassidy hadn't wanted to discuss it. Soon after, she left. I'd been harboring unfriendly thoughts about how I was responsible for her leaving, and Rose all but confirmed my fears.

Merry leaned over me. "That doesn't explain why she didn't tell *me*. I was closest to her in the group. She kept my secret for me."

Rose shrugged. "I doubt it. No one knew except Emily. But nothing gets past Emily."

"You're using this to further your career, aren't you? This is just to look 'diverse' so that FPZ picks you over Yumi for the *Sing It* reboot." Merry shook her head in exasperation. "You never change. You screw over your friends at the first dollar opportunity. Look at Viv."

"Viv had *cancer*," Rose hissed. "What would you have me do?"

"Give her back her spot when Cassidy left? She was in remission by then."

"I thought Cass was coming back."

"Whatever." Merry stood up and Soleil scrambled to her feet.

"Oh Sunny," Rose said in a singsongy voice. "I want my letter back now."

Soleil set her jaw and shuffled out of the pew. She and her mother moved closer to the front of the church, leaving Rose and me by ourselves near the middle. The crowd hushed as the priest appeared at the lectern.

"What letter?" I whispered.

Rose ignored me.

The priest cleared his throat and began his homily.

"Rose, what letter?"

"Nothing. Just an old letter that would confirm Cassidy's being in love with me."

"That I guess you're going to use to extend this story that you were lovers. All this for a ridiculous job?"

"A ridiculous job worth eight figures? Sure."

I seethed. The priest introduced Cassidy's sister, one of the twins whom we'd met a couple of times when we'd passed through Texas on tour. Then, "What, you think that one cameo in a comedy movie and being a judge on television is going to increase your social currency? This is *the real world*. You are in your thirties now. Be realistic."

"This isn't the real world, this is *Hollywood*. It is never realistic. It's about who you know and who you're seen with. We were pop royalty."

I laughed with contempt. "You're nothing without Gloss. You've been using us for years. Any time you need to feel relevant, you bring us back into the public eye. And now you're dragging Cassidy into this, and she's dead. You are toxic."

"Shh! You're being very disrespectful." Rose looked ahead and listened to the eulogy. I sat with a burning in my chest.

I did not want to be on *Sing It,* I realized. I did not want to be a part of the entertainment machine. I didn't want to associate with these people, I didn't want to shake Henry Grafton's hand, I didn't want to be on the stage again.

But then again, I did not want Rose to get the seat. I didn't want her to whisper toxic, friendship-ending things into her mentees' ears. I didn't want her to think she could win by invoking her dead friend's name. And I didn't want Stephen St. James to not get called out for what he had done.

I slid out of the seat and walked out of the church. On the front steps, I dialed Mike Parsons. When I saw the bobbing lenses from the small crowd across the street, I turned and headed into the courtyard, away from the cameras.

"Ms. Otsuka!" he said brightly. "To what do I owe the pleasure?"

"I accept the job, under two conditions."

"That's wonderful news! What might those conditions be?"

"Tell me, how much was Rose McGill countering her salary to be?"

"Ah . . ." he paused. "I'm not at liberty to say."

"But she *was* countering." I said it as a statement. Rose was always holding out for more. "She was not happy with what she was offered."

"Well, ye-es . . ."

"I'll do it for the amount you offered *her*. Send the offer to my lawyer."

They had *not* quoted me eight figures. But they'd told her something in the teen millions.

"And the second?"

"You release a statement of *why* you decided against hiring Stephen St. James," I said. "I even came up with the wording for you: 'That while *Sing It* is proud of its alumni and past contestants, you don't support or condone any actions that include beating women.' If you don't, I'll have a press release of my own about what I know."

There was a beat of silence. Then, a resigned, "I'll pass this along to my boss, Ms. Otsuka."

"Tell them that I'm a reasonable person. These are the only demands I'll make during my tenure as judge. But the St. James statement is nonnegotiable. And it should be easy to align yourself with what is right, don't you think?"

I hung up. The pressure on my chest released and I breathed deeply in and out a few times, trying to slow my heart rate. Then I snuck back into the church and stood at the back as Melanie finished speaking and sat down. I realized that the casket had made its way up the aisle while we'd been whispering, and I'd missed it. We'd been arguing in front of Cassidy this entire time; shame made my throat tighten. I whispered toward her spirit, *I'm sorry.* Sorry for Alex. Sorry for my mistake. Sorry, sorry, sorry.

# EPILOGUE

# Melanie

"Thank you for coming." Melanie speaks into the microphone. "My family and I appreciate your presence today in celebrating my sister's life.

"We gather in memory of Cassidy May Holmes. She grew up here in Houston with my two older brothers and me and my twin. She sang and danced. She loved Drew Barrymore movies.

"I blinked and she was gone.

"My sister."

Melanie had watched her parents walk together up the stairs of the church, leaning heavily on each other, tired in a way that it hurt her bones to see them. The family had elected Melanie to give the eulogy. So she begins to talk about Cass's childhood, her formative years. Melanie recognizes her anger. As she speaks, she thinks, *Cassidy had been born, which in itself is lucky enough. She grew. Meal after meal, tiny body growing like a weed, the audacity of her lungs taking in breath and nourishing her blood.*

"During her last year of high school, she had the opportunity to compete in a nationally televised singing competition, which was the springboard for her career. Though she didn't win, she impressed the judges enough that one offered her a job a little while later. And so the global phenomenon of Gloss was born."

At the mention of Gloss, Melanie's eyes roam the crowd of black-suited mourners, looking for the members. Merry is easy to find, with her halo of white-blond hair, and after another glance up from her notes, Melanie spots Rose sitting demurely in the back. The story about Rose and Cassidy's relationship had come out the day before, and Melanie wonders how Rose has the audacity to show up. None of her family had known about Cassidy's sexuality, but then again, Cassidy hadn't discussed her personal life with them much.

"But while Cassidy's professional life was at an all-time high, her personal one was more subdued. People who knew Cassidy, the person—not Cassidy, the performer—reflected on her quiet nature, her love of baking, and how much she enjoyed being at home. And in her years since leaving the music industry—"

Her eyes alight on Joanna, seated next to Alex, his hand resting on a cane. His leg is stretched out in front of him, his ankle in the aisle. Edie is nowhere to be seen.

People have this notion that depressed people are shut-ins. Antisocial. That they have no families and no friends. It's true, Cassidy pushed her family aside often—eschewing home visits, skipping Thanksgivings—but she always made it back for Christmas. She'd laugh and smile, they'd go to the movies on Christmas Eve, she'd bake her signature cookies.

Melanie flew out to see her, maybe once a year. The last time she saw Cassidy was several months ago. The sisters took turns petting Cass's old dog, Penny, the only other relic from her Gloss days besides an MVA statuette in her bathroom cabinet, which almost took Melanie's eye out when it fell from a high shelf as she searched for makeup wipes. "Shit!" she'd shrieked, and Cassidy came running, bursting into the bathroom.

"Oh, that thing," she'd said, stooping to pick up the statuette, which was now dented slightly.

"Don't you have a better place for that?"

"Nah. Where would I put it?"

Her house in Pasadena was on the smaller side.

"Out, somewhere, maybe? On your coffee table? On a bookshelf?"

Cassidy stuffed it precariously back into the bathroom cabinet. "I don't really care about it," she said, closing the door as the statue thumped against it.

But she must have—right? She saw it every time she had to get toilet paper. It was hidden, but it wasn't forgotten.

She had weathered the fallout from Gloss, she *hadn't* moved back to Texas, and Melanie couldn't understand why.

At the pulpit, Melanie continues: "—in her years since leaving the music industry, Cassidy had an active life. She sought roles without high profiles, like volunteer positions at soup kitchens and senior living centers, behind the scenes. I think she wanted to do things that mattered and help individual people." She swallows.

Their parents' faces in the front row are tear-streaked. Melanie's twin sits stoically, trying not to cry, holding her husband

and son. Patrick and his boyfriend, Robbie and his wife, they're all passing a pack of travel tissues down the pew.

The last time Melanie saw Cassidy, she asked her, "If you still have that mansion in Hollywood, why not stay there when I come to visit?" They were sitting on the porch of the small house. Cassidy passed her a can of lemonade. "It's huge. I wouldn't have to take over your bed and you could sleep on something besides a couch. I mean, you basically use it as an off-site hotel for Mom and Dad when they come."

"But then we'd have to *be* in that house. I should just sell it." She smirked, her Sassy Cassy grin.

"Well, why don't you sell it? What good is it doing you?"

She shrugged. She clearly didn't need the money. In her will she gave the bulk of it away to charities and an equal share to their parents and every one of her siblings. She'd made the will years ago, before her nephew had been born, and hadn't updated it. Even the small slice Melanie received was enough to retire on.

Melanie had returned home, not realizing it would be the last time she saw her sister in person. It was such an ordinary interaction. Sure, she'd noticed that Cassidy was slow to answer emails and phone calls. Her voice was subdued when they talked and sometimes she seemed tired. But other times, she sounded completely fine.

It breaks Melanie's heart now to think that she was hurting. That she only saw the strong, pleasant side of her sister that she would paint on for the few days they were together.

Melanie remembers that a couple of days before she passed, Cassidy called unexpectedly. Her voice was calm and detached.

"Penny died," she'd murmured, and Melanie expressed her sympathies. She was quiet for so long that Melanie thought the line had been disconnected, but then her voice came again. "Mel? Do you think I'm a good person?"

"Of course I do," Melanie answered, not sure why the question had been asked. Cassidy didn't bring it up again and her younger sister let it slide from her thoughts.

But when her father called her, his voice breaking, Melanie knew immediately what had happened. Although she hadn't recognized the signs before, they all stacked up now. She beat herself up over her obtuseness. She should have checked on her more often. She should have done more, been there more.

She had gone to L.A. with their parents after the suicide, to identify Cassidy as well as help the police with any questions. Melanie had walked up the driveway of the gated mansion with a uniformed escort and peeked inside. She'd never been there before, but there was one thing that she knew was out of place: the MVA statuette, sitting on the coffee table.

Melanie still didn't know what it meant.

Blink, and Cassidy was gone. All those years. Her multi-platinum records, her dozens of televised appearances, her outfits on display at the Smithsonian—none of that mattered; they were done fifteen years ago. But the delicate tap when she dented a sugar cookie dough ball with one finger, the delight she had when scratching a dog under the chin, the way she made people feel when they were around her—that had disappeared. Evaporated like ether.

"She was vivacious and amazing, and she will be missed," Melanie concludes. "I wish I had known what Cassidy was going through. We love her and her memory will live on with us. Thank you."

She returns to her seat, swiping away tears.

And that's why Melanie unlocked her sister's social media. She wanted people to know that the real Cassidy—the woman who had been such an integral part of Gloss—was not a taciturn introvert in the years following her rift with the rest of the group. It's just, her mind fought against her. Had it been another day, if she hadn't felt a certain despair already, if Penny hadn't died of old age, if she'd read a different book, if she'd heard a different song on the radio, would she have reconsidered her plan?

Would she still be here now?

THE FAMILY FILED away from the service, the beige building reflecting too cheerily bright in the afternoon light; the camera people kept an almost-respectful lawn's-distance away from the procession.

As the group, from one somber car to the next, wound its way to the cemetery, garish updates were already being made to cable network Twitter accounts and websites: Cassidy Holmes's final resting place, Cassidy Holmes's thirty-nine car procession, Cassidy Holmes's hearse stopped traffic on Main for forty solemn minutes. Blurry, grainy images of the black car were posted as well, not remarkable at all except for the contents inside.

Houston's channel 26 followed the car in a traffic helicopter, out of deference, perhaps, to their station's affiliation with Big Disc. Having brought Cassidy Holmes into people's televisions for the first time on *Sing It, America!* some fifteen-odd years ago, they thought it would be fitting to show her last journey across town before being set into the ground.

At the cemetery, passengers spilled out of their dark cars. Yumi could see a light smattering of paparazzi from the corner of her eye; it was a well-honed instinct of being able to recognize a telephoto just from the glinting reflection off the spherical lens. She ignored them as best she could, gripping her own arms so tight that she unknowingly drew a crescent-shaped slick of blood from digging in with an overgrown fingernail.

Meredith stood next to her as the priest made his comments and invited family to toss rose petals. She watched impassively as Mr. Holmes, his face slack with grief, brushed a handful of petals onto the gravestone, and held Soleil closer to her body.

A simple black hat with a half-veil shadowed Rose's eyes. She was away from the other two women, on the opposite side of the mound of earth excavated for the fallen Cassidy. Her hands were clasped in front of her body, her cell phone tucked inward toward her palm.

If the photographers outside of the cemetery gates could magnify Rose's face with their telephoto lenses, they might have seen a slight flickering of one cheek.

It could have been a smile.

It could have been her weeping.

# ACKNOWLEDGMENTS

Thank you to my brilliant editor, Asanté Simons, who understood the final, clarified vision for this novel and helped me get it there. I also appreciate everything that the exceptional team at William Morrow—including Stephanie Vallejo, Rita Madrigal, Kaitie Leary, Rhina Garcia, Jennifer Hart, Yeon Kim—did to bring this book out into the world.

I owe the warmest thanks to my agent, Kelly Van Sant, whose wisdom is unmatched and to whom I'm more grateful than words could describe.

Thank you to secondary readers Cora Godfrey and Katharine Forsyth, and sensitivity reader Dill Werner for their valuable input. Bao Vo and Marcos Varela listened to me ask detailed questions about the music industry and tried to steer me right; Dr. Ann Kuo researched when I asked medical questions; and my uncle, Larry Sloan, gave his valuable insight on police procedure (all inaccuracies are mine). I had additional help from Jodi and Jason Kingsley, Aurora Gordon, Jessica Schilling, David Kvasnicka, and Laura Lee Anderson.

Thank you to Cathryn Ibarra, Beka Vinogradov, Kristan Hoffman, the Nosies—especially Ang Jandak, Soleil Howard, Cindy Savage, Erin Gettler, Sharon Hsu, Alix Bannon,

Rebecca Wright Iverson, Jacqueline WayneGuite, Kristin
Maffei, and Kinzie Ferguson—and the crews of my two
book clubs for their continued encouragement. (I'd also like
to thank all friends whose names I borrowed for this story
without permission.)

Additional thanks to Julie Sugar, Rebecca Lammons, Sarah
Clarke Menendez, and Matt Mullenweg for their love and support over the years.

I'm so lucky to be surrounded by supportive family. So much
love goes to my parents, who instilled in me a habit of reading and nurtured my creativity from an early age. Additional
shout-outs go to my sister Chieko and my in-laws Donna, Bill,
and Max.

To my life partner Walt, who has supported me through
writing this book and other endeavors, thank you.

Most of all, thank YOU for reading this novel.

## About the author

## About the book

Insights,
Interviews
& More . . .

# Meet Elissa R. Sloan

Caitlin McWeeney

ELISSA R. SLOAN is a Texas-native Japanese American with a penchant for reading books and celebrity gossip. She lives in Austin with her husband and two cats in a house with a rolling library ladder. *The Unraveling of Cassidy Holmes* is her debut novel.

Follow her on Instagram at @elissareads. ⌒

# Behind the Book

I began paying attention to popular music in middle school. My first concert was *NSYNC; my first album, Mariah Carey. Somewhere in the jumble of pop and R&B came the Spice Girls and their movie *Spice World*, which I saw in theaters. That, and a pair of ankle-breaking platform shoes, was about the extent of their influence on me. Or so I thought.

Fast-forward to 2014. I'd been reading celebrity gossip for about a decade at that point and I knew the ins and outs of Mel B's ongoing, horrible divorce. Around the same time, I caught a showing of *Spice World* on TV. It was an interesting dichotomy, seeing the face she presented to the world as Scary Spice in the movie, filmed more than fifteen years before, compared to the very publicized private battle that Mel B was waging with her ex in the present.

And I began to wonder. What would it would be like if something more devastating happened in the news, like if a once-popular girl group member *died* unexpectedly, years after the group's messy breakup?

The first line popped into my head while I was in the shower: *The day that Cassidy died, the rest of us were in London.* . . . And somehow, a hazy outline of the rest of the story did, too. ▶

3

**Behind the Book** *(continued)*

When I began writing, I knew I wanted the story to be set in two timelines—then and now. I did not start out with Cassidy as the main character, despite the opening sentence. At the beginning, Yumi was my focus, and she was a different character entirely—a woman named Jazzy who was going through a bad divorce. Jazzy's life was going to have a clear delineation between married and divorced; during and after Gloss; before and after Cassidy's death, and how that affected Jazzy. It was absolutely dull. I realized that I was trying so hard *not* to insert any of myself in the storytelling, that the story itself was bland and impersonal. I decided to change Jazzy to Yumi in the third draft, shrank her role, and rewrote Jazzy-as-Yumi to give her more of my personality. I then included subtle instances of racism that she encountered. As a half-Japanese woman, I could relate to Yumi in ways I couldn't relate to Jazzy, and I think it made the story stronger.

I began writing in 2014, but my revisions took longer and longer, and #MeToo erupted in 2017. When I saw that I could talk about the toxicity that women, especially female performers, dealt with in a male-dominated field, I aged Soleil up from toddler to adolescent so that she had more autonomy and there would be a real danger of her becoming a young model. Soleil's revised age also meant that her conception would have to happen while Gloss was still together, bringing a dynamic that affected the rest of the members as well. Merry's character was inspired by so many big gossip articles. As the Gloss girl who got herself written up in all the tabloids, it seemed natural that her stories were also ripped from the headlines. I removed several of her boyfriends, a few of her drunken club nights out, and one sweet moment where the Gloss girls all hear their single for the first time while out dancing and react accordingly—a nod to the scene in 1997's *Selena* when J. Lo-as-Selena hears her song on the radio.

Rose was an interesting character to discover. At first, she was just the mean girl, needlessly cruel to Cassidy. But over time, I wanted them to find a friendship—and more. I wanted her to be headstrong and the most focused of the girls on Gloss's career, at the expense of her finding happiness in her personal life. I think we've seen stars who sacrifice so much of themselves that they lose who they really are, people who we think of as robotic or soulless. Above all, I wanted Rose to be complicated; I wanted some readers to root for her and others to absolutely hate her.

Like, I said, it became clear to me ▶

after I started writing that the real story was about Cassidy. Over the years, I dealt with undiagnosed depression, and it wasn't until I gave a voice to Cassidy and wrote out her spiral that I understood there was something actually going on with me. I did not understand *how* I could be depressed; my personal life was great! I was in love, my relationships were all strong, and the business I owned was doing well. But that's just the thing, isn't it? Sometimes brains are just complicated, fickle things that don't create the right combination of chemicals to keep us happy. I wrote Cassidy's character in a way that didn't *blame* her depression on anything; it just *was*. She had a supportive family. She was close with her siblings. She had enough money. She did something with her life—she was involved with charities after Gloss broke up. But she still struggled with her mental health.

After I finished the final draft of this novel, I knew I needed to talk to someone and I found a therapist. One of my early readers asked me why Cassidy didn't go to therapy or try medication. To that person I said, I don't want anyone to read this book and worry that therapy or medication won't work for them. It's true that some days are harder than others, but I didn't want to write Cassidy as someone who

died even though she took major steps
to feel better. I'd rather it be open-ended;
maybe therapy could have saved her,
like it helped Merry.

Who knew that a seemingly fluffy
girl-group book would draw out so
many heavy themes?

I am not musical in the slightest,
so I read up on musician biographies to
understand the world better and asked
musician friends for help. I enjoyed
combing through old Oscars photos
to brush up on the fashion of the times.
I especially loved Cassidy's Oscar dress,
inspired by Gwyneth Paltrow's 1999
pink Ralph Lauren gown! I also liked
describing the tech before everyone
owned iPhones—when Paris Hilton
and her Sidekick were all the rage.
I hope you enjoyed the nostalgia as
much as I liked writing it! ∾

# Elissa's '90s–2000s Playlist

- "Ray of Light"—Madonna
- "Everybody"—Backstreet Boys
- "Independent Women"—Destiny's Child
- "Wannabe"—Spice Girls
- "If You Had My Love"—Jennifer Lopez
- "Believe"—Cher
- "No Scrubs"—TLC
- "Get Over Yourself"—Eden's Crush
- "I Know Where It's At"—All Saints
- "Absolutely"—Nine Days
- "It's Gonna Be Me"—*NSYNC
- "Back Here"—BBMak
- "I Try"—Macy Gray

# Reading Group Guide

1. Given everything that happened after Cassidy joined Gloss and signed with Big Disc Records— the highs *and* the lows—do you think she should have never chased a music career after *Sing It*?

2. Do you think that being busy and being a celebrity are the only reasons why Cassidy lost touch with her childhood friends, Edie and Joanna?

3. What did you think of Cassidy's relationship with Alex? Should she have stayed "just friends" with him? Should she have pulled the plug on their relationship much earlier, like Joanna suggested?

4. Do you think Yumi was truly acting in Cassidy's best interest by going to the press about Alex?

5. Rose says that she can't be with anyone who loves her. What does that really mean and why do you think Rose feels that way? ▶

6. In the present, we see where each of the Gloss girls is in terms of their fame. Merry is very successful, with multiple brands, career ventures, and opportunities coming in. Yumi voluntarily gave up being a celebrity in the mid-2000s and is simply enjoying her life. Rose is still desperately trying to be a Somebody and not a Has-Been. Why did each of them end up on such different career and life paths? What influenced their decisions and the way the world sees them?

7. Even at the height of their fame, none of the Gloss girls ever spoke up about the abusive behavior of the people working with or around them. What reasons do you think made them keep quiet?

8. By the end of the novel, we start to see the abusive male characters get their comeuppance. What more do you think we should have seen in the book?

9. After everything, what do you think of Rose? Do you think she was just hungry for any ounce of fame and was willing to do any and everything for it? Or were there other things that made her who she was and do the things she did? ～